THE RAVE

Nicky Black

Published by Nicky Black Ltd

Copyright © 2018 Nicky Black Ltd

All rights reserved. No portion of this book may be reproduced, by any process or technique, without the express written consent of the publisher.

This is a work of fiction inspired by the author's experiences. Any similarity of these names to the names of any living person is purely coincidental.

The publisher can be contacted at nickyblack2016@gmail.com

"If music be the food of love, play on,
Give me excess of it."

- William Shakespeare

For Dad

PROLOGUE

TUCKER

Newcastle upon Tyne
June 1989

I didn't go to Tommy's rave. I wouldn't have been welcome there, all things considered, so I'm here instead, shotgun in hand, the unarmed coppers in their car burying their heads under the dashboard.

Cowards.

There's only a single bullet left, so just one of these men I despise will die today. They're standing like waxworks, all three of them, looking at me and wondering who it's going to be: Paul Smart, my boss, my mentor. My betrayer. I've learnt everything from this man who's staring me square in the eye, not a glimmer of fear. He doesn't feel fear. Paul Smart doesn't feel anything.

The copper's here too – the Chief Inspector, wearing that cliched beige Mac like the tosser he is. He doesn't look scared either. He's been trained not to show fear, but I've clocked the tiny beads of sweat on his forehead. I hate all coppers. I loathe them. They've hurt me physically, but I can take that. It's their words that do the damage: *coon, darkie, half-cast, nig-nog.* I've heard it all from their filthy mouths while they search my pockets, asking if it's true what people say about the size of my dick. I would happily put this bullet into the Chief Inspector's chest. He could take it for the team.

And here's the third man on my list.

Tommy Collins is scared all right. He's shitting himself. I bet young Tommy didn't think he'd be staring down the barrel of a shotgun this time last week. But he's only got himself to blame for that, because there's one thing that hurts me more than ignorance.

Rejection.

I think I might hate Tommy Collins more than Paul Smart and the copper put together.

Tommy's saying something, but I can hardly hear it, what with the blood in my ears. I strain to listen, try to look like I'm not listening at all.

'*Do the right thing,*' Tommy's saying.

He's trying to be friendly, but I wasn't born yesterday. I know he doesn't really mean it.

I will, Tommy, I think. *I'll do the right thing all right.*

8 DAYS EARLIER
SATURDAY

TOMMY

The wall pulsed to the beat of the music pounding from inside the small, disused warehouse. It echoed in the calm night, the trickle of the Ouseburn river below the only other sound. It had been a sweltering summer so far, the hottest for a generation, and some of the rivers and burns were all but dried up.

Tommy Collins leant back against the wall, rubbing at his shorn head, drinking in the rhythm and breathing out the white fog of his cigarette as he reminded himself of *The Rules*, running them over in his head as he did most days. He'd read them in a magazine a couple of years before – one of those men's mags; the sort that made anyone with a pigeon chest feel inadequate. The article was about an American billionaire who said making money was "nothing but a game." He'd even set out his own rules of play.

Tommy knew them by heart.

One: work hard, play hard.

Barely eleven o'clock and the warehouse was rammed inside. He heard the music melt into a slower, Balearic beat – Herp Alpert: one of his all-time favourites. He bounced his head in time to the beat, felt his chest swell, energy charging his fingertips. He didn't need the drugs or the booze; they were for mugs who had no ambition. The music was his addiction, and he was happily drowning in his dependence on it.

Two: treat others with the respect they deserve.

The fire door flew open and a bare-chested youth was tossed out by the bouncers. Tommy looked on impassively as the kid picked himself up in a swirl of profanity and crashed down the fire escape's metal stairs. Tommy's security could sniff out dealers like bloodhounds.

The music ramped up again, and he felt the warehouse throb to its foundations. He smiled as the cheers and whistles of the ravers inside rose above the beat. They were having the night of their lives, thanks to Tommy Collins.

Three: know your enemies.

He saw it before he heard it: the jarring blue flicker of the police tearing over Byker Bank. He swore under his breath, and flicked his cigarette onto the cobbled bank below, the bouncers throwing the doors open on cue when his fists pounded.

The concrete stairs smelt of piss, and Tommy put his hand to his nose as he skipped down them onto the mezzanine level, inching his way through the throng of jerking dancers. Below him, an ocean of bodies faced the MC, Jimmy Lyric, who stood motionless in his own personal spotlight, his tattooed arms stretched wide like Christ the Redeemer while the music halted for a few beats then slammed back in, bass heavy as concrete, and a thousand hands reached up in unison.

Tommy leant over the balcony, arms signalling to Jimmy, but Jimmy's lips remained fastened to the microphone, unaware of any other ego but his own.

Jimmy would have to wing it.

The storeroom at the end of the mezzanine was just a few yards away, where Tommy's right-hand man and best friend in the world was guarding the takings, his first DJ set over and done with an hour ago. Jed would be bored out of his skull by now, waiting for the second set that wasn't going to happen.

Four: expect the unexpected.

Bursting into the storeroom, Tommy found Jed – not staring at the walls or playing Patience with the pack of cards he'd brought to keep him occupied – but taking a woman from behind over some old beer barrels, his tall, athletic frame grinding in perfect time with Jimmy Lyric's incomprehensible words.

Grimacing at the sight of buttocks he hadn't seen since childhood, Tommy whistled sharply, and Jed turned his hot face over his shoulder, his silky dark hair framing a face as striking as any Levi's model.

Jed winked, displaying a blissful smile before turning back to his prize – oh so close.

'Oy!' Tommy grabbed the plastic carrier bag of money from one of the barrels. 'The cops, man!'

Jed's head dropped. 'Ah, you're fucking joking!' He stepped back, snapping off the condom and throwing it into the corner of the room. Pulling up his jeans awkwardly, he planted a kiss on the woman's arse cheek before running out the door after Tommy who headed for the fire exit; their quickest route out.

But they were too late.

Tommy glimpsed a uniform at the fire exit door, felt the adrenaline kick in as he looked over the balcony onto a stream of fluorescent hats wading through the sea of bodies who danced on, oblivious. Pushing his way through the ravers on the mezzanine, he dragged Jed back into the storeroom where they shoved some barrels up against the door and walked to an arched window that reached from floor to ceiling. It opened easily, flakes of paint falling onto the rotten wood of the sill as it had when they'd trialled their Plan B escape route that afternoon.

Five: and remember, it's only a game.

They'd had a blast, jumping from the window onto the flat roof below, ducking like SAS soldiers as they crept towards the rusty ladder that would lead them to a yard full of scrap metal. A hole in the yard's fence would take them down the hill to Frankie, their trusty driver and lover of all things on wheels. It had seemed easy to Tommy in the light of day, but now hearts were pumping, the rozzers were everywhere, and the flat roof, just a few feet below the window, had assumed the dimensions of the black abyss.

The two friends' eyes met when the music came to a sudden stop, and the sound of whistling and dissenting jeers filled the warehouse.

Jed, fit as a lop, was out the window in a matter of seconds.

'Are you Tommy Collins?'

Tommy had forgotten about Jed's prize, skulking in the shadows, still holding her blouse together at the neck. She emerged into the moonlight, cheekbones like wings, one side of her short black hair falling over one eye.

'Aye,' said Tommy, climbing onto the sill. 'The one and only.'

Below him, Jed waited, and he hit the roof soundlessly. They crouched like Neanderthals, looking into the whites of each other's eyes as a voice bellowed from below.

'Hey! Ye cannit take me decks, it's not my do!' Jimmy Lyric was beyond furious.

'Illegal do, the gear gets confiscated.' A different voice, low and gravelly.

'It's not my fucking do, man. It's not my do!'

'Tough!'

Something in Tommy's memory jarred at the sound of the voice that wasn't Jimmy's. He pushed the bag of money under this jacket, crawled to the edge of the roof, and peeked over the metal barrier that encased it. He could see Jimmy gesticulating angrily, his bleached Mohican glowing yellow in the beam of a single streetlight as he marched away from a tall man, grey hair falling in waves over the collar of a beige Mackintosh.

Tommy felt his stomach somersault. It was him, he was sure of it.

'*Jed! Jed!*' The girl with the cheekbones was at the open window, leaning out like a scene from *Romeo and Juliet*. Tommy gulped silently and pushed his body deeper into the asphalt, eyes fixed on the man in the Mac who had turned his head towards the sound. Tommy watched him for a moment, recognising the face instantly.

Peach.

Their eyes didn't have time to meet, and Tommy scuttled crab-like towards Jed who hung from the ladder, waving frantically. They climbed down, hit the ground, and ran like hell.

***

The lime green bonnet of the Mini Metro was poking out from behind a mountain of tyres. The interior light was on and Tommy could see Frankie at the wheel, his receding ginger hair tied back in a scraggly pony tail. Frankie held a magazine on his lap, open at its centre, his tongue running over his lips as his finger followed the curvy outline of a shiny, red Rover 200 series, released recently to rival his favourite car of all time: the Ford Sierra.

'Frankie, man!' Tommy hammered on the window.

'Open the doors, you daft twat!' Jed's handsome face took on a Hulk-like appearance as Frankie closed the magazine and fumbled with the lock of the passenger door. Tommy peeked around the mound of tyres, watching with alarm as officers poured through the hole in the fence like spiders, holding onto their hats as they scampered down the hill towards them.

As Tommy shouted his warning, the passenger door sprang open and Jed jumped in, reaching over to unlock one of the back doors.

'Why are the pissing doors locked?!' yelled Jed.

'Safety first,' said Frankie in his usual long drawl.

Tommy hurled himself onto the back seat, lying face down with his feet still sticking out the open door as Frankie started the engine and revved the car, only to stutter a couple of yards before the engine cut out.

'Howay, Kermit, don't let me down.' Frankie named all his borrowed cars. It was his thing.

'Fucking move!' screamed Tommy, feeling hands on his feet. He kicked out as the engine started again and Frankie screeched away, the back door still swinging open, and one of Tommy's trainers in the hand of a panting officer.

Scrambling into a sitting position, Tommy reached out and pulled the car door shut, made all the more difficult as the wheels bounced over pot holes and discarded metal. He turned and gaped out the back window at the growing crowd of police, some with their hands on their hips, most clutching their knees, wishing they were younger and fitter. They were joined by the man in the Mac, who held a carrier bag aloft, his face lit red in the car's rear lights as it roared up the hill towards freedom.

Tommy spun back around, frantically rummaging under his jacket, panic almost bringing tears to his eyes.

The money was gone.

'Shit!' he sputtered.

Jed's face said it all as he turned to look over his shoulder at Tommy's empty hands; a thin smile that said, *I told you so.*

Tommy sighed and threw his head back against the leather of the seat as the car swerved onto Byker Bank. This was the second time they'd been raided by the police, only this time there were more of them and they'd got there sooner. And this time, DCI Peach was in charge.

'Back to base, Frankie,' Tommy said, leaning forward and patting their driver on the shoulder.

As the car sped through the empty streets, Tommy stared out the window. He'd taken the billionaire's rules and applied them to a new game: raves. A release for hundreds – thousands – of cooped-up young people, gagging for it, anything to escape the toil of angry parents, dead end jobs or no job at all. Young people who had found their expression.

Young people like him.

PEACH

Detective Chief Inspector Peach stared after the disappearing car at the head of a cluster of uniforms, sprawled behind him like a formation of geese. He held open the handles of the carrier bag, examining its contents under the weak beam of the streetlight: a couple of grand, maybe less, hardly worth him working past midnight for. He turned to the gaggle of officers behind him, watching a ruddy-faced PC approaching, holding out a white trainer.

'Why, thank you, Cinderella.' Peach grabbed the trainer and cuffed the officer over the head with it, knocking his hat to the ground. 'Anybody get the registration?'

The officers shuffled and coughed, avoiding eye contact and responsibility for their failure.

Peach looked away from them, turning his attention to the streams of youths piling out of the warehouse onto the cobbles. They hung off each other's necks, chewing ferociously, grinning like goons. Some danced in the flashing lights of the squad cars, their euphoric cries like a call to arms. They chanted, arms and legs jerking, whistles blowing. This, thought Peach, was their ludicrous idea of enjoyment.

'Get them out of here,' he said to Cinderella.

'But, sir, there's hundreds of them!'

Peach's glare had Cinderella scampering away, and he watched glumly as the officers attempted to round up the youths like dogs herding disobedient sheep.

Turning away from the chaos, he stared up the hill, pulling at his grey horseshoe moustache with a finger and thumb. These kids were running wild, drugged up to the eyeballs, roaming the streets at all hours. This is what he'd been brought to; a game of cat and mouse, chasing yobs who should be working for a living instead of creating mayhem on the city's streets. But it was only a matter of time before he found the organisers, caught them in the act. They were hardly bright after all. *Just like this bloody lot,* he thought, looking over his shoulder, unable to distinguish a single uniform. They'd been submerged into the mass of bodies, drowned by louts.

A low growl settled in his throat. If he had a decent team he could delegate the legwork, take command and dole out the orders as warranted his position. But here he was, standing around in the middle of the night, dispersing a bunch of dopey students and council riff-raff. What were the parents thinking, anyway, letting their bairns out 'till all hours? They had no control these days. They had no sense.

A throat cleared behind him, and he turned, looking down into the half-hidden face of a young man wearing a long sweatshirt and baggy jeans that bunched like concertinas around booted ankles. The chin was aloft, a white cotton hat pulled down over the eyes. It took Peach a few seconds to recognise DS Murphy, his new sergeant, freshly seconded from Manchester, and, if Peach had his way, straight back on the next National Express.

This was his team.

'You need to come inside, sir. They're saying it's your young 'un,' said Murphy.

'Follow them,' Peach replied, nodding up the hill. But Murphy didn't move.

'They're well gone, boss. But your kid ...'

Murphy was looking back at the warehouse and Peach followed his gaze, his face falling into a puzzled scowl. His daughter was at home, tucked up in bed like she always was at this time of night, and he turned to Murphy to tell him so.

But Murphy continued to look at him from under his hat, something in his droopy eyes halting Peach's words.

Murphy swallowed. 'You need come inside, sir.'

TOMMY

The granite eyes of George Stephenson followed Tommy and his friends as they passed the Central Railway Station on their way to Phutures, their night club of choice on account of the guaranteed free entry. Harold "Hadgy" Dodds, bouncer and provider of said free entry, stood at the top of the stairs, his jet-black hair standing on end as if he were plugged into a socket.

Frankie skipped up the stairs first.

'Thought you had a do on tonight?' said Hadgy.

Frankie gave him a warning look and walked into the club.

Jed followed, and Hadgy tried again. 'You're sharp back, no totty?'

Jed walked past without a word, and Tommy brought up the rear, his one remaining trainer in his hand, a toe sticking through a hole in his sock.

The bouncer raised the thick monobrow that sprouted on a face so big the eyes were all but slits. 'Go all right?' he asked Tommy.

'Fuck off, Hadgy.'

The club was chocka, but only a handful of women danced self-consciously to Sonia on the kidney-shaped dance floor. The lads headed for their usual table where two women sat, sisters by the looks of it, one still in her teens, the other a good few years older, more Frankie's age than Tommy and Jed's.

'Hiya, Tommy,' said the younger one.

Tommy had never seen her before in his life, but his dented pride took some pleasure in the greeting. Her eyes soon left his to linger on Newcastle's answer to Rob Lowe.

Jed, white teeth and T-shirt glowing in the neon light, bent down and whispered into her ear. The girl suppressed a smile, and, with a jerk of her head, she and her sister moved away from the table.

'Cheers, lasses,' said Tommy. Jed's prowess came in handy at times.

Tommy plonked himself down, Jed flinging himself heavily on the stool opposite. Frankie was left standing, dressed head to foot in stone-washed denim, collar up and thick ginger hair poking out at the neck of his open shirt.

'Get the drinks in, Shakey,' ordered Jed, handing a fiver to Frankie.

Frankie was happy to head to the bar, his gait taking on a Travolta-like strut, much to the amusement of the two women who giggled and stuck their fingers down their throats.

Jed pouted. 'That's the end of that then.' Jed's huffs were legendary, his sarcasm even worse.

Tommy looked away; it wasn't the end, they were barely getting started. They just needed to think smarter; be not one, but two steps ahead of the police. But Jed continued to gripe.

'That's us back to the grindstone.'

'There's only one grindstone you know,' said Tommy.

Jed ignored the dig. 'So, who can we not pay, then?'

Tommy blew out his cheeks. 'Bouncers, riggers, DJs—'

'Jesus.'

Tommy was running out of favours. His blagging and Jed's film-star smile could only get them so far before people wanted hard cash.

He leant forward, meaning business. 'Look, if we're gonna do this, we can't piss about. We need to be professional.'

'Let's do something else,' moaned Jed.

Tommy stared hard at his friend whose face perked up in a

light bulb moment.

'Hey, I've got the knock-off trainers.'

Tommy blinked at him, eyebrows raised, but Jed was on a roll.

'Or Northern Soul nights, we were good at that.'

'We're good at this,' Tommy argued. 'This is the future, man. The youth of the nation coming together. Black, white, rich, poor, for the love of the music.'

Jed raised his eyes to the ceiling.

'Howay, mate,' said Tommy. 'These people *need* us.'

'It's finished, Tommy,' said Jed, firmly, 'the police are all over us.'

'Then we'll do it legit. Get leases, licenses—'

'What with? Fresh air?'

Tommy clasped his lips together. He couldn't stop now; it was all he could do, all he was good at, his opportunity to have a life outside of fiddle jobs and youth training schemes. It was the one thing in his life that gave him any status.

'Just needs some lateral thinking,' he said, touching his temple.

'Needs money, and that's something we categorically don't have,' said Jed, the look in his eyes one of blame.

Tommy heaved a sigh and looked over Jed's shoulder, watching Frankie weave his way through clubbers who were rushing to the dance floor to the sounds of S'Express.

Frankie placed a tray of two pints and a Coke carefully on the table, lining it up squarely before rubbing his hands together, ready for his pint. Tommy reached for the Coke. He'd never been much of a drinker, didn't like the taste of the stuff aside from the odd cocktail he'd tried on his only ever holiday abroad. But it didn't do to be seen supping lass's drinks in Newcastle. And besides, this business needed a clear head at all times.

Jed grabbed his drink, taking a few long glugs and standing up, wiping the frothy lager from his lips. 'See yez.' He headed to the dance floor, casually turning back to Tommy and Frankie with a shrug as girls moved in on him like pins to a magnet and Frankie moved in on his empty stool.

***

The night wore on. Hands were shaken, backs slapped in appreciation and commiseration, another tremendous night thwarted by pigs put on this earth to stifle the freedom of ideas. Jed danced on without a care, white T-shirt sticking to his broad, solid chest, nipples visibly erect. Tommy accepted the praise and wisecracks from stragglers from his rave who'd found a second-rate solution to dancing off their energies. But the undertone of disappointment didn't go unnoticed.

The return of chart music had Jed ambling back to the table, Frankie swaying and grinning, happy to be a member of such an eminent team. Tommy eyed Jed with a mixture of confusion and suspicion – he should have pulled by now, have his tongue down some poor cow's throat on the promise of seeing her again. Not likely. Instead, Frankie was ordered back to the bar and more pints arrived.

It was after 1.00 a.m. when Tommy noticed Jed's face fall into a frown. It was nothing unusual, but Tommy followed his friend's gaze anyway and caught the back of a familiar head emerging from the gents' toilets and approaching the bar: the sharp, blond flat-top of Paul Smart, dressed in a black trench coat despite the raging heat, and by his side, a sleek greyhound on a leash. Paul Smart was Valley Park Estate's very own high street bank, a loan shark with a fondness for breaking bones and slicing flesh.

Behind the bar, a door opened, and Paul's side-kick and bodyguard of sorts beckoned to his boss. Tucker, a mixed-race, green-eyed thug with scars on his cheeks and the flattened nose of a bare-knuckled fighter, pierced the room with razor-like eyes as Paul made his way towards him, and they both disappeared through the door.

'What's that nutcase doing here?' Jed asked, his frown lines deepening. This wasn't the sort of place people like Paul Smart frequented. There were fancier, more elegant clubs in town that served people with money to burn. If he was here, he was here for a reason, and it wasn't the dancing.

'Set my hair on fire coz I owed him a fiver,' said Frankie, stroking his pony tail fondly and muttering an apology when Tommy's eyes rested on his. Frankie didn't need to say sorry; there was no love lost, and there wasn't much Tommy could do about the family connection. Young as he was, Tommy had a wife at home, and a damn lovely one at that – only Paul Smart was her uncle, the younger brother of a mother-in-law Tommy would happily see banished to Mars. Not that they would have her, and not that anybody ever spoke of Uncle Paul – he was as good as disowned on account of his reputation for being a psychotic twat.

'Shit, look busy.' Jed turned back to the table and took a cigarette from Tommy's packet as Tommy looked over his friend's shoulder towards the bar. Tucker was walking towards them, eventually stopping at their table and throwing a glance at Tommy before leaning down to Jed's ear. The glint of a blade pressed against Jed's side made Frankie freeze, pint halfway to his mouth.

'Mr Smart wants to see Tommy,' Tucker said.

Jed didn't budge. 'Do I look like Tommy?'

Tucker hesitated, not used to being challenged. 'No.'

'Well, fuck off, then.'

Tommy held his breath, trying to suppress the grin that threatened to expose his disrespect as Tucker straightened up, flicked the blade closed, and slid it into his bomber jacket pocket.

After a long stare in Tommy's direction, he grunted and walked back to the bar.

Jed lifted his pint with a 'you're welcome,' and Tommy raised his Coke in return, feeling a ripple of apprehension run down his spine. Paul Smart's hold on Valley Park and other estates in the west end of Newcastle had gone unchallenged for ten years or more. He bled people dry, frightened their children and their grannies half to death if they didn't pay up what was owed, and if that didn't work, you could say goodbye to your dole, your telly, and your legs. In that order. Tommy kept his distance. He liked his legs; they might be skinny, but they got him where he wanted to be.

Tommy glanced towards the bar where Tucker stood, staring over, his very presence a menace.

Tucker Brown had materialised on Valley Park about five years earlier, the only black face around, no family, no friends, a twenty-year-old with cheeks full of scars that were cause for much speculation: were they acne welts, or were they tribal marks that some witch doctor had sliced into his face with the tooth of a tiger? Tucker had arrived with tales of Liverpool gangsters and the price on his head that saw him fleeing to Newcastle, his accent so thick that if you weren't a fan of *Brookside*, you wouldn't understand a word he said.

But the stories didn't ring true; he'd been awkward, friendly to the point of needy, hanging around like a bad smell, always on their tails. But, at sixteen, Tommy and Jed had been too tight. They'd ignored him, lied to him about where they would be, crossed the street or turned on their heels to avoid him, openly running in the opposite direction as he approached them. An outsider was something they'd neither wanted nor needed, especially one with such an air of *otherness* about him; especially when Tommy was wading his way through the worst year of his life.

1984 was a year Tommy would never forget. It was the year Peach had handcuffed his father, driven him away, locked him up. Three months later his mother was dead, his grandfather had taken up residence in his house, and Tucker was roaming the streets of Valley Park on the hunt for friends who didn't want him. Eventually, Tucker had left Tommy and Jed to it, but still he would hang around the estate and stare at them with glassy, emerald eyes, saying nothing – just as he was doing right now.

In 1984 Tommy had grown up, had his eyes reluctantly opened, and Valley Park and all its offensiveness had become his prison. In his mind, there was only one way out of the place: money.

And DCI Peach had just confiscated it.

PEACH

Sally's swollen hand was limp in his. It felt cold to the touch even though her temperature still raged.

The nurse touched his shoulder. He knew it was meant to be kind but still he shrank from it. Every strand of her frizzy red hair, every smile meant to give him comfort put his frayed nerves on a knife edge.

He'd just been through two hours of hell.

By the time he was allowed into the cubicle, Sally had been stripped to her underwear. Soaking from head to foot, she'd squirmed on a metal-framed bed, her feet twisted behind her, and her spine bent backwards into the unnatural curve of a gymnast. Then the wailing began – a deep, animal sound which started as a low growl then climbed to the high-pitched cry of a newborn. Nurses and paramedics had swarmed the cubicle, throwing wet towels and sheets over Sally's writhing body while she pulled her head back, eyes rolling, the wail unremitting and unnerving.

'Mr Peach?' A doctor entered the cubicle with a burst of authority, her fair hair tied back, her face freakishly void of eyebrows and eyelashes.

'What the hell's going on?' Peach demanded.

The doctor gave him a look that said she didn't appreciate his belligerent tone. 'We need blood,' she ordered. 'Is your daughter a drug user?'

'She just finished her O Levels for Christ's sake.'

'Is she sporty?' The doctor stood back as a nurse began drawing blood from Sally's arm, four others holding her still.

Peach barged forward, but the doctor took his arm firmly and held him back.

'Please, Mr Peach,' she said.

He swallowed, thinking. 'Plays netball – or used to, I don't know.' He tried to remember the last time he'd seen Sally's PE kit in the wash or hanging on the line, but his head was full of sand.

'Severe overheating on this scale is usually associated with high impact athletics in very hot conditions.' The doctor stated her facts as if reading from a text book. 'So, unless she's been running a marathon—'

'She doesn't run bloody marathons!' Peach spat. 'Now, are you going to tell me what the hell's happening here?'

A temperature of over forty-three degrees and a heart rate of two hundred and twenty, he was told. Unfamiliar with things medical, the words were meaningless to him, but the tone indicated their gravity.

'You really need to stay back for now,' the doctor said with a direct stare that rooted his feet to the floor. She turned to the nurse holding the vial of Sally's blood and told her to get it to the poisons unit immediately.

'Poison? Jesus.' Peach ran his hand though his hair, clutching it at the crown and pulling it hard as if causing himself pain might ease some of Sally's distress. It didn't, and convulsions began to rattle her body, her eyes startled, bubbles of foam appearing at the sides of her mouth.

The doctor took a syringe, filled it with fluid from a glass vial and flicked it with her finger. She injected the fluid into Sally's arm and the convulsions slowed until she stopped moving all together.

'Temperature's down to 42.9,' said the nurse with the frizz.

The statement brought no sighs of relief, no victorious smiles between the medics who stood around with their hands over their mouths.

The doctor stood over Sally, the only sound the dripping of water onto the floor.

Then all hell broke loose.

'She's stopped breathing,' he heard, and he was ushered out of the cubicle and into the corridor.

***

An hour later, he sat in a waiting room. It contained only a sink, four chairs, and a small table, upon which a box of tissues idled, waiting to be plucked. The room screamed *bad news*, the sort of place people were brought to grieve and cling to each other. Alone, he stared at a tall window which let in the yellow light of the hospital car park, willing Sally to be strong, to survive.

When the doctor finally walked in, Peach felt his breathing become shallow. She took a seat opposite him, her face the picture of concern.

'She's breathing,' she said, 'but she needs help, she can't breathe on her own.'

His relief was short lived as he searched the doctor's face for hope but saw none.

'Your daughter is very sick, Mr Peach.'

'I can see that,' he replied, staring at her name badge: *Doctor Lucy Flynn.*

'You're a police officer?'

'Detective Chief Inspector,' he said, relieved his rank was known, and he wouldn't be treated like a dimwit.

Doctor Flynn was unimpressed. 'People suffering this sort of hyperthermia rarely recover. In fact, I've never known a case—'

'I thought you said she was too hot,' said Peach, unable to buck the instinct to jump on inconsistency.

'*Hyper,*' she said. 'Not *hypo.*'

He felt himself flinch at the correction, and the knot in his stomach threatened to cut his breath short as he listened to her explanation of a body overheating to compensate for loss of fluid, the brain ceasing to regulate the body's temperature, and the organs starting to fail. Normally, he would welcome a straight reporting of the facts, but this was brutal, the words winding him.

'We'll do everything we can,' the doctor said, 'but you might want to let the rest of the family know.' She inhaled deeply. 'It's unlikely she'll survive, Mr Peach,' she said on the out-breath, 'and if she does, well …'

She was lying. She was some sort of incompetent.

Peach leant forward, the way he would to the criminal filth he'd interviewed a thousand times. The woman needed to do her job and save his daughter's life.

'If she dies,' he said, 'I will hold you wholly responsible.'

'If she dies, you might want to find out who gave her the drugs.'

Peach's face flamed, his counter-attack evaporating.

'You can stay here for now,' said Dr Flynn. 'We're just taking her up to intensive care.' The doctor stood, but Peach kept his eyes on her vacated chair. He couldn't look at her. He didn't like what he saw in her face: defeat.

Her voice became gentler, a little sad. 'I'm sorry,' she said, and she left the room.

Peach stared at the imprint she'd left on the padded chair, fear and rage making it impossible to move.

The rest of the family. She was wondering where the mother was, no doubt.

His stomach rolled, his forehead prickling with a sickly sweat. He stumbled to the sink in the corner of the room and retched. There was nothing to come out, nothing but air and guilt.

His hands clasped the sides of the basin as his legs weakened and the acid throttled him. When the spasms had subsided, he shrank back and sat on the wide window sill, his head against the cool glass.

Sally. Sensible, kind, hard-working.

She would not touch drugs. And she would not die.

TOMMY

The second slow dance was crawling to its final, painful crescendo, Jed finally in the throes of snogging a girl who resembled the woman with the cheekbones from the warehouse storeroom, only shorter, stouter, and considerably more pissed.

Tommy sat opposite Frankie, arms crossed, tapping his fingers on non-existent biceps as he looked around the emptying club. It was small but popular, and Tommy knew the lease was up for sale. His own nightclub; it was a dream he'd harboured for years, the thought of a nine-to-five job in a shop or an office filling him with horror. Not that he'd get one even if he wanted to. He'd tried and failed on many occasions, the boredom and the bitching driving him to near insanity. The bosses would send him packing for the smallest mistake or the first time he was five minutes late. They'd taken a chance on him, they'd say. Not often they would take on someone from "that end of town." He'd let them down; he'd let his *community* down.

All he had now was the fiddle job cleaning the Metrocentre a couple of mornings a week which kept his head above water. Just.

A hand on his shoulder made him start. Jed, his elbow hooked around the girl's neck, was retrieving his jacket from the stool, asking him if he fancied a house party. Tommy shook his head. House parties weren't his thing these days. Full of bad home-brew and dope-fuelled epiphanies.

'Suit yourself.' Jed looked like he too could crawl into his bed, but old habits die hard. The girl was hammered, her eyes barely open, oblivious to Jed's apparent disappointment at his conquest.

Jed whipped his jacket over his shoulder and led the girl away.

'That's all right, I didn't want to go anyway,' muttered Frankie, turning to Tommy. 'Lift?'

'Aye, cheers, mate.'

'Right, I'll just have a slash.'

Frankie stood, hiking up his already high-waisted jeans and heading to the gents' while Tommy sunk back onto the stool, resting his arm on the wooden bannister that enclosed the dance floor. He imagined Jed at the decks, Hadgy Dodds on the door, Frankie driving him home at the end of the night. A club like this would be perfect – a little goldmine. The flock wallpaper would have to go, the sound system replaced, the bar reconfigured. He could fill this place to the rafters, no bother.

The club's houselights flickered on, revealing Tucker, one blood-red Doctor Martin boot flat against the scuffed panel of the bar, his eyes on the door of the gents'. Tucker had beefed up in the last couple of years; he trained hard and fought easy.

With an ominous glance at Tommy, Tucker pushed himself away from the bar with his foot, the flash of the blade making an appearance once more as he made a beeline for the men's toilets.

Tommy flew from his seat, running to Tucker's side. 'What you doing?'

'What I'm told.'

Tommy stuck with him, and they stopped at the toilet door, Tommy pushing his way ahead of Tucker, arms held out, barring access to Frankie. 'Howay, Tucker, he's not done anything.'

Tucker raised his chin in challenge. Nobody said "no" to Paul Smart, the man that now had Tucker's undying loyalty.

Tommy's eyes flicked towards the door behind the bar and the man it harboured. 'What does he want?'

'It's business,' said Tucker. 'Maybe it's *family* business,' he added with an orphan's bitterness.

Tommy thought for a moment too long, and Tucker swirled the knife in his fingers, pushing Tommy to one side, and throwing the door of the gents' open.

'Wait!' Tommy pulled on Tucker's arm and to his surprise, Tucker relented, his hostile eyes taking on a warning. It wasn't Frankie he wanted. Paul Smart wanted Tommy, and Tucker would never let his boss down.

'Don't be a dick'ead, Tommy,' Tucker said, the "ck" rumbling in his throat like gravel. 'When he wants to see you, he wants to fucking see you.'

***

Paul Smart and half a dozen men played cards, a pile of notes and a bottle of whisky in the middle of a round table. The room was windowless and stuffy, the dense smoke making Tommy cough.

Paul was facing him, his eyes fixed in concentration on his cards. He raised his hand and Tommy stood still, knowing not to interrupt a man about to play a hand. Four of the men were sitting back in their chairs, arms folded, tumblers empty of their scotch. Tucker took up his post by the door, the greyhound standing motionless by his side, staring at a single point on the floor.

Tommy put his hands in his pockets and waited, a small trickle of sweat weaving its way down his back. He'd hear what the man had to say, answer his questions, and walk away. *Simple,* he told himself.

Paul was dressed in black, his high shirt collar tipped with platinum python heads. The wide pink tie would have looked ridiculous on anyone else, but Paul Smart carried off colour unapologetically. He bore more than a passing resemblance to a clown, Tommy thought. His forehead was wide and high, his nose and chin so close together they squashed his mouth into a pouting line, forcing premature ripples to form around his mouth like rows of brackets. Paul Smart could win any gurning competition hands down.

'I'll see you,' said Paul to his opponent.

A bald man with no neck laid his cards on the table with a self-satisfied expression.

Paul regarded the full house, knocking back his whisky, and glancing at Tommy before laying down his cards.

'Four of a kind.'

'Fucking hell.' His opponent pushed the cards away and Paul smiled, revealing short, gapped teeth. He pulled the money towards him as the bald man stood, grabbed his jacket from the back of the chair, and pushed past Tommy, leaving the room in quiet rage. The other men began to file out, shaking Paul's hand, heading back to their wives with empty pockets and a few lies to think up.

Without looking at Tommy, Paul beckoned him over. Tommy sat on the chair furthest away from him, hands still in his pockets.

'Drink?' asked Paul.

Tommy shook his head, wondering how to play this. Friendly? Cocky? He decided on a bit of both.

'Bit low brow for you this, isn't it?' he said, looking around the room.

'Thought I might find you here,' Paul replied, pouring himself a generous drink. 'I hear you got raided tonight, by Peach himself.' Tommy's blank look brought a frown to Paul's face. 'You know, big 'tash, googly eyes.'

'I know who he is,' said Tommy.

'Of course, you do.' Paul offered a half smile of insight, but he left it there, hanging in the air like a bare bulb. 'I suppose as long as they're chasing you, it keeps them out of my hair.' He tapped his lacquered flat-top and Tommy wondered if it was mowed to perfection daily like a tennis court – it never got any longer, and it never got any shorter.

'I hear there's money to be made at these parties,' said Paul. 'Public-school boys down south, raking it in, eh? Posh kids with university degrees? The rich getting richer?'

Tommy attempted a bored expression but wasn't sure he pulled it off. 'Tucker said you wanted to talk business. What sort of business?'

'Funny business,' said Paul. 'Keeps me laughing, all the way to the bank.' He smiled, and Tucker snorted like a wart hog, the brown-nosing twat. Looking over his shoulder, Tommy noticed that even the greyhound had lifted its head as if trained to laugh at Paul Smart's jokes. The whole scenario was becoming offensive – Tucker, Smartie, the stink of sweat and whisky, the heat.

He turned back to Paul. 'What, lending to people with nowt? Aye, that's a right laugh.'

Paul's face became stern. 'I offer a service to the community,' he said, 'one your old man was more than happy to take advantage of.'

And just like that, the light bulb sparked into life, and Tommy's skin prickled. His father, Reggie, had been an abysmal gambler, in debt to Paul Smart for thousands. But still he'd kept on betting, despite his better nature.

'He had a problem,' said Tommy, his defences up despite his aversion to his father and his crime.

'Oh, so do I.' Paul put his hand on the pile of notes next to him. 'Only I win.'

Tommy wasn't sure whether it was the heat or the memory of his father, long pushed to the back of his mind, that made his lungs tighten.

'What do you want?' he asked, attempting to expedite matters.

'A new venture,' said Paul, his blue eyes suddenly animated. 'Something with a bit more – what do you say – panache. I'm expanding my interests.'

Paul was watching him keenly, waiting for what Tommy would say next, which was nothing.

'Raves, man!' said Paul. 'All-nighters! They're all the rage.'

Tommy frowned, curled his lip a little. 'What do you know about it?'

'Nowt,' said Paul. 'But you do.'

'Bit out of your league, isn't it?'

An intake of breath came from behind him – Tucker, making it clear Tommy had taken the challenge too far. It didn't do to patronise the likes of Mr Smart, but Paul let out a rumbling laugh that seemed to go on for minutes rather than seconds.

'You should be on the fucking telly, you,' he said. 'Now, here's something you should know.' The smile was gone, and he was leaning forward, pointing a manicured finger. 'Nothing, I repeat, nothing, is out of my league, laddie. Now, you've got a problem. You're being shut down, am I right?' He leaned further over the table and Tommy pushed back into the hard wood of the chair. 'But,' Paul continued, his tone beginning to coax, 'if you can get a few thousand to one of your dos they'd have to leave you to it. Wouldn't want a riot on their hands – bad for community relations.'

The trickle of sweat had turned into a river and was running into the crack of Tommy's arse. The conversation was going in a direction he didn't like one bit.

He shifted uncomfortably. 'Actually, Smartie, we're not doing any more,' he lied. 'So, if you'll excuse me.' He made to get to his feet.

'*Sit down!*' Paul's voice cracked like a whip and Tommy's wet arse cheeks hit the chair hard. 'And it's *Mister* Smart to you.' His steely eyes remained on Tommy as he bent to pick up a shoe box from beside his chair. 'Here. Watch these.' Paul slid the box across the table. '*Proper* raves from down south. And one of yours.'

Tommy attempted to keep his hands steady as he opened the box and looked down at two videocassettes.

'Had some of my lads at your dos these last few weeks.' Paul indicated the videos with his head. 'Thought I'd see what all the fuss is about.'

Tommy recalled one of his raves at the old Wallsend shipyard – abandoned only a year earlier and still in good nick – some bloke with a video camera who'd been escorted from the premises. Tommy had thought he was police until he noticed the Borstal spot on the fella's temple.

'Load of fucking bollocks if you ask me,' Paul said, visibly tetchy. 'But hey, who am I to argue with a whole generation?'

Paul Smart was barely into his thirties, and yet he seemed a whole generation away from Tommy. People were getting old before their time. You were lucky if you made it to fifty on Valley Park.

'There's always money to be made from rebellion.' Paul smiled, relaxing somewhat, as if the very thought of profit relieved his anxieties. He sat back and crossed his legs, grasping his knee with knitted fingers. 'Right, so, who supplies your drugs?'

There it was: the interests that Paul Smart was expanding, the *panache* he so desired.

Contempt settled in Tommy's gut. 'There's no drugs at our dos,' he said.

Paul snorted. 'Get away to Gateshead.'

'Everybody's searched, and if there's 'owt dodgy they don't get in.' He knew what was coming: Paul Smart supplying drugs to his raves. *His* raves. He'd rather buff the floors of the Metrocentre for the rest of his life.

'Are you taking the piss?' Paul was scratching at his forehead.

'That's the policy.'

'Policy? Jesus.' Paul pointed at the shoe box. 'They're all off their fucking heads, man, are you blind?'

Tommy blinked, hesitated. He knew the drugs were part and parcel of the scene, just as it had been for the hippies twenty years earlier, but for him it was about the music, the integrity of it, the way it brought people together in dance; the rhythm of language without words; musical freedom. And where better to express it than in the city's forgotten warehouses, monuments of decay, of toil and sweat. He couldn't control what they took before they got there, and a couple of pills changing hands didn't bother him but dealing on the scale Paul Smart was interested in was something else altogether. It was seeped in greed and violence, the very things the acid-house movement rejected, and the very things Paul Smart represented.

'We make the money off the door,' Tommy said, flatly.

Paul rubbed a hand over his mouth. 'You're not a very good business man, are you?'

'That's a matter of opinion,' Tommy replied.

'That's fact, laddie. You've not even got any shoes.'

Tommy looked down at his socked feet, the toe bulging, and he felt the heat of embarrassment rising up his neck.

'How much does it cost, to put on one of these all-nighters?' Paul asked. 'A proper one. Lights, bouncy castles, Frankie Fucking Knuckles?'

'So, you do know something about it.'

'Not as daft as I look,' said Paul. 'Five, ten grand? You'd get a hell of a party for that.'

He would, there was no denying it. With thousands of punters they'd make tens of thousands of pounds. But Tommy wasn't daft, he knew what it meant to involve someone like Paul Smart. It would never end.

'I don't need a loan,' he said, 'but thanks for the offer, I appreciate it.'

Paul stared at him full-on for some moments, Tommy unable to read his expression, his nerves starting to fray. He flinched when Paul rose from his chair, but the blow didn't come. Instead, Paul strode over to the dog, getting down on one knee and ruffling its ears, leaving Tommy wondering if the conversation was finally over.

'Bought this beauty from Hadgy Dodds,' Paul said. 'She's going to make me some serious cash.'

Tommy thought he spotted worry on the dog's face, as if she knew her fate if she didn't live up to expectations. 'I wouldn't buy nowt off Hadgy Dodds,' he said, the attempt at banter signalling his relief at being able to stand; at still having his legs.

Paul was looking into the dog's eyes. 'I'm calling her Peach Surprise, just for you.'

The door and Frankie beyond it beckoned, and Tommy felt like a child in the headmaster's office, wondering if he should wait to be dismissed.

'And tell your friend with the bonny hair that I've bought the debt for the dodgy trainers,' Paul said.

Tommy's mind wandered to Jed and the shoe boxes that lined the walls of his bedroom.

'Tucker's collecting the money from now on, and he'll be wanting five hundred quid in the next two days.' Paul grinned up at Tommy. 'See? Diversification. Don't forget your videos.'

Tommy snatched the videotapes from the box and walked to

the door, grasping the handle. He wasn't quite sure how he'd done it, but he'd got away with saying "no" to Paul Smart; a tiny triumph on a night of failure.

But his foot was barely over the threshold when he heard Paul's voice at his shoulder.

'If you don't do it for me, do it for your *family.*'

***

Tommy's garden wall was cool and damp with dew as he sat next to Frankie, sharing a cigarette, the first signs of dawn visible over the chimney tops of Valley Park. Across the road, a burnt-out car still smoked from last night's mischief. The estate was quiet now, the daylight tranquil enough. It was the nights that came alive, the estate holding its breath during dusk until the fire, the bottles, and the joy-riders took control.

Tommy slouched and bounced his heels off the wall, his trainer and Paul Smart's videos next to him. 'Look, Frankie, if you couldn't get cars, it wouldn't bother me. I'd get a taxi.'

'You can't afford taxis,' Frankie mumbled.

'No, but I would, if I could.'

Frankie was rubbing at his palm with the thumb of his other hand.

'What?' asked Tommy.

'Well, sometimes I feel like, you know … I don't fit in.'

Frankie was the butt of everyone's jokes, especially Jed's, but Tommy liked him. He was loyal and protective, and at twenty-eight years old, he was like the big brother Tommy never had but knew existed out there somewhere. He'd failed to extricate the right information from his mother, always frightened he'd bring on the tears and the days – sometimes weeks – in bed the boy's memory seemed to induce. She'd given the child up before Tommy was even a glint in her eye, and now she was gone the information would lie forever unknown. His father had similarly remained silent on the issue, and he could hardly ask Reggie about it now. Tommy hadn't seen his father in five years, and nor did he want to.

He straightened his back and put a hand on Frankie's shoulder. 'What the fuck are you on about? 'Course you fit in. It's good you can get cars, but you're a mate first, right? Hundred per center.'

Frankie rubbed at his mouth, trying to hide a small smile. He'd been a regular attender at Tommy and Jed's Northern Soul revivals back in '87. Frankie had the moves down to a fine art despite his short, round stature, and his spins had become not only renowned but expected. He'd worked cash-in-hand for Honest Jim's Motors for ten years, and Jim trusted him with the array of his customers' bangers and classic cars. The odd lift to their venues had turned into a regular chauffeur job, Frankie happy to talk for hours about his favourite music and spend more time doing something he loved even more than dancing: driving cars.

Tommy handed the cigarette back to Frankie, and they both looked to their right at the sound of scraping. A young boy walked towards them, dragging a stick across the walls and garden gates. It was one of the Logans – the youngest one, Carl. He was naked bar a pair of dirty Y-fronts, his brown eyes, massive in his gaunt head, cast down to the pavement. Snot caked his upper lip, drying to a crust.

Tommy kept his eyes on little Carl, wary of any of the Logans, even the seven-year-old. 'What you up to, then?' he ventured.

'Camping,' said Carl, keeping his eyes lowered and walking on down the street, the stick running over their legs and back to the walls and railings of the front gardens.

Tommy swallowed a pang of guilt; guilt that wasn't his to bear. The child was fatherless these last five years, just like him.

When Carl was out of sight, Tommy jumped down from the wall.

'What did Smartie want, like?' asked Frankie.

'Nowt,' said Tommy. What could he say? That Paul Smart wanted to be his new business partner? Joint bank accounts? Champagne with Paul Smart at night clubs with telephones on the tables? 'Just keep it to yourself, all right?'

'Aye, aye, I'll keep shtum,' said Frankie. 'He's a heed-the-ball, mind.'

Tommy hardly needed to be reminded.

As Frankie drove away, Tommy stepped into his dark hallway and crept upstairs, pushing open the door to the baby's room. He looked down over the edges of the cot. She slept with her mouth slightly open, her dimpled hands twitching in dream. He kissed two fingers and placed them on her perfect, button nose.

In the bedroom, he slipped off his jeans and T-shirt and slid into bed beside Sam, only a sheet covering her ivory back in the sticky dawn. He traced a finger down her arm and she stirred, hitting out behind her with a '*Gerroff!*'

He put his arm over her body, filling his nose with her damp neck, curling his body around hers.

Her hand took his, and she kissed it, putting it under her chin where she held it tightly until sleep took her again and he felt her grasp loosen.

His family.

Through the open window, he heard the chiming of the stick on railings once more: little Carl Logan back on his patrol of the street. Try as he might, Tommy couldn't erase from his mind the image of Carl's dad, Billy, lying on the ground, riddled with bullets, Tommy's own father standing over him with the gun in his hand.

He held Sam tighter to him, easing the spreading sense of shame.

'Love you,' he whispered, and he closed his eyes.

SUNDAY

PEACH

The scuffed trainer rested amid the circular stains of countless mugs of tea on Peach's desk, the bag of money lying open at his feet. He still wore the long Mac over his shirt and jacket, his attention to appropriate summer attire hardly his top priority. There was nothing he could do, they'd said at the hospital. He should go home and get some rest.

As if he could rest.

He stared at the greenish glass screen of a computer that had appeared on his desk a few months earlier. It served no purpose other than to offer a distorted image of his own face. He'd never switched it on. He had everything he needed in the filing cabinets and the archives. In his head. The invitation to the computer course in his in-tray had gone unanswered since Easter.

The shadow of a figure drew his eyes to the window which overlooked the wide corridor of the ancient police station. There was no natural light, the grey Venetian blinds broken and bent, the imprints of fingers exposing a thick layer of dust. He was told that fancy new "vertical" blinds were coming. There'd been a meeting about it.

The figure's face was at the window and Peach quickly dropped the trainer into the bag at his feet before the door opened and Detective Superintendent McNally stood in the doorway in a pair of grey shorts and some sort of Hawaiian shirt. His black hair was greased back as always, collecting in a bunch of short curls at the nape of his neck. The dyed hair looked absurd on a man approaching sixty, and Peach wondered how his boss had the metal to walk into a chemist and buy the stuff. Perhaps the wife got it for him. Perhaps he had no choice in the matter. Some called Mrs McNally assertive; Peach thought her a ball-breaker.

'What the hell are you doing here?' McNally's accent was southern, some might say posh.

'Could ask the same of you, sir.'

'Paperwork, bane of my bloody life,' said McNally.

And an opportunity to get out of some household chores, thought Peach.

'How's Sally?'

Peach thought he heard a cheery tone to his boss's voice. He kept his eyes lowered. Sally was in an induced coma, machines breathing for her, her brain barely functioning.

McNally sighed. 'Look at the state of you, go home, will you?'

Home. Peach couldn't think of anything worse. He'd never liked the place, but his wife had wanted a bungalow, detached from any other properties. Terraces were for a different class of people, and a detached house had been out of their range of affordability.

'Just as soon as I've finished up here,' he muttered, pushing some paper around his desk.

'What did you get last night?'

'An hour at the hospital,' said Peach, rubbing at his eyes.

'I meant the raid.'

Peach had to think for a moment, fatigue hanging like a fog in his head. 'Sound equipment, decks.'

'Drugs?'

Peach chewed at the inside of his cheek and McNally plunged his hands into his pockets.

'Look,' he said, 'I've got to take you off these rave things. You know the procedure. You should take some leave, people will understand.'

Peach's chin jutted in offence. He'd hardly taken a day's leave in his life and he wasn't about to start now, not while the crime kept going up and the number of bodies required to fight it kept going down. It was resources he needed, not a bloody holiday.

He eyeballed McNally. 'Got someone else to put on it, have you?' He stopped there. He shouldn't speak to his superior like that, but McNally was non-confrontational. A wimp.

McNally flushed a little and stammered something about getting a temporary replacement Detective Inspector as soon as the next sick note came in. Peach's DI had been off for a month already – stress they said. That's what happened when you put women in charge, either off on maternity leave with their feet up or struck down with the pressure.

'You need to stay well away,' McNally said. 'Get Murphy to do the legwork, that's what he's here for. But there's no crime here, not unless …'

Not unless she dies.

Peach watched McNally bite back the words and begin to back away.

'Ten minutes and I want you out of here,' he said. 'And don't make me say "that's an order", but it is.'

Peach conceded with a nod of the head, eyes following McNally as he left the office and disappeared down the corridor.

When his boss was out of sight, he glanced down at the trainer hanging out of the carrier bag. It should be bagged and evidenced, but who was to notice? It would only lie on a shelf while more important crimes took priority.

With his DI at home watching *Richard and Judy*, he'd been trying to track down the organisers of these parties alone for the best part of two months. The system was so slow that by the time he got wind of a party, got the officers and resources approved and organised, the damn thing was over. Last night had been a one-off, the city unusually quiet and plenty of officers chewing their nails with nothing to do. After months of whinging, McNally had finally agreed to a temporary secondment, a sergeant from outside the area who could do some undercover work – someone the organisers wouldn't recognise. And look who he'd got – DS Andrew Murphy, a detective Manchester CID had no doubt wanted rid of, a greasy-haired streak of piss with dopey eyes and the enthusiasm of a sloth.

His eyes settled on a school picture of Sally on his desk, aged around ten. She'd decorated the frame herself with crepe paper flowers and leaves – red, yellow, and green now faded to insipidness. It was taken just before everything went pear-shaped. She grinned rather than smiled, her mousy hair brushed over to one side, curling cutely at her ears.

He couldn't look, and he turned away from the face, so like her mother's. As she'd grown up, Sally had become more like Kathleen in both appearance and character – Kathleen's old character, the one she had when he first met her.

He felt the weight of his sleepless night and was about to stand when the office door opened, and DS Murphy stood in the doorway. He was a short, stocky man of around thirty, with eyes that sunk at the edges in a way that reminded Peach of the rabbit from the *Magic Roundabout*. Murphy was wearing the same clothes as last night and Peach wondered if he'd been to bed at all. The hat was gone, and his basin-cut brown hair hung like a pair of curtains over his face.

Peach frowned and waved him away.

'Just came to see if you were all right, sir,' said Murphy, entering the office, and closing the door.

The nasal Mancunian accent grated on Peach, the *"sir"*

coming out like *"soh"*, but Murphy's failure to act on his gesture irritated him more. 'Go home,' he said. 'And don't come to this office dressed like that again.'

Murphy looked down at his baggy jeans and sweatshirt. 'Got to blend in, innit?' he said. 'Can hardly turn up to a rave in me best clobber, soh.' Murphy threw himself into the chair opposite Peach's desk, hands clasped across his chest, legs spread wide. 'How's erm …?' His voice tapered off as Peach's eyes warned him not to cross the line into personal matters.

Murphy seemed to understand, and his expression changed from concern to its usual nothing. 'Got info on your organiser, if you want it.' He lifted his hips and thrust his hand into the front pocket of his jeans, pulling out a scrap of paper and leaning forward with it.

Peach snatched the paper from him and looked down at it. 'Is this it?' A scrawled list of two names, nothing else. *Tommy, Jed.*

'Yup.' Murphy slunk back into the chair. 'Took me all night to get them, boss. Ain't easy with this lot. Tight as a nun's fanny, I'm not kidding.'

Peach pinched the bridge of his nose with distaste.

'That's the point, though, ain't it?' added Murphy.

'What's the point? I see no point.'

'Well, it's all top secret, soh.'

'I'm quite aware of that. That's why we have *detectives*.' Peach handed the piece of paper back to Murphy. 'I'll need more than this,' he said, 'and it's *sir*, if you don't mind.'

'No problem, mate. How about "chief?"' Clearly "sir" was out of his reach.

'Please yourself,' said Peach. As long as he didn't call him "Guv." They weren't on an episode of *The Bill*.

'Sound.' Murphy yawned and stretched, saying that was him

off.

'Off?'

'You told me to piss off, chief, so I'm pissing off.' Murphy shrugged his logic at him.

Peach blinked his dry eyes at his sergeant, rubbed his tongue over his teeth. Now he had names he wanted more.

He pushed back his chair. 'Get me more on these organisers,' he said.

'Wha? It's Sunday, boss, they're all in fookin' bed!'

'Do it, or I'll have you back in Moss Side before you can say *barm cake.* And less of the language,' he added with a stern look.

Murphy threw his head back, clearly wishing he'd never come in to see how his boss was after all. 'Prefer your stottie bread anyway, chief,' he said. 'They're more *spongy,* know what I mean?' He indicated the word with his fingers and thumb, then dragged himself from the chair.

Peach's stomach rumbled a plea for food. He felt simultaneously sick and hungry, anxiety ebbing and flowing in waves. 'And get changed, you look like a bleeding hippy,' he grumbled. 'Smell like one too.'

'Brutal.' Murphy was at the office door, where he turned and held up two fingers in the peace sign. 'Have a groovy day, chief,' he said.

When the door had closed, Peach scooped up the bag from his feet, took the trainer from it and held it up. It was all he had to identify the loser who organised these all-night raves. He'd been indignant at first when McNally assigned him the job – a PR exercise to appease the city's angry residents who called at five in the morning complaining of the noise. It wasn't even a case he could investigate properly, the warehouses empty by the time he got there, the organisers long gone, counting their cash. But now, as he stared at the trainer in his hand, he felt the bitter surge of repulsion, the same repulsion he felt for rapists and murderers.

Hearing McNally's voice in the corridor, he opened the desk's top drawer and dropped the trainer into it, locking it with the bunch of keys that sat forever heavy in his trouser pocket. The handle of the door moved, and the carrier bag of money was under his Mac before the door opened and McNally's black head appeared.

'Home!' McNally ordered, opening the door wider and standing back.

Peach rose from his desk, hugging his Mac close to him as he left his office.

Five minutes later, he sat behind the wheel of his car, the morning sun dazzling his tired eyes. He pulled some of the bank notes from the bag and held them up, fanning them out and dropping them like floating leaves onto his lap. Profit from his daughter's mangled brain.

A loud bang on the window startled him. Trevor Logan, the eighteen-year-old bane of every copper's life, was staring through the driver's window, a manic smile across his face. Here was everything Peach hated about places like Valley Park. Trevor's face was raw with booze despite his tender years, his body emaciated, his eyes tiny holes of worthlessness. Trevor wavered, no doubt high on his latest fix as he stared at the cash on Peach's lap. Peach pushed the money back into the bag, shoving it under the passenger seat as a splash of spit hit the glass. Another fist to the window, and Trevor was walking away, his stride hyper, his filthy mouth effing and blinding at nobody at all.

'*Understand them*,' the social workers said. But Peach would never understand. Trevor Logan had been dealt a shit hand, his father murdered in front of his eyes. But everyone was dealt a shit hand at some point in their lives. Plenty of people witnessed horror, death, and pain, but not everyone turned out like Trevor Logan.

TOMMY

The red squares of the radio alarm clock glowed 12.31 p.m. when Tommy peeled his eyes open. Senses recovering one by one, he pulled a pillow over his head. The vacuum cleaner droned, the baby howled, the theme tune to *Countryfile* blared from the television which meant only one thing: Sam's mother, Denise, who thought a few years living in Northumberland afforded her some sort of authority on all things rural.

He turned onto his back, looking up at a familiar water stain on the ceiling. He liked to stare at it, creating the faces of aliens from its mushrooming outline.

His meeting with Paul Smart seemed like a murky dream now. Tommy had walked away, he'd agreed to nothing and nor would he, and Paul Smart would find some other mug to do business with. But the conversation had set his mind ticking – *lights, bouncy castles, Frankie Fucking Knuckles.*

His heart chimed. How incredible would that be? He could picture it clearly: the rave to end all raves. Jed was right after all; they needed to change tactics, but they couldn't step down, they needed to step up.

The familiar ambiance of his house helped dispel the foreboding he'd felt the night before. He felt himself blush, feeling foolish to have shown fear in what was probably Paul Smart's tenth meeting of the day.

He swung his legs over the side of the bed, sitting for a minute, the steady hammering of next door's windows being boarded up adding to the unremitting noise. He rose and stood in front of the warped wardrobe mirror, wiping at the sleep that matted the corners of his blue eyes, sticking his spidery long lashes together. *'Lassies' eyes',* his class mates had taunted.

His father's eyes.

His skin was white as cotton, punctuated with dimpled cheeks that had ensured a life of getting away with anything from cadging sweets from the tuck shop to blagging weed off some serious hard men from South Shields. Tommy ran his hand over his head, giving it a good scratch at the back. Only when his mother had shaved off his Leif Garret-like curls at the age of twelve had he looked like someone from Valley Park should: hard, poor. She couldn't be arsed with the nits anymore, she'd said, the letters from the school, the knocks on the door from the anti-nit do-gooders. So off it came. He'd grown to like it, eventually.

He breathed deeply, jutting out his ribs and slapping his bare, white chest like a primate about to do battle with his mother-in-law. He grinned cheekily at his scrawny frame, mimicking a body builder's pose – first left, then right. He might be poor, he might be useless, but he was all man.

Opening the bedroom door, he tiptoed across the landing, sliding stealthy fingers around the bathroom door handle, but the vacuum cleaner rumbled into the downstairs hallway, quickly followed by the peep-toe shoes of Sam's mother. Her hair was swathed with black dye, a band of white cotton wool framing a face thick with make-up. An old towel hugged her shoulders, held together with a clothes peg, protecting the silk blouse and pencil skirt that was her usual uniform. Denise was elegant, he supposed, in a Cruella De Vil sort of way. She could afford hairdressers, he knew that; any excuse to poke her nose in where it wasn't wanted.

Denise glanced up the stairs and Tommy froze, mid-tiptoe, looking down into her fake face. It was Paul Smart's face, only female. Sort of.

Paul's older sister had been estranged from her brother for years. They lived barely a mile apart now and yet they couldn't bear the sight of each other. Sam, ever protective of her mother, ever hateful of her Uncle Paul, wouldn't even hear his name spoken in her presence.

Aware of the baggy boxer shorts sliding down his backside, Tommy waved a timid hand.

'Christ almighty.' Denise switched off the vacuum cleaner with her foot and marched back into the living room. 'I've seen more meat on a butcher's pencil,' he heard her say, purposefully louder than necessary.

Sam's face appeared at the doorway. That face: hazel eyes and round cheeks, smooth and tanned by the sun. Sometimes he thought she was so gorgeous he could eat her up.

'Looks quite sexy, actually,' smiled Sam. She shooed him into the bathroom, mouthing *'half an hour'* to him with a lustful grin.

Inside the bathroom, Tommy stood at the cracked sink and examined his face in the mirror, mottled from years of steamy baths and a window you couldn't open for fear it would come off its hinges. He pulled a face, gave his cheeks a slap. They needed some colour, but that was about to come. His skin tingled in anticipation; there was nothing he liked better than hearing his wife panting in his ear. He turned on the tap to wash his face and bits, ready for action, but it twirled in his fingers pointlessly, nothing coming out.

Lips pursed in irritation, he gave the pipe a kick. It clattered, brown gunk sputtering into his hands and falling through his fingers. He stared at it indignantly.

What a shit-hole this place was.

***

An hour later, Tommy and Sam had the house to themselves,

Ashleigh, all trussed up in a frilly frock and mop cap, carted off by Denise to be shown off to her chums. Since Ashleigh was born, daytime sex came at a premium, the long days in bed eating toast, drinking tea, and shagging a distant memory to him now. Still, they took the opportunity whenever it arose.

Sam's head rested on Tommy's chest. 'You are a sex machine,' she purred.

Tommy tightened his arms around her and kissed the top of her head. 'Aye, you're a lucky woman.'

They chuckled and cuddled closer, Tommy running the tips of his fingers over the bones of her shoulders, the warmth and comfort of her body making him sleepy despite only waking up an hour ago. The contentment was short lived, however, as the sound of raised voices began to seep through the open window, an argument spilling out onto the street.

The Logans were at it again.

Tommy closed his eyes, feeling a deep unease at the sound of their mutual insults, reliving memories of Trevor Logan's onslaught on this house which started the very day Tommy's father was arrested.

Trevor, Carl the Camper's big brother, had just been released from youth detention, and Mrs Logan, a loud-mouthed woman who ran the estate's resident's association where she sold her knock-off cigarettes and anything else she could get off the back of a lorry, was coming down hard on her son now he was eighteen and responsible for his own actions. Trevor's appetite for heroin and cider, burglary and thieving from his mother's purse had driven her to shop him to the police herself on many occasions despite her own dodgy goings-on.

And Trevor hated her for it. Sometimes the fights turned physical, and the pair had to be prised apart by neighbours. Mrs

Logan came off the better these days, Trevor's strength eaten away by the poisons he inflicted on himself. Little Carl would watch on quietly, observant and mute, having barely spoken a word since witnessing the murder of his father five years earlier. He'd been a toddler, not even out of nappies, and the experience had shut down what few words he'd learnt by then.

It was a murder they'd all paid for: Tommy's father in jail, his mother dead, the Logans damaged beyond all repair.

Sam had stopped talking, her tightening grasp failing to soothe Tommy's growing restlessness as he listened to Trevor let rip a string of obscenities so vile he found his eyes closing tighter.

Trevor was outside the house now, driven from his own front door by the fire poker Mrs Logan kept at the bottom of the stairs for these very occasions. Tommy braced himself for the sound of breaking glass, a brick through the window, and he wondered if Sam was asking herself the same question he was: Ashleigh. What life would she have? What protection could they offer?

'Just ignore him,' he heard Sam say, gently.

It was easier said than done. Trevor Logan, though barely a teenager at the time, had taken it upon himself to make Tommy and his mother's lives hell once Peach had dragged Reggie away. Like Mrs Logan, Tommy's mother had been a mainstay of the estate, loved and respected, if not a little bonkers. Despite her big personality, though, she'd had times of deep, deep despair; a sorrow that seemed to come from nowhere and have her in her bed with the light off for weeks on end. The trigger generally involved babies, he knew now in hindsight – news of a new arrival, a storyline on a soap opera. She'd been immersed in this gloom already when Reggie had committed his crime, and Trevor Logan had as good as finished her off.

An eye for an eye.

When he opened his eyes, Sam was up on her elbow, looking down at him.

'What's wrong?' she asked.

'Nowt.'

'Tommy …' There was a hint of warning in the tone.

'Just … that.' He pointed his thumb towards the window.

Sam shook her head. 'Nah – ah.'

Sometimes Tommy thought she knew him too well. But if he raised the subject again, he risked the cold shoulder. Sam was an expert at it, and they'd had the conversation before: Tommy desperate to escape, Sam happy enough with her lot; a man she loved, a baby she adored, a roof over her head. Her bloody mother nearby.

Sam's raised eyebrows dared him to speak.

'What?' he asked, all innocence.

'You can be a right annoying little shit.'

'I'm just thinking.'

'What about?'

A beat. Why not have the conversation again? 'Money,' he said.

Sam dropped her head, her dark hair falling onto his chest. 'We'll manage,' she mumbled, as if for the millionth time.

'I don't want to just manage. You deserve more.'

'Don't bring me into it,' she said, lifting her head.

'*We* deserve more then.' He sat up, reaching for the cigarettes on the bedside table but finding the packet empty. 'Ashleigh deserves more.' He felt Sam's hand on his back. It gave him the confidence he was looking for. 'I've got all these ideas, Sam,' he said. 'I'm bursting with them. For a rave, a big one, like no one's ever done up here before.' He glanced back at her, testing the water.

Sam sat up next to him. 'How much?'

Tommy hesitated. It scared him to say it out loud. 'I reckon I could do it for five grand, maybe more. Probably more.'

'Well, that's that then,' said Sam, lying back down.

Tommy's head fell next to hers and they stared up at the stained ceiling. He thought he could make out Denise's ugly mug in one of the expanding brown lines. 'I just thought,' he said, cautiously, 'maybe your mam …'

Denise seemed to buy anything she wanted, always wearing something new, furniture delivered on what seemed like a weekly basis. She had the cash, no doubt about it. The pause was long and obstinate, but he'd started now. With the takings of a full-on rave, they could get out of this dump, move somewhere nice – Wideopen or Morpeth. He put it to Sam, hoping for once she would show some enthusiasm for the idea.

'You know what she said,' was her response.

He did. No more bail outs until he got a proper job and faced up to his responsibilities. Fat chance – on the first count. Still, he took the tentative next step. They had no secrets from each other, and he wanted her to know he'd been summoned last night at Phutures. Word might get out, and that cold shoulder might go on for days. 'Your Uncle Paul—'

Sam sat up sharply, cutting him short. 'Don't you dare. He's bad news, you stay away from him.'

Tommy held up his hands. 'All right, all right!'

Sam had told him of the day Paul had punched her mother with such force she'd lost a tooth. She'd described it with gruesome precision, the tale bringing tears of anger to her eyes. Sam had been twelve years old when it happened, had never been able to rid herself of the image of her uncle standing there, pure hatred in his eyes, calling her mother a whore and a bitch. It must have been going on for years, Sam had said, all the black eyes and bruises that only appeared after a visit from Uncle Paul. He was a brute, and Sam had never forgiven him.

Her body felt tense next to him now, and he regretted mentioning it. She was right, of course, getting involved with Paul Smart would be nuts.

'Hey,' he said, grinning at Sam, his hands disappearing under the sheet. 'Wanna see my impression of a tent pole?'

Sam looked down at her husband's proud erection and gave a pantomime gasp.

'*Samantha!*' The voice spewed through the letter box, making Tommy's skin bristle like a hedgehog, and his proud erection shrivel to nothing.

'Coming, Mam!' Sam called, pulling back the sheet with an apologetic look at Tommy.

Tommy sighed and puffed up the pillows behind him, sitting up to admire Sam's bare backside as she pulled on her dressing gown.

'No harm in asking,' he said. 'Shy bairns get nowt.'

Fastening her dressing gown, she bent down, and kissed him on the lips. 'You're radge,' she said.

Tommy pulled a crazy face in agreement.

'And I don't want to live in fucking Morpeth,' she added with a hiss.

And with that, she was gone.

PEACH

The beeps and blips of the machines that kept Sally alive still resonated in Peach's ears when he arrived home from the hospital mid-afternoon. There was no change in Sally's condition. She remained prostrate, arms by her sides, mouth hanging open around the breathing tube, lips and eyes swollen.

He entered the empty bungalow, numb with tiredness, stepping over half a dozen envelopes lying on the doormat. He needed a shower; he needed to rest. He'd sleep for a couple of hours in the chair by the telephone in the living room, just in case.

He headed for the kitchen and filled the kettle, setting it to boil next to a sink piled high with mugs and plates. He picked up one of the mugs, lipstick staining its rim. A milky film had formed on the dregs of the coffee inside and he wondered when Sally started wearing lipstick.

He put a tea bag in a mug then walked down the hallway to Sally's room, where he held the handle in one hand, the other raised, knuckle ready to knock. It was automatic.

It was a typical sixteen-year-old's bedroom. A large, framed picture of a bare-chested man holding a baby dominated the chimney breast wall, the others strewn with posters of pop stars he'd neither seen nor heard of: male or female, he couldn't tell with some of them. Her unmade bed sat against the radiator under the window, the curtains still drawn. He pulled them open and sat on the bed, opening the drawer of the bedside cabinet. He took out a small make-up bag. It was dirty inside, a few eyeshadows without their lids, a mascara, and a couple of pencils, a bobbin of black thread with a needle weaved through the cotton. On the floor by her bed was a long leather case full of neat rows of cassettes. He picked one up, *"Sunrise 1989"* scrawled in black ink across the label. He picked up another, *"Genesis 1988,"* it read. So, she had some taste after all.

He put the tape into the cassette player on the bedside cabinet and pressed *play*, but instead of the dulcet tones of Phil Collins he heard a racket so unmusical he wondered if the tape had got stuck like a scratched record. He wound it forward and pressed *play* again, the same nasty din hitting his ears. He fumbled with the buttons, unable to press *stop* quickly enough. It set his teeth on edge, the relentless repetition of the same notes.

Getting to his feet, he scoured the room. On one of the wardrobe doors was a collage of photographs, pink and red paper hearts interspersed between them. He strode over to it, searching out familiar faces he could put names to, friends who would have answers to questions that had begun to bombard his mind like midges, but they were all strangers to him except one. *Sarah, Sandra* – something beginning with an 'S' – a girl who used to come to tea after school. They'd been inseparable a few years ago, but what was her damned name? He wracked his weary brain but couldn't remember the last time anyone had come for tea.

At the bottom left of the collage was a photograph of a bare-shouldered girl with mean, blackened eyes, blond hair stuck to the sides of her face, tongue sticking out at the photographer, and middle finger raised aggressively. He tore it from the wardrobe door and held it closer to his face, scarcely able to believe the lairy face belonged to his child. It was another person, and yet it was her.

His chest constricting, he shoved the photograph into his trouser pocket, rubbing at the grey stubble that clung angrily to his jaw with his other hand. He looked around the room.

If there were drugs, he would find them.

***

Twenty minutes of rifling and plundering followed. When every draw had been turned out, every cupboard ransacked, every box emptied, he stood by Sally's bed, swimming in adrenaline and relief. He was right. Of course, he was right. There were no drugs. There was nothing in Sally's room but school books, clothes, trinkets, and magazines; nothing to make him distrust her.

He glimpsed his reflection in the mirror on Sally's wall. The skin around his eyes hung in folds, his grey hair stood up where his fingers had gripped and pulled at it. He flattened it down, remembering how Sally had once told him he looked like a TV cop from the seventies with his middle parting and moustache. He hadn't minded. Those were the days when coppers were coppers; the days when they could dish out a good thrashing and call the lesbians *butch*.

He gave himself a long, hard stare, recalling the numerous warnings he'd issued to Sally over the past year about drugs, alcohol, and, as much as it pained him, safe sex. Sally's response would be a roll of the eyes and assurances that she wasn't an imbecile. All he could hope was that the message got through. And it had got through, he was sure of it. Sally was blossoming, on the cusp of womanhood, doing well at school, about to embark on A levels. She wanted to be a television producer, and now she might not live to see tomorrow.

His chest began to sizzle. Someone had given her the drugs, someone had told her it would be fine.

He turned away from the mirror and sat on the bed, falling to his side and laying his head on Sally's pillow. McNally was right, he'd have to pull himself together, because when he found out who was responsible, he was going to make them wish they'd never been born.

***

It was past five o'clock when he awoke with a jolt, his face buried in the pillow. Like a jack-in-the-box, he was up on his feet and stumbling down the hall into the living room, where he sat in the armchair and fumbled in his pocket for the hospital's phone number. He picked up the telephone receiver with a trembling hand and dialled, terrified he might have missed a call, horrified he might be too late, that he hadn't been there to hold her hand as she slipped away.

The words "no change" were starting to eat away at him. He dropped the receiver into its cradle, the armchair creaking from its belly as it always did. It had been his wife's chair, and it had creaked from the day they bought it – Kathleen bending down to pick up her knitting; Kathleen reaching forward for the *Radio Times*; Kathleen standing up and stretching after the *News at Ten*.

It had been almost six years since he'd sat in that chair, preferring to stand if he ever needed to use the phone. Sally, however, had commandeered it. She curled up in it to watch TV, read books, or do her homework.

As if a shock ran through him, he jumped from the chair, almost hearing the *clickety-clack* of Kathleen's knitting needles.

***

When he entered his office, Peach found Murphy balancing on the edge of the visitor's chair with his cheek resting on the desk, the hood of a sweatshirt covering his head. He was dead to the world, mouth open, snoring.

Peach hung up his coat and sat in his chair. When he cleared his throat, Murphy's head shot up, a piece of paper stuck to the side of his cheek with saliva.

'Chief,' Murphy said, finding his composure.

Peach picked up the telephone and dialled reception. 'Tea,' he said, 'strong, two sugars.' He stared at Murphy who was blinking the sleep from his eyes and peeling the paper from his face.

'Got any Tizer?' he asked.

'Just the tea.' Peach hung up and folded his hands on the desk, a '*Well?*' in his eyes.

'Collins,' said Murphy, still somewhat disorientated. 'That's your man.'

'Who is he?'

'The organiser. Tommy Collins.'

Peach creased his brow and turned his head slightly, his mind flitting back to the night before, the brief glimpse of a young man on the flat roof of the warehouse's extension. Not the same Tommy Collins, surely?

The door opened, and the desk sergeant put a mug of tea in front of Peach and a can of Tizer in front of Murphy.

'Cheers, Shazza,' said Murphy, looking up at her with a wink. The older woman's grin and pat on the shoulder were almost motherly. Murphy had them eating out of his hands already.

The door closed, and Murphy hissed open his can of pop, taking a long drink. 'Got in with the Goths at that shopping centre in town,' he said, not before letting out a long, cavernous belch. 'They might look 'ard, but they're all nancies. One look at my ID and they were pissing themselves. Wouldn't be seen dead at a rave, like, but they knew who he was.'

'Where's he from?' Peach asked.

'Valley Park, wherever that is.'

Peach's hands cradled his mug of tea. 'Well, I'll be damned.'

'You know him, then?'

'I know the father.' Peach took a sip of his tea and looked at Murphy over the rim of the mug. 'He's a murderer.'

'Fukin' 'ell,' said Murphy with a short laugh.

Peach remembered it well. Reggie Collins, convicted of murdering Billy Logan outside his home on Valley Park in 1984, was currently serving a life sentence in Durham prison. Peach had spent more time than he would have liked on Valley Park Estate in 1984, back when he was a Detective Inspector on the hunt for weapons and bloodied clothes. The striking miners were vicious enough, but with any excuse for a scrap, the Valley Park skinheads didn't waste any time getting in on the pursuit of scabs. Two junior officers had had their faces slashed at Easington, and Victor, PC Smithy's German Shepherd, had been stabbed to death. Not by the starving miners, mind you – oh no – by yobs who had never done a day's hard graft in their lives. He remembered the houses of the estate, stinking of damp and dirty chip pans, the beds bare of sheets, the children half naked with the round bellies of the Ethiopians everyone was chucking money at back then.

'Want me to look him up on the computer?' Murphy's voice interrupted his thoughts.

'No need,' said Peach. 'It's all up here,' he tapped his temple.

'Fair dos,' said Murphy. 'Oh, here you go.' He leant down to the floor beneath the chair. 'I got you a sarnie.' He threw a white paper bag spotted with grease onto the desk. 'Cheese savoury stottie,' he said, prodding the bag with a proud finger.

'I don't like cheese,' mumbled Peach.

Murphy grimaced. 'Eh? Who doesn't like fookin' cheese?'

'Me,' said Peach. 'And swearing is a sign of limited vocabulary.' It was a saying of Kathleen's and it was out before he'd even realised. He cringed at the pomposity of it. 'You can go,' he added, and he was sure he heard the words *"grumpy old bastard"* as Murphy closed the door behind him.

***

With Murphy gone, Peach sat back in his chair and cast his mind back five years. Billy Logan had been mowed down in one of the most botched assassinations he'd ever investigated. It had taken six shots to kill him – two bullets missed, hitting the man's front door frame, the third and fourth catching Billy's shoulder and arm. Reggie Collins had had to walk right up to Logan to finish him off. But even then, Reggie's hand shook so much the next one hit his victim in the stomach – not fatal. The last shot, the final bullet, went straight into the chest, but still Billy wouldn't die, not for a long five minutes. The older boy, Trevor, and the toddler, Carl, had stood at the window and watched their father plead for his life, the mother out at bingo with her hoard of sisters. She'd come home to a river of blood that would see her on her knees with a scrubbing brush for weeks.

Peach had found Reggie Collins on his front door step within the hour, just three doors down from the Logans', bleating like an infant, begging the forgiveness of all the saints in Heaven. The gun was in the dustbin buried in ash but still bearing his fingerprints. Not a single witness from Valley Park came forward, but still, Peach had secured the guilty plea after very little negotiation, Reggie compliant and dazed. Collins' wife and teenage son had borne the brunt of the older Logan boy's anger for months after: shit through the letter box, the dustbins set on fire, broken windows, graffiti. Death threats. Everything short of firebombing the house itself and he'd tried that once or twice. Trevor Logan was a serial pain in the arse and had done about as much time as Reggie by the time he was sixteen, invariably back inside within days of his release. Trevor had just finished a two year stretch for nicking motorbikes, removing the engines, and dumping the carcases in the Tyne, all in the name of funding an insatiable drug and alcohol habit that would probably see him dead by the time he was twenty. Jean Collins, Reggie's wife, had killed herself in the end, he'd heard. Forty sleeping tablets prescribed that morning by the doctor. The reason for Reggie's crime remained a mystery. Some said it was a crime of passion, most shrugged their shoulders and got on with their lives.

Peach tried to remember Tommy's face. The boy had been there that day, a scrawny teenager standing on the doorstep as Peach led Reggie away in handcuffs, the mother on her knees in the hallway behind her son. Tommy had looked hard-faced, if he remembered, malnourished like the rest of them.

Tommy Collins. The name suddenly brought his blood to boiling point.

Criminals breeding criminals. Murderers breeding murderers. It was all par for the course in places like Valley Park.

DENISE

Denise Morris couldn't quite believe what she was hearing. *An investment,* he was saying: three hundred, maybe four-hundred per cent return. For someone.

Once the subtext of Tommy's inane chatter had sunk in, she began to enjoy herself; watching his eager little face, all animated as he explained the size of the event, the colours, the stage, what would go where, who would do what. She listened, she played along, nodding her head as if interested in a damn thing the useless pile of shite was saying.

'Easy money. For someone,' Tommy said. 'Just needs an investor with a few grand going spare.'

The arrogance of it.

Denise glanced now and then at her daughter who avoided her eyes, little flushes of red creeping up her neck. Denise was embarrassed for her. The clip on him: the T-shirt washed to within an inch of its life, the jeans torn at the knees, the socks ... She turned her face sideways, feeling a bit sick at the toe sticking through the hole.

And this house. Oh, she hated it. So dull, so dreary. She rued the day she ever took Sam to that caravan at Sandy Bay. At sixteen, her daughter still carried the puppy fat of her childhood and had the gorgeous, smooth round cheeks of a babe in arms. She'd kept Sam close to her, her hourglass figure starting to attract the attention of boys and a few grown men who should have known better. She'd had friends with daughters of the same age, off the rails and barking at their mothers as if they were the Devil incarnate. Hitting them, some of the little bitches, slapping their mothers' faces and calling them sluts. Sam was different: lively without the need to dominate, loving without the need for profit, and gentle. Gentle as a lamb. They'd been as close as mother and daughter could be.

Best friends.

This piece of work had changed all that. She'd thought Tommy harmless when she first saw him; like the runt of the litter, he wouldn't last long and not many would want him. But she'd been wrong. Sam had spent one minute in the glow of those sad blue eyes and she was a goner. Him too. Smitten. And from Valley Park to boot, as if it couldn't get any worse. What were the chances? The lovebirds had something in common instantly – the hell on Earth she'd escaped at seventeen years old.

But then Tommy Collins happened, and she was back. She wouldn't leave her only child alone in this place, even if it had meant being nearer her little brother – the brother who shunned her, the brother she missed so much it hurt.

She was happy for Sam to believe she was the one who had turned her back, walked away from the violence. It had gained her Sam's respect; her daughter thought her strong and resilient. But there was no truth in it, and when Sam fell in love, what little strength and resilience she had was replaced with an icy fear that she would lose her only child to this lazy lump of lard.

But it was worse than that. Turned out her daughter's new love had nothing, not a qualification to his name, not a chance of a real job, no future whatsoever. Three years on, he still had nothing, and her nineteen-year-old child was turning into a dowdy housewife in front of her very eyes. He had a fiddle job like everyone else of his calibre; a quid an hour, cash in hand, a fiver a week, if that. She'd wanted so much more for her daughter, wanted her to live a life of comfort, to strive for the life Denise never had as a young woman, and yet here Sam was, married too young, a single parent in the making; history repeating itself. Her daughter's general demeanour, however, was one of happiness which confused her. It didn't make sense. Denise had never been happy poor. Poverty was nothing to laugh about. It brought you down, it ate away at your dignity.

Give her time, Denise had thought; give her time and she'd see Tommy for what he really was: a waste of space. But she hadn't. Not yet.

He'd finished prattling now, leaning forward in the chair, waiting for her to tell him what a fine businessman he was and how lucky they all were to have such a clever man among them. Sam, too, had expectation in her eyes.

'Well,' Denise said, reaching for her handbag. She sensed Tommy stiffen, felt his hopeful eyes meet Sam's as he imagined his mother-in-law's fingers clasping the cheque book and asking him how much he needed. Instead, she pulled out a vanity mirror and a lipstick which she applied carefully, wiping the stray red away with her little finger. She snapped the mirror closed and rubbed her lips together. What Sam and Tommy didn't know was that she couldn't give it to him even if she wanted to. She had no money in the bank, not a penny to her name. Cash was so last decade. Credit was the way forward, and it was so easy to come by. 'Sounds like a no-brainer,' she said. 'For *someone*.' She smirked a little as she dropped the lipstick and mirror back into her bag, clicking it shut and sitting back onto the sofa. 'Any tea going?' she asked.

Sam's eyes were closed, and Tommy's face was turning a satisfying shade of pink.

'I'll make it then, shall I?'

Denise rose from the sofa and headed for the kitchen. By the time she came back, Tommy was standing at the small, round dining table in the corner of the living room. He was touching the new baby clothes Denise should have put out of sight, knowing how much it pained him when she indulged in Ashleigh. She might not want to invest in Tommy's stupid parties, but the baby didn't have to go around looking like something out of a Catherine Cookson novel. She'd put the clothes on top of a great pile of letters, unpaid bills, and the Visiting Order that Sam still requested every month on Tommy's behalf. Not that he'd ever been to see his murdering father; one small thing she could give him credit for.

'What's this?' Tommy asked.

'Little tights with diamonds on.' Sam was walking on egg shells, Denise could tell.

'Aren't they cute?' Denise smiled at Tommy. 'We got some lovely stuff, yesterday, didn't we, love?'

Sam's smile was weak, a mixture of gratitude and worry. She'd tried to stop Denise buying the clothes – 'maybe just something little,' she'd said, but Denise had hushed her, asked her why she wasn't allowed to buy her grandchild nice things. Sam didn't have an answer, and the basket had filled up. Denise knew it would rile Tommy, make him feel inadequate. But he was inadequate, and someone needed to make that clear.

Tommy's fingers were rifling through the shopping, labels still displaying their unaffordable prices. 'Don't suppose there's any food in the house?' he said.

Sam flushed red. 'There's enough 'till we get your giro tomorrow.'

'Well, first things first, eh?' He dropped the clothes onto the table as Ashleigh stirred in her buggy, letting out a feeble whimper. Tommy walked past the buggy towards the living room door.

'Where you going now?' asked Sam.

'I'm knackered.'

'You're always bloody knackered. I'm knackered!' She was on her feet.

'It's all the excitement you get spending your mother's money.' Tommy was walking out into the hallway.

'The only excitement I get is when the washing basket's empty! What is your problem?' Sam shouted after him.

'I'm married to you, that's my problem!' he called from the top of the stairs.

The bedroom door slammed, and Denise lifted Ashleigh from her buggy as the room fell silent. 'There is something the matter with him,' she said.

Sam threw herself onto the sofa, her eyes filling up, and Denise sat next to her, rubbed her hand up and down her daughter's arm while Ashleigh wriggled for her mam. She thought she felt Sam flinch, which only made her grab her arm tighter.

'I just want you to be happy, love,' she said.

'I am happy,' said Sam, pulling her arm free and taking the baby. But she wasn't. How could she be?

Denise looked around the room, void of colour, unlike her own house which shone with pinks and purples, reds and yellows. Colour was life. This house still stank of death, the furniture dating back to the sixties, the walls bare of décor or pictures aside from a framed photograph of Tommy's grandfather. It hung over the fireplace, yellow and shabby. She had to admit, it had a certain charm, him standing stiffly in his RAF uniform in the shadow of an aircraft hangar, chest proudly thrust out towards the camera. But it was so old, so bland, so *passe*.

She turned to Sam who was wiping at her eyes. She should offer comfort, tell her daughter everything would be all right. But Sam would never have the life she deserved if she thought it would all work out in the end, which, inevitably, it wouldn't. 'Why don't you come home, love? Your room's still there,' she said instead.

'Mam...' Sam growled, but she didn't finish the sentence, and Denise wondered if it was through pride, loyalty, or fear that her own pink bedroom was exactly what she wanted. Either way, the rejection smarted.

'Well, I've got to go, love. You know where I am.' Denise sighed, glancing at the window. The sun was getting low in the sky, and she needed to get herself ready for her visitor.

At last, her brother was yielding. They'd met twice already at Mark Tony's in town, the conversation stilted and cautious at first. The telephone call had come out of the blue, his voice – so very familiar – bringing a lump to her throat and a shudder to her spine. As they'd sipped at their frothy coffee, she'd wanted to ask so many questions but didn't know where to start. On their second meeting he'd been more at ease, and he did the asking; question after question about her life, her home, her work at the building society. She'd gushed her replies, the words cascading in the torrent of a waterfall, just happy to be near him again, to be in his company. Perhaps he would learn to forgive her now if he got to know her again.

Denise kissed Ashleigh on the cheek and picked up her bag, heading into the dreary hallway and opening the front door, leaving her daughter to her useless husband and her house that smelt of death.

TOMMY

Upstairs, a veil of failure was enveloping Tommy. It happened more often these days – anything from a busted tap to the coin-operated meter running out and not a fifty-pence to his name. Other people providing for his child.

It came down like an avalanche, but he hid it most of the time, taking to his bedroom or his friends, not wanting to hurt Sam with his disappointment in life. She would take it personally, think she was the problem. She didn't understand his need to branch out into the world, or at least beyond the confines of Valley Park. He wanted to do something; he wanted to be someone. But he'd messed up, missed his chance, didn't finish school. Twenty-one years old and a has-been before he'd even got there.

He should be grateful after all. He had Sam; he had Ashleigh. He had Jed and Jed's family who were like his second home. He even had Frankie, but he knew it wasn't enough. Something in him was busting to be free; to be successful. He thought he'd found it, the recognition he craved – that feeling in his chest that bordered on pain but made him fly. Over the last six months, once a week on a Saturday night, he was truly *happy*. But it appeared Peach had other ideas.

Tommy was lying on his stomach, flopped over the side of the bed. He reached out, pressing *play* on the beat box under the window. He hung there for a while as the rhythm of his thoughts began to synchronise with the beat. It baffled him how others didn't understand it – the vibe, the music, how it spoke to him in a voice of its own, how all the best sensations in the world could be wrapped up into one spectacular feeling on one night, shared by hundreds, thousands of others. Like a new religion, it was the closest he'd ever come to divinity. One hundred and twenty beats per minute of pure love.

His arms reached under the bed and he slid out a dusty, black art folder. He opened it and pulled out some posters, fanning them out on the threadbare carpet. He touched them: *'Class of 85'* – a soul all-nighter – their first gig and his first printed design. He smelt it, remembering the hours he'd spent on it, time and food forgotten. There were others: mod revivals, raves, even discos at the youth centre.

Noticing something poking out from the back of the portfolio, he eased out a sketchbook with his fingers. He'd forgotten it was there and touching it took him back to a school he'd barely attended towards the end. A few scribbled designs of aliens occupied the first few pages. Flicking through it, his eyes fell on a charcoal drawing: a striking UFO scene – not the usual flying saucer crap – a fearsome dome, shards of white light carving a tripod into the twilight. The dark sky protested, grumbling clouds churning out their alien intruders. His teacher had applauded that sky – literally clapped her hands and held it up to the class.

Space Generation.

He imagined the words lit up in purple neon, forming an arch at the entrance to a spectacle that would draw in fans of the movement from across the whole of the north. But it was pie in the sky, and he pouted gloomily as he reached under the bed again, straining his eyes. He spotted the little white box in a mound of fluff next to the skirting board, and he stretched further, easing it out with his fingertips.

Sitting up on the bed, he blew the dust from it and opened it carefully. A set of charcoal pencils lay inside, deserted and unused. On the inside of the lid was a message:

Dead proud of you, son, Mam xx

Son. Such a simple word, so full of affection. But he knew there was another son, the one she'd given up, and he knew she was proud of him too. She'd rarely mentioned him; only now and then from her weeping bed. The dark gloom would descend and take her upstairs for days or weeks at a time. He'd hated it, but now and then, at least he would get a snippet of information about his big brother.

'Such a beautiful boy,' she'd cried once, clutching Tommy's hand. 'Such a lovely family that took him. I think he's going to be someone very special, someone amazing.' She'd been so young, she said, and if she'd known Tommy's father was just around the corner, she'd have kept him.

'That's enough, Jean,' his father's voice had come from the doorway, and ten-year-old Tommy had been led out of the room.

It had sent his mind into dreamy overdrive, and ever since, when he thought of his brother, he imagined an intrepid explorer, a scientific genius, or an astronaut – that was his favourite. The first time he'd mentioned the astronaut to Jed, Jed had sulked for weeks, so he'd never mentioned him again. Jed's mother, Jean's best friend, had ignored any hints he dropped over the years – all it did was make her clatter crockery around as if it angered her, and Betty Foster angry was such a rare occurrence he didn't want to feel the responsibility.

His fingers ran over the edges of the spaceship in the drawing. The face of the boy staring up at it looked just like him, but it wasn't him. It was the astronaut without his helmet, the successful older brother who made Tommy strive to accomplish something - anything.

Tommy never finished the O level art exam; hadn't finished any of them. He'd had more important things to contend with, like a father in jail, a dead mother, and an interloping grandfather who arrived with nothing but his pipe and slippers and his RAF photograph under his arm which he hung above the fireplace before taking to Jean's chair and demanding a blanket for his legs.

Sitting up on the bed, Tommy emptied the pencils onto the sheet. This had always been his escape, and he'd neglected it for too long. As dusk crept into the bedroom, he picked out one of the pencils, turned to a fresh page of the sketch pad and started to draw.

DENISE

Paul sat stiff as a board, cradling a whisky in one of her best tumblers, the pink leather of the armchair squeaking as he lifted the glass to his mouth. The suite was only a few years old, but Denise had her eye on a new three-piece from Bainbridge's – buy now, pay in six months. She was describing it to him, but his expression of boredom shut her down and she felt herself flush awkwardly.

'You look well,' was all he'd said so far, but she'd liked the compliment. She often thanked her lucky stars she'd kept the weight off, avoided the middle-aged spread most women her age suffered. She wasn't skinny by any means, but she was no heifer either.

'Hey, mind, ye divven't look bad for thorty,' a man of tender years had said to her in a bar on Friday night. She often lied to young men. And she *didn't* look bad for thirty. She didn't look bad for thirty-eight either which was her actual age.

'Samantha all right?' Paul asked now, his tone brightening. 'Still with Tommy, I see.'

He hadn't asked about Sam until now, but when he did, she felt her heart, a stone in her chest for so many years, begin to thaw. She imagined them all together, out for a meal or on holiday somewhere warm. The family – Paul, her, Sam, and Ashleigh – all together again. Tommy didn't figure in her fantasy.

'Oh!' Denise shook her head. 'Don't get me started on Samantha.'

With no further enquiries from Paul, silence loomed, so she filled the void, recounting her chat with Tommy earlier that evening, how he had it all worked out - the figures, the *return on investment* from his ridiculous parties. As if Tommy Collins would amount to anything, she said. The last lot of money was confiscated by the police, he couldn't even get that right.

Paul emptied his glass and set it down on the coffee table. 'Confiscated?'

'Lost the lot,' she said. 'I mean, would you invest in Tommy?' Her laugh was brittle.

Paul shrugged. 'Not my kind of thing.'

She sensed his mood darkening. It was a warning sign she recognised, the same black energy that had haunted their childhood.

'Spends all his time with his waster mates,' she said. 'I swear, Sam might as well be a single parent.'

'Maybe she loves him,' Paul said.

The word jolted her. Coming from her brother, it sounded cold, bitter.

'I expect she does,' said Denise. 'But Tommy loves his friends more, believe me. If it came down to it, he'd choose Jed Foster over Sam any day.'

'How much did he ask for?' Paul was looking into the empty glass on the table and she wondered if it was a sign he wanted another one. She knew she did, but she'd already had a couple for Dutch courage before he arrived. Okay, three.

'Oh, he didn't get that far,' she said. 'I told him in no uncertain terms that he wouldn't get a penny out of me.' That uneasy silence again, putting her nerves on edge. 'Jed bloody Foster,' she repeated. 'That's his family, not Sam and the baby. I call him *wifey*.' She chuckled, a nervous thing that came out like a snort. 'Tommy would sell his soul for that man.'

At last, she thought she saw a smile on Paul's lips as he lifted his steady gaze to hers. Gone were the pleading, tearful eyes of his younger years, that look of sheer terror as their father beat the living shit out of their mother, the fear that the fists would come their way, the knowledge that they wouldn't so long as they did what was asked of them. And so, they would watch, forced to sit still and witness what could happen to them if they uttered a word or moved a muscle, Paul clinging to her, terrified, his head buried into her chest. But Paul soon became desensitised, and by the time he was nine years old he was throwing himself at their father, raking his nails down the old man's face, and he'd paid the price while she sat back and watched.

The guilt overwhelmed her at times. Paul had wanted her protection, her solidarity; she was older than him by six years, two babies kicked from her mother's womb before they had a chance at life. But Paul had wanted to live; he'd demanded it, clung to that umbilical cord with the same heavy-duty fists that had rained down on her for years. But she'd deserved it. She should have sheltered him, but instead, she'd abandoned him. The minute Charlie Morris came into her life, she was gone; married at seventeen, pregnant at eighteen, living in the countryside with all its stenches and bitter winds, her father's insatiable love of violence locked away in a box in her brain. Her eleven-year-old brother left to his fate.

But the violence had come back into her life when Charlie left her, and Paul turned up on her doorstep at the age of eighteen, a grown man, a cold man. Every six months he paid her a visit, as if he'd let the rage build up to the point of bursting. And she'd taken it. Just like her mother.

'Ready for some dinner?' she asked now. She'd cooked lasagne; she thought it quite exotic. 'We could eat it in the garden,' she said. 'Mind, it's a bit of a mess, green fingers I do not have.' She chuckled, hoping it would rub off on him, ease his tense muscles. But Paul's expression didn't change. His eyes were on hers, and she guessed that he too was thinking back to their mother's front garden, her haven for many years before she'd given up on it along with everything else.

'I'd love a beautiful garden,' Denise said, warmly, scrutinising her brother's face for any expression of sorrow. But he seemed unaffected, and he drank her in, looking at her so intensely she thought he might swallow her whole.

Then, with the flash of a smile he said, 'The garden it is.'

MONDAY

TOMMY

'Hello, pet!'

Jed's house was a rose among thorns, his mother, Betty, a precious ray of welcome sunshine even on the brightest of days. The tidy, well-trimmed garden, Betty's pride and joy, was glowing with colour, the smell of baking cakes hanging in the air even at ten o'clock in the morning.

Betty Foster stood in the doorway in a long fleecy dressing gown, two curlers lodged at the fringe of dark hair that was starting to whiten at the roots. The Fosters didn't rise so early these days, not since Jed's father had been laid off from the Neptune Yard the year before.

Betty stood back to let Tommy in just as a long, anguished wail echoed from upstairs. 'Having his hair washed,' said Betty, referring to Jed's younger brother, Barry. She shook her head stoically. 'Just go up, flower, I don't think he's awake.'

Jed lay on his back, his tall frame too big for his single bed, his feet hanging over the edge by at least a foot. Jed was still dressed in yesterday's clothes: blue 501s, black T-shirt, and a blue satin waist coat.

The room was dark, but daylight framed the curtains and Tommy could make out the walls, lined with floor-to-ceiling shelves of vinyl records, carefully catalogued A-Z by music genre and style. Three towers of shoe boxes containing the knock-off trainers balanced precariously in an alcove. On the chimney breast wall hung a cork board thick with music play lists, in the centre a photograph of Jed with his father, Davie, who wore a sweater draped over his shoulders, looking like something from a knitting pattern. Jed was about ten years old in the picture, and they smiled, fishing tackle proudly standing to attention by their sides. The cosy intimacy of the image had been spoiled by a single dart that hung from the centre of Davie Foster's forehead. Jed and Davie had been at loggerheads for the best part of a year, and Jed had been practicing, hitting his target with precision.

Leaning over the bed, Tommy pulled back the curtains, making Jed groan and cover his face with his hands.

'What time is it?' he croaked.

'Job o'clock,' said Tommy.

'Fuck off and die.' Jed turned his face away from the light.

'Howay, chop chop, I need me money.' Tommy had run out of cigarettes and the cravings were starting to gnaw, aggravating his sense of disappointment. The big rave, the night club, the dream of turning them into a reality had lasted a mere jiffy. He was doomed to live the Valley Park life forever.

'I'll be down in a minute,' he heard from under the pillow Jed had thrown over his head to drown out Barry's shrieks.

'Don't sit there, hinny, come in and sit down.'

Tommy was sitting at the bottom of the stairs waiting for Jed, and he peered through the spindles of the staircase to see Betty standing in the kitchen doorway.

'I wish you lads would find yourselves jobs,' Betty said as Tommy followed her into the kitchen. 'Anything's got to be better than having to go to that place every week.'

The Job Centre was a place Jed's father also frequented regularly now, his tales of lazy bastards who thought the world owed them something filling Betty's ears day and night.

'Davie tells Jed all the time,' she said.

Tommy knew he did. Jed's father would phone numbers from the local paper's job adverts on a Thursday, making appointments, telling them his son had skills in computer programming, teaching, bread-making. He knew it drove Jed to distraction.

A mint Club biscuit and a beaker of orange squash landed in front of him, awaking nostalgic memories of holidays at the Fosters' caravan. Betty and Tommy's mother, Jean, had been as inseparable as their sons, their husbands tolerating each other on pain of divorce, such was the bond between the two women.

'Thanks, Mrs Foster.' Tommy smiled up at Jed's mother who patted him gently on the shoulder and went back to her chores.

As he sipped his weak squash, feet pounded down the stairs like a round of artillery, and Jed entered the kitchen, tucking a Beasty Boys T-shirt into his jeans, his teenage brother, Barry, close on his heels, flattening down the wet, wayward hair that had obeyed its own rules since birth.

Barry Foster had the face of an angel, his Down's features displaying a cuteness that instilled maternal longing in women whose children had long fled the nest. They cooed over him, Barry lapping it up, the women wishing they could have a Barry in their lives forever.

Little did they know.

Barry clutched his Walkman in one hand, the fingers of the other pressing one of the earphones to his bouncing head as he chanted, '*Aceeeiid! Aceeeiid!*'

'Oh, for the love of God!' Betty cried. With a stern look at Jed, she ripped the earphones from Barry's head.

'Nooo! I like it!' Barry whined, fighting with Betty for the earphones.

'If you're going out, take him with you,' said Betty.

Jed looked up at the ceiling and mouthed, *fucking hell.* 'Right,' he said.

Barry's petulant pout turned to joy in an instant, a wide smile stretching across his entire face. It was a smile that never failed to cheer Tommy up.

Tommy got to his feet and punched Barry playfully on the arm. 'Howay, Worzel Gummidge,' he said.

***

The obnoxious orange sign of the Job Centre loomed over them as they stood outside its doors, Tommy ripping the cellophane from a packet of twenty, his eyes on the papers Jed had rolled into a baton in his hands.

'What do you want to work at Nissan for?' Tommy asked, twisting his face. 'You'd be better off on a YTS.'

'Oh aye, get treated like a twat for a tenner a week.'

Barry giggled and covered his mouth with his hands.

'Can't see you in a factory, like,' said Tommy. 'You'd have to get out of fucking bed for a start.'

'It's project management, actually,' said Jed.

Tommy frowned. He didn't know what project management was, but it sounded poncy. Besides, people like Jed didn't stand a cat in hell's chance at places like Nissan despite his seven O levels. They'd take one look at the postcode and chuck the application straight in the bin, throwing Jed's dreams of independence and his own bachelor pad away with it.

'Darren wants you for the disco,' said Barry, skipping up to Jed's side as they set off up the hill.

'Not this time, kidda.'

Jed was at his best behind the decks at their all-nighters, and DJing at the youth club discos pained him. Nobody danced, nobody whistled or cheered or made him feel like God Almighty. But the youth worker had him over a barrel. Darren, every young person's friend, had given Barry a volunteer's job in the kitchen, serving crisps and cartons of Um Bongo to unruly youths.

Tommy glanced at Jed, who he couldn't see losing himself in project management either, whatever the hell it was.

Lights, bouncy castles, Frankie Fucking Knuckles. Just five grand and Jed could have his night of glory.

Tommy took in a lung full of nicotine and strode on, feeling Barry's arm go through his. He looked down to give him a smile, but Barry was staring up at him with doleful eyes, tears forming, lip trembling. He'd seen it before; Barry Foster could turn on the tears like Sue Ellen Ewing.

'Don't look at me,' said Tommy, 'I can't DJ.'

Barry's expression fell into a great huffy sulk. 'Shit,' he said.

'Don't say that,' said Tommy. 'Just grown-ups can say that, right?'

'Right.' Barry said. 'No shit.'

'Good lad.'

The dust from the roadworks stung their eyes as they headed home. A new dual carriageway was under construction, one that would cut Valley Park off from the rest of the city. At least that seemed to be the intention. The noise was so loud Tommy didn't hear the voice that bellowed behind him until the hand was on his arm and he was spun around.

Jimmy Lyric, the MC from Saturday night's rave, was glaring at him with the eyes of a serial killer. Peach had confiscated Jimmy's decks; Tommy hadn't paid him, and Jimmy was a big lad, bleached Mohican, tattooed from head to foot, even the face. Rumour had it he'd gone straight after his last stint in prison. Some said he'd been buggered one too many times, others said he was bent and enjoyed it. Either way, Tommy was too scared to ask.

'You've destroyed my livelihood, pal,' Jimmy said.

Tommy held up his hands, cigarette still burning between his fingers. 'Jimmy, I'm sorry about your gear—'

'You will be, coz I've got gigs, gigs I can't do coz I've got no fucking decks.'

Tommy shrugged, looked sorry. What else could he do?

'If they're not on my doorstep by tomorrow night, I'll rip you a new arsehole, got it?'

Tommy's jaw dropped. A new arsehole was something he could do without. 'Where am I gonna get decks from?'

'Tomorrow,' Jimmy said, his face just millimetres from Tommy's.

'Everything all right here?'

A voice came from behind Tommy's shoulder. He froze, and Jimmy started to back off, his posture taking on a less aggressive stance before he turned and walked away with a warning stare at Tommy, who turned slowly to face DCI Peach.

'Beautiful day,' said Peach, squinting up at the cloudless blue sky.

Tommy's eyes were glued like Pritt Stick to Peach's face. It was older, a lot older, as if life had been unkind to him, the hair longer and greyer, the moustache curling over his top lip, twitching like the legs of an earwig.

He felt Jed's hand on his arm, but his feet had grown roots. He was sixteen years old again, his father being led down the path, his mother's pleas over the following months to do something about Trevor Logan's retaliation ignored.

'No evidence,' Peach had said. 'Get some witnesses and I'll see what we can do.'

He'd seemed distracted, disinterested, as if he'd grown bored with the constant moaning of a woman whose husband had committed such a terrible deed. The fear and dread of that time rushed though Tommy once more, just about knocking him sideways.

It was Peach who broke the stand-off now. He leant down to Tommy's ear. 'I'm watching you,' he said.

The skin on Tommy's neck crawled in protest, and his arms hung stiffly by his sides as he narrowed his eyes in the wake of the beige Mackintosh which fluttered in the breeze as Peach headed back down the hill. Humiliation muted him. He should have been the one to turn his back and walk away – been the bigger man, instead of standing there, immobilised like a wanker.

'Is that ...?' Jed asked.

Tommy nodded slowly. 'Aye,' he said. 'And he's got our money.'

***

'Pleeease!'

Barry wasn't letting up on the youth club disco and Jed's patience was wearing thin.

Tommy grinned at Jed half-heartedly, Peach's cold, colourless eyes still wedged in his mind. 'It's for the bairns, man, go on,' he said.

'You can shut up, an' all,' Jed snapped.

'*Pleeeease, Jed, it's for the bairns!*' wailed Barry.

Jed gave Tommy a stern look that indicated he was less than impressed. 'For Christ's sake, I'll think about it,' he grumbled.

Barry whooped with glee, and he skipped ahead, but he stopped dead at his garden gate. The wail returned, genuine this time, and Tommy's face turned to horror as they approached Jed's house.

They stood at the gate with Barry, mouths gaping.

'What the fuck?' gasped Jed.

The garden had been stripped of its flowers, the grass torn up, the contents of the dustbin strewn across what was left of it. But worse than that, someone had scrawled a message in spray paint on the pebble-dash under the living room window.

"*MONGOL.*"

While Jed stormed up the path, Tommy pulled Barry around to face him, hoping he hadn't understood what the word meant. Barry did, and his face contorted in pain. Tommy's mind tumbled, and he looked around for any sign of Trevor Logan, but the street was deserted save a couple of stray children digging in the drains with sticks.

'Come on,' Tommy said, his fingers trembling as he took Barry's hand and led him down the path.

Jed opened the door, pushing Barry and Tommy inside, calling out to his parents. Neither were home, the house silent bar Barry's frantic cries.

As Tommy closed the door behind him, he noticed a folded piece of paper on the hallway floor which Jed bent to pick up. They exchanged a glance before Jed opened it, his face falling into a curious frown. He handed it to Tommy who looked down at a page torn from that morning's *Racing Post*. It meant nothing to Jed, but Tommy's eyes were drawn to one of the fixtures:

"*6.34 p.m. PEACH SURPRISE.*"

PEACH

Funny how the unemployed could afford their smokes but complained of having no money for food.

A morning spent on Valley Park was one thing, but the Intensive Care Unit at the Royal Victoria Infirmary was quite another when it came to hopelessness. The ward was quiet as a graveyard, six beds containing near-corpses emitting no sound other than the beeps and clunks of apparatus.

It had been two days and still Sally's temperature refused to subside. Unable to breathe for herself, a machine caused her chest to rise and fall unnaturally like clockwork. Tests had confirmed not only ecstasy in her system, but cocaine too, and Doctor Flynn had regarded him with eyes that told a story he didn't want to hear. Just a couple of more days, she'd said, and they'd have to think about their options.

The nurse with the frizzy red hair, whose name he'd learnt was Pamela, had grown fond of Sally. He could tell by the way she stroked her hand and spoke to her about the poor girl who'd been brought in the night before and had her legs amputated. Sally was lucky to still have her legs, she'd said. She would be back up dancing in no time.

'Here's her things, Mr Peach.' Pamela held out a hospital-issue bag. He took it from her and looked inside: Sally's white dress, now dirty and soiled, a small, white shoulder purse and a pink camera. 'I'll get you some tea,' Pamela said.

'Strong, two sugars,' he replied, robotically.

Sitting on Sally's bed, he took the camera from the bag, checking the magnified window on its rear to see how many photographs she'd taken. Twenty. The camera could provide clues; perhaps she'd taken some snaps on the night of the rave. Maybe Collins was in them, dancing with her, putting a pill onto her tongue.

He switched the camera on, listening to the high-pitched whine of the flash warming up. He pointed the camera at Sally's face, *clicked* and wound on, repeating the process until the film was finished.

He'd had to explain to the staff that Sally's mother was dead, but he hadn't given them the whole, gruesome story. The nurse, Pamela, was desperate to know; she was a nosey parker, no doubt about it.

'What a shame, not to have your mam at a time like this,' she'd said with a morose shake of the head. She was digging for information, so she could talk to her pals about the poor girl who'd overdosed – an overworked father and a dead mother. *Cancer. Car accident. Suicide.*

Tragic.

Sally's sickly face brought back memories Peach would rather remained buried.

Try starved herself to death.

But they didn't need to know that. None of their business.

He hadn't noticed it at first, his wife's self-absorption, the fussing over every stray hair or broken nail, pinching at the flesh under her arms, assessing its size with a tape measure, tapping at it with the back of her hand. It had got to the point where he became so tired of the constant need for reassurance, he'd stopped commenting all together, choosing to ignore her or walk away from any remark about a new line on her forehead or dimple on the back of her thigh. This served only to increase the amount of time she spent examining herself in mirrors, picking herself to pieces.

They were seven years into their marriage when Sally came along. He understood now that it wasn't motherhood she avoided, but pregnancy, the idea of getting fat triggering a level of anxiety and simmering rage he only ever saw in criminals who realised there was no way out. Once Sally was born he'd watched in horror as Kathleen wasted away, hospitalised on many occasions, years of swings and roundabouts. For ten years she hopped from one diet to the next, one crisis to the next. In those final months, refusing all offers of help, she'd retreated from them both.

He hadn't understood it; it didn't compute, and it had scared the life out of him. To him she'd been beautiful, and he'd been lucky to find her, sitting shyly in the typing pool of the police station, her short hair curled around the backs of her ears in the style of the time.

'*Like Twiggy,*' she'd said.

He'd tried everything: persuasion, flattery, force. He'd ignore it, eating alone and making out it was perfectly normal. Eventually, he'd run out of options. He hadn't known what to do, so he did nothing at all.

The hospital cubicle was heating up as the morning wore on, a fan whirring air around it to keep Sally cool. He'd picked up the post from the doormat that morning. Among the bills were half a dozen cards addressed to Sally. He opened them now, one by one, reading them aloud and placing them on the bed next to him. There was only one name he recognised: Selina, the girl who used to come for tea.

'Such lovely friends.' He hadn't noticed Pamela return with his tea. She was reading the cards without asking if she could.

He reached up and snatched the cards from her, putting them into the bag with Sally's other things. As he did so, he noticed another card, already sitting on the bedside table next to his steaming tea. He picked it up, his face flushing a livid red. A stick girl with a smiley yellow face for a head danced. '*Little Raver!*' it read.

Furious, he shoved the card into the bag, but then his breath caught, shut off like a stopcock. Sally's hand twitched and rose a few inches from the bed, and he felt his stomach pitch as her forefinger pointed to the curtain like a ghoul in an episode of *Scooby Doo*. Pamela held onto his arm as he lunged towards Sally, grabbing her shoulders and shaking her, scouring her face for life. He felt the nurse's hand pulling him back, but he resisted, wrenching his arm from Pamela's grasp, his hands cupping Sally's cheeks.

'It's me, it's dad,' he said.

'It happens all the time, Mr Peach.'

'She moved,' he said, turning angrily to Pamela. 'She bloody moved!'

'It's just a reflex,' Pamela insisted.

Fire burnt his face. 'Don't just stand there, you idiot, get the doctor!'

Affronted, Pamela drew back her shoulders. 'You know, you should talk to her,' she said. 'They can often hear what's going on around them.'

Turning his back on her, he heard the soft-soled shoes withdraw as he looked at his daughter, absorbing a face that was starting to look like someone else's.

He should talk to her, but words of endearment muddled themselves in his throat. They forever throttled him and stuck to the roof of his mouth. He took in Sally's pale face, hearing the right words in his head, but feeling awkward, as if facing a headstone and wondering what to say, worried someone might be listening.

He wondered, while he struggled to free his tongue, if he could ever be the sort of man who could show how he felt, say the right thing at the right time. It had lost him his wife, it could lose him his daughter.

He gathered his courage and leant forward, brushing Sally's hair from her brow. He put his mouth to her ear.

'I'm going to get who did this to you,' he said.

***

'I told you to leave it, Mike, it might have nothing to do with him.'

Superintendent McNally was signing a pile of letters, and Peach winced at the use of his first name. Was this a *telling off*?

'Oh, it's got everything to do with him,' he said, throwing a newspaper onto McNally's never-ending pile of paperwork. "*Spaced Out!*" the headline read, "*11,000 youngsters go drug crazy at Britain's biggest ever acid party.*"

McNally pulled the newspaper towards him, his eyes scanning it for barely a second before pushing it away. 'He's a nobody from a council estate. He can't pull off something like this. Now let it go.'

Peach pushed the newspaper back across the desk. 'Sir, I know—'

'What? What do you know?' McNally sighed and put his pen down, finally focusing on Peach. 'That some two-bit party organiser may or may not have given MDMA to your daughter? Do I really need to mention the word *evidence* to you? I am up to my ears in unsolved crimes.'

'That's what I mean,' said Peach, leaning forward and putting his palms on McNally's desk. 'If I can get a warrant to search Collins's house—'

'On what basis?' McNally asked, tight-lipped. 'What are you going to arrest him for? Being a smart arse?'

'I'll get him to come in voluntarily.'

'You'll stay away from him; do you hear me? You are too close to this. Give me time and I'll get something sorted.'

Pushing himself away from the desk, Peach clenched his jaw. Time was something he didn't have.

McNally's eyes were bloodshot, and Peach noticed a slight tremor in his hand as he picked up his pen and pointed it. 'And one more incident like this morning and you're going home.'

He wouldn't have called it an incident as such. He'd only just walked through the station door and she'd started on him. The woman had a mouth like a sewer, arms and legs riddled with track marks like a dire case of scabies, so when the addict spat in his face and called his mother a whore, what was he supposed to do? Give her a cup of tea and some sympathy? She deserved a clip around the ear and that's what she got.

'I'm giving you the building society robbery from Friday, we're getting nowhere,' said McNally. 'Murphy's got the file.'

'That's way below my rank, sir,' said Peach, angrily.

'We're all mucking in right now.'

'Sir—'

'You'll take it, or you'll take leave.' McNally's tone indicated that the conversation was over.

***

Back in his office, Peach threw himself onto his chair, kicking at the bin, sending it scuttling across the room.

Tommy Collins.

He'd think of something. He'd arrest the little toe rag for breathing if he could.

He picked up Sally's framed picture, something in him wanting to snap it in two. He quickly dropped it back into place as his office door opened, and DS Murphy entered wearing some semblance of a suit, the sleeves of the creased, linen jacket pushed up to his elbows, the legs of his trousers an inch too short revealing sockless ankles and brown loafers. He looked like a bag of spuds.

'Don't they knock in Manchester?' Peach grumbled.

'The Tyne Building Society, chief,' Murphy said, ignoring the question and holding up a file and a videocassette. 'And this.' He held up another folder in his other hand, a wonky grin on his face.

Peach looked at it, guessing what it contained. 'Shut the door,' he said.

Murphy cast furtive glances up and down the corridor before closing the door and sitting in the chair opposite Peach's desk, passing the folder to him. Peach opened it and looked down into a full-face image of Tommy Collins, long-lashed eyes looking slightly to the left of the camera.

'Got the CCTV tapes from a night club called Phutures,' said Murphy. It was the only club in town that played house music, he said, and Peach remembered the tuneless rubbish he'd heard from Sally's cassette player.

'Said I was from the brewery and the lass let me into the office,' said Murphy, who drew a long breath, waiting for his boss's response.

But Peach's eyes were trained on Tommy's face.

'It's a right dive,' Murphy continued, 'but then that's all part of the scene, ain't it?' Another pause that wasn't filled. 'She knew two of them, though, the lass – names, addresses, their mothers' knicker size.'

Peach held up a hand, tired of the wittering. He turned to the next photograph in the file: an attractive young man stood next to a smiling teenager who bore the hallmark Chinaman's eyes and jutting chin of Down Syndrome.

'Second in command, Jed Foster,' said Murphy, leaning

forward and tapping a finger on Jed's face. 'DJs at the club sometimes.'

Peach remembered the Fosters from the Reggie Collins case. The older brother was Tommy's friend; joined at the hip they were.

'Kept his head down, so the club's CCTV didn't catch his face,' said Murphy. 'Once I had the name it wasn't hard to find him. That's from the *Northern Gazette* a few months back, the re-opening of some youth centre.'

Peach scanned the image, saying nothing. In the photograph, the mayor and a diminutive white man with a black man's afro and John Lennon-style glasses stood next to Jed and his brother.

He heard Murphy huff like a horse and sit back in his chair, peevishly. Peach sensed what he wanted, but expressions of appreciation weren't his style. They somehow made him feel exposed, as if the respect he'd garnered over the years would disintegrate the instant such words were uttered.

'I've been right busy this morning, boss. Not even stopped for a butty,' Murphy said, grouchily.

Ignoring Murphy's disappointment at not getting a round of applause, Peach turned to the next image of a man in his late twenties, receding hair tied back, his large, freckled face almost a perfect circle. He was completely unfamiliar, and Peach glanced up at Murphy, nodding his head to indicate he could speak again.

Murphy gave him the story with a little less enthusiasm. The girl from the club didn't know this fella's name, so he'd presented the face to some of the officers in the station until he got one: Frankie Donahue, known not for any criminal behaviour, but for his reputation for fixing just about anything with an engine. Even tractors apparently. Did a lot of "helping out" at Honest Jim's in Benwell.

'What else?' Peach asked, snapping the folder shut.

'All right, give us a chance, I ain't Sherlock Holmes.'

He certainly wasn't, and half a story was no good. He wanted to know everything about Collins; where he went, who he talked to, what colour his piss was.

'What about the building society, boss?' Murphy's hooded eyes were on the other file. 'McNally wants progress by the end of the day.'

'*Superintendent* McNally,' Peach corrected. 'And you work for me, not him.'

Murphy sucked in his lips, hiding a smile. 'I know what they meant now, boss,' he said.

Peach stared back at him.

'You know, that you could be … *difficult.*'

'Hm.' Peach looked back down into Tommy's face. Difficult was no skin off his nose.

'But that's sound, chief.' Peach could hear the brazen grin in Murphy's voice. 'I kinda like difficult.'

'Go,' said Peach, looking up and nodding towards the door.

'No problemo.' Murphy heaved himself from the chair, pushed up the arms of his jacket and sauntered from the office.

Peach peeled his eyes away from the door, a rare smile playing on his lips. Something about Murphy amused him. Most of his detectives flinched when he barked at them, most approached him with trepidation. He wasn't one for doling out praise, the absence of a berating being his usual method of imparting a positive message. It had come up in his first "annual appraisal" with McNally earlier that year, a pointless new exercise intended to patronise and create excuses for Human Resources to move the shit people around as often as possible, all under the guise of "increasing opportunities." They wittered on about personal goals, objectives and "key indicators of performance." Waste of bloody time.

He looked up at the wall to his left where he'd pinned a map of the city, a series of red dots indicating the venues of the last three months' all-night parties: three in the east end, two at Gateshead quays, one in Newburn and one to the north near the airport. There was no obvious pattern to it – opportunistic choices, but there had to be some logic. Warehouses mostly, abandoned, easy to access from the main routes around the city.

He took the photographs of Tommy and his team mates from the folder and walked to the wall, tearing Sellotape from its reel with his teeth and sticking the photographs as well as he could to the peeling paint.

Sitting back down, he took in their faces. What had started as a minor infraction of the peace, a bunch of bored dole-wallers making a quick buck, was now up there in his mind with the major incident files on his desk: stabbings, shootings, armed robberies. McNally had ordered him to stay away, but anger was tugging at his gut. He was all too aware of the protocol around investigating crimes that involved victims who were family members. If he didn't keep his distance he could face a disciplinary at worst, get a black mark on his ridiculous annual appraisal at best.

His fingers hovered over the building society file. Wouldn't take him five minutes to flick through it he supposed, get a tick in the box.

The file was thin and flimsy, and he opened it, running his finger over statements from the staff and customers. He picked up one of the fuzzy stills from the CCTV: two figures were dressed in cagoules, the toggles tied tightly around their faces so only their eyes were visible. He looked closer at one of the robbers, a skinny lad with hunched shoulders and bulging, white knuckles. Peach could just make out the robber's feet: white trainers, with a flash of lightening up the side.

His heart quickening, he opened the top drawer of his desk to retrieve Tommy's trainer, looking from it to the photograph then back again. The sigh was one of satisfaction as he picked up the phone and dialled the desk sergeant.

'Bring one of those video players and a television to my office,' he said. 'And tea – strong—' He didn't finish the sentence as the desk sergeant confirmed she knew exactly how he took his tea after all these years.

Hanging up, he sat back, a few hairs coming free as he tugged at his moustache in a habit that had driven his wife to distraction. He picked up another black and white still from the CCTV, the skinny robber looking slightly to the left of the camera. The eyes were arrogant, the lashes long, the irises translucent.

Anticipation roused a thin smile.

'Gotcha,' he said to himself.

TOMMY

'It can be done,' Tommy said.

It had just gone two o'clock, that time in the afternoon when the sun shone directly into the living room making the dust motes swirl at the slightest movement. Tommy sat in the armchair under the window, looking expectantly into the faces of his two friends who sat next to each other on the sofa.

Tommy had shoved the torn page from the *Racing Post* into his back pocket. The message was clear, and Paul Smart's words ran circles around his brain.

Do it for your family.

This was a warning of worse to come and he'd spent the last two hours weighing up his limited options. He could do nothing at all and wait for Paul to send Tucker to hurt Jed's family – then his. Or he could take Paul's money and do the best job he could. But he couldn't do it without Jed. Jed had a head for figures, he was organised and efficient. Tommy was the ideas man, the visionary. They made a good team, but unbeknownst to Jed, Tommy had brought trouble to his door. He wished like hell he'd never gone to Phutures on Saturday night. Should have gone home to bed like a grown-up.

'It *can't* be done,' said Jed, his face still sullen.

They'd given up waiting for the police. Instead, they'd cleared the garden of the rubbish, tried to soothe Barry's wails, waited for Jed's parents to arrive home from his nana's. Davie went ballistic while Betty made tea and got the scones out, her face drawn, tears brimming, doing the only thing that seemed to calm her nerves: feed people.

Tommy rubbed at his forehead, trying not to lose patience with Jed's negativity. 'Make us a cup of tea, will you?' he ordered.

'Frankie, three teas, pal,' said Jed.

Frankie rose from Tommy's sofa without question and headed for the kitchen.

'Here, what about the knock-off trainers?' said Jed. 'We could be entrepreneurs – imports, exports.' He was dodging the subject.

'Hey, I'm a pioneer of music, not a door-to-door salesman,' said Tommy. He hadn't told Jed the good news that Tucker was collecting the trainer money; that Paul Smart was taking over the counterfeit footware business. He'd keep that to himself for now. Jed was pissed off enough as it was.

'A few hundred in a warehouse is a bit different to pulling off a full-scale rave.' Jed slumped back.

'You just multiply everything, stupid,' said Tommy.

'Don't call me stupid,' Jed snapped. 'You'll need sound gear, marquees, generators, the works. Where's the money coming from?'

Tommy held his stare. 'What if I can get a backer?'

'Oh aye, what's in it for them?' asked Jed. 'And more to the point, who is it?'

Tommy threw his arms in the air. 'Fucking Barclays, does it matter?'

'Aye, it matters!' Jed turned the argument on Frankie who had arrived back from the kitchen with a tray of three mugs and a bag of sugar. 'Spoons?' barked Jed before Frankie's arse had the chance to hit the sofa.

'Got to know who you're getting into bed with,' said Frankie in his slow drawl.

'Well, in your case, nobody,' sneered Jed. 'Virgil. That's what your mother should have called you.'

Frankie was back up on his feet, two fingers up at Jed, talking so slowly his next sentence seemed eternal. 'Just because I don't go around poking every orifice in sight. You want to charge for it, Foster, you'd be a millionaire by now.' Frankie headed to the kitchen once more, shouting, 'I hope your dick drops off!'

'At least I've got one,' muttered Jed.

Tommy clicked his fingers, bringing Jed's attention back to him. 'Seriously, mate. The biggest party to hit the north-east? We'll be heroes, man.'

Jed folded his arms across his chest, his tongue in his cheek.

'Howay,' goaded Tommy, 'what've you got to lose?'

'Erm, my reputation?'

Frankie threw three spoons onto the coffee table. 'Listen to Vinyl Richie here,' he mocked as he sat down.

Jed ignored him. 'I'm telling you now, it'll be a disaster.'

Everything in Jed's body language, his expression, the slight curl of his lip, denoted his resistance. He was sick as a chip, his father out spending the milk money on paint, his mother and his brother in tears. Like Tommy, he was at breaking point when it came to Valley Park and what it had to offer. A big fat nowt.

'This is our chance,' said Tommy, seizing on Jed's discontent.

'Yours, you mean,' came the reply.

'No,' said Tommy firmly, sitting forward. 'Ours.' He glanced at Frankie, making sure he knew he was part of the deal.

Jed looked away and Tommy played his trump card.

'You get to DJ,' he said in a sing-song voice. 'Some big names. A whole set.'

Jed sighed, leant forward, spooned four sugars into his tea and stirred it.

'Well, I think it's a great idea, me,' said Frankie. 'I'll DJ if you want.'

Jed's head shot up. 'You can't have Belinda fucking Carlisle at a rave!'

Frankie shrunk back into his denim jacket.

'Remember the Hacienda?' said Tommy. They'd hitch-hiked to Manchester earlier that year, walked through the industrial plastic-strip curtains into a haze of dry ice, the bass setting their teeth on edge, the overwhelming sensation of *coming home* throwing them into each other arms as the music drew them into the centre of the universe.

'Fucking awesome,' said Jed with a nostalgic sigh.

'That could be you,' said Tommy.

Jed continued to stir his tea then threw the spoon onto the tray.

'Okay. Two sets,' Tommy relented.

'The Carl Cox of the Toon!' said Frankie.

Jed was in awe of DJs like Carl Cox and Danny Rampling. They were his Gods. He raised his eyebrows as he took a slurp of his tea. 'Cash up front?'

'Cash up front,' said Tommy, without hesitation.

'Legit? I can't be fucking up my chances with Nissan.'

Tommy hoped Jed didn't notice him faltering. 'Legit,' he said. 'Are we in?'

'In!' Frankie raised a hand.

Tommy's eyes were on Jed, who took a series of gulps from his tea and smacked his lips. 'Aye, gan on then,' he said.

He should jump from his seat, shout *'Yes! Yes!'* but something kept Tommy's backside pinned to the cushion – relief that they would be spared Paul Smart's retaliation; fear that if he didn't pull off what Smartie wanted, he'd be indebted to him forever. Or was it the overpowering illusion of hope? Hope that by this time next week, even if it meant taking Paul Smart's money, he could be free of all this shit.

Frankie did the jumping for him. 'Belter!' he cried, pulling Jed to his feet and embracing him, much to Jed's horror.

Finally, the springs in Tommy's legs were unleashed, and he leapt towards them, joining the communal hug.

'Woah, hold on,' said Jed, pushing Frankie away and holding up his hands. Tommy and Frankie froze, mid-celebration, Tommy's stomach falling; Jed was having second thoughts already. 'What the hell's that?' Jed creased his nose, sniffing around him.

Tommy's nose began to twitch too, and their attention fell on Frankie. 'How dare you fart in my house,' said Tommy.

Frankie's eyes widened. 'It was the dog!'

'I haven't got a dog! Get away to the bog, man,' said Tommy.

As Frankie dragged himself out of the living room, muttering to himself, Tommy sunk onto the arm of the chair while Jed fell back onto the sofa. It was beginning to feel real, and with the right amount of backing, it could be immense.

'Christ,' Tommy said, wistfully. 'Imagine. We're part of a movement. We're making memories. We're making fucking *history*.'

While they simultaneously lifted their tea to their mouths, Tommy wondered if Jed could read his thoughts, see the spectacle: the party to end all parties. Fame, admiration, profit. Escape.

They pondered the moment until Jed broke the silence. 'What about this cash, then?'

'Sam's mam,' said Tommy, thinking on his feet. 'I'm going to sweet talk her.'

Jed scrunched up his face in puzzlement and Tommy avoided his eyes. Denise Morris couldn't stand the sight of him, and everybody knew it.

Just in time, the front door opened, and Sam shouted a cheery hello. 'What youse lot up to?' she asked, rolling Ashleigh's buggy into the living room.

'Nothing, my love,' smiled Tommy.

Sam threw him a suspicious look as Frankie re-appeared at the living room door.

'By, that took some flushing,' he said, fastening his belt, a cigarette hanging from the side of his mouth. 'Thought I was gonna have to get a coat hanger.'

They all looked at Frankie quizzically.

'To chop it up,' he explained.

'He's disgusting.' Denise stood in the doorway behind Frankie, laden down with shopping bags. 'Come on, you lot, hop it.' She pushed past Frankie, and Jed sprung to his feet.

Tommy felt heat on his face. Sam's mother wasn't the boss of this house, yet she seemed to railroad her way in whenever she pleased, doling out the orders, taking over. Much to his frustration, they were seeing more of her recently. Some robbery at the building society she worked for had left her traumatised. That's what she'd told the bosses anyway – got herself a sick note for two weeks to give her a bit more time to spend the money she wouldn't give him. Looked perfectly unaffected as far as he could see. The happy expression on Sam's face quelled any urge to tell Denise to sling her hook, and Tommy forced a smile across his face, a smile that fell the instant Denise walked past him with a stare that would freeze mercury.

Sam, Ashleigh in her arms, walked up to him and planted a warm kiss on his lips. 'Love you,' she said, wiping the kiss away with her thumb. And suddenly, it didn't seem so bad after all. He watched her walk into the kitchen after her mother; they laughed and chatted, as if carrying on a conversation that had lasted all day.

Sam had been sixteen when he'd first clocked her in an orange sundress so long she'd had to hold it up to walk. At eighteen he'd had his share of girlfriends. He'd even liked some of them, and some of them had liked him before they met Jed.

It was one of the long summer weekends they'd spent in Sandy Bay at Jed's parents' caravan. They'd come of an age where Tommy and Jed had been allowed to stay there on their own for weekends during the summer. Tommy would bring crackly cassette recordings of the newest Chicago House, a new underground sound that was rippling through America. Soon a bunch of teenage youths, bored out of their skulls with the "entertainment" provided at the Sandy Bay Pavilion Bar, had found their way to the sounds of this new, raw mix which seemed designed for one thing and one thing only: dancing. Each visit to the caravan brought new beats, new mixes, evolving so fast that every new track was pulled to pieces, discussed, and analysed by a bunch of young lads who'd been brought up on disco and The Beatles. This was special, and it felt like nobody else knew of it but them.

It was the morning after one of these nights when Tommy sat alone on the steps of the caravan, watching old folk set out their deck chairs. She was walking towards The Pavilion for breakfast with a woman with raven-black hair who resembled an older, portlier version of Joan Jett. He watched the wobble of the girl's backside in the orange sundress and the bounce of her curly perm. She'd looked at him over her bare shoulder and he'd tried his best to be cool, lifting one side of his mouth into a grin, raising one hand in the way Jed did, and hoping like hell she liked house music because he had sod all else to talk about. Joan Jett had given him the daggers and quickened her pace, pulling the girl along by the arm.

That night, the lads had got on with it on their own, and he'd lumbered down to The Pavilion Bar to suffer the Frankie Valley tribute act and buy the lass a drink once Joan Jett had staggered off to the ladies with a belly full of Babycham.

The rest was history.

Tommy walked to the open front door now and watched his friends strolling down the path, Frankie turning to the right and Jed to the left. He'd begun to close the door when he spotted the camper, little Carl Logan, and four or five other children under ten pulling radiators from the boarded-up house opposite. Trevor Logan emerged from the door of the empty house, bare chested, his spindly arms laden with kitchen cupboard doors. The two brothers stopped and stared, Trevor spitting on the ground before walking off, eyes still fixed on Tommy.

Tommy peered over at the empty house, remembering the days when every property was occupied, when he could play out in the street without his mother having to watch through the window. It could all work out if he kept his head, kept shtum about Smartie. This was his chance.

Hope.

He'd always thought you couldn't buy that shit. Until now.

PEACH

The CCTV footage was grainy and blurred to buggery – no sound, just some poor middle-aged woman in a cardigan being dragged from her chair by the skinny robber and shoved in among a huddle of people who gathered at a display board boasting fixed-rate mortgages of thirteen and a half per cent. The second robber was so short his cagoule reached his knees. He was fat and dumpy, nervous and alert, keeping the terrified customers and staff at bay with a sawn-off shotgun.

Then a third one came into the frame. No cheap, lightweight weatherproof for this one. He stood in a thigh-length, double-breasted coat, the collar turned up and a bowler hat pulled down over his ears. A woman's scarf covered his face like an old, Western bandana. Thought he was a right Bobby Dazzler this one.

Then, like the cowboy he imagined he was, the Bobby Dazzler bent his knees and drew two penknives from the deep pockets of the coat. He flicked them open, took one step forward and the huddle in the corner fell collectively to the floor like dynamited chimneys while the skinny one picked up the holdall and ran around the back of the counter, the seconds ticking by endlessly before he ran back out again.

Peach paused the video when all three of them were in the frame. He let out a sound, halfway between a sigh and a grunt. The Bobby Dazzler: Jed Foster; the short, fat one: Frankie Donahue; the skinny one in the trainers: Tommy Collins.

He fast forwarded to the footage of the outside camera. It was better quality, clear as day, in fact. The getaway car was parked on the double yellow lines, hazard lights blinking innocently. Once they were all inside, the car indicated and pulled out into the passing traffic, casual as you like. According to the file, the three-year-old BMW was registered to a Mrs Rebecca Cooper from Windy Nook who'd confirmed that the vehicle had been at Honest Jim's Motors on the date in question having the bumper repaired.

He stared up at the photographs on his wall, a long, wheezy breath emptying his lungs. So, this was how they were financing their little enterprise.

Fingers tapping the desk, he glanced across at Sally's photograph before gathering the papers together and placing them back in the folder. If he could get an identification …

Putting the file under his arm, he switched off the desk lamp and left his office, pausing at McNally's door as he walked down the corridor. He hesitated, fingers hovering above the handle. He'd never disobeyed an order from a superior officer in all his thirty years on the force. The chain of command was sacrosanct. Biting at the inside of his cheek, he drew his hand away and carried on walking.

At the reception, a small man with a middle parting and weasel-like face was attempting to flirt with Sharon, the desk sergeant, who eyed him with bored aloofness. He was young, studenty-looking, and he bounced away from the desk as Peach approached.

'DCI Peach?' he said, throwing himself into Peach's path.

Peach walked around him without giving him the time of day, but the weedy voice continued.

'I was sorry to hear about your daughter, Inspector.'

Peach stopped and turned. The man was spotty, skin shining across the forehead and chin.

'Mind if I ask you some questions?' A small note pad was produced from a leather bag that hung from the weasel's shoulder.

'I can't talk about an ongoing investigation.' Peach turned back to reception, handing the file to Sharon. 'Get these witnesses in,' he said.

'So, you're treating it as a crime?' The reporter was in front of him again, the smile fastened to his face. 'Ben Stone, the *Northern Gazette*.' He held out his hand, eager as a bitch in heat. 'I'd like to tell your side of the story, Inspector … sir.'

Peach ignored his outstretched hand. 'What story?'

'Your daughter, Sally.' Ben's tone had changed into something more supercilious and he withdrew his hand.

Peach gave him a black look, and Ben touched his nose, speaking in a low voice.

'Nurses like to talk,' he said, 'given the right reward.'

Peach's moustache twitched with antagonism. 'And what side is there other than mine?'

Frowning in puzzlement, the reporter pulled back his chin. 'The side the people want to hear, Inspector. Daughter of a decorated copper, bigging it up at raves, doing drugs—'

The reporter's wince was audible when Peach took him by the upper arm, his fingers digging through the un-ironed cotton shirt and into Ben's skin in a way that was meant to hurt. He pulled him out the door, led him down the station steps, releasing his arm only when they'd reached the bottom.

He towered over the ratty little shit. 'I'll tell you my side of the story all right,' he said, 'there's people out there shoving their sordid lifestyles in our faces, in our bairns' faces.' He dug into his trouser pocket and pulled out the photograph of Sally he'd torn from her wardrobe door. He shoved it in the reporter's face, too close for him to focus on it. 'We've been shat on up here, my lad. We've had our industries ripped out from under our feet. But they'll have our youngsters over my dead body.'

'Quite the Socialist,' said Ben.

'This isn't about politics, moron,' said Peach. 'How about you write about a whole generation of brains wrecked by a drug we know nothing about.'

'We know quite a lot about it, actually,' said Ben, pushing Peach's hand from his face.

Peach's brow puckered, looking from one of Ben's eyes to the other, but the reporter looked right back at him, unflinching and conceited.

'What evidence is there that ecstasy's any more dangerous than paracetamol?' Ben asked. 'They say you're more likely to die falling off a horse.'

Peach pushed him backwards, people on the street starting to take an interest. 'Oh, I've got evidence,' he snarled. 'I've got a sixteen-year-old who doesn't know what day it is because decent kids can't go out without getting drugs shoved in their faces.' He held the photograph up again. 'It's evidence I'd rather not have.'

Ben gathered himself, dusting down the arms of his shirt. 'Well,' he said, 'when she comes round—'

'When she comes round?' Peach pushed Ben again, his back hitting a parked car with a thud, his shoulder bag falling to the pavement. '*If* she comes around. *If* she's got any brain left.'

Unease bristled on the reporter's forehead, and Peach waited for the next inept claim, but Ben Stone seemed to have nothing more to say as he looked around at the small crowd of curious onlookers.

Peach took a step back to allow the reporter to pick up his bag and walk away.

Ben Stone could crawl right back under the rock he came from.

No story in bloody paracetamol.

TOMMY

Floodlights illuminated the parched greyhound track despite the blinding sun. Tommy shielded his eyes and searched, and as he made his way through the crowds of gamblers, he couldn't shake the feeling he was being watched. He felt exposed, eyes of condemnation all around him. *Mug.* They burnt into the back of his head as he tried to pick out Paul Smart.

He soon spotted him at the fence that bordered the race track, towering above the other gamblers with the poise of a prince. Paul was surrounded by his associates, grizzly men employed to guard his integrity as well as his body. Tucker was one of them, his sharp eyes weighing up the various huddles of men around the stadium, all in the same formation: one main man in love with his own villainy and a collection of thugs.

Tommy approached with caution. A few feet away from Paul, he stopped and hesitated. Paul had his back to him, an angry, red spot on the back of his neck interfering with the outline tattoo of a dove in flight.

On Tucker's nod, Paul half turned, his eyes not meeting Tommy's. He turned back to the track and stood taller, straightening his shoulders as the names of the dogs came over the loudspeaker:

'*Number six, Peach Surprise.*'

Paul rocked from his heels to his patent leather toes, dressed in an ivory-coloured suit, the short jacket wide at the shoulders and tapered into his slim waist. Tucker moved to one side when Tommy tapped him on the shoulder, allowing him access to the pack.

'Got your message,' said Tommy irritated at how apprehensive he sounded.

'Shhhh!' Paul held a pair of small binoculars to his eyes. 'Got three grand on number six to win.'

Tommy felt the discomfort of Tucker's stare, and he found himself moving a little closer to Paul as if this would offer some protection against Tucker's pointed teeth. Tucker had found his niche now. Paul Smart was far too well dressed to get blood on his hands, and Tucker was just what was needed, someone who'd get their hands dirty and sod the consequences. Perhaps Tucker hadn't been lying about the Scouse gangsters after all.

The claxon sounded, and the gates swung open in the distance, Paul's tiny, blue eyes narrowing as Peach Surprise was last out of the stalls. Tommy could see the villains further down the fence sniggering as the dog started to lag further and further behind, her faltering limp slowing her to a lurching gait.

Paul's voice remained frostily calm. 'Get on there and get that fucking dog off,' he said.

Tommy and Tucker glanced at each other, not sure who Paul was talking to.

'Now!'

Tucker was taking no chances. He vaulted over the barrier and sprinted onto the track as the dogs flew past, taking hold of Peach Surprise and carrying her under his arm to the other side. Tommy looked on in astonishment as Tucker leapt over the opposite barrier with the stealth of a ninja and ran across the yellowing grass towards the far side of the track.

Paul turned to one of his associates. 'Pick up the stake, Geordie, race invalidated.'

The crowd began to jeer as Geordie meandered his way through the masses, and Paul put an arm around Tommy's shoulders, leading him away from his men. He stopped and faced Tommy, holding out a folded piece of paper between two fingers.

'Middle of nowhere,' he said. 'Farmer's been paid to take a little holiday.'

Tommy looked down at it uneasily. He wasn't so sure now he stood face to face with someone who could make him or break his legs. He reached for the paper tentatively, but Paul snapped it away.

'Can't hack it? Know some lads from Sunderland who'd be well up for it.'

Tommy breathed out heavily, not wanting his unease to show. If he was going to take Paul Smart's money, he couldn't show weakness.

Paul lowered his arm again and Tommy took the slip of paper. He unfolded it: a hand-drawn map and directions to a Groat Hall Farm in Northumberland, just south of Hexham. Tommy had never heard of the farm, had never been out of Newcastle apart from the delayed honeymoon in Ibiza Denise had paid for less than a year ago, back in the days when she was a bit more flash with the cash, and only on the understanding that she could come too. He'd taken some persuading, Sam insisting that her mother was an early-to-bed/early-riser, which meant she could babysit and they could party like they did before Ashleigh was born. He'd relented, not wanting to disappoint, and, as it turned out, they'd had the time of their lives for a couple of nights before he started shitting green water. Ashleigh, just a couple of months old, was as good as gold, her grandmother a miserable, demanding cow as always.

'Listen,' said Paul, the tone a little more reassuring as if he could sense Tommy's apprehension. 'It's a business deal. I put up the cash, you organise the rave, we split the profit.'

Tommy nodded. 'And then we're done?'

Paul grunted, cynically. 'Once you get a sniff of money, laddie, you're never done.'

'It's a one-off, Smartie, that's the deal. And you leave my mates alone.'

Paul put a hand on Tommy's shoulder, eyes locked on his. 'You'll get forty-grand in your pocket, more if you do a good job, then you can piss off and do whatever you want.'

Forty-grand? Tommy blinked rapidly.

'Five thousand people, twenty quid entry, take off the costs. You don't have to be a mastermind.' Paul peered around him before taking a wad of cash from his trouser pocket. He peeled off some notes, thinking carefully as he counted it, then held it out.

Tommy looked down at it. *Forty-grand.* It was life-changing money. His club, his future, his freedom.

He bit the bullet, and took the money from Paul's fingers, flicking through it quickly – about two thousand. 'I'll need more than this,' he said.

Paul snapped one of the twenty-pound notes back and folded it into the rest of cash, shoving it into his trouser pocket where it bulged like a hard-on. 'Let's see how you get on first, eh?'

Tommy slid the money into his own pocket before he spoke again. 'When?' he asked.

'This Saturday.'

'Jesus.'

'Like I say—'

'Nar, nar, I can do it,' Tommy asserted. Five days. Fucking hell.

'Here you go, Mr Smart.' Geordie was back, holding out another wad of cash. 'They're talking about an inquiry.'

Taking the money, Paul sniffed. 'I very much doubt that,' he said with a wink at Tommy.

Geordie, offering a little bow of courtesy, turned away and Paul made to follow him.

'One condition,' Tommy said.

Paul turned back, eyebrow cocked.

'No dealers.'

Paul's brow knitted together as he took a step back towards Tommy. 'Are you negotiating with me?'

'No dealers,' Tommy repeated. 'The cops aren't interested in the raves, they're interested in the drugs. No drugs, no trail, no police.' His mind was all over it already. The best DJs, the best sound system, professional dancers. 'And I want my own security,' he added.

'But the police aren't going to find out where it is,' Paul stated in a tell-me-I'm-right sort of way.

'As long as they're not trailing drug dealers, no,' said Tommy. 'They know who they are, and if they get a whiff of something big, we're fucked.' *We*? It nearly made him gag.

Paul sucked in his cheeks, flicked his jaw from side to side as he pondered. 'Whatever you say,' he said.

A flurry of victory brought a faint smile to Tommy's face. It was bitter sweet; his and Jed's families would be safe, he'd make his money, he'd buy the lease to his club, have a life. But he couldn't help thinking that Paul Smart would be back for more.

Paul turned away from him, a backward wave of his hand dismissing Tommy as he blended back into his men, the group closing around him like liquid.

Tommy stood for a while as the next race got underway, the cheers of the crowds rising in parallel with his growing anticipation. A farm in Northumberland would be a lot easier to keep hush-hush than the warehouses they were using now. No complaining nimbies, the nearest police station at least twenty miles away.

As he made his way through the crowds and left the stadium, his feet felt heavy beneath him, but as he reached the main road and headed for the bus stop, the ground seemed to turn to air and he felt he might take off.

Five days. He could do it.

TUESDAY

PEACH

Drumming his fingers on the steering wheel, DCI Peach watched a long line of vehicles bleed black and blue uniforms onto the pavement and into the school yard. The girls linked arms, their strides synchronised like troopers, the boys pushing and slapping each other, dishevelled and ungainly. With Sally unable to communicate, he needed answers. He needed this Selina's address, so she could verify that Tommy Collins was dishing out the drugs. It would bring him the resources he needed. Armed robbery *and* drug dealing. That was a nice long stretch right there.

Switching off the engine and stepping out of the car, he surveyed the low wall and high railings that surrounded the school yard. The place felt foreign to him, and he checked the sign above the plinth of the school gate. The ensign was familiar enough: a root and branch tree flanked by the Northumbrian flag and the city's three turreted castle, the same logo that adorned Sally's blazer pocket.

Inside, the reception was milling with teenagers, the smell of meat pie wafting through the corridors. Sally's year had finished their exams and were free to do as they pleased, but the lower grades still had to wait another few weeks for their much-awaited freedom.

'Can I help you?' came a voice from his right. A tiny woman approaching sixty with a belly bigger than her breasts stood at the reception window, her face riddled with self-importance.

Ignoring her, he turned to a dense-looking boy and asked him where the head teacher's office was. The boy pointed up the stairs, and he ran towards them, sprinting up two at a time. A chewing girl with a shock of black hair pointed down a corridor to his left when asked the same question.

He legged it before the receptionist could reach him, stopping at a door sporting a "Headmistress" sign, underneath it, her name:

"Miss C. Lindsay, BA(Hons), PGCE, MEd, MPQH."

He opened the door without knocking.

'Oh!' Miss Lindsay had a china tea cup halfway to her mouth. He'd never seen her before, and he guessed she was one of those so-called leaders who kept themselves locked away, liking to remain enigmatic to give the impression of control. She wasn't what he'd expected – some sort of *Mrs Pepperpot* with a grey bun and spectacles on a chain. Instead, she was relatively young, with thick, hay-coloured curly hair, brushed into waves that swamped her head like *Crystal Tips*.

He was holding up his ID when the receptionist appeared at the door, breathless and giddy to the point of choking, asking if everything was all right and should she call the police. Judging by the melodramatic look on her face, she would have liked nothing better.

'No, thank you, Connie.' Miss Lindsay put her tea cup on its saucer.

'More tea, miss?' The nosey cow didn't want to miss a minute of it.

Miss Lindsay looked at Peach with mild curiosity then back towards the door. 'No, Connie, that won't be necessary.'

Peach turned to the receptionist. 'Strong, two sugars,' he said.

With the receptionist's disappointment hanging in the air, Miss Lindsay pulled her chair closer to her desk. Everything about her was abrupt and stiff. 'I'm very busy,' she said, 'so please be quick.'

'It'll take as long as it takes,' Peach replied, putting his hands in his Mac pockets and pulling the coat around his hips as he sat down opposite her.

Miss Lindsay huffed a little. 'About three minutes would be nice. I've got a meeting.' She glanced up at the clock on the wall. 'Now, how can I help you, officer ...?'

'Detective Chief Inspector,' he said.

'Gosh,' said Miss Lindsay with a mocking smile. 'What an honour.' She was trying to be clever, and he felt his hackles rise.

He got straight to the point. 'One of your students is sick. We think she may have been given something.'

Miss Lindsay frowned. 'I'm not aware—'

'Her name is Sally Peach,' he interrupted. 'Do you have a drug problem at this school, Miss Lindsay?'

'Certainly not!' Like a cat on the defence, her hackles were up too, her tail all puffed out. 'If Sally Peach has been dabbling in drugs – which, by the way, wouldn't surprise me – she most certainly didn't get them here.'

Peach paused, squinting. 'What do you mean?' The words came out like a growl, low and challenging.

'I mean, we have strict policies—'

'I was talking about Sally Peach.'

The headmistress lifted one shoulder, then another, an automated movement that seemed designed to relieve stress or rebut anger. 'She was a troubled girl,' she said. 'And *troublesome,* if I remember rightly.'

Peach stiffened. *Sally?*

'In what way, troublesome?' he asked.

'Stealing, fighting, bullying. You name it.'

She was confusing Sally with someone else.

'Oh, no.' The reply was confident. 'No confusion. I know who Sally Peach is.'

She was assessing him now with her eyes, questioning his

motives. Women like this got his goat, always trying to read your thoughts, always ready with an answer, looking at you as if your whole life was already known to them. It was no wonder the woman was still a spinster.

'So, what has she done now?' Miss Lindsay asked with a sigh.

'She's in a coma,' Peach said. It caught her off guard, just as he wanted, and the shoulders twitched again.

'I'm sorry to hear that,' Miss Lindsay said. 'Must be hard. I believe her mother passed away in difficult circumstances.'

Difficult didn't even come close.

The door opened, and Connie arrived with the tea, half of it lapping at the sides of the saucer. Miss Lindsay's eyes flicked up to the clock again, and they both waited for Connie to creep away and close the door.

Peach took a sip of his tea and winced. Like Miss Lindsay, it was cold and a bit too milky for his liking.

He put the cup and saucer on the desk. 'If she was causing so much trouble, why wasn't I—?'

'The father couldn't give two hoots,' said Miss Lindsay.

Peach felt himself flounder, and he realised she had no idea who he was. The name on his ID had been too small for her to see when he'd held it up. He wavered. He should tell her, but something stopped him; he wanted her to be honest, but he wasn't sure he wanted to hear any more.

Miss Lindsay's gaze was steady on his. 'I'm very sorry, Inspector. I'm sorry she's sick and I hope she pulls through. But since she's no longer a pupil at this school, the responsibility isn't ours. We have plenty other students to think about.'

Peach sat forward, confusion drawing his brow into deep lines. Sally was coming back to do her A levels: French, art, English Literature. He'd signed the forms.

He grasped the desk with iron fingers. 'What do you mean, no longer a pupil?'

'I mean, she left the school.' Another glance up at the clock.

'Listen to me, lady …' he said.

The head teacher visibly bristled. 'Sally Peach decided not to come back to school after the Easter break, she didn't want to take her GCSEs—'

Peach held up a hand to stop her, his heart rate notching up a pace. But Miss Lindsay didn't take kindly to the patriarchal interruption.

'They're the new O levels as of last year,' she said with condescension.

'I know that.' He didn't; had never heard of GCSEs.

Miss Lindsay was looking at his open palm and he let it drop. 'Why are you here, Inspector?' she asked. 'Have we done anything wrong? Or are you just after a bit of background on the girl? Because if you are, you're best off speaking to the head of year. Only, I'd make an appointment next time, he's got a lot on.'

Her voice had started to sound muffled in Peach's ears, and he fought hard to maintain his composure. 'She had a friend,' he managed. 'Selina someone.'

'Selina Blackhurst,' Miss Lindsay said. 'Lives in the Old Vicarage on Newcastle Road. Nice girl.' She offered a lop-sided grin. 'Mother's an award-winning architect.'

The dig riled him. 'You have a duty of care …' he said, needing to get one last word in, see her come down a peg or two.

'And so do parents,' she replied. 'Sally's father came in with her. He agreed with everything she wanted to do. Totally irresponsible.'

A hush descended on the room, a chasm of disbelief opening up beneath Peach's feet. 'Her father?'

'Her father,' echoed Miss Lindsay. 'Horrible man. Creepy as

hell. Now, if you'll excuse me.' The pen was back in her hand.

Peach's face was frozen; he wanted to speak but his mouth was dry as bone. Looking through the window into the school yard, he realised it was alien to him, all of it; as unfamiliar as Timbuktu. He'd never set foot in the place, never dropped Sally off at the school gates, never picked her up, never attended a performance or a sports day. He had never been to her school in the three years she'd been here.

Feeling weak as a newborn, he listed as he stood, holding the arm of the chair to steady himself. He ought to get a description at least, tell the woman that *he* was her father. But shame shut the words down. 'I'll, erm, I'll need to see her school file,' he stammered.

'See Connie,' Miss Lindsay said without looking up.

The school corridor seemed to lengthen as he walked towards the stairs, the walls gliding past him at a slower pace than his steps. Questions bombarded him like missiles. Where had Sally been every day in her school uniform? The Saturday job, the weekend sleepovers, the studying late at friends' houses, the notes to say she was at netball practice, drama, choir?

Gathering himself at the top of the stairs, he looked down at the now quiet school reception.

Her father?

Miss Lindsay was mistaken. Either that, or his child was a barefaced liar.

TOMMY

It had been many years since Tommy had experienced peace and tranquillity quite like this. To the north, the hills lumbered upwards in a patchwork of yellow, green, and brown, past the horizon and onwards to Scotland. To the south, they fell away into dense forest. Birds chirped and squawked ceaselessly, interrupted only by the intermittent bleat of a sheep or low of a cow.

Frankie whistled the theme tune to *Last of the Summer Wine* while they sat on a dry-stone wall eating Betty's chopped pork sandwiches from Tupperware, Jed tapping figures into a calculator and jotting the numbers onto a spiral pad. Fatty, an orange Mini Coupe, was parked on a gravel path nearby, Frankie under orders from Honest Jim to drive it as far and as fast as possible in a low gear to cause maximum damage. There was a tenner in it for Frankie if Fatty arrived back needing a hundred and fifty pounds worth of work rather than the fifty originally quoted.

Fatty had done nothing for Jed's street cred, folded into the back seat, his knees high, his head bent low. 'Two grand?' Jed had complained, hugging his knees. 'We'll need more than that, comrade.'

They would have to call in some favours, Tommy had said.

'We haven't paid anyone for the last one yet,' came Jed's mumbled reply.

The thought of going back to Paul Smart for more money was making Tommy's neck itch.

'Anyhow, what we gonna call it?' Jed looked up from his calculator.

'What?' said Frankie.

'The rave, numb-nuts.' Jed went back to his pad of paper and underlined the final figure with a pen, letting out a whistle. 'Six and a half grand,' he said.

'We'll have to get stuff on credit,' said Tommy.

'Your credit ran out long ago, pal.'

It seemed no matter how much Jed manipulated the figures, it was proving impossible to keep to the two-grand budget.

Tommy scratched at the skin under his chin with the back of his nails and told Jed to keep trying.

'Anyway, what did you have to do to get money from Denise?' Jed nodded at the cash in Tommy's inside pocket, and Tommy looked away from Frankie's fleeting glance, the realisation that he would have to lie to Jed settling hesitantly in his throat. He'd never lied to Jed.

'Ahhh, for fuck's sake!' Frankie exclaimed from nowhere. 'There's no cake!' He held the empty Tupperware upside down, the last sandwich firmly clenched in his hand.

'So, put in a complaint!' snapped Jed, but his eyes were still waiting for Tommy's answer.

'Profit is a great motivator, Gerald,' said Tommy, ignoring the evil eyes Jed employed when anyone used his full name. He leant into Jed and whispered. 'She wants no one to know, so not a word.' Another lie, and he wondered when it might end.

'Just so long as it's legit,' said Jed. 'I can't afford to be getting mixed up with shite, not with a proper job on the cards.'

Jed sounded deadly serious and Tommy had to stifle a laugh, not quite sure what to do with the little stab of jealousy that caught him unawares. 'Better get rid of the knock-off trainers, then,' he said, cynically. 'Tucker wants his money. He's threatening your manhood.'

Jed hadn't taken the news well that morning, his head banging off Fatty's roof when Tommy told him of Tucker's new position in Paul Smart Incorporated.

'I did,' said Jed, 'I used the money to buy the safe.' It was meant to provoke guilt, and it hit the mark.

'Christ, it doesn't have to be Fort Knox,' Tommy said. 'Why can't we just use a safe house?'

Jed indicated the vast countryside with an outstretched arm and Tommy squinted around him, drawing his lips together in acknowledgement. He'd been to the countryside only once before – a school outing to Vindolanda. It was a far cry from Valley Park's recreation ground, the only piece of green space the estate could boast as a park. He'd walked through the rec that morning to meet Jed, Frankie, and Fatty. Barely ten o'clock in the morning and Trevor Logan and half a dozen street drinkers and junkies were heading towards the protection of the oak tree, little Carl trudging along a few yards behind his brother, straining to pull an old tartan shopping trolley. The group had gathered around the massive trunk of the tree to wait for Carl, T-shirts hanging from their back pockets.

'Howay, Hulk Fucking Hogan!' Trevor jeered at Carl, his lackeys laughing like howler monkeys, scratching at their balls, and drawing hard on their fag ends. When Carl reached them, he opened the flap of the trolley and they all dived in, pulling out six packs and cartons of cigarettes.

Trevor held two of the six packs aloft, turning towards Tommy and gyrating his hips in a dance of sorts. 'Wor bairn!' he shouted. 'Best little thief in Valley Park, eh?!' Turning back to Carl, Trevor handed him one of the six packs and pushed him away. 'Now fuck off, you manky bastard,' he'd spat.

The high-pitched cry of a lone buzzard brought Tommy's eyes to the cloudless sky now, Frankie shielding his sandwich, afraid the bird would rob the food from his fingers. The sense of space and liberty was overwhelming, and Tommy hopped onto the dry-stone wall, stretching his back, stiff and sore from the buffer machine he'd been tied to that morning, up at the crack of dawn and down at the Metrocentre by six o'clock.

Putting his hands on his hips, he surveyed the fields. 'We should put the marquee over there,' he said, pointing to the field to his right. It was huge and flat.

'No marquees,' said Jed. 'All sold out.'

'Open air,' Tommy said. 'Al fresco raving.'

'Circus tent?' said Frankie.

Jed baulked. 'Make that seven and a half grand,' he said, shoving the calculator into a sports bag that lay at his feet.

The bickering went over Tommy's head. He imagined the scene: the sky inky-black, stars twinkling, the night alight with colour. Jed was at the decks and people were dancing, sweating, faces aglow. Thousands of people.

'I'm going to have an office, business cards, the works,' said Tommy. 'And youse can all have jobs.'

'Even me?' asked Frankie.

'First refusal, Frankie,' said Tommy.

'Does that mean I'm not getting one?'

'You daft twat,' said Jed. 'It means you get the first job offer, you can refuse it if you want.'

'Nah, nah, I'll take it,' said Frankie.

Tommy jumped down from the wall. '*Space Generation*,' he said. 'That's what we're calling it.' He reached into the back pocket of his jeans, pulled out a piece of paper and held it up. 'Wait 'till you see this.' He unfolded the paper and spread it out on the wall, feeling two lots of breath on his face as his friends put their heads next to his. He'd recreated the UFO drawing, the spaceship now the DJ at his decks, suspended high in the rumbling clouds, spilling liquid light onto a mass of elated faces below. Behind the ship, in a patch of clear, black sky, a bright moon glowed, half of it spherical and cratered, the other half a partial alien face with one wide, tilted eye and half a tiny nose and mouth. It smiled in supernatural triumph.

'Jesus,' he heard Jed whisper. 'That's the dog's bollocks.'

'You're a goddam genius,' said Frankie.

'Who needs marquees, when you've got nature?' said Tommy, clutching the drawing and standing up straight, filling his lungs with the fresh air.

'And aliens,' said Frankie.

'And cake,' added Jed, bending down and taking another plastic tub from his sports bag.

'Thank Christ for that!' said Frankie, grabbing the tub and opening the lid.

They laughed, their voices lost in the breezy air as Tommy folded the drawing and put it into his pocket.

Genius. He could live with that.

PEACH

Unable to take Sally's file off the school premises, he'd demanded a copy from the receptionist, a demand that had Connie doing the slowest job possible. Eventually, she'd handed him a pile of loose papers with a look that would cut glass.

He'd gone straight to the hospital, his hope of finding Sally alert and able to talk quashed instantly at the sight of her lifeless form. He'd sat with her for an hour or more, just watching, the letters from the school folded into a thick wad in his coat pocket.

At his desk now, he felt sick to his stomach. Among the reports of detentions for bad behaviour were copies of several letters addressed to him. None of them had reached him, and he recalled picking up the post from the doormat the day before, realising it was a task he hadn't done for some time. He would always leave the house before Sally, and before the first post. She would be home by four o'clock in time to pick up the second. Even on Saturdays he would be at the station more often than not.

According to the correspondence, staff had called to the bungalow on more than one occasion to speak to him, but there'd never been anyone home. The letters painted a grim picture – concern about Sally's growing absence from class, her aggression, and her propensity to fall asleep at her desk on the rare times she was there. The typed notes of the meeting with "her father" were brief, dated 17 March 1989, stating that Sally, at sixteen, had the right to leave full-time education if she so wished, and that her one remaining parent had agreed to the decision.

There was only one person who could enlighten him, and there was still no change in her condition, the options Doctor Flynn wanted to discuss shunted to the back of his mind. They would have to stay there for the time being, because now there were two men he wanted to string up by their bollocks, and they would require all his energy.

He looked up at the sound of knocking, quickly sliding the papers under the building society file as the door opened and Murphy swaggered his way to the chair opposite the desk. He dropped into it and assumed his usual position: hands clasped on his chest, legs akimbo.

'Saturday night,' he said. 'The rave, boss,' he added when Peach's expression remained blank.

Peach frowned. 'This Saturday?' Surely, they couldn't organise something of any significance in just a few days.

Murphy nodded his affirmation. 'According to the busty young lady at Hitsville USA, yeah. It's a record shop in town, boss. I bought a tape, got some bouncin' tracks on it: garage, house, techno, back beats, the lot.'

He was talking gobbledygook.

'So, where is it?'

'We'll have to wait 'till we get the flyers, then we should get a team to sit and call the number. Not too early mind, we'll have to wait 'till the real punters start ringing.'

Peach scoffed. *Team?*

'And they'll have to learn the lingo an'all,' said Murphy. 'None of this, *"excuse me, this is City CID, can you tell me where the rave is please?"*'

Peach regarded Murphy for a moment: young, hip, if you liked that kind of thing. This was a whole new world, and he suddenly felt his age.

'Got an idea, chief,' said Murphy. 'Wanna hear it?'

Peach barely nodded, bone tired.

'How about I do a ring around, call some of the forces down south, see how they're handling it? I could get some inside information, stuff they don't talk about in the press.'

'That's not how we do things,' Peach replied, disappointed at the futility of the idea. 'What happens here, stays here.' Not only that, but he could do without being the laughing stock of the well-heeled forces south of the M25.

'Well, I get that, boss, it's the same in Manchester. But what if I said I knew the Deputy Commissioner in *Laandon, innit?*'

Peach sighed, losing patience. 'How on earth would you know him?'

'She's me mam, boss.'

Murphy didn't hide his grin when Peach's eyebrows shot up, not quite sure how to respond. Thankfully, his desk phone rang, and he picked it up brusquely as he shooed Murphy from his office with a dismissive hand.

'Sir, there's a couple of ladies in reception to see you,' Sharon said.

In the reception area, two women were sitting with handbags on their laps, covering the rolls of belly flab they'd rather not have. One was in her sixties, drowning in a blue twin-set. The other much younger, mutton dressed as lamb.

'Yes?' Peach said.

'I'm Mrs Bailey, this is Denise Morris. We're from the Tyne Building Society,' the older woman said proudly.

His witnesses. But only two of them, where the hell were all the others? Too lazy, too scared.

'Follow me,' he said.

DENISE

They were a good ten minutes into the interview before the inspector's fingers started to tear at his moustache. It hadn't taken long to give their account of that day: they'd gone to work, had a cuppa, served the early morning customers and suddenly there they were – three men brandishing weapons. They'd done as they were told, got onto the floor, and then the men were gone.

Denise had relayed this information in twenty seconds flat, Mary Bailey taking up the remaining minutes – who she'd made tea for, how they took it, who preferred coffee et cetera et cetera. It was no wonder the man was starting to cause himself pain.

She was here for one reason, and one reason only. To make sure the police were put well and truly on the wrong track. The armed robber in the coat and the bowler hat had said nothing, and she wasn't entirely sure she was right, but there was something so familiar about the man's posture, the way he stood as if he owned the place. Paul had been too curious about her job, more interested in that than her own life. But still, she wouldn't let him go down for it. He'd had enough pain in his life already. Denise had watched enough cop shows to know not to incriminate herself or raise suspicion, to wait for the right questions, and it didn't take long for them to come.

'Any specific accents?' the copper asked. 'Stammers, lisps?'

Mrs Bailey had to apologise; her memory wasn't what it was, but Denise set her face to pondering.

'The tall one wasn't local,' she said. 'Sounded foreign to me, do you not think, Mary?'

Mrs Bailey was looking at the inspector, her not-what-it-was memory reeling back in time. 'Eeeh, I don't know.'

'When he told us to get down,' Denise insisted, her tone just on the right side of encouragement. 'Remember that?'

'Yes, yes,' said Mrs Bailey, 'now you come to mention it.'

'What sort of foreign?' Peach asked. 'American? French? What?'

He was irritated, she could tell. They weren't giving him what he wanted.

Denise shrugged. 'Just foreign. Not Geordie, that's a definite. And his eyes were brown.'

He kept on about the other one, the one who ran to get the money, but their noses were touching the carpet by then, and she'd already said it once and didn't appreciate repeating it again.

The inspector sighed and jotted all of three words on a note pad – *Not Geordie. Brown.*

Then the trainer was produced, a scuffed old thing that all the kids were wearing. He picked it up from the chair next to him and placed it on the table. 'One of the perpetrators was wearing a pair of these. Recognise it?'

'Never seen it before,' said Denise, looking away. She done her bit, now she needed to go.

Mrs Bailey, however, concentrated on it. 'Seen something like them on our Janice's lad,' she said eventually. 'You should see him, mind, got this thing, here, stuck in his nose, and a thing, here, right through his eyebrow.' She hoisted up her breasts in a way that reminded Denise of Les Dawson. 'You got bairns, Mr Peach?' Mrs Bailey asked.

Peach hesitated. 'A girl,' he said, 'sixteen.'

Mrs Bailey nodded, then continued rambling. 'So, there he is, our Janice's lad, eating his tea and I think, I never put any silver dragoons on that cake, and he's got this bloomin' thing through his tongue!' She stuck out her tongue and pointed at it while Denise made a meal of looking at her watch. But Mrs Bailey jabbered on. 'So, I says, "What do you want with him?" And she says, "Gran, there's nowt the matter with him," and I says, "Why, there's nowt the matter with donkeys but they divven't let them on the bus, do they?!"'

'You can't tell them nothing,' said Denise, shuffling in her chair, the heat making her sweat in unladylike places. 'They'll just do what they want, anyway.' The bitterness in her voice brought a glance from the inspector, a sour look of hostility with a hint of agreement. 'I've got stuff on, Mary, I need to go,' she said, fanning her face with her hand.

But Mary Bailey's thoughts were elsewhere. 'Blue eyes,' she said, decisively, suddenly sitting upright as if enlightenment had struck. 'One of the lads from the robbery. I remember that if nothing else. He was thin as a rake. Big blue eyes, like a lassie.'

The sourness in the inspector's face morphed into something else, something altogether more optimistic. He put his hand on a folder which had rested unopened on the table until now, looking intently at Mrs Bailey while Denise sighed and trained her eyes on the ceiling.

'I want you to look at something very carefully for me,' he said. 'You too, Mrs Morris.'

She brought her eyes down and found herself looking at his back while he shuffled about with the file. This was all she needed, another twenty minutes in the stifling heat of this wretched place. But when he turned around, and put a photograph in front of them, she couldn't stop her hand reaching for her throat. He'd covered the face bar the eyes with bits of paper, and they were Tommy's eyes, clear as day.

'Are these the eyes you saw?'

Mrs Bailey leant forward, all renewed confidence. 'Hey, Denise, is that him?'

Denise let the air leave her lungs, felt the sweat tickle her brow. It was an opportunity too good to miss. 'That's him,' she said.

'Are you sure?'

Denise looked right at the DCI. 'I'm sure.'

'Eeeh, it is, it's him,' said Mrs Bailey. 'Mind, these bairns; they should put them in the army, that'll lorn them a thing or two.'

The inspector looked like he'd often thought so himself, and a smile crept over his lips. 'Thank you, ladies, you've been most helpful.'

He'd pulled the photograph back towards him before Denise could change her mind. If the inspector came for Tommy, they'd soon learn of the family connection. It would lead them back to her – and back to Paul.

She felt her legs turn to stone, and she opened her mouth, ready to take another look at the photograph, but the interview room door was flung open and another detective stood in the doorway – older, his hair black as coal.

He strode in and threw a newspaper on the table, telling Denise and Mrs Bailey they should leave. She didn't get much of a chance to look at the front page, but she saw the headline before the inspector with the moustache grabbed it from the table.

"SENIOR POLICE OFFICER VOWS TO GET THE SCUM WHO HURT HIS INNOCENT GIRL."

Then there was a uniform at the door, the woman from the reception, her face all red and stressed.

'I've got the RVI on the phone for DCI Peach. They said it's urgent.'

And the inspector was jumping from his seat and running out of the room like his life depended on it.

PEACH

As he stood at the foot of Sally's bed, disappointment and revulsion crept up his throat, overriding the trill of adrenaline he'd felt when the witnesses had identified his man. It was an addictive rush that had kept him in the force for thirty years. It might not come as often as he would have liked, and much of the time it was short lived as some lead went dead or some witness got cold feet or disappeared altogether. But that just made him strive all the harder. He lived for it: that feeling of victory when toe rags like Tommy Collins were put behind bars where they belonged.

He waited while the nurse, Pamela, fussed about, putting objects in the heavy metal bin, straightening the bed sheets. *Humming*, a tad overexcited considering the sight that lay before him. If this was his daughter "coming round" then some sodding doctor needed sacking.

Peach grabbed the nurse firmly by the arm as she walked past him, and she looked down at his fingers.

'Was it you?' he said, producing the newspaper.

She looked at it, then up at him, her face puckering into a look of extreme offence. 'No. Now, take your hand off me right this minute.'

He loosened his grasp, and she strode off, leaving him to wonder who the hell he could trust in this place.

Sally was free of the mask that had been attached to her face for days, her skin still baring the marks of the tape across her nose and cheeks. A thin tube had replaced it, sitting snugly under her nostrils, and making a little wheezing noise as the oxygen snaked its way into her lungs.

He moved to the side of the bed, unable to tear his eyes away from the alien face. Gone were the healthy round cheeks, and her hair hung in greasy tentacles over her shoulders. Her eyes flickered open, but they rolled, their focus in another world altogether. Her mouth opened and closed, her tongue trying to form words that were beyond the reach of the dry, cracked lips. A sound emerged, human only in so much that it wasn't the sound of any animal he knew. And yet, the voice was hers. It was Sally's warped voice wedged in the back of that throat.

The curtain was pulled back and drawn again, and Doctor Flynn was by his side. She spoke in a steady tone; factual, composed, objective. Details of core temperature, blood pressure, liver function, the production of urine. He wasn't sure if what he was hearing was good, bad, or disastrous. He caught the words: *vegetative state, brain damage, lifelong care.* The doctor seemed to talk for an age and perhaps he didn't hear *still hope* and *more time,* because when he nodded that he understood what she'd said, and Doctor Flynn was gone, he felt only dread.

Taking hold of Sally's hand, he sat on the bed. 'Shhhh,' he said in a scratchy whisper. 'It's Dad.'

He stroked her hand, recalling the last time he'd seen her. It was last week, Wednesday or Thursday. She'd eaten jam on toast and gone to her room to study. It was her last exam the next day she'd said. He'd wished her good luck, and she'd responded with a blunt *thanks*. He couldn't remember what the exam was. She hadn't told him. He hadn't asked.

Young as she'd been, at just ten years old, Sally had handled Kathleen's death far better than him. He'd never seen her weep or mourn. She'd been strong as an ox and he'd admired her for it. She'd cried more when the cat died - broke her heart. Finnegan - the crusty old ginger tom who spat and growled at him but purred like a tractor in Sally and Kathleen's arms. But even Finnegan had feared Kathleen's unpredictable moods and Peach had often noticed Sally shrink from her mother's skeletal hands, taking no comfort in cuddles from a bag of bones. He'd assumed Sally had felt the same guilty relief he had when it was all over, and if anything, she'd flourished these last few years.

He looked down at the grainy picture of Sally on the front page of the newspaper, the one he'd torn from her wardrobe door, the one he must have dropped to the ground when he was in the reporter's face. Next to it was his official police photograph, around ten years old, his hair shorter and darker, the moustache neat and trimmed.

He folded the paper in half and looked back at his daughter. He didn't know how long he'd been there, watching her stare into an infinity beyond his vision when she finally spoke. He couldn't make it out at first; it was like a baby trying to utter its first words:

'*Mmmuh. Mmmuh.*'

He squeezed her hand and thought he felt her fingers tighten around his. 'That's it,' he said, wiping a tear from her cheek with his thumb. 'Your dad's here.'

He leant forward, and he heard it clearly at the end of a fizz of breath.

'*Mam.*'

***

She wanted her mother.

As Peach walked away from the hospital towards his car, he felt an old sensation of helplessness take hold, a feeling he thought he'd put behind him, a sensation he'd never wanted to experience again as long as he lived. It made him feel weak, inept. Kathleen had put them through hell and forgiveness was still well out of his reach. The years of worry, anger, and blame; her inability to understand basic logic: we eat, we live; we don't, we die. She hadn't wanted to die. Death had terrified her, but not as much as putting a spoonful of soup to her lips.

Seething, Peach thumped the roof of the car, dropping his head onto the knuckle of his thumb, feeling it dig painfully into his forehead.

Lifelong care.

The words stung like nettles. He wouldn't be around forever. Who would take care of Sally after he'd gone?

His skin crawled as if insects had invaded the lining of his clothes. He couldn't breathe for the rage that was holding every muscle taut. Someone was to blame: this bogus father who'd paraded into the school unchallenged. Kathleen. Tommy Collins.

All of them were to blame.

DENISE

She'd lugged the tins of paint all the way from the bus stop. Perhaps it was a sort of apology, or an impulse buy, she wasn't quite sure. Either way, she would have expected a bit more gratitude.

'It's pink,' Tommy said, deadpan.

'It's free.' The ungracious shit.

She dropped the tins onto the hallway floor, rubbing at the indentations they'd made across the inside of her fingers. Tommy stood in her way as if he didn't want her to come in. Nowt new there.

Pushing past him into the living room, she sneered inwardly at the sight of Jed Foster sitting at the dining table, pen in his mouth, hunched over a calculator and a pad of paper. Here he was again: *Wifey*.

Ashleigh was sitting in her playpen surrounded by soft bricks and wearing one of the new dresses Denise had bought her. She swooped down to pick her up as Tommy strode past her and stood over Jed, telling him they should call it a day in a low voice she wasn't meant to hear.

'Eh? We're not finished!' Jed complained. He needed a few more minutes, he said, and he went back to his calculator.

Tommy hesitated then sat on the chair next to him, all jittery and nervous. Didn't take a genius to see he was up to something, but armed robbery was way out of his league. He didn't have it in him – didn't have the nerve or the confidence. He didn't have that kind of power, and she felt an unexpected wave of pride for her brother as she watched Tommy draw his fingers over his lips in a *zip it* movement.

The man was transparent as cling film.

'Is everybody ignoring you, poppet?' Denise chimed, bouncing Ashleigh on her hip.

'Sam's upstairs,' said Tommy.

She might as well be on another planet for all the attention she got, Denise thought. And the baby. They'd be better off with her – Sam would never have to lift a finger.

She sat on the sofa with Ashleigh, her eyes falling on the corner of the newspaper that poked out of her bag. She'd seen something in that copper's face when he'd looked down at Tommy's eyes – a kindred spirit. He hated Tommy, too, and now she knew why. It was plastered all over the front page, the story depicting nights of drug-fuelled parties in warehouses that could collapse at any minute onto the heads of the innocent. Parties organised by Tommy.

She understood the DCI perfectly; his child had been violated, and parents would do anything to protect their children. Her own father seemed to have bypassed that gene, but her mother had been different – in the early days, anyway. Denise had seen it in her eyes, felt it in her comforting arms many times before it was knocked out of her.

Her stomach curdled, and she closed her eyes against the memories.

Open the box, put them inside, close, lock, click.

Looking down at Ashleigh she felt the nausea subside, only to be replaced by the peevish nips of anxiety. She hadn't thought it through. She'd seen Tommy's eyes and blurted out the lie, but if Sam discovered Denise had betrayed Tommy, it would never be the same. Even if he was guilty, you didn't grass on your own.

'Cuppa?' Sam had come into the living room, blowing her

fringe from her forehead, furniture polish and old rag in hand.

'Oh, yes love,' said Denise. 'Let Tommy do it, you have five minutes.'

'It's all right,' said Sam, happily, disappearing through the door into the kitchen.

'Ahh, don't you look pretty,' Denise sang to Ashleigh. 'Not like your mam, eh? She looks *knackered*, yes she does!' She glanced at Tommy who was rubbing his eyes with a thumb and finger. 'You haven't seen the new garden yet, love!' she shouted. 'Hey, mind, it's bloody lovely! You should get Tommy to do yours up.' There was a long silence, and she heard the dining chairs creak as the boys shifted in their seats, a secret glance passing between them.

'He's busy, mam,' said Sam, coming into the room and putting two cups of tea on the coffee table. 'He was at work this morning. Anyway, I don't mind doing it.'

You could hardly call it work, cleaning the floors and the bogs at the Metrocentre. She had a mind to say so but kept it to herself while Sam headed back into the kitchen to fetch tea for the lazy arses at the table.

She shook her head with a sigh. Sam could have been anything she wanted to be; she played the piano, had the voice of an angel. She could have been a pop star, travelled the world, maybe taken her old mam with her on tour. But here she was, her talented little girl, playing house and using an old pair of knickers to polish rickety furniture from the dark ages.

When Sam sat next to her, she noticed she didn't look so knackered after all, in fact, she was positively beaming.

'It's never another one of these dos, is it?' Denise asked in a low voice.

'Don't ask me,' said Sam, but she knew what was going on all right, and Denise wondered why she didn't trust her to just say so.

'Four and a half grand,' Denise heard Jed say. 'We might get away with four, if we can get these on tick.'

The boys high-fived each other before they got up from their chairs, smiles all round.

'Don't be going on my account,' said Denise, 'I'm not staying.' She kicked off her shoes, put her feet up on the coffee table and wiggled her toes, making herself a little more comfortable. She dug into her handbag and retrieved the newspaper. 'Terrible about this lassie,' she said, 'look at the state of her.' She looked up at Jed who was standing behind the sofa, his smile vanishing as he stared down at the picture of the policeman and the girl in the white dress, all black eyeliner and attitude. 'Sixteen,' she said, 'just a bairn.' She could almost feel the heat of Jed's face burning her neck.

'You wouldn't think it to look at her,' said Sam, stealing a glance at her husband.

'Drugs,' said Denise. 'I'm pleased you never got involved in any of that, mind.' She patted Sam on the knee. 'You were a good girl.'

'I still am,' said Sam with a nervous laugh.

Denise heard the front door slam, and the newspaper was swept from her hands by Tommy. She watched him blanche as he dropped it onto the coffee table then ran out the door after Jed.

She shrugged at Sam who was reading the article and rubbing at her mouth. Oh yes, she would protect her child, come hell or high water. And she would protect her brother too.

This time.

TOMMY

It was gone half-past five and the after-school disco at the youth club was in full swing. A group of teenage girls danced energetically to Jive Bunny's latest medley, the boys lined up around the walls like chess pieces. Barry twirled and bounced in an old man's shirt and tie, the pockets of the shirt adorned with an array of badges, the largest of which shouted a warning of *"Just Say No!"* to his peers.

Darren, the youth worker, stood at the double doors. Always dressed in the same tweed jacket and sensible shoes, he was a sciency-looking man in his forties with round glasses and brown hair that grew out of his head like the foam cover of a microphone.

'Just make sure he doesn't play any of that poxy House shit,' Darren said when Tommy asked if he could steal Jed for five minutes. 'Makes my ears bleed.' Darren was another one of the old school fraternity. He'd come to one of Tommy's raves in the early days – his attempt to get down with the kids. He'd stayed ten minutes then run from the warehouse with his hands over his bleeding ears.

'Will do, boss,' said Tommy with a wink.

Tommy approached Jed who sat on a plastic chair behind the decks looking miserable as sin. He'd stormed away from Tommy earlier, not wanting to engage in conversation, but now his eyes followed Tommy with the precision of an Exocet missile.

A few minutes later, a Kylie twelve inch was on the turntable and they stood in the corridor.

'What if she dies?' Jed was saying, hands firmly on his hips.

'She won't die.'

'She might.'

'She won't.'

'She *might.*'

Tommy had recognised Sally Peach's face immediately. She'd been at their dos before, almost every one, but she'd appeared mature in both age and conduct, and now he knew why Peach was watching him, and why Jed was glaring at him with eyes that accused.

'What?' Tommy said. 'I didn't give her drugs. Howay, Jed, we both know what goes on.'

Jed looked down at his feet with a sigh. Something was bugging him. Something bigger than Peach's kid.

'You need a shag,' said Tommy, trying to chivvy his spirits. It must have been four days. Unthinkable.

'She's sixteen, man, how did that happen?' Jed asked, looking through the glass of the doors where Barry headed up a long line of girls winding their way around the hall to the 'Locomotion'.

Tommy followed his eyes. 'We'll be more careful, all right?' he said. He was already careful. The number of kids being turned away from his raves was growing, some of them not even teenagers yet, desperate to know what their older brothers and sisters had been up to when they snuck back into the house at breakfast time, buzzing like sparklers on Bonfire Night. But Jed's face was still bleak. 'Howay, mate, what's up?' Tommy gave him a nudge with his elbow.

'Nowt,' said Jed, looking away.

'Tell Uncle Tommy.'

'Fuck off, perve.'

'That's the spirit,' said Tommy, slapping him on the arm.

Jed couldn't help but grin. 'Honestly, it's nowt,' he said, his face flushing. 'There's this lass …'

Tommy frowned humorously. 'Have you been dumped?'

As if, Jed's face said. 'She's just playing hard to get,' he explained.

'Must've found out about your huffs.'

'Very funny,' smirked Jed. He put his face up to the glass of the door again, and Tommy put his cheek next to his.

'What time does it finish?' he asked.

'Seven-thirty, why?'

They had their planning meeting at nine o'clock in The Crown, their favourite drinking hole on the Quayside. And there was the question of Jimmy Lyric's ability to create arseholes where they weren't needed.

Tommy flattened his nose against the glass, eyes on the decks.

'Nah, nah, nah. Howay, Tommy, not Darren,' said Jed, pulling him away from the doors. The decks at the youth centre had just been replaced after a recent burglary. They were new, they were state-of-the-art. *Technics.* It wasn't as if Darren had paid for them himself, they were covered by the council's insurance, so the Government had coughed up, and Tommy reckoned the Tories owned him one.

Jed's frown was full of warning. 'Touch those decks, and you're dead,' he said, and he pushed open the doors and made his way back to equipment that would be in the hands of Jimmy Lyric by eight-thirty whether Jed liked it or not, the window to the toilets jemmied open a few minutes after Darren pulled away in his car. Tommy needed Jimmy on Saturday. Jimmy had contacts, a generator, and he was the best MC this side of the Pennines.

Inside the hall, Tommy joined the back of the long line of girls, waving to Jed, but Jed had his eye on the next record. He held the vinyl up to the light before placing it on the turntable and pushing up the sliders on the mixer. Even from this distance, Tommy could see the glint in his friend's eyes.

The rasping refrain of Black Box pounded from the speakers, Jed's head flipping forward in time to the beat, teeth biting at his bottom lip. Tommy whooped and threw his arms up, palms pushing upwards with the rhythm. Barry joined him and soon even the boys surrounded him, faces serious as they concentrated on copying Tommy's moves: *big fish, little fish, cardboard box.*

He felt Darren's eyes stinging his neck but fuck him. Fuck Peach, fuck Smartie, fuck Denise, fuck them all. He had a right to dance to the music he wanted to dance to. No such thing as society? Fine. They'd made their own, and, for one night a week, it was Heaven.

***

Tommy caught sight of Jed and Frankie sitting on stools at their usual table by the cigarette machine in The Crown. The pub was lively, the music barely audible over the sound of raised laughter and chatter. Tommy was almost an hour late, Darren wanting to stay behind and chat about his plans for a job club for young people on the estate, Tommy eventually wheeling the decks in a shopping trolley all the way to Jimmy's house in Arthur's Hill. No one batted an eyelid.

His friends looked bored as hell as he approached, and Jed raised his hands in exasperation.

'Here, man, sit down,' he ordered, 'and don't ever leave me alone with this man again. He's got nee patter.'

'I'll remember that next time you want a lift,' sniffed Frankie.

Tommy pulled up a stool and sat next to Jed, taking a sip from the Coke that had already been bought for him. 'What the fuck's that?' Tommy pointed at a brown leather satchel at Jed's feet. 'You going back to school or what?'

Frankie grinned. 'It's a bag,' he said, 'for a man.'

'A man's bag?' Tommy's face was a spectacle.

'It's called style,' said Jed, who appeared oddly distracted.

Frankie chuckled. 'You big puff.'

Jed wasn't listening, his eyes, all round and moony, fixed on a spot in the distance. Tommy followed his eye line to the bar and recognised the woman with the cheekbones and sleek black hair from the storeroom at the rave. She was an unusually tall woman of around Frankie's age, sipping a glass of wine and ignoring Jed.

'Bit different, isn't she? Name's *Shona*.' Jed pronounced the name with affection. 'She's spiritual. Into all that afterlife shit. She can hypnotise anyone.'

'Hadaway and shite,' said Tommy.

'It's true, I've seen it!' insisted Jed. She'd been at Phutures the night before, he said. All over him, couldn't get enough of him. Then she'd hypnotised the barman, and they'd got a free drink.

'Looks like she's had enough of you now,' said Frankie, puffing out his chest as he raised his pint to his mouth.

Jed sneered at him. 'What would you know about it, Francis Rossi?'

'Talented man,' said Frankie, nodding slowly, not insulted in the least.

Tommy picked up his rucksack, pulling out a handful of crumpled sheets of paper. He lay them flat on the table. What had started out as a to-do list now resembled the musings of a mad man.

'When's the rest of the cash coming?' demanded Jed, frowning at the list.

'First things first,' said Tommy.

'Err, no. Cash first, bookings later.'

'Are you gonna trust me, or what?'

Jed pulled a cynical face and focused on the bar once more.

'Right,' Tommy ran his fingers down the list. 'Jed. Dancers. There's auditions tomorrow at the Tyne Theatre for some musical shite.' He looked up, slapped Jed on the arm, and Jed turned his attention from Shona to the paper on the table, eyeing it with a confused frown and a tiny smile Tommy couldn't quite decipher. 'I want professionals, no charvers,' said Tommy. 'Take Frankie with you.'

'Eh? Howay!' Jed threw his arms in the air.

'He might be an ugly get, but he can dance.'

Frankie grinned with a wise nod of the head.

'Coaches?' Tommy's eyes were back on his list.

'I'll need cash for the deposits,' said Frankie. 'And we'll need shed loads of water. I'll store it at the works.'

'Good man,' said Tommy, and he awaited Jed's childish response to the praise, but Jed's eyes were hooked on Shona who was now reeling him in like a fresh-water fish.

Tommy looked back his scrawls, turning the paper sideways so he could read his jumbled notes. He grimaced, berating himself for not being more organised. It didn't come naturally to him. Not like Jed.

He pressed on anyway, Frankie nodding and agreeing to whatever was allocated his way.

'Generators,' said Tommy, facing Jed.

'You'd love this lass,' Jed mused in response, his chin resting on his knuckles. 'She's into all that *Space Generation* stuff – time travel, parallel universes. She's trying to get a show on at the City Hall.'

Tommy wondered if Shona had hypnotised Jed, turned him into proper boyfriend material, which would be nice for him at some point, but Tommy could do with his real friend back right now.

'Mebbies she was abducted,' said Frankie, winking at Tommy.

'Aye,' replied Jed. 'That would explain lots of things.'

Tommy was just about losing it. 'Well, go and talk to her about fucking aliens!'

'I don't fuck aliens,' said Jed, mesmerised.

'Only 'coz they haven't landed yet.'

Frankie howled, and Tommy put his hands to his head in distraction. They had four days, and he needed Jed to be on the ball. He pulled his fingers over his eyes, pushing so hard he could see a kaleidoscope of white lights. As he whined in frustration, he heard something clatter onto the table through the din of raised voices. He peeked through his fingers at a clip board, a piece of white paper attached containing neat tables and coloured stickers, dates, times, and contacts, tasks and timelines. He frowned at Jed who was putting his man-bag back onto the floor, a sly grin on his face as he sat up straight and nodded down at the clipboard.

'Project management, my friend,' he said.

***

It was closing time and Jed and Frankie had had a skin full. Tommy's glass of Coke had lasted him all night as usual. No one questioned or expected a round from him.

With Jed's meticulous inventory of tasks guiding him, Tommy had doled out the orders, and Smartie's two thousand pounds was distributed in a toilet cubicle, away from thieving eyes, the three of them squashed in, trying not to touch each other in the wrong places. Every penny was to be accounted for – sale or return, each task costed to the penny. Various scenarios even showed potential profit ranges.

Frankie's eyes had bulged at the highest income forecast of eighty thousand pounds, Tommy staying quiet about the fact that half of it would be going to Paul Smart.

Tommy leant into the cigarette machine now, arms folded, smiling at his friends, drunk and happy. As they staggered to their feet, Jed took a small card from his back pocket and held it up.

'Youth Club's cash and carry card,' he said with a lop-sided grin.

Tommy grabbed at it. 'I fucking love you.'

'Ooooohh!' said Frankie, camping it up.

Jed snatched it back, leant into Tommy and slurred, 'Just another few grand up front, and I'm all yours, baby.' He pointed the card at Tommy's chest. 'If there's no more cash, mate, I'm out.'

Tommy made to speak, but Jed held up a hand.

'I know. I trust you,' he said.

Tommy quickly threw off the sense of unease that made the hairs rise on his arms. Not only was Jed the organised one, but Tommy simply couldn't imagine doing it without him. It was their enterprise; they did it together. That's just how it was.

'What's this lad, Frankie?' he said, putting his arm around Jed's shoulders.

'Fanny magnet,' said Frankie, no one mentioning that Shona had left the pub without him.

'Nar, he's a brick,' said Tommy, pulling Jed towards him. 'A fucking wall!'

'The three amigos!' Frankie cried. Then he paused, held out his arms, his expression one of drunken affection. 'In the words of our kinsman, Knopfler,' his arms stretched wider. 'Brothers in arms.'

Frankie moved in for a hug, but Jed held him back with his outstretched hand.

'You, mate, have got enough brothers to sink a ship, so back off.'

'Aye,' nodded Frankie, 'but they're all off at university, or at their bloody jobs, man. Black sheep, me.'

Jed grinned and pointed a finger at him. 'That's because you're adopted.'

'Pack it in,' said Tommy, pulling Jed away.

'Actually,' said Frankie, his eyes suddenly forlorn. 'Me mam did say something about the rag-and-bone man.' After a moment, his face spread into a wide smile and he belly laughed, leaning back with his hands on his round stomach. Jed joined him, and Tommy couldn't help but smile. He pulled them towards the door of the pub, Frankie giving one of his all-star Northern Soul spins as they passed Hadgy Dodds, who Tommy grabbed by the arm, leading him down the steps onto the Quayside to talk about the supply of security while Jed hovered at the edge of the pavement watching the river, Frankie stumbling off to fetch his latest car.

'Twenty men?' Hadgy creased his huge brow. 'This Saturday?' He shook his head. 'Depends if there's a match on.'

'Well, is there?' Tommy was no lover of football.

Hadgy thought for a minute. 'Nope.'

'Twenty-five, then, just to be on the safe side.'

'Must be a big do, is it?'

'The biggest,' said Tommy, with a slap on Hadgy's back, 'and the best.'

He was all pumped up, ready to face Paul Smart and relieve him of some more cash – minimum two-and-a-half grand, though Tommy reckoned he should go in higher. Five maybe.

Tommy shook Hadgy's mammoth hand and joined Jed at the edge of the pavement. They stood in silence for a while, Tommy deep in thought before he said, 'Hey, what if he is adopted?' Frankie was the only one in his family with the carrot top, and once his older siblings were gone, Frankie's parents had fostered a dozen little worky-tickets. It was a long-shot, but possible.

'Give over,' growled Jed, as headlights appeared around the

corner of one of the narrow roads that curved from the River Tyne up to the city centre. But the lights didn't belong to Mr Miyagi, Frankie's Nissan Sunny.

Tommy pulled Jed back as the wheels mounted the pavement, and the bumper of a gleaming black Range Rover pinned Hadgy against the wall. Tucker emerged stiffly from the vehicle and opened the boot of the car, pulling a large white suit bag from it, the words "Peach Surprise" written on it in what looked like red finger paint. Tommy tried and failed to shield the words from Jed, almost hearing Jed's mind ticking backwards to Monday and the page from the *Racing Post*.

Dropping the bag to the ground, Tucker bent down to unzip it. The dog was all but decapitated, its teeth bared, its eyes bulging. Hadgy gagged into his palm and a few women leaving the pub shrieked.

Tucker straightened his back and faced Hadgy.

'Mr Smart wants a refund by nine,' he said.

WEDNESDAY

TOMMY

'Rule number one. Never come to my house.'

Paul Smart wasn't long out of bed, a short Japanese-print kimono gaping open at his smooth chest. Despite the early hour, his hair stood up in perfect symmetry and his icy blue eyes glistened harshly.

The houses on this side of the street were large and semi-detached, set some way back from the pavement, elevated above steep front gardens and drives. They had once housed the shipyards' management, the great and the good, living high above the long lines of working men's two-up, two-down terraces, most of which had been cleared to build Valley Park in the sixties: *a new, modern way of living.* Now, every other one of these houses was empty, unkempt, or burnt down; apart from Paul Smart's, which stood behind ten-foot brick walls and an iron gate, two pit bull terriers adorning the plinths of the entrance to a drive which was home to Paul's cars: a black Range Rover with tinted windows and a silver MG sports car that would have Frankie pissing himself if he ever got the chance to drive it.

Paul grabbed Tommy by the shoulder and pulled him inside.

The house was large and spacious, Tommy's footsteps echoing off the empty walls of a cavernous hallway. Two properties had been knocked into one, the heavy wooden door at its centre flanked by elaborate pillars. Paul had moved away from Valley Park at the earliest opportunity but stayed close enough to maintain control of his customers. He might have loathed the place, but the business opportunities were too great; as the jobs got scarcer, the people got poorer. All the better for financial gain.

Tommy followed Paul into the living room, bare of furniture other than a smoked glass coffee table and two leather swivel chairs that rested on a zebra-patterned rug. A mirrored bar, fronted with padded, black leather, hugged the corner of the room, its shelves lined with optics and sparkling crystal glasses. It was a world away from the bleakness of Tommy's council house not twenty minutes up the road, and he felt dwarfed by its opulence.

'What do you want?' Paul stretched, reaching his fingers up to the ceiling, forcing Tommy to look away as the kimono rode up, threatening to expose more than was decent.

'You said if I needed more money—'

'What do you think I am, a fucking cash point?' Paul's arms fell in a gush of air.

'Well, now you come to mention it.' Tommy let out a nervous laugh, thinking better of it when he saw Paul's poker-faced expression.

'What've you done with the last lot?'

'Deposits for the stage, dancers, DJs, got to get them sorted first.'

'How many tickets you sold?'

Tommy screwed up his face. 'It's not the Theatre Royal, Smartie.'

'*Mister. Smart*,' said Paul, leaning forward, annunciating the words. 'It's not difficult.' He was petulant, an expression of boredom across his face as he whined on. If it was cash on the door, he expected security to be tight so his profits didn't go down the swanny, he said. What if twenty people turned up? Where was his return coming from then?

'That's it, see,' said Tommy. He wasn't used to seeing Paul Smart in a childish sulk; wasn't quite sure which way it would go. 'I need flyers, proper lighting, marquees. I only need another five grand.' Tommy plastered on a smile, but Paul wasn't mollified by his friendliness.

'Five hundred per cent on any further loan.'

'I'll take it.' Tommy held out his hand, unable to compute the figures in his head, and not wanting to spend any more time in Paul Smart's volatile company than was necessary.

Paul breathed a sigh of extreme tedium. 'Fair enough, but you'll have to take it in kind.' He ignored Tommy's outstretched hand and ambled from the room in his bare feet before Tommy could ask what he meant.

Left alone, Tommy took the opportunity to soak up his surroundings. The room shone with minimalist glamour, and he imagined himself sprawled on a plush sofa with Sam, the kids tucked up in their own rooms, a home-cooked dinner sitting heavy in his expanding belly. He sidled up to the bar and ran his fingers over a bottle of champagne that lazed in a silver bucket.

He turned abruptly at the sound of a whistle and dogs barking, followed by the scraping of claws on lino. He threw himself back against the bar, eyes wide, arms raised as if a gun was pointed right at him. The stumpy, bandy-legged dogs stopped just short of him, staring up with the eyes of Satan. He whimpered, knowing for a fact dogs could smell fear.

'Terry! June!' Paul had re-appeared at the living room door, holding two tins of baked beans. The dogs ran to him, sitting at his heels, tongues lolling. Paul unscrewed the bottom of the tins and extracted four tubes of Smarties. He threw them to Tommy who caught them clumsily one by one. 'There's about eight hundred quid's worth in each of them. I'm told they go down well around the schools.'

Tommy removed the plastic top of one of the Smarties tubes and poured the contents into the palm of his hand: small, blue pills displaying an imprint of the Playboy Bunny. His heart just about stopped. 'Howay, man, I can't—'

'Or you could flog them to Tucker and he'll give you five hundred.'

'That's not enough,' said Tommy. He couldn't do it, he couldn't deal drugs; what would that make him? His mind turned foggy. He'd have to give up; his dream of the big rave and the profit it would bring him disappearing fast.

'Some advice, though,' said Paul. 'Be careful of the competition. Some people will have your legs off if they catch you selling on their patch.'

Exactly.

'Or,' said Paul, 'you can give me my two-grand back plus interest by Friday. And if you don't, then Tucker will see to you. Sound reasonable?' Paul tightened the belt of his kimono and folded his arms across his chest, his white, downy legs splayed wide.

The two hundred per cent interest on two-grand. That was probably a lot, and Friday would be impossible.

The drugs in Tommy's hands were like hot pokers. His father's face flashed before him, then Sam's, Jed's, his mother's, the astronaut's, like some weird slide show of cinematic proportions. Their eyes warned and judged, and he heard the gavel smash down on the block, heard the snapping of his femur.

Guilty.

He let the cardboard tubes fall to the floor, some of the contents scattering across the bare, wooden boards. He wouldn't go down that path. He wouldn't be taken for some sort of Laurel to Paul Smart's Hardy. He had his principles, and he had his dignity.

Drawing the confidence he needed into his lungs, he walked past Paul, one eye on the dogs that guarded the door and one on

Paul's gaping chest, fearing any eye contact would drain him of his new-found brawn. He found himself in the hall, then at the front door. He pulled on the handle, but the door wouldn't open. Wiping sweat from his brow, headed towards the back of the house, not another peep from Terry, June, or Paul Smart as he walked through more pristine white gloss, across the kitchen and towards French doors that opened onto an immaculate garden. Outside, Tucker stood to one side of the doors like a sentry, green eyes, sharp as blades, following Tommy's every step.

Tommy looked around him for a gate, but there was none. There seemed to be no other way out but over the tall, mesh fence that kept Paul Smart safe. Hearing growls and the sound of claws once more, he ran towards the fence and leapt onto it, his jacket catching on the green wire that bit into his hands as he struggled to grasp it with his fingers and the tips of his trainers. He summoned every ounce of strength he could muster and swore painfully as he pulled himself up. Then, as if invisible hands were under his feet, he was at the top and falling into the overrun garden of the empty house that backed onto Paul's.

Winded and gasping, he drew himself up onto his knees, taking a moment to get his breath before staggering to his feet. On the other side of the fence stood Tucker, dangerously silent.

Looking around him, and knowing he was safe from Tucker's teeth, Tommy gave him a fierce glare and ran.

PEACH

'My God, you're serious.'

Superintendent McNally was looking at him as if he'd lost the plot. But Peach stood his ground. Murphy had been on the phone to police forces across the south of England: London, Kent, Essex. Turned out his mother was, indeed, someone of clout, as was his father, his grandfather, and his great grandfather. Three generations of senior officers completely undetectable in Murphy's sluggish character.

Peach knew now what resources he needed, and he needed authorisation for them now – today: a dozen staff, a few computers, phone taps, monitoring equipment, helicopters …

Bewildered laughter silenced him mid-sentence, and McNally rummaged in the pile of paper on his desk, found what he was looking for and held it aloft. 'See this?'

Peach cocked his head to read the print.

'Police priorities,' McNally stated. 'And I quote: "*Burglary, car crime, organised crime, armed robbery, and football related violence.*" Nothing here about house parties. I won't even go into the arrest and conviction rates.'

Peach's grasp tightened around the envelope of photographs in his hand, developed that morning at Happy Snaps who would produce your prints in an hour – quicker if you held up your police ID. The photographs from Sally's camera were worthless; most were blurred, and those that weren't showed the faces of silly young men in silly hats he'd never laid eyes on before. He'd scoured each and every one for a glimpse of Collins. Nothing. The final four photographs of Sally's inert face were so horrifying he could barely look at them.

'Give me one night,' he said, 'and I'll have half a dozen dealers behind bars, not to mention breaches of fire regulations, health and safety, trespass, you name it.'

'Have you listened to a word I've said? You're stepping over a line, here. The Drug Squad would have to assess it.'

Peach bit back his vexed response. The last people he wanted involved was the Drug Squad. They were only interested in nailing the big-time gangsters, the ones who would generate the kind of veneration the Drug Squad detectives' egos required. They weren't interested in the likes of Collins, and Peach would rather keep the long-haired, ear-ringed louts at arms-length. What he needed was a team and equipment.

'Larry,' he said, ignoring McNally's warning eyes. 'We are going to look like fools when this all kicks off and we're not ready. *You* are going to look like a bloody fool!'

McNally stared evenly at Peach. 'A bunch of halfwits without an O level between them are going to humiliate an entire police force?'

'Yes!' exploded Peach. 'My point, exactly!' He began to pace, anything to keep himself from going off like a mortar.

'My hands are tied, Mike, here's what we need to work to.' The superintendent lifted the document again then dropped it onto his desk. 'What's happening with the building society?'

Peach halted his patrol of the room and pursed his lips. He'd already sent two officers out to find Collins to persuade him to come in and "help with their enquiries." Once he was here, they would coerce him into a line-up, bring in the witnesses and, once Collins was picked out, he'd arrest him, search his house, find what he was looking for and chuck him in a cell.

Peach considered his response, knowing McNally would warn

him off before he could even get a sniff of a result. He scoured McNally's walls: photographs of a career spanning forty years; handshakes, awards, and accolades, pictures of his son's graduation and his daughter's wedding. The beam of the bride's smile plunged into Peach's chest like a jagged blade.

'It's progressing,' he said.

McNally's eyes lingered on his before he picked up his pen again. 'Without substantial evidence, I can't give you extra resources, I'm sorry.'

'I'll speak to the Area Commander—'

'You'll do no such bloody thing!'

The rebuke hit Peach like a slap in the face, and he froze for a moment before opening the envelope of photographs, slowly taking out the picture of Sally in her hospital bed and handing it to McNally. 'That could be someone else's bairn next week,' he said.

'Mike …'

'I know,' said Peach, taking the photograph from McNally's fingers. 'It's not a priority.' He backed away, taking hold of the door handle. If it wasn't a priority for the top brass, he'd have to make it one, and he thought he knew how. 'I'll have an update on the building society by the end of the day.'

He opened the door and left McNally's office.

***

Within the hour, major news desks in the United Kingdom had been sent photographs of an innocent, middle-class white girl, lifeless if it weren't for the machines that kept her body's essentials working. A personal statement was included, an abstract of a happy, healthy girl, near death due to the ingestion of some "love drug" – a drug freely available at parties, cheap as chips and spreading through a whole generation like cancer. It called for vigilance, for the outright banning of illegal all-night parties,

criminal charges for those involved in organising them, and, most of all, a subliminal message to all law-abiding parents:
She could be yours. You could be next.

TOMMY

The cash and carry car park was littered with trolleys and plastic bags which stuck to the bushes lining its borders. The store was vast, a mammoth structure on the outskirts of the city.

Tommy was the last to climb down the steps of the yellow minibus, its doors emblazoned with the words "Sunshine Society," the logo of a teddy bear peeling from its sides. The bear's eyes were all but gone, giving the logo an air of the macabre. Tommy could see why Frankie had named it Chucky.

He'd spent the morning weighing up new options. They were sorely limited. But one thing was for sure: Paul Smart needed him if he wanted his forty-grand profit, and profit was what drove Paul Smart. He'd settled on this option: he'd carry on until the money ran out, catch Smartie in a better mood and have his reasoning straight. He'd prove himself to be a good investment and Paul would be too impressed to say no.

But then there was Jed, who was proving as much of a challenge. Tommy had spent the journey to the cash and carry bouncing around on Chucky's bad suspension and trying to convince Jed that he hadn't seen the name Peach Surprise before.

'Sounds familiar, that's all,' Jed had pondered, looking out the window.

Tommy had tried to change the subject, but Jed continued to wrack his brains, never satisfied until he was proven right about everything.

'Sounds like one of your ma's cakes,' Frankie had offered, with a glance at Tommy.

Jed had nodded his agreement, but the jury was still out, and

Jed was standing in the cash and carry car park now with his hands on his hips, staring at the minibus with distaste, swearing that Frankie was humiliating him on purpose.

'Saves us doing a few trips,' said Frankie, patting the minibus's bonnet.

'Sound, Frankie, you're a star,' said Tommy, staring up at the huge store entrance.

'Hey, where's my kiss for getting the card?' Jed held up the store card, lips puckered.

'Right, ladies,' Tommy grinned, 'let's go shopping.'

Inside the store, Tommy led the way up and down the aisles, each of them in charge of loading their trolleys with chewing gum, cans of pop, Pot Noodles, and luminous toys. They'd pick up the pre-ordered water at the back entrance once they'd paid at the till. Tinny music played over the store's sound system, and MC Hammer had Jed dancing *the Running Man* in the confection aisle, his mouth spread into a comedian's look-what-I-can-do smile while the women stacking the shelves giggled behind their hands.

An hour had passed, and the trolleys were brimming when Tommy drew his team together at the back of the checkout queue, clipboard and pen at the ready as if about to badger passers-by into buying double glazing.

He started his countdown: the generators were booked, the cash needed by Friday; rigging, lighting, screen, and projector. *Tick.* Security, coaches, directions, pirate radio content. *Tick.* The dancers were on board. 'Like Legs and Co on speed!' laughed Frankie. Walkie-talkies, phone lines, and recorded messages; all were sorted or on order, hardly any of it paid for. The flyers were ready to go, but Tommy would have to sweet talk Macca at the printers. Again.

'Good work, lads.' Tommy hugged the clipboard to his chest,

hoping that when Smartie saw the progress he was making, he'd hand over the cash, no bother.

The hefty woman at the till eyed their piled-high trolleys with dismay as they approached her. She blinked a *you've got to be kidding me* from behind thick glasses, and even Jed's roguish smile did nothing to release the cheek flesh she bit between her molars.

Forty minutes later, looking like she could kill each one of them with her bare hands, she sat back. 'That'll be six hundred and eight-four pounds and twenty-three pence all together please.'

There was silence while they took in the total, then Jed held out a hand to Tommy and demanded the cash.

'Eh?' Tommy frowned at him.

'You said you'd have cash.'

'You've got a card, haven't you?'

Jed turned away from the cashier. 'It's fucking membership, not plastic!' he hissed. 'How we going to pay for this?'

Tommy felt his Adam's apple rise and fall.

'For fuck's sake,' said Jed. 'Shift.'

Tommy sidled up to Frankie's side as Jed turned back to the cashier, leaning one arm on the edge of the conveyor belt, employing the charm of James Bond himself. After a brief chat, Jed waved a hand to Tommy and piped up in his poshest accent.

'Darren!? Do you want this putting on the youth club account or what?'

Tommy matched Jed posh for posh. 'Yes, super, if that's okay! I've gone and left the cheque book in the office!'

The checkout woman snatched the membership card from Jed, turned it over in her hands then pressed the button on a small microphone beside the till.

'*Store manager to checkout ten.*'

Jed mouthed *fuck*, turning to Tommy as if he were about to

throttle him.

'Is there a problem?'

Tommy felt his scalp shrivel as he recognised Paul Smart's voice, and the lads' faces turned towards the long queue of people who were starting to grumble and move away to other checkouts.

Paul stepped out, a shopping basket hanging over his arm.

Tommy shrugged at his friends, an *I don't know what's happening* look on his face while his heart battered his ribs.

Paul reached the till and pushed Jed aside, dumping the basket at his feet and leaning into the cashier. Her head strained backwards, her eyes crossing as Paul's face closed in on hers.

'Something I can help with?' he asked.

She stammered – something about this man reeked of criminal. 'I'm just getting verification,' she swallowed.

Paul held out his hand for the card and she passed it over, snapping her hand away as Paul took it. He smiled at her, digging into his pocket, and bringing out a roll of cash, only half the size of the wad he'd had at the greyhound track, Tommy noticed. Paul looked at the till display, licked a finger and started counting. There was just enough, and he sniffed as he handed the cash over.

'Keep the change,' he said, 'for being such a canny lass.'

She swallowed again, eyes massive behind scratched lenses, the *thank you* stuck behind frightened lips.

Paul smiled at her before walking to Tommy's side. 'You changed your mind yet?' The voice was low and sinister. 'Eight hundred per cent for that little lot.' He looked back at Jed and raised his voice. 'The gardening isle's that way,' he said.

Jed's eyes emptied, his face falling into a scowl which he directed at Tommy once the automatic doors had slid closed behind Paul's back.

Tommy dropped his head, eyes falling on the basket at his feet and the jumbo-sized packet of double-edged razor blades that lay in it. He kicked the basket under the counter and took hold of his trolley, avoiding Jed's eyes as he attempted to manoeuvre it forward. Frankie took hold of the side of the trolley to help get it going, and when Tommy looked into his face, there was a warning there.

You have to tell him.

***

Outside the back of the store, Jed's bare chest was drawing attention from a crowd of women who had gathered at one of the upstairs windows. They pointed and leered, enjoying their tea break with a bit of extra eye candy. The lads hauled their purchases chain-gang style onto the minibus where Frankie stacked trays and boxes into every available space.

'I've got to go back to that youth club,' grumbled Jed.

'I'll handle it,' said Tommy. Eight hundred per cent on six hundred quid. Maths wasn't exactly his forte, and he could hardly ask Jed to tot it up on the calculator.

'That's Darren in the shit now.' Jed wasn't letting it lie, and judging by the piercing look he gave Tommy, Tommy had a feeling he'd already put two and two together. He braced himself as Jed took the trays of Pot Noodles from him, turning to hand them to Frankie. But Frankie's sullen glance at Tommy seemed to tell Jed everything he needed to know. It was the last straw, and Jed rounded on Tommy.

'You better tell me who this backer is.'

'I've told you,' said Tommy. It was pitiful, he could hear it in his own voice, but he was holding on to that one per cent chance that Jed hadn't clicked.

'You've told me shite.' Jed's mouth pursed in fury. 'Do you think I'm thick?'

'Sometimes,' said Tommy, attempting a grin, hoping for rescue.

'Who's the backer, Tommy?'

Tommy could see in Jed's eyes that he knew; just wanted to hear it from his best mate's mouth. But Tommy swallowed, coloured, and looked away.

'Peach Fucking Surprise, Paul Fucking Smart, my mother's fucking garden.' Jed dropped the Pot Noodles to the ground, kicked them away.

'Jed, man!' Tommy brought up his arms in a beseeching gesture, but Jed pointed at him, face spitting.

'Fuck you, liar,' he said.

Pushing Tommy backwards, Jed stormed away, tripping over as the sole fell off one of his knock-off trainers. He bent down and tore the trainers from his feet, turning and hurling them at Tommy.

'Christ, we can't do this without The Chancellor,' said Frankie as they watched Jed hop onto a wall and disappear over the other side, just as a police squad car screeched into the car park, stopping a few feet from the minibus and giving Tommy no time to think of a solution.

'Thomas James Collins?' Within seconds, two uniforms were in Tommy's face. 'Can we talk?'

'I'd rather eat my own feet,' Tommy replied, his eyes still on Jed's retreating figure.

'We'd like to ask you some questions about a robbery.'

He looked right at them, irritated. 'What you on about?'

'Don't be a twat, just come with us,' said the other officer, puny by comparison and looking like he'd barely left school.

'I haven't done anything,' said Tommy, trying to push past them.

'An armed robbery.' The chunky officer forced him back.

'Eh?'

'We can do it at your house, or at the station, it's up to you.'

'I'm not having you in my house,' said Tommy, looking the officer up and down. 'Are you arresting me?'

The officers exchanged a glance. 'No—'

'Well, get lost then.'

'But we will if you assault us in any way.' The baby-faced officer had his hand on his baton and a look in his eye that goaded.

This was the last thing Tommy needed. An illegal rave to plan and him in a cell.

'I'll crack on,' said Frankie, his eyes warning Tommy not to kick off.

'It's a mistake, Frankie.'

'Aye, I knaa,' Frankie reassured him.

Tommy sighed and threw up his arms in submission. Flanked by the officers, he walked to the squad car and folded himself into the back seat. The car pulled out of the car park and into the traffic, passing Paul Smart's silver MG and Jed as he stomped toward the bus stop in his socks. Tommy watched from the back window as Jed shrunk to the size of a toy soldier before the officer floored the accelerator and his head was thrown back with the force of the speed.

Arsewipes.

PEACH

Pacing was becoming a habit, fuelled by impatience and sheer dogmatism. Peach had rolled up his shirtsleeves, the windowless viewing room thick with heat. It was all over the news, this heatwave; people splashing around in the fountains at Trafalgar Square, the beaches packed to bursting, warnings of sunstroke and skin cancer. He thought it was tosh; '76 had been hotter in his recollection, back when he had a whirlwind toddler, a wife, and ironed shirts. The woman who was paid to housekeep now wasn't a patch on Kathleen when it came to the crease on the arms of his shirtsleeves, so it didn't matter if he rolled them up and spoiled them.

Collins had kicked up a fuss by all accounts. It seemed he was eager to get away, so Peach made sure the detectives conducting the interview took their sweet time. He'd stood at the air vent in the corridor of the station's cells, listening in, enjoying Tommy's rising frustration at being asked the same questions twenty times over. They'd got him to agree to the ID parade after four hours of interrogation. He had nothing to hide, he'd said. He'd done *nothing wrong.*

While officers were hunting down Collins that morning, Peach was hunting down Sally's friend, Selina. Her mother, Fiona Blackhurst, had been potting plants on wooden decking, a ghastly veranda, constructed around the ground floor of the Old Vicarage, a beautiful piece of the city's history ruined. Selina's mother didn't look quite forty and didn't resemble any architect he'd ever seen. She had that bohemian vibe, all Indian-print cotton and Jesus sandals.

Peach had approached her with a thin smile which soon faded when he was informed that Selina was away with friends. She'd left on Monday and wasn't due back for three weeks. Now the exams were over, they were all off "interrailing." The woman appeared to show no concern that her sixteen-year-old was out in the big wide world, unsupervised, nor that a senior police officer was standing on her vile decking asking questions.

'Sally Peach,' Fiona had mused. 'Haven't seen her for, gosh, a year at least.'

'To your knowledge, has your daughter ever dabbled in drugs?' he'd asked.

'Oh, I expect so,' was her response. 'Haven't we all?'

No, thought Peach, *we haven't.* His own mother had just about flipped when he lit a joss stick back in the early sixties.

'Young people need freedom,' Fiona said when she saw the judgement in his eyes.

The woman was a moron, and he'd left her to get on with her potting, hoping that if he ever saw her again, she'd have the decency to wear a bra.

The door to the viewing room opened and Mrs Bailey entered, accompanied by DS Murphy who wore a yellow and purple tracksuit top over a black polo neck and army combat trousers. The man must have been melting.

'Here's the rabble, chief,' said Murphy, tipping his invisible cap and winking at Mrs Bailey, making her blush.

'Come in, come in,' said Peach, eager to get on with proceedings. Peering at the door, he saw no one else. 'Where's the other one?' he asked Murphy when he reached his side.

'Gone AWOL, boss,' said Murphy from the side of his mouth.

Peach's lips tightened. Denise Morris was the one who'd identified the eyes. He needed her here. 'Well, go and find her!' he hissed. He couldn't keep Collins for much longer; didn't want him disappearing or demanding a brief.

'You need me here, boss,' said Murphy.

Peach let out a frustrated sigh, knowing Murphy was right, that he couldn't conduct a line-up alone. He'd just have to get on with it for now, hope for the best; hope those eyes were somewhere in Mrs Bailey's fading memory.

Mrs Bailey was at his side, now, ringing her hands anxiously. He put a steadying hand on her shoulder, speaking gently. 'We're going to show you two line-ups. Take your time, look carefully, and touch the shoulder of the man you saw.' He nodded at Murphy who walked to the door, opened it, and beckoned to someone unseen.

'Are they coming in here?' Mrs Bailey's voice shook, and her hand grabbed Peach's bare forearm. 'I didn't know they'd see me!'

Peach had purposefully forgotten the witness briefing, fearful they would change their minds if they knew the reality of the procedure. They might get scared, pull out at the last minute. He wasn't having any of that.

'I'm here with you, and so is Detective Sergeant Murphy. You'll be just fine, I promise.'

'Oh!' Mrs Bailey let out a small cry and grasped her handbag in both hands as Murphy stepped back into the room, followed by eight young men rounded up from the local estates, most of them tired-looking, puffy-eyed, and scratching at themselves. Collins was among them. He avoided Peach's eyes, his face stern and his cheeks hollow, looking like he needed a good feed.

'Eeeh, there's our Shaun,' said Mrs Bailey with a gush of relief, raising an arm to wave. Peach brought it down quickly and glanced over at Murphy. If any witness knew one of the line-up it would be invalid. But Murphy was lighting a roll-up, his eyes fixed on the flame of his match.

'You can start now,' said Peach, holding out an arm which invited her to walk forward. Giving her the nudge she needed, he watched Mrs Bailey shuffle forward to the edge of the line to begin her promenade.

The room utterly silent, Peach wrapped his arms around his ribs, shoulders hunched as he watched closely. Mrs Bailey stopped, her eyes on the wrong man, probably "our Shaun." He willed her to move on. To the seventh man. He repeated the number in his head: *seven, seven, seven.*

The heavy tension was interrupted when the door was flung open and Superintendent McNally strode in on a warm gust of air. Pulling Peach to one side by the arm, he raised his chin in challenge. 'What the hell are you doing?'

Peach looked at his witness then back at McNally, keeping his voice low so as not to interrupt Mrs Bailey who had reached the end of the line and was wiping her forehead with a handkerchief. 'I'm getting on with the building society job, sir. I recognised his trainers.'

'Trainers? Is that it?' McNally was trying to confine his voice to within the four walls. 'The market's flooded with the damn things. Have you lost your wits?'

'And two witnesses have both mentioned striking blue eyes—'

'You can't do a line-up of eyes!'

Peach's own eyes questioned McNally's. Hadn't they done the very same thing before? 1986 – the robbery of a war hero in his own home, beaten to a purple pulp, blinded in one eye, dead a few months later. All the old man had seen were the eyes, and they'd got their conviction before the poor bugger died of fear.

'He needs money,' hissed Peach. 'Where else is he going to get it?'

McNally didn't respond, beckoning Murphy over instead and ordering him to get the witness out of there. Peach began to colour as Murphy led the woman out, closing the door quietly behind him. He could almost smell the bollocking about to be unleashed, and he was sure that if the lads in the line-up weren't still in the room, McNally would have burst like a water pipe.

'You are fucking this up,' said McNally. 'The woman's on the verge of tears, what if she makes a complaint? Use your brain, man.'

'There's nowt wrong with my brain.'

'No? Where are the background checks on these witnesses, then?'

Peach remained silent, and McNally pulled him to the back of the room with a glance at the line of youths, some of whom giggled behind their hands, sharing a joke. Not Collins, though, who stared at his feet.

'Denise Morris,' McNally muttered, 'is Collins's mother-in-law.'

The humid air turned pungent, and Peach felt Tommy evaporating from his grasp like mist. In his haste to get his man where he wanted him, he'd ignored basic procedure. He'd ignored almost all procedure.

'If it wasn't for him, my daughter wouldn't be lying there, useless.' Peach thought he heard his own voice crack as he turned to look at Tommy, searching his face for guilt, regret – insolence even – but seeing only the top of his shorn head.

McNally heard it too, and his voice lost its urgency. 'Come on, you've got a tenuous link, she was out with friends.'

'At one of his dos!' Peach made to walk towards the line-up, but McNally restrained him.

'Let him go. This is your last warning. Don't make me do

something I don't want to do.'

Peach felt anger twist in his gut, a swirl of acidic hatred. He turned his back on Tommy as McNally walked away, opened the door, and the young men filed out. He walked to the wall at the back of the room, pressing his palms flat against the cool gloss and closing his eyes, staying there until he heard a voice behind him.

'You all right, chief?' Murphy held out a cup of tea.

Peach dropped his hands from the wall and looked into Murphy's young face, void of lines, void of worry. 'Apparently not,' he said. 'Apparently, I'm all wrong.'

'Look, why don't you go home for a bit? You've been here non-stop.'

Peach took the mug and turned away from Murphy, his eyes fixed on the space the line-up had left empty. He sipped the hot liquid and said nothing until Murphy's discomfort eventually pulled him from the room.

He waited for the door to close.

'Because there's nothing to go home to,' he said.

***

Peach had seen his fair share of drug addicts, their eyes rolling in their heads, skin peppered with lesions, vomit dripping down their chins. *Junkie,* was his first thought when he stood at the foot of Sally's bed two hours later. She was propped up against the pillows, the sockets of her unfocused eyes sunken and dark, her mouth dribbling fluid onto her hospital gown. At the side of the bed was a bag of urine, full to bursting.

The humiliation of the failed ID parade was eating away at him from the inside, and he imagined bloody wounds inside his gut, his spleen. His voice bellowed down the corridor and Pamela came running, her hand holding the watch at her breast to stop it jiggling. The look on his face must have startled her because she slowed her pace as she approached him.

Why was his daughter being left like this? he bawled. Why was she allowed to lie there, slavering like some spastic?

'Mr Peach!' Pamela's mouth hung open in shock. She barged past him, took a tissue from a box by the bed and wiped Sally's mouth. 'There you go, sweetheart.' She touched Sally's cheek before standing again.

'Shouldn't this thing be emptied?' Peach pointed at the urine.

'You a nurse, now, are you?'

There was a warning in Pamela's voice, but Peach kept going. 'I need to speak to her.' He looked at Sally, knowing the possibility was remote. 'Has she said anything?'

The odd word, apparently, nothing coherent yet.

Yet? It made him shoot a look at Pamela who was searching his face, something in it making her soften.

'Look, why don't you sit with her for a while,' she said. 'I think she's been looking forward to seeing you.' She patted Sally's hand, the intimacy of it excluding him.

'Leave us alone,' he said.

With an acquiescent sigh, the nurse left the cubicle, and when she was out of sight, he closed the curtains and sat on Sally's bed. He pulled the hospital-issue bag from under his coat. He'd locked himself in his office after the line-up, poured the contents of the bag Pamela had given him on Monday onto his desk – the cards, the dress, and the small white bag Sally wore constantly strapped across her chest. The items had lain there for some time before he'd picked up the handbag, his fingers touching the edge of the zipper. He'd opened it and put his hand inside, drawing out a five-pound note, a few coins, and her house key. Other than that, it was empty. He'd opened the zip of the inside pocket and searched with his fingers. A lipstick, nothing else. But then he'd felt it, a hole in the corner of the lining, stitched loosely with the black thread he'd seen in Sally's make-up bag when he'd searched her room. He'd torn at the lining, turning the bag upside down, shaking it. It fell onto his desk: a tiny seal bag containing small blue pills, the Playboy bunnies laughing up at him.

But it was the *Little Raver!* card that had his heart in his mouth. He'd opened it, stared down at the spidery capitals.

"WHAT WILL I DO WITHOUT MY BEST GIRL?
GET WELL SOON. LOVE DAD. X"

Sally's groan brought him back to the dreary cubical, sending his mind whirring back in time, back to Kathleen, choking and gagging as the liquid food was forced into her. He hadn't been able to watch or listen. He hadn't known whether to pull the nurses off her and let her die or let them get on with prizing her mouth open and forcing the tube down her throat.

Pain swelled in his chest, the sharp pain of sorrow that often took him unawares. It coursed down his arms and into his fingertips where it rested. There was nowhere else for it to go. If only he could forgive her, he might be free of it.

If only he could forgive himself.

He reached out and took the box of tissues from the cabinet, pulling one out and gently dabbing it on Sally's lips, and for a second, as her head rolled, she looked at him. He leant forward to kiss her forehead. It was only meant to be a peck, but his lips stayed there, and the box of tissues felt to the floor as his hand slid behind her head.

'*Da,*' he heard, and although he tried with every thread of strength he had, his eyes clouded, and a sob wedged in his throat.

He pulled Sally's head to his chest and drew his arms around her, rocking slowly.

'I'm sorry,' he'd whispered, 'I'm so, so sorry.'

TOMMY

They were there, just as they always were, the rolled shutters of the youth centre a magnet to anyone with spray paint and time on their hands. A beat box thumped out hardcore techno, three lads painting the largest shutter while others tackled the silver bins that lined the back of the building. Hoods up and masks over their faces, they were lost in their art, and Tommy approached them without challenge.

'Easy, Mobz,' said Tommy to their leader.

Mobz and Tommy had been in the same class at school – or not as the case may be. They'd skive together, ride their bikes into town to steal from the student's art shop at the Haymarket. Mobz was a man of few words and he controlled his flock of apprentice graffiti artists with his talent alone.

Tommy stared up at their corrugated canvas. *"Crash 'n' Burn"* read the zig-zag words in yellow, red, and purple, human limbs protruding from the letters, some climbing the red brick, some clinging to the great metal boxes that held the shutters.

'You look fucked,' said Mobz.

He did, and he felt it, too. Despite his bath, the sickly stench of the police station still plagued his nostrils. He was tired to the bone, barely an hour of the last few days stress free, his sleep broken, his dreams disturbing. How people lived in constant fear was beyond him. It made him think of battered wives, Holocaust survivors. Prisoners.

Mobz raked his fingers through his straggly beard as he considered the mock-up flyer Tommy had handed over. On his command, the young artists stopped what they were doing and crowded around Tommy's drawing. They muttered among themselves, following the lines of the alien images with paint-stained fingers. After a few long moments, each of the crew gave Mobz one mechanical nod of the head before walking back to their stations.

'How much?' Mobz asked.

'Cash on the day. Saturday,' said Tommy. 'Hundred quid.'

'Fuck off,'

'Two,' said Tommy. 'And free entry for the crew.'

Mobz drew on a fat joint. 'Two-fifty.' It came out as a croak as he exhaled.

Two-fifty, five, a grand. It didn't matter to Tommy; he didn't have it. And now going back to Smartie for more money was making him feel sick to his stomach.

'Can you DJ?' asked Tommy, 'on the radio, and that?'

'Nar.'

Without Jed there would be no pirate radio on Friday night from Frankie's family's high-rise flat in Cruddas Park, the roof home to the vast transmitter that pulled in listeners as far away as Dunston.

'I can,' he heard from behind him. He turned, surprised at the girl's voice, and more surprised at her posh accent and clear skin. She wasn't from around here.

'What's your top tunes?' he asked, cautiously.

She didn't hesitate. 'Armando, Mr Fingers, 808 State.'

Tommy smiled in surprise. 'You're in. Friday night.'

She gave him a nod of accord and she walked away, Tommy holding out his fist to Mobz who pushed his own into it before donning his mask again and heading back to his squad. Tommy watched with aching envy as Mobz climbed a ladder and drew out his spray can – doing what he loved and fuck the consequences. He trudged away, ready for another sleepless night before he faced Paul Smart the next morning.

He'd just stepped through the gates of the youth centre when the Range Rover flew onto the pavement and blocked his path. He turned and ran, but vice-like arms were around his waist before he could manage a few yards, his arms pinned down, his feet lifted from the ground before he was bundled into the back seat where Paul Smart sat, straight-backed, sunglasses on.

'You and me need a little chat,' he said.

***

The empty warehouse was familiar. It was within spitting distance of Valley Park, and the location of Tommy's first rave six months earlier. What had started out as a hedonistic enterprise was quickly turning into a nightmare.

Tommy had been pulled from the car by Tucker, thrown up against a skip piled high with abandoned furniture and carpets. The stench of rot was overpowering, the heat putrefying the mounds of discarded rubbish, the sound of seagulls caterwauling overhead like vultures adding to the sense of remoteness.

'I've got things to do, Smartie,' said Tommy nervously, wondering how he could protect himself, wondering who would hear him scream.

'Shut your fucking mouth,' said Paul, striding back and forth in front of him, dressed in a shiny silver suit and crisp white shirt. 'I really didn't want to have to do this, Tommy, but you've left me no choice.'

Tommy felt his legs go numb as if readying themselves for the blows. He could beg, he could plead, but he had no doubt it would make little difference. 'I just need a bit more cash,' he said, 'and it'll all be tickety-boo, I swear.'

'What did you tell them?' Paul asked.

Tommy glanced around him, even looking to Tucker for help.

'Peach,' said Paul, squaring up to him. 'What did you tell him?'

'Nowt,' Tommy said, hearing the pitch of his voice rise.

Paul leant into him and Tommy felt his eyelids stretch to their limits, his heart throbbing, his throat dry. 'He let you go?'

Tommy nodded, unable to speak.

'You've got me to thank for that, and don't you forget it,' said Paul. 'It was my sister that shopped you, but I've taken care of it. Can't be having you locked up, know what I mean?' He stood back, lifted his finger and pointed into Tommy's face. 'And let me make this clear. There is no more cash, so stop fucking asking.'

'Just a couple of grand—'

The back of Paul's hand hit his face with a thwacking clout so hard Tommy felt his teeth move in their gums.

'I don't think you're listening to me, laddie,' growled Paul. 'There's no more fucking cash.'

Tommy, shocked and slumped to his side with his palm to his face, held his breath as the pain radiated into his head and neck. He'd never been hit before in his life. Even his parents had never lifted a hand to him.

He straightened up, looked into Paul's serious face, a fact dawning on him.

Was Paul Smart skint?

'We can call it off,' he stammered. 'I'll pay you back, a few quid a week. I'll get some of the deposits back and we'll be sorted in no time.'

Paul's face was like stone. He grabbed Tommy's T-shirt, rolled it in his hand until it started to throttle him. 'Here's what's going to happen,' he said. 'You're going to take those drugs. You're going to sell them. You're going to put on this rave and make me some money. And if you don't, I'll sort out your mate and his window-licking brother first, then your bonny wife's face.' He leant in. 'Then you.'

'She ... she's your niece!' Tommy said.

'I don't give a flying fuck who she is.' The chill in Paul's eyes confirmed that he didn't, and Tommy uttered a small cry, tears threatening to spill from his eyes if he wasn't careful.

'Please, Smartie,' Tommy breathed, 'I can't—'

'Tucker?!' Paul called over his shoulder, and Tucker was by his side in an instant. 'Hit him until he says yes.'

The tears were brimming now, hot and untethered. 'No,' Tommy said. 'Howay, we can sort something out.'

'Hit him.'

Tucker stood in front of Tommy, drew back his fist, and Tommy closed his eyes, his bladder threatening to empty its contents down his legs. But the blow didn't come.

Daring to open his eyes just a slither, he saw Paul's hand wrapped around Tucker's fist, holding it back. He felt a brief sense of relief until Paul released Tucker's hand, removed the silver jacket, and roll up his sleeves.

Oh, Jesus.

Tommy closed his eyes again tightly.

'Black bastard!' he heard Paul bellow.

He opened his eyes just in time to see Paul's fist collide with Tucker's face, snapping his head back like a bent spoon. Tucker staggered backwards, the next punch sending him spinning to the ground.

'Why didn't you hit him?' Paul yelled.

'I didn't—'

'You need to be quicker than that, laddie! Have you learnt nowt?'

Spitting blood from his mouth, Tucker stumbled to his feet. 'I'll be quicker next time—'

Another blow to Tucker's face had him reeling backwards, then another, and another, on and on to the ribs, the face, the kidneys. Tucker offered no defence, eventually falling to the ground, unconscious.

Paul, breathing heavily, wiped sweat from his forehead, leaving a streak of blood across his brow. He kicked out at Tucker's legs, grunting with each blow, but Tucker remained still, the blood from his smashed nose dripping onto the hot tarmac.

Paul turned to Tommy. 'See what happens when you don't do what you're told?'

Tommy's stomach contracted, and he gagged, trying to swallow the vomit that was forcing its way up his gullet. His head began to swim as he watched Paul wipe his hands down his shirt, then heard the unmistakable sound of a blade leaving its casing. Paul bent over Tucker, pulled the blade down one of his cheeks, then the other, the blood oozing out and joining the drops beneath Tucker's ears.

Two Paul Smarts stood up and approached him. He was seeing double, the world around him disappearing, a high-pitched ringing in his ears blotting out all other sound. He saw the fuzzy shape of the tubes of Smarties, felt them being shoved into his jeans pockets as he tried to focus on the bloody blade Paul held up in front of his face.

'You've ruined my best fucking shirt,' Paul said.

The world spun out of view, and Tommy hit the deck like a raggedy doll.

DENISE

Denise turned her head away from Sam's ancient television that didn't even have a remote control; *Boys from the Blackstuff*, a depressing excuse for a programme if ever she'd seen one. Yosser Hughes had nothing on this oaf though. At least he'd had a job to lose in the first place.

Her son-in-law had just walked in the door, his skin pasty white, making the bruise on his cheekbone appear all the more garish. Sam was on her feet immediately, all over him, touching his face, her mother entirely forgotten after she'd given up her evening to keep her daughter company while her so-called husband was out all day and all night getting up to God knows what.

Something dodgy was going on; she could smell it. You didn't grow up with a father like hers and not know trouble when you saw it – the drunken brawls, the no-questions-asked return after long stretches of absence, the sudden appearance of money then months and months of want. The never-ending violence. But she had to confess to rather liking the odour of deceit that was coming off her son-in-law. If Tommy was getting into trouble, she wanted to be the first to know about it.

Tommy was pushing Sam's hands away, telling her to leave him alone, and her daughter's expression was changing.

'Where've you been?' Sam asked. 'We've not seen you all day.'

'Not now.'

He looked wasted, probably on drugs. That's what they were all doing, these youngsters; couldn't face up to their hard lives so they drowned it out with opiates. *Hard lives*, she thought resentfully. They didn't know the half of it.

'And what's she doing here?' Tommy was looking at Denise with downright hatred.

'Tommy!' Sam berated.

'It's all right, love,' said Denise. 'Let him go to bed, he's had a long day.'

He'd obviously been let go by the inspector. She wasn't surprised, especially when she herself hadn't shown up to the ID parade. Mary Bailey had called her, and she'd promised to be there, so Mary wouldn't be alone, but it had been a lie. They seemed to come so easily to her these days, so easily that sometimes she forgot what was true and what wasn't. But Paul had made it clear to her that she was to stay well away; that getting involved as a witness could have terrible consequences. He was just looking out for her, he'd said, didn't want her getting into any bother, not now that they were *reconnecting*. He'd said the word with a touch of his hand to her arm, and she'd felt the warmth of it through her blouse, felt tears prick her eyes. She wasn't going to turn up anyway, but she thanked him for his advice, regardless. She wanted him to feel useful, and she was pleased to see his smile when she touched his cheek and said, 'What would I do without you?'

After that, they'd had a smashing afternoon together. They'd sat in her lovely new garden, just the rose bushes left to go in, and chatted for hours. By the end of the afternoon, he'd told her of his plans. He'd had enough of Valley Park, enough of being surrounded by poverty. He was about to make some serious money from an investment and he was planning on moving away – a villa in Spain, maybe.

'What, all by yourself?' she asked.

'I'll take the dogs,' he replied, and she'd quickly masked the fleeting pain that surely showed on her face.

She knew loneliness when she saw it. Her brother had no real friends to speak of, no talk of a girlfriend. He had his associates, and he spoke of a Tucker Brown once or twice, but he kept his cards close to his chest when it came to personal affairs. It wasn't as though she hadn't enquired about him over the years they were apart. She knew people who knew him or knew of him. She knew his reputation, his business. She'd even heard the word "evil" once. But no one was born evil. Everyone had some good in them, and she saw good in Paul; and more than that, she understood him. Living through what they had, she understood his need to keep his distance, to not get too close to people. But she could help him come out of his shell. She'd seen it on the TV: *Oprah* and *Montel*, programmes she watched with the intensity of any serial drama. She watched the way they broke down emotional barriers with an expression, a touch, or a few words, chosen at just the right moment, tearing the wall down with a simple, *"that must be so hard for you."* She would make him a better man – he was already a better man, and it warmed her to think she might have had a part to play in it.

And so, she let him think it was his idea that she didn't turn up to the police station. It was better that way. It would bring them closer, and one day, they'd all be together; she'd just have to bide her time a little longer. And not too long, she thought now, because Tommy was up to no good and she was going to find out what it was.

He was upstairs now supposedly washing his face, but she could hear no clunking of pipes. Sam had disappeared into the kitchen, probably crying as she washed up the tea dishes. She wished her daughter was stronger like her. Crying over men was pointless.

Turning down the volume of the television, she strained her

ears. She could hear footsteps from above, the wardrobe door opening and closing, drawers banging shut, then footsteps on the landing. A pause, then the creaking of the airing cupboard door. She'd seen the way he'd stood when he came home, his hands tight over the pockets of his jeans. There was something in there he didn't want Sam to see, and, when she heard the airing cupboard door creak closed, she knew exactly where to look for whatever it was he was hiding.

His feet came thudding down the stairs again, and she turned up the volume on the television, sitting back on the sofa just in time.

'You'll be starting the decorating soon, will you?' she said, breezily, as Tommy walked in.

The miserable programme had finished, and the news was on. Two hundred and fifty people had been arrested at Stonehenge, an attempt to avoid a repeat of last year's riots. She tutted and shook her head as she watched a handful of muddy hippies being rounded up by hundreds of uniforms in riot gear while Druids in white robes hugged the stones.

'Acid-house parties,' the reporter said as the scene switched to the large chimney of an old cotton mill. Tommy had stopped behind the sofa, and she glanced behind her to see his eyes trained on the TV.

The reporter went on: a growing fear for public safety, drugs, and noise levels; city centres besieged by thousands of cars, traffic jams worse than during the rush hour, scenes of mayhem; *disasters waiting to happen*. Denise took in the images of youths in baggy clothes, silhouetted against smoky white light, dancing anonymously as if only their own worlds existed.

Hundreds of officers were being drafted in at weekends, the reporter said, to prevent the parties even starting. Thousands were being sent home disappointed – just like the hippies at Stonehenge.

'*Not only that,*' the reporter's face had turned stern, '*but there are growing concerns over the involvement of organised criminal gangs cashing in on this new craze that seems to have taken the country by storm. Shootings have been reported in Blackpool and Bolton. "The Summer of Love," some are calling it. Others fear it could be The Summer of Death.*'

Tommy's feet scuttled towards the kitchen, its door closing with a crash, and Denise was up the stairs and in the airing cupboard in ten seconds flat.

THURSDAY

PEACH

His mind had been on this "father" all night, a man who remained faceless in his dreams and his reality. He lifted his shattered eyes to Murphy who stood with a satisfied grin on his face, looking down at the photographs he'd thrown onto Peach's desk.

Peach picked one up and stared down into two familiar faces. 'When was this?' he asked.

'Eight o'clock yesterday morning, boss, set me alarm and everything,' Murphy said, looking pleased with himself.

'Why didn't I see these yesterday?'

Murphy had wanted to check out who it was, he said. 'Half a story and all that.'

Peach looked down at the image, blurred from the enlargement, a railing blocking a good chunk of the photograph. But it was unmistakable: Paul Smart and Tommy Collins, all pally-pally on Paul Smart's door step.

'Loan shark,' said Murphy.

And the rest, thought Peach. Smart was well known in the west end. The police had their eye on him, but like most people of his standing, there would be no grassing.

'Anyone could have told you who he is,' he said.

'They did,' said Murphy, taking a seat, 'but I wanted to check summat else.' He leant forward and put another image in front of Peach: Paul Smart entering Phutures night club on Saturday night. Murphy had been through the CCTV again; he never forgot a face, he said, and when he saw who Tommy was visiting, something clicked. 'It's like a special talent,' he said. 'God given, me mam says.'

Peach wasn't listening to his vanity. 'You think Collins is dealing for Smart?'

Murphy shrugged.

'Nahh,' said Peach. 'Smart would have his legs taken off getting into that game.' Everybody knew the big dealers, the organised criminals who ran the protection rackets, and Paul Smart was way down in the pecking order.

'Worth a look,' said Murphy.

Maybe Murphy was right. Perhaps they were all in it together. Perhaps Paul Smart could shed some light on Tommy's activities.

Murphy leant forward, face serious. 'Got a feeling in me waters, boss.'

Peach glanced up at his sergeant, his own waters stirring. 'Bring him in,' he said. 'Today.'

***

Sally's cheeks glowed pink as she walked towards him, dragging her feet like the octogenarians that occupied the other beds on the ward. She was supported by Pamela on one side and assisted on the other by a male nurse who hailed from Nigeria. Peach eyed this new nurse in his crisp white tunic with suspicion. He detected a hint of flirtation on Pamela's part; what she didn't realise was that the man would have three wives back in Africa and was unlikely to want much to do with a pasty Geordie a bit past her sell-by date.

'There you go,' said Pamela, holding Sally around the waist as she sat her on the bed. 'You'll be doing the Great North Run next.'

'I'll take it from here,' said Peach, placing a hand on Pamela's arm as she bent to lift Sally's legs.

Pamela straightened up and exchanged a look with the African which led Peach to believe he'd been the topic of conversation over their morning tea break.

'Make sure you wash your hands,' the African said with an

accent laden with the sort of authority Peach didn't much care for. He gave Pamela a grim look which she seemed to find amusing.

'Sink's just in the corner, there,' she said.

Sally sat slumped on the edge of the bed while he washed his hands. She was in a "normal" ward now, Doctor Flynn deeming her recovery quite the miracle. She was going to write an article about it, she said. Might even get published in the *British Medical Journal*. She seemed very pleased with herself for a woman who'd called his daughter Sarah on more than one occasion.

After drying his hands, he helped Sally into bed, pushing her shoulders back against plump pillows. She smiled. It was meagre and frail, but it was a smile nonetheless.

'Won't be long before you can talk, they say,' Peach said, sitting on the bed and straightening the sheet around her waist.

Sally's smile faded, but her eyes stayed on his.

'And you know, there's nothing you can't tell me.'

She looked down quickly, pointed at her throat. 'Hurts,' she croaked.

'Your headmistress is a bit uptight.'

Sally sank further down into the bed.

'That's okay.' Peach rubbed her arm, reading her face; there were always clues in faces. 'You rest, I'll be back later. And tomorrow morning. And tomorrow night, and the day after, and the day after that.'

Her eyes glazed over.

'And when you're strong enough, we'll talk,' he added pointedly.

'Mr Peach?' Pamela stood at the curtain. 'There's a phone call for you.'

With a wink at Sally, Peach rose from the bed and followed Pamela to the nurses' station, picking up the receiver of the telephone.

'Thought I'd give you the heads-up.' Murphy's voice was low and conspiring. *'McNally's looking for you, and between you and me, boss, he's going fookin'* mental.'

Minutes later, Peach strode out of the hospital where Ben Stone from the *Northern Gazette* and the African nurse smoked and drank tea from polystyrene cups, their smiles fading as Peach walked across the ambulance bay. Behind them a small crowd of men and women in sharp suits stood at cars and vans displaying various logos: BBC, ITN, and some he'd never heard of. Peach paused for a second, and the African's smile returned – too bright, too shiny, and Peach wondered if he was telling Ben Stone the whole story about Sally's recovery, or whether he was milking the *Northern Gazette* for every penny they were prepared to give.

He pulled up the collar of his Mac as he headed to his car, but to no avail. He heard the squalling cries of the mob approaching him and he quickened his pace.

'Detective Chief Inspector? How is your daughter? Do you know who supplied the drugs? Will the police be making any arrests?'

Reaching his car in the nick of time, he opened the door into one of the polystyrene cups that sent brown liquid coursing down Ben Stone's shirt. He turned the key in the ignition as the microphones bounced off the windows, reversing the car without regard for the reporters who sprung out of its path. He wouldn't tell them she was on the mend. Not just yet. Not when it might get him what he wanted.

***

At the station, he took a deep breath before opening Superintendent McNally's door. Murphy was right, his boss was livid, and McNally commenced his rant before Peach had even stepped over the threshold.

'I am *this* far away from putting you on gardening leave.' McNally held up a forefinger and thumb to get his point across. 'That's if you're not suspended immediately, which is possible. No, probable.'

Another armed robbery on a petrol station and a ram raid at the Metrocentre over the last two days had been added to the mounting catalogue of serious crimes that were going uninvestigated. And now a "moral panic" was swarming the media, and everyone was up in arms. Sally's half-dead face was plastered on every newspaper in the land and every television news item carried it as their headline, and the Chief Super was on his way to bollock them both.

Detective Chief Superintendent Forbes was a rough-as-you-come man with broad cheeks and a shiny, bald head. Brought up on the Meadows Estate in North Tyneside – a place that made Valley Park look like Disney Land – he had a look of Buster Bloodvessel and didn't take shit from anyone. Forbes' use of slang words and phrases had left McNally mystified in his early years in the north-east, and Peach had often had to step in to translate.

'You better keep quiet and let me explain,' said McNally, every word straining on a leash. 'You've been under a lot of stress, so we might get away with some extended sick leave.' He was talking to himself now, thinking about how he could explain away his own ineptitude. 'But you've crossed the line, Mike. I'm … I'm *disappointed.*'

Peach took a chair opposite McNally. They'd been friends once. Their wives had tried being friends. There was a time Kathleen had talked non-stop about Patricia McNally as if she were some sort of goddess: a career, kids, lovely home, great cook, witty, clever, beautiful. The list went on. He looked at McNally now: knackered, cynical, and old. That's what happened when you married Wonder

Woman.

Seeing McNally stiffen, Peach turned as the door was flung open and the chief superintendent stood in the doorway in full uniform, his hat under his arm. He didn't say a word, just stood there in all his fatness. *Breathing.* His face was frighteningly taut, and Peach thought he heard McNally whimper as Forbes strode in and sat next to Peach in a chair that creaked under his weight.

The chief super didn't believe in pleasantries. 'What in the name of *fuck* is going on?' He threw his hat onto McNally's desk.

Peach kept his eyes down, hands clasped, rolling his thumbs around one another.

'You bollocking idiot,' he heard Forbes snarl. 'You've let this get completely out of hand.'

Peach glanced up to find the chief super's eyes trained on McNally.

'My bastard phone's never stopped all night. Fucking MPs calling me at all hours. And you know what I'm like when I don't get my sleep!' A bit of spit hit McNally's desk as Forbes pronounced the "p" of sleep.

McNally flushed. 'DCI Peach and his team have put a stop to the last two warehouse parties—'

Team?

'One of which put his bairn in hospital,' said Forbes. 'Why didn't I know about it?'

'I didn't want to bother you with it, sir,' said Peach.

McNally's shoulders fell, and Peach felt his boss's betrayed eyes burning into him.

'Sir.' Peach spoke directly to Forbes, 'if I may.'

'Get on with it,' said Forbes.

Peach leant forward, elbows resting on his knees. 'These raves are highly dangerous, held in totally unsuitable locations. There's considerable organisation involved, but, equally, the amount of deception and disregard for safety and the concerns of the local community are outrageous.' He'd rehearsed it, more than once.

'Doesn't bear thinking about,' sniffed Forbes. 'Death-traps for thousands.'

'Hundreds, sir,' said McNally. 'Let's not get sensational—'

'We have reason to believe that the next rave will attract many thousands, and that some serious criminals are involved,' said Peach.

'Drugs?' barked Forbes.

'Sir,' McNally said with renewed assurance. 'Every time we've raided one of these parties, there's been no evidence of mass drug distribution, no more than you'd find in a regular night club. We'll struggle to back up all this media hype with statistics of young people dropping like flies at all-night parties.'

Forbes took no heed. 'When's the next one?' he asked. 'I'm hearing all sorts of horror stories and I'll not have this city debated in Parliament as an example of depravity and lawlessness. I want it stopped.'

McNally interceded once more. They needed to be careful, he said, needed to think about the consequences of thousands of angry youths stranded. As far as he was concerned that was a bigger risk to public safety than the parties themselves.

Forbes looked away from him and faced Peach, searching for the answers he really wanted.

'We're trying to find out,' said Peach, 'but without the resources …'

Three minutes later Peach had his resources: a team of six dedicated full-time officers of his choosing, use of the new Air Support Unit, and priority access to whatever back-up he needed from Northumbria and neighbouring forces, including the Armed

Response Unit.

'We'll need search warrants,' said Peach.

'Whatever you need, you've got,' said Forbes.

McNally's face was almost forlorn, no doubt thinking about the budget implications. 'Sir, I—'

But Forbes was getting to his feet. 'This is coming from the top,' he said. 'And, when I say the top, I mean *The Top*. Good work, Inspector.'

Peach stood and shook Forbes's hand, mentally thanking Mrs Thatcher herself for her astuteness and foresight; and there was him thinking the old hag was a pompous idiot.

'I'll see you tonight, Larry.' The Chief Super turned away from McNally and winked at Peach, patting his stomach. 'Mrs McNally's doing one of her fondues,' he said. 'My missus is just about pissing herself. She loves a fondue.'

As the door closed, Peach stood quietly as the metaphorical tumbleweed blew across McNally's office. Humiliation had left its blotchy residue on his boss's neck and McNally peered at Peach with the unveiled resentment of a defeated man.

'That was uncalled for,' he said.

TOMMY

Three: know your enemies.

Tommy hadn't heeded the billionaire's rules and now he was in the deepest shit possible.

The breaks of the single-decker bus squealed like the dying birds Paul Smart would peg to the clothes line back in the days when Tommy and Jed would be dragged to weekend coffee mornings by their gossiping mams, Barry in his pram, eliciting the stares of the ignorant.

The Smarts had lived two doors down from the church hall in the seventies, a far cry from the plush manor Paul now called home. It was the only house in the street with a tree growing out front. And grow it did, year on year, morbidly shielding windows whose curtains were perpetually drawn. Like every other house on the street, it had a backyard, housing an outside toilet and a pigeon coop, the smell of bird shit overpowering anyone walking down the back lane.

Old Mr Smart was a morose man, his wife a fragile jumble of nerves who always walked two steps behind her husband. In the summer, when a window was open or a door of the Smarts' house ajar, the howls of the teenage Paul could be heard over the roars of Mr Smart and the screams of Mrs Smart, and people walked by, heads lowered, their pace quickening in an attempt to rid themselves of the images the sounds induced.

'That poor lad,' he'd heard his mother mutter to Betty, and they too would hurry past, their chins wagging about the sister who was long gone by then, never visited, was living up in Longhouton, middle of nowhere, couldn't get away quick enough.

Six-year-old Tommy had done it for a dare – a Caramac up for grabs for the one who had the guts to scale the wall of the Smarts' back yard. A weird squawking noise had been heard by Jed and the McFall brothers the weekend before, and rumours were rife that old Mr Smart was murdering his pigeons and selling the meat to Chinese restaurants. The same disturbing sound had been heard that spring morning and Jed was soon dragging Tommy down the back lane.

Mr Smart spent every Saturday in the pub with his toothless wife who spent the entire afternoon cradling a bitter lemon, awaiting the bitter tang of blood that would inevitably fill her mouth later in the day when Mr Smart had had one too many.

Jed had balanced on a dustbin, Tommy standing precariously on his shoulders, peering over the top of the Smarts' backyard wall, scared half to death but with the sweet taste of caramel urging him on. The pigeons flapped and cooed safely in their cages, feathers and white faeces littering the ground.

That was when he saw the birds, a row of half a dozen fledglings, wings broken, pinned with wooden pegs to the blue string that reached from the gate post to the edge of the pigeon coop. Tommy had gasped and clung to the wall, the sugary anticipation turning horribly sour.

Then, a shadow had appeared at the kitchen window, morphing into Paul's face like an apparition as he pushed his nose up to the dirty glass. Tommy had toppled backwards, hitting the ground with a crash as he, Jed, and the bin tumbled. They'd run like the wind, the weird, squawking noise clarified, and the Caramac completely forgotten.

Birds, dogs, people. Paul Smart had a thirst for pain, so long as it wasn't his own.

The drugs were safely hidden for now in the airing cupboard

behind a mound of towels in a pair of never-worn pixie boots Sam was hoarding until they came back into fashion. There they would stay until he had a buyer for them. With Peach on his back, he couldn't afford to be accosted by the cops with a pocket full of Es.

Not being acquainted with drug dealers other than the self-appointed Paul Smart, he had limited options. Jimmy Lyric had as good as thrown him out of his house that morning.

'I'm on license,' he'd said. 'Do you think I'm a mug, or what?'

'I only want two grand for them.' A couple of grand would get Tommy the deposits he needed for the rigging and lighting, the chippies to build the stage. Maybe the sound too if he was canny enough. Jed had been right: a few hundred in a warehouse was a different kettle of fish to a full-scale rave. He needed professionals, people with the right amount of gear and the right amount of personnel to be able to work quickly.

'Tommy, you're a nice lad,' Jimmy had said. 'What you getting messed up in drugs for? You're looking at a three-year stretch.'

The last thing Tommy needed right now was a preachy ex-con going straight, and he'd put fifteen hundred forward. Last offer.

'Tommy.' Jimmy had circled a tattooed finger around his mouth. 'Watch my lips. No fucking way.'

Hadgy Dodds had been next on his list – a long shot, he knew, and Hadgy had looked at Tommy like he'd been asked to complete a trigonometry problem, such was his confusion. *Drugs? Fuck off, Tommy.*

Out of desperation, he'd even approached Darren who was out on the streets of Valley Park doing his "detached youth work," an attempt to persuade kids who'd known nothing but crime and drugs that there was another way of life. But the anger and disappointment in the youth worker's face had sent him scuttling away with his tail between his legs.

The bus exhaled into its final stop. There was only one person Tommy knew who wouldn't baulk at the selling of drugs, or who would find him a buyer at least. And he knew exactly where Trevor Logan spent his days sticking needles into his arms.

***

The stench of the railway arches was enough to turn even the strongest of stomachs. Covering his nose with his arm, Tommy clambered over the sodden sleeping bags and cardboard boxes. It didn't seem to matter what time of year it was, the arches were forever dank and wet.

Movement under a grey blanket caught his eye. Standing over the mound, he pulled the blanket to one side with the tips of a thumb and finger. A young girl's face blinked up at him, couldn't have been any older than Jed's brother, Barry. Fifteen tops.

'Fiver to suck you off,' she said, sleepily.

'Nar, you're all right,' Tommy replied. He mentioned Trevor's name, and the girl waved a hand in no direction at all.

'Next one down,' she grumbled, pulling the blanket back over her head.

He found Trevor Logan slumped against the cold, grey sandstone of the next arch. It was a pitiful sight, Trevor's ribs rising and falling in his bare chest, one hand trembling against his thigh, his cheeks streaked as if he'd been crying. Tommy thought back to a time when Trevor would play out on the street with himself and Jed and the other kids, kicking a football about, gliding over self-assembled ramps on a home-made skateboard fashioned by Billy from bits and bobs. There were only a few years between them. They could have been friends.

Tommy, feeling no sense of danger from the lifeless Trevor, sat next to him, stretching his legs out parallel to his, and with a sigh of sheer exhaustion, Trevor turned his head away from him. He looked tired and vulnerable – spent, as if any movement at all was beyond his capability. It was a far cry from the whirlwind of fury and abuse he usually exhibited. Here in his cave, Trevor Logan could be someone entirely different.

Trevor mumbled quietly, 'What the fuck do you want?'

'Need a favour.'

'Fuck you,' came the inevitable reply.

Trevor coughed, and Tommy noticed a trickle of sweat run down his neck and onto his chest.

'I need a buyer,' said Tommy. 'Ten per cent for you.'

Trevor's head turned in lazy side glance, but Tommy could sense his desperation. 'What is it?'

'Ecstasy.'

Trevor waved a fragile hand. 'It's smack people want, man.'

'Hey, don't knock it 'till you've tried it,' Tommy said. 'Here.' He took a single pill from his pocket, held it out like a peace offering. 'Make you so happy you won't know how miserable you are.'

Trevor knocked it from his hand. 'Bollocks to that,' he slurred dismissively. 'I'll be back inside soon, anyhow. Then I'll be sorted. This is nee life, this.'

Tommy leant forward and picked up the pill, dropping it back into his pocket as Trevor's head slumped to his chest. Guilt and pity were feelings Tommy hadn't anticipated.

'Couple of hundred quid,' he tried again. 'Tide you over.'

Trevor's head stayed bowed. 'Need to know the supplier.'

Tommy hesitated, unsure if it was wise to mention Paul's name, unconvinced by Trevor's current calm demeanour.

Trevor lifted his waxen face. 'No point selling drugs to someone who's already sold them to you.'

Tommy imagined Trevor handing the tubes of drugs out to Paul Smart and asking for money. 'Smartie,' he said.

Trevor's glazed eyes met Tommy's and he let out a short laugh which grew into a hacking, phlegm-ridden cough that doubled him over, making his eyes stream. Not tears then.

'Fucking hell.' Trevor laughed again once the coughing had subsided, 'after what he did to your da?'

Tommy's brow furrowed in confusion. 'Eh?'

'Thick as mince, you, mind.'

Tommy straightened his spine. Was he thick? He didn't think so. 'You better tell me,' he said, suddenly fearful of what he might hear.

'You'll find out soon enough,' said Trevor. 'Smartie, eh?' He paused, then his eyes turned sly. 'Tell you what. I'll get you a buyer if you tell me where the rave is.'

Tommy glared at him with annoyance.

'Everybody knows, man,' said Trevor. 'Tommy's rave this, Tommy's rave that. Where is it?'

'Without a buyer, there won't be any rave.'

Trevor gave a little snort and shook his head. 'Paul Smart supplying drugs to your rave. You fucking doylem.'

Tommy felt his heart drop like a dead weight of realisation. Paul had agreed there wouldn't be any drugs, but since when was he a man of his word? A doylem Tommy wasn't, a complete and utter idiot, he was. 'What did he do?' he asked again.

Trevor looked at him with an *I-know-something-you-don't* expression. 'Maybe you should ask your da.' With some effort, Trevor raised his body up and rested his head against the wall, closing his eyes, shutting Tommy out.

Having the cash was more important than unscrambling Trevor's riddles right now, and he felt Trevor's desperation seep into his own skin. 'I need a buyer, howay, Trevor.'

'We need to know where the rave is, but.' He didn't open his eyes.

'Who's we?'

Trevor grinned a little, eyes still closed. 'I'm not saying 'owt else, so don't bother.' He swung his head towards Tommy, his face bordering on gratification. 'I'll be at the rec at nine o'clock with your buyer. But remember. No venue, no money.'

Trevor twisted away from Tommy, pulling up his knees and curling into a ball against the wall of the arch. Tommy stared at the jutting vertebrae of Trevor's spine, the bruises and scrapes, the veins of his neck shot to fuck, and the guilt settled in his gut once more.

Looking around him at the filth, Tommy thought back to the days before Paul Smart, before his father's addiction took hold, when his family was hardly rich, but getting by, when there was laughter and Meccano and the Ramones on the record player. It felt like a lifetime ago.

He pulled himself to his feet, feeling a hundred years old. Just a few days ago he'd had the brawn and the confidence; cocky as hell. Now his family was in danger, his best friend had shunned him, and he'd done a deal with the Devil. Two Devils in fact, for Trevor Logan was no angel.

DENISE

Her son-in-law was a drug dealer. How crass was that? What sort of low-life was her daughter in love with?

A sewing basket rested by one of the pink leather armchairs, mostly for effect. Mending things wasn't her style. Poor people mended things, and if there was one thing she wouldn't be seen as, it was poor. She'd grown up wanting, hungry, other kids taking the piss out of the jumble sale clothes they recognised as their own cast-offs. Shame and mortification had left their scars and now everything had to be new; the best. The basket was where she threw the useless stuff, like credit card bills and repayment demands written in big red letters designed to intimidate.

Tommy's drugs had joined the trash, and she stared at the basket now, wondering how long the dealing had been going on. A few weeks? Six months? Since before Sam married him?

She remembered the cheap, nasty wedding at the Civic Centre, her daughter dressed in a borrowed two-piece, the bump that was to become Ashleigh evident to everyone. Even as the mother of the bride, Denise had felt entirely overdressed at the pub dinner that followed, Sam tucking into scampi and chips and a knickerbocker glory. No evening do, no cake, no going-away outfits.

Did it start in that godawful place they'd gone on the belated honeymoon? All the girls wearing next to nothing, out 'till all hours, pissed out of their tiny minds? Tommy and Sam had thought to join them, but she'd put a stop to that. As if she was some sort of glorified babysitter. Tap water in Tommy's water bottle had kept his arse glued to the toilet for the best part of three days.

Hearing her brother call her name, Denise eased herself out of the armchair and walked into the kitchen where Paul watched his men through the window, his stance one of satisfaction. He'd turned up unannounced with a kiss for her cheek and a couple of ugly looking creatures with wheelbarrows of full of rose bushes and black bin bags of compost. Looking through the window now, she gasped, the blood-red rose garden exquisite, but reminiscent of things more brutal.

'*Oh, my love is like a red, red rose,*' Paul sang quietly.

The hairs on Denise's arms rose to meet the tune, goose bumps prickling in recollection. It was a song their mother had sung, sometimes serenely to them at bed time, more often through tears to comfort herself.

As if he knew the effect the song would have, Paul's arm went around her shoulder. 'Thank you,' he said.

Still reeling from the clarity of the memory, she stammered, 'What for?'

'For letting me do this. For you.'

The prickling sensation erupted all over; it stung her skin, raced through her blood. The arm around her felt secure, safe, and she hoped it would stay there a little longer, all the while knowing she was the one who should be strong. She should have taken him with her all those years ago, got him out of that hell. But her husband would have none of it. He wanted her all to himself, he'd said, and at the end of the day, she had to save herself, otherwise she would surely have died of terror.

The tears rose from the hollow depths of a heart she had long thought empty. All the years she'd been convinced her brother didn't love her any more fell in streams down her cheeks. That was all she'd ever wanted; to be loved, and since Tommy had taken her daughter away from her, she'd been adrift.

'I'm sorry,' she sputtered, the back of her hand at her nose.

Paul still watched his men through the window. 'No need to apologise,' he said. It was as if he'd expected the tears, and she yearned for him to hold her tighter, tell her everything would be all right. But who was she to expect such affection? She'd betrayed him and now he didn't know how to offer comfort. She could forgive him that.

'I won't tell anyone,' she said, lifting her head to look at him, 'about the building society.'

She counted the beats of his silence. He didn't flinch, didn't say "thanks, sis," or pat her arm with gratitude. He just stared through the glass and said, 'Don't know what you're talking about.' He tightened his arm at last, perhaps too much. 'Don't spoil it,' he said, before walking away.

***

Alone now, vodka bottle half empty, the curtains closed against the relentless afternoon sun, Denise let the fierce, quiet tears run free. About once a year it possessed her, the need to let herself fall to the bottom so she could crawl her way back up again. As always, she did it by herself. No one needed to see this. She was Denise Morris, she could get through anything, but now and then the accumulation of regret, guilt, and fear had to be allowed out.

She cried for her friendless brother, her mother lying in her early grave, her rotten father, decaying in a nursing home with some alcohol induced dementia. Her daughter, her damned ex-husband, and shithead boyfriends.

Her husband, Charlie, had been a rotten twat if ever there was one. '*A Jack the Lad,*' she'd laughed with her friends, thinking she'd be the one to change him. Hindsight wasn't a luxury you could fall back on when you were barely a woman yourself and had no experience of the world beyond your own grisly front door.

He'd thought her frigid, unexciting, always wanting her to *let herself go*. Then he'd met Angela, a bland woman with a face like a foot who clearly hid her lust for spontaneity.

'She's just so *uninhibited*,' he'd said. Decided he wanted another family. Decided he wanted to emigrate to New Zealand with *Angela*.

Just like that. Divorced.

Then there was Adrian, nice as pie until he was found with his trousers down with a thirteen-year-old. Sam had been ten years old at the time, avoided him like the plague, called him a creep. Denise had wondered – oh, she'd wondered – but had been too much of a coward to ask Sam directly if he'd ever touched her.

She was still a coward, she realised, and the tears of self-pity coursed down her face.

Marvin had been kind, sweet; so nice it drove her to hate him, as if conflict were a necessity to her, like food, water, shelter. The infernal comb-over and his ability to bore even the Pope had driven her to near insanity.

Kevin had been the final straw. Wanted to buy a house for them, he'd said, up in High Heaton. Even showed her around it, all bay windows, cornices and ceiling roses. All he needed was a ten per cent deposit, he'd said. She'd handed it over, her life savings. Then, like something off *Rentaghost*, poof! He was gone.

She was a monumental failure, and she sobbed like a baby as she stared into the glass of clear alcohol – the abyss of her future. They said you should face your fears head on. But she couldn't face hers. She couldn't keep a man, she was losing her daughter, her brother could walk away from her at any moment if she put a foot wrong.

She filled the tumbler to the top. She would numb the fear instead – the fear that she would die alone.

PEACH

Paul Smart had a face only his mother could love. Perhaps it was the wealth, ill-gotten or not, that gained him the respect of the brutes who seemed to colonise him like head lice. He wasn't stupid either, so the decision not to have some brief sat next to him had to be for a reason which, Peach was sure, would become clear soon enough.

Paul sat opposite the DCI with his hands clasped on the table, dressed in a tight sports top, revealing the shoulders and arms of a man who spent much of his time with his nose to the floor doing press-ups. He was tall, well over six feet, his legs barely fitting under the table. How old was he? Peach wondered. Thirty, perhaps a bit older. Ten years ago, the man was just some small-time lender, but it soon became clear that Paul Smart had ambitions, and that he would do whatever it took to make money and be the Big Man. His dirty work was done by others, however, people who would rather die than grass on their mentor.

With the tape running and DS Murphy spread-eagled in a chair by his side, Peach pushed the photograph across the table. Paul sat forward, looked at it, then sat back again.

'Want to tell me why a certain Thomas James Collins was at your house yesterday morning?' Peach asked.

'He's a mate,' Paul replied.

'Spend a lot of time together, do you?'

Paul shrugged. 'Not really.'

'Not a mate, then.'

Sucking in air, Paul lifted one side of his mouth like Popeye. 'An acquaintance,' he clarified.

'Bit early to be receiving acquaintances, eight o'clock?' Peach pointed at the photograph and Paul looked down at it with a sigh of tedium.

'He wanted money, I told him to piss off.'

'Money for what?' Murphy picked up the questioning.

'Fucked if I know. People want money for all sorts.'

'Do you know the prison sentence for supplying class A drugs, Mister Smart?' asked Murphy.

'Drugs?' Paul cocked an eyebrow. 'Err, nope.'

'You might be about to find out,' said Peach, 'because my officers are tearing up your floorboards right now.' Tommy Collins was meeting with him in nightclubs and at his house, and these raves needed the fuel of MDMA. Didn't take a brain surgeon to work out the connections.

Paul blinked slowly from Peach to Murphy. 'I'm not arrested, I know my rights,' he said.

'You might want to tell that bodyguard of yours not to invite police officers into your house, then,' said Murphy.

They'd had nothing to arrest Smart for, but the dark-skinned man with the stitched-up face that guarded Paul's front door had believed the uniformed officers. As soon as Paul was signed in, Peach had sent them to Smart's house with orders to wave a piece of letterheaded paper around and lie to the man that his boss was under arrest and they had the right to search the house. Not everyone was as well informed about the law as Paul Smart, who was now scratching under his chin and looking down his nose at Peach, the fleeting look of cold hostility gone.

'I know you don't like me,' Paul said. 'You're a bit of a leftie, you don't like people making money. It's *distasteful* to you. But surely you don't think I'm some sort of muttonhead? Drugs? Mugs game.'

'Making money from your line of work is distasteful to me, yes,' said Peach.

Paul held up his hands. 'I run a legitimate business. I even pay my taxes, so you can waste them on my floorboards.' He looked at Murphy. 'I'll be looking for compensation.'

'How long have you known Collins?' Murphy sat forward.

'Erm, let's see,' said Paul, rubbing his chin in mock thought. 'Since the little prick was born, probably.'

'So, you don't like him?' said Murphy with surprise. 'Thought you said you were mates.'

'An acquaintance,' Peach corrected.

Murphy nodded. 'Go clubbing, do you? You know, throwing some shapes on the dance floor and that?' He gave a little example of what he meant.

Paul eyed Murphy with scorn. 'I leave that to the bairns.'

Murphy slid another photograph towards him. 'Phutures, last Saturday night,' he said.

Peach watched Paul carefully. Not a flicker.

'I had a game,' said Paul.

Another photograph.

'With your acquaintance?'

Paul glanced down at the photograph of Tommy entering the club and scoffed again.

'Coz, the bird behind the bar said he joined you for a little tête-à-tête. Lasted about, what?' Murphy looked at Peach for the answer.

'Ten, twelve minutes,' said Peach.

Paul's hands had slid into his pockets. *Making sure he doesn't fidget,* thought Peach.

'Like I said,' Paul maintained, 'he wants money, and I'm not into lending to people who can't pay me back.'

'Well, knock me down with a fucking feather,' said Murphy. 'I thought that's exactly what loan sharks did. Have I been wrong all this time, boss?'

'No, you're not wrong.' Peach couldn't take his eyes off Paul's face. The man was made of iron. Didn't give a thing away.

'Let's just say it's not a very good business model these days,' said Paul.

'So, you need to make your money elsewhere,' Peach stated rather than questioned. 'That's quite a lifestyle you've got to fund.'

Watching Paul shrug again, Peach dug into the breast pocket of his shirt and brought out the seal bag he'd found in Sally's handbag. He threw it onto the table, sensing Murphy staring at them, hearing him clear his throat a little. 'Are you supplying drugs to Tommy Collins to sell at his raves?'

Paul looked at the seal bag blankly. 'No. But he wants to be careful getting into that game. I mean, the lad's got a wife and bairn. Families are fair game to drug dealers. Nasty people.'

'You know we can trace the batches of these things, don't you?' said Peach. 'I mean, it's a bit daft putting the stamp on it.'

'I wouldn't know, would I?'

At last, some emotion, albeit irritation.

'So, if I arrest Collins and search his house, I won't find any of these?' Peach held up the bag.

'If Tommy's stupid enough to keep drugs in his house, that's his problem.'

'And yours, when we find them buried under your floorboards,' said Murphy.

This drew a smile onto Paul's face; teeth this time, gappy, like the milk teeth of a five-year-old.

Peach leant forward, his own teeth displayed, his patience running out. 'Stop playing with me,' he seethed.

Paul just continued to smile, and Peach's fists smashed into the table making Murphy jump beside him.

Paul sighed, long and hard. 'I'm a bit bored now, can I go?'

A knock on the door had Murphy pulling himself from his chair and up onto his feet, the long, hooded stare at their interviewee bringing a wider smile to Paul's face.

The door closed with a quiet click, and Peach pushed air through his nose in heavy bursts.

'Interview suspended, five forty-three p.m.' Peach pressed the *stop* button on the tape recorder and reached for the photographs and the seal bag, but Paul's hand came down on his, his slate-blue eyes beckoning him in.

'I know it's not me you want,' he said. 'You want Collins? I'll give you Collins.'

'Stay here.' Peach made to stand but Paul's grip tightened.

'I'll do you a deal.'

Peach sat back in his chair, felt Paul's fingers loosen, and he withdrew his hand, pulling the photographs and seal bag slowly towards him.

'I know what Collins is up to,' Paul said, 'and I know people. I can make sure he has plenty drugs on him when you bust that rave. You just give me the sign and I'll take care of it.'

'There won't be any rave,' said Peach.

'You going to stop it, are you? You and Bugs Bunny out there?'

'Why would you want to stitch up Collins?'

Paul held up a hand and rubbed two fingers and a thumb together. 'It's a big do. Thousands of people. You let me out the back door with the cash and I'll make sure Collins has the drugs on him. I'll lead you right to him. I get my money, you get your man. It's a win-win.'

Peach creased his brow. 'You're bankrolling him?'

But Paul's face remained blank. 'This is a one-off opportunity. You might get him for theft one day, might get him for pissing up a lamp post, but you'll never get him for dealing on this scale.'

Peach continued watching him, that growl settling in his throat once more. 'Where is it?'

'Well, that's for me to know and you to find out,' said Paul. 'These raves have run their course. They're pissing all over them down south.' His eyes darkened. 'Someone will die, and it'll all be over.'

Peach felt himself flinch, and Paul tilted his head to one side.

'I was sorry to hear about your bairn. Terrible business.'

A stone struck the pit of Peach's stomach. He should have got that description from the head teacher. Did Paul Smart look old enough to pass as Sally's father? He had an authority about him for sure, and fathering children as teenagers was hardly a rare occurrence in Valley Park.

Raging, Peach sprung across the table, grabbing the neck of Paul's top as the door of the interview room opened, and Murphy sprinted over.

'Chief!' he urged, trying to prize Peach's fingers away. 'Chief! Stop! There's nothing there, they didn't find 'owt.'

His face a flaming red, Peach released Paul who let out an ugly laugh.

'That's made my day, that has. I take it I'm free to go?'

Murphy pulled Peach towards the interview room door. 'He's clean, boss,' he said.

Staring hard at Paul, Peach recalled the head teacher's words: *'Horrible man, creepy as hell.'* He watched Paul get to his feet. There was nothing clean about him.

Paul was ambling towards him, stopping at the door. 'Do me a deal and I'll give you the venue,' he said, voice barely above a whisper. He pushed a business card into Peach's hand. 'And I'll give you Collins.'

TOMMY

Something caustic smouldered in Tommy's insides, even though his evening bartering with suppliers had given him some hope. They still wanted deposits, some insurance against a nobody asking for staging and lighting on the scale of a West End production. Thanks to Trevor Logan, he'd have it for them in the morning, and they'd shaken hands, giving Tommy a brief glimpse of what life could be like as a professional club owner with money to do business with.

'*After what he did to your da?*'

The words throbbed in Tommy's head like a toothache as he opened his front door. He'd been sixteen, his exams only a few months away. He'd kuckled down those last few months, his mother adamant it would be his only way out, Jed insisting he wouldn't remain friends with a thicko.

Billy Logan had sold fish from the back of a van; Tommy remembered the smell of the fresh cod his mother would buy on a Friday, an odour that lingered in the house for days after it had been steamed with butter on a dinner plate over a pan of boiling water. Billy was an innocuous man; gentle, nervous, wouldn't say boo to a goose. In contrast, Tommy's father was a loud-mouth with a fog horn laugh and a liking for dirty jokes. His gambling had crippled them, brought his mother to her knees on occasion. Sometimes Reggie would cry, pull at his hair, promise to get himself straight. But the addiction was too much to resist, and Reggie Collins, for all his arrogance and cheek, was weak as water, and his debt to Paul Smart had spiralled out of control. But Paul had written it off after his conviction, and he'd never bothered the family for repayments.

Unheard of.

In the living room, Sam was lying on her back on the sofa, Ashleigh sprawled across her, both sleeping soundly as if their world were a place of peace and contentment. But the sight of them brought no joy, only fear and a smattering of relief that the drugs would be out of the house at last. It was already gone eight-thirty, and his heart pounded. He was getting used to the feeling of it hammering against his ribs day and night.

He walked to the table in the corner of the room, dropping his jacket onto the back of one of the chairs. As he did so, his eyes rested on the Visiting Order which had been issued for this coming Friday. Sam never failed to request it every month, and he wondered if his father still waited for him, sitting by himself at a table, watching other families greet each other, argue, point the finger in blame.

Sam had been his redemption. After his mother took her own life, his grandad had moved in with his pipe and tales of the war, his farts and his dicky hip. It had secured the tenancy from the council, stability for the grieving teenager, but Tommy had spent much of his time at Jed's where Betty would let them watch *Danger Mouse* undisturbed and spread a sleeping bag out on Jed's bedroom floor, giving him a pat on the arm as he crawled into it.

'I miss her too, pet,' she'd say.

"Missing" was an understatement. Tommy had felt his mother's absence in his bones. At sixteen, he hadn't even begun to appreciate her role in his young life: pocket money, food, clothes ironed. She did everything for him and he would never have the opportunity to thank her now he was older and knew what it was like to love a child – now that he understood her grief, the pain of having to hand over something born of your own flesh. Even the absence of the dark times had left a hole. They were the only times she would mention the big brother Tommy missed now more than ever. Big brothers were there to advise and protect, and he often envied Barry his lifetime of Jed, and Frankie his brood of older siblings.

But then he'd met Sam, and the sun began to shine once more. Within six months she'd moved in, and, when she'd discovered she was pregnant, they'd married, Sam defying her pretentious mother and pulling the whole thing off for under fifty quid. Impending parenthood hadn't scared them, young as they were. They'd been so happy they'd talked of little else. Almost a year ago, Ashleigh came into their lives and he had even more to live for – something to protect. A family of his own.

But that morning, Sam's concern over his bruised face and short temper had turned into questions he couldn't, wouldn't answer, and now she was giving him a wide berth with her one-word responses.

Two: treat others with the respect they deserve.

He hadn't respected Sam, and he couldn't bring himself to tell her what a colossal mess he'd made of things. But maybe it would be all right. Just maybe he could give them the life they deserved. All he needed was the cash, and it was waiting for him at the rec.

Closing the living room door quietly, he headed up the stairs to the airing cupboard, the door delivering its usual horror-movie creak as it opened. He reached up and pulled one of the boots from the top shelf. It fell from his hand to the floor and he bent to pick it up, frowning at its emptiness. He shook it out.

Nothing.

Panic rising, he grabbed at the other boot and brought it down.

Empty.

Towels and sheets fell to the floor as he raked inside the airing cupboard. At the back of the middle shelf was a box of Christmas decorations, and his dread subsided as he dragged it out, took it into the bedroom and emptied the contents onto the floor. The cardboard tubes had fallen out of the boots and into the box, it was the only explanation. On his hands and knees, he rummaged through tinsel and baubles, heat engulfing his face as he realised the drugs were gone.

'What you doing?'

He looked up to see Sam standing at the bedroom door, Ashleigh still sleeping with her head on her mother's shoulder. The look of sheer terror on his face had Sam's eyes widening.

'Tommy,' she demanded, 'what are you looking for?'

'What have you done with them?' She'd been standoffish that morning. She'd gone looking. Flushed them down the toilet.

Face searing, he jumped to his feet and grabbed her arms. 'The Smarties. Where've you put them?'

'Get off me!' She stepped back, a palm over Ashleigh's ear. 'Smarties?' Her face changed from confusion to fear. 'What've you done, Tommy?'

He let go of her arms, tasting dread. They were gone. He was finished.

'I saw Jed today,' Sam said, voice trembling. 'He crossed the street to avoid us. Something's going on, and you better tell me what it is.'

'Or what?' hissed Tommy. 'You'll go tappy-lapping back to your mam?' Deep down he'd always feared it, that Denise would get her way, that Sam would start to believe her.

'Maybe,' said Sam, her wet eyes on the bruise on his face. 'Maybe I will.'

At least she had a mother to run to.

He felt the dull ache of grief wrap itself around his ribs. Sam would leave him, just like everyone else. It suddenly felt inevitable.

'Go on then, pack your stuff,' he said.

Sam's sob caught in her throat as she clung to Ashleigh and fought back tears.

'*Bastard!*' Tommy heard as he passed her and ran down the stairs and out the front door.

PEACH

Ten o'clock couldn't have come soon enough. The half-moon rose as he turned into Holly Drive and pulled up a few doors down from Tommy's house. The curtains were drawn, no light on inside.

Murphy put out his hand to open the car door.

'Stay put,' said Peach, 'I don't want him seeing you.'

Confident as he was he'd find what he wanted, until he had Tommy in custody he couldn't risk him recognising Murphy. Should it all go wrong, he would still need him undercover.

Murphy looked a little disappointed not to be in on the action. 'Might get some kip in,' he said, withdrawing his hand and pulling the hood of his sweatshirt over his head, cracking the joints of his fingers in a stretch.

There wouldn't be time for snoozing. They'd arrest Collins and have him back at the station in half an hour.

Two officers emerged from a police van that had pulled up behind, one of them holding a battering ram. Grasping the warrant in his hand, Peach emerged from the car and gave the officers their instructions: after he'd read Collins his rights, they were to search for drugs, large amounts of cash and weapons. They could do whatever damage they wanted.

Valley Park was quiet. Birds chirped, an aeroplane flew overhead in the distance. If Peach closed his eyes, he could have been in any leafy suburb of the city. Instead, he regarded the derelict property opposite Tommy's house, the windows boarded up with mesh grating. It stood slumped like a corpse, it's carcass scarred and disfigured by spray paint and repeated purging. The Collins' home, too, looked forlorn in the dusk, the houses either side of it newly boarded up, ready to be pillaged of their meagre contents.

A few youths holding cans of Special Brew were gathered at Tommy's gate, and as Peach approached with the officers, the youths sidled away, one or two of them glancing over their shoulders as they slunk around the corner.

Peach turned at the sound of a pair of mopeds tearing down the street. They whizzed past him like wasps, the skinny drivers bare chested, their faces concealed with red bandanas. The street light above him buzzed and flickered, and he saw movement from the garden of the abandoned house opposite. A dog wandered out onto the road, stopping to look at him before trotting down the street and into the Logan's garden.

'Let's go,' he said to the officers.

As he followed them down the path to Tommy's front door, the mopeds flew down the road again, four of them now, then five, six. The drivers, now wearing T-shirts and backpacks, whooped and held up their middle fingers. The dog appeared again, then darted back into the garden, head down and tail between its legs. The street light flickered and died.

'Police! Open the door!' The officers pounded, glancing around them, as the mopeds continued to fly past.

Kids, out to cause a nuisance, nothing better to do, thought Peach as the officers pounded again; no response.

'Break it down,' he ordered.

'Shouldn't we—'

'Do it!'

One thrust of the battering ram and the door was open, the officers inside, their shouts causing curtains up and down the street to twitch. Then, one by one, doors opened, and people began to trickle out. Peach looked around him, saw children, naked from the waist down, standing in lit doorways with their fingers in their mouths while their parents and older siblings gathered nearby. Some people held back, curious, while others strode towards Tommy's house, men and women in vests, shorts, and flip-flops.

'*Chief,*' he heard on his radio.

'Go ahead.'

'*I don't like the look of this.*'

'Stay where you are.'

One of the officers was at the door. 'No one here,' he said.

Peach looked behind him at the sullen, angry faces of Valley Park's residents, standing their ground as the mopeds weaved around them. He heard the sound of breaking glass. He should abort, get his officers to safety. 'Get what you can and get out of there,' he said.

The people gathered in small clusters, talking in hushed voices, pointing. His head spun at the sound of vehicles screeching to a halt at the end of the street. Two cars, each of them booming out a non-musical bass, manoeuvred in rapid three-point turns to block the western entrance of Holly Drive. Inside the vehicles, Peach spotted the lit ends of cigarettes, glowing like the eyes of wolves.

The officers were tramping out of Tommy's house, carrying evidence bags of whatever they'd been able to get their hands on in the short time they'd been inside. Peach followed them to the garden gate and put his radio to his mouth, eyeballing the crowd which had doubled in numbers in the space of a couple of minutes.

'Calling your mates, are you?'

He faced a squat woman, barely the height of his chest, tiny eyes in a red, football face, lines running from the edges of her nose to her chin like a ventriloquist's dummy.

'Don't fucking expect them 'till the morra,' she sneered.

'Or next week,' said her friend.

Another bottle landed in the road, this time with a splash of fire.

'For Christ's sake,' said the woman. 'Happy now?!'

'Just stand back and we'll be out of your hair,' said Peach.

'You lot are never out our hair.' The woman was squaring up to him. 'You come here, you stop and search our bairns every five minutes, walk into our houses, take what the fuck you want. But when you're wanted, when there's some old biddy getting burgled for her pension, where are you, eh? Where the fuck are you then?'

Grumbles of agreement rose from the throng.

'Howay, Dawn, there's no point,' said the woman's friend.

'They've got parents, haven't they?' said Peach, nodding at the youths lining the street, revving their bikes. 'Maybe it's them you want to be screeching at.'

'Parents?' The woman's face was getting redder. 'They're all off their heads on smack or booze just to get through the day, man. They're on every corner selling it, and *you lot*.' She pointed a finger at him. 'Do fuck all.'

The officers were climbing into the police van, and he could see Murphy gesturing to him from the open car window. The swelling crowd mumbled and groaned, raised voices igniting others until individual voices were indiscernible. The pounding bass from the cars joined the din as the vehicles' doors were thrown open.

A few seconds later, Murphy was at his side, pulling at his arm, but he wasn't going to leave yet, not without his man.

Then, as if some covert order had been given, bottles, stones, and bricks came raining down. Murphy pulled harder, and the square woman ducked and started to move away with her friend.

'Mind, you've done yourself proud this time!' she shouted. 'Bastards, the lot of you!'

Shielding his head with his arm, Peach pushed Murphy away.

'Get in the car and call for back up,' he said.

'Already did,' said Murphy over the din. 'And I'm not leaving you here to get lynched!'

More screeching of tyres, and Peach peered through the smoke. Three more vehicles blocked the eastern end of the street, a pack of youths climbing onto their roofs and bonnets, leaping on the metal and shrieking their war cries. He turned his head, the other cars at the western end still stationary, lads leaning against them, huddled over flames.

The noise was intense, the night raining down arrows of glass and grit amidst the din of baying voices, barking dogs, and screaming children. Facing the derelict house opposite Tommy's, he saw the flicker of orange flames from inside as the metal grates of the windows begin to fall away, two or three children hanging from each of them like chimpanzees.

The officers stepped down from the van, batons aloft – but they were surrounded, completely outnumbered, and there was no way out.

'Come on, boss.' He felt the tug on his sleeve again, heat on his face as a blazing bottle landed in Tommy's garden.

Then, he spotted him, about twenty feet away: Collins forcing his way through the crowd which was moving in waves, the older ones falling back, the younger ones moving forward, lobbing their burning bottles and bricks in quick succession. Tommy was walking towards his house, mouth open, his eyes on the broken windows and shattered door.

Murphy's hood was up over his face again and he turned his back on Tommy as Peach began to stride towards his target. As he got closer, the squat woman and her friend leapt between them, others, braving the falling debris, joining the two women, forming a human shield around Tommy, and within a few seconds, he had disappeared altogether.

Blue lights flashed at each end of the street, their entry blocked by the parked cars, the spinning lights now the focus of the descending missiles and firebombs. The two officers were back in the van which was being rocked by a dozen youths, and the thundering of a helicopter overhead had the children dropping from the windows of the derelict house, scattering from the garden like cockroaches from a newly lit room.

The chopper's propellers fanned the flames, and the explosion blew them all off their feet. The house burst into a ball of fire that mushroomed into the air, and Peach dropped to the ground, Murphy falling next to him amidst a shower of glass, bricks, and slate.

A few long moments passed as they lay face down, hands protecting the backs of their heads. Eventually, Murphy looked up at him.

'You all right?' he breathed.

Peach nodded. 'You?'

'Didn't get much kip, boss.'

The people dispersed as quickly as they'd arrived and by the time Peach was on his feet, the street was almost deserted, the barricades abandoned, officers rolling the dumped vehicles onto the pavement to give them and their dogs access. Only Tommy remained, just ten feet away, his face blackened with soot, the whites of his dazed eyes on his house.

Peach fumbled in his pockets for the warrant; he still had time, he still had authorisation, but his pockets were empty. He scoured the ground frantically, his shoes crunching on broken glass as he searched, but the road and pavement were littered with debris – it was like looking for a needle in a haystack.

He turned to face Tommy, and they remained still, the chopper pounding out its rhythm overhead. The stand-off was broken by the arrival of a woman in a long coat over a high-necked nightie, her hair in curlers under a scarf.

She held Tommy's shoulders with trembling fingers, shouting over the crackling of the burning house. 'Tommy, love!'

Tommy's eyes remained on Peach. *Why?*

'Where's our Jed, Tommy?'

Tommy shrugged.

'He's not here?'

He shook his head.

The woman looked relieved, then asked, 'Are you hurt?'

Tommy didn't answer, and Peach watched her try to move him, but Tommy was resisting, eyes turning reluctantly away from Peach and onto his house.

'Oh, Tommy, love,' the woman said again. 'Are Sam and the bairn safe?'

Tommy nodded, and the woman lifted a hand to Tommy's cheek. 'Howay back to ours, then.'

She was going to take him, and Peach's eyes were back on the ground, but instead of the warrant he was searching for, he saw a pair of red Doctor Martin boots, laced up as far as they could be before they hit a pair of calves like shanks of meat. He looked back up into the face of Paul Smart's bodyguard, his cheeks a gnarly criss-cross of black stitching, his thick body and the glint in his fierce eyes screaming, *brute, bully*. He was one of them – one of the lowlifes who thought they owned this city; men who thought they could get what they wanted through fear and violence, murder and corruption.

'I'm here for Tommy,' the man said, accent thick with Liverpool.

Like Hell. If anyone was taking Tommy anywhere, it was Peach.

He began to move away towards Tommy, who stood next to the woman in the nightie, staring at the bodyguard like a frightened rabbit.

'Not without a warrant, pig.'

Spinning around, he saw the man holding up a sheet of scorched paper in one hand and a cigarette lighter in the other. The flames took hold quickly, and the warrant blew from his hand in the hot, gusty wind of the burning house.

As fire engines hurtled down the street, Peach felt his face fall into a snarl. He walked up to the scarred man, looked him up and down as if he were the lowest of the low, let his nostrils flare at the stench of him. 'As if this place wasn't bad enough,' he growled.

The man's face twitched, his eyes flicking over Peach's shoulder in Tommy's direction. He wasn't getting the message, and Peach towered over him, felt the spittle on his lips as he drew them back to reveal his teeth. 'I said piss off, and crawl back to whatever stinking hole you came from.'

Their eyes locked.

'Now!' Peach yelled.

The man huffed a small, derisive laugh. 'You'll regret that,' he said.

'The only thing I regret is letting scum like you into this city.'

The man's face took on an expression of deep hatred, and he took a step back with another glance at Tommy, then he turned and walked away, the billowing smoke taking him within a few seconds.

Turning back around, Peach found Collins' relieved eyes back on his. They were glistening with tears and grit, but there was something else there too, Peach noticed: the deep, deep sorrow of someone who had lost everything.

It was a look Mike Peach recognised all too well.

FRIDAY

TOMMY

For a few blissful seconds, Tommy was in his own bed, Sam's head on his chest, his feet sticking out the end of the sheet. His eyes swivelled in their sockets as he came too, and reality stung his nostrils in the form of burnt toast.

Snapping his head sideways, he found Barry bending forward on a pouffe, reading *Smash Hits* magazine. Looking at his watch, Tommy noticed his blackened hands and realised he'd slept for ten hours on Betty's sofa. He vaguely remembered lying down, Betty trying to persuade him to take off his clothes and have a wash, but that was the last thing he could recall.

'Jed's been bad,' Barry said, looking up from his magazine. 'Didn't come home.' He blinked at Tommy, tearfully. 'I think he's dead.'

Tommy sat up and rubbed at his eyes, noticing the array of sheets marked with soot and dirt covering the sofa, armchairs, and the entire carpet.

'He's not dead, Barry,' he reassured.

'How do you know?'

'I just do, all right? It's me, remember?'

Barry smiled, his fear evaporating. Tommy's word was Gospel. 'Your face is proper black!' Barry sprang from the pouffe and skipped towards the door, bumping into Betty who held a tray aloft. She let Barry past and came into the room, setting the tray down on the pouffe.

Tommy looked hungrily at the pile of toast, stacked like a block of flats.

'There's someone here to see you,' Betty said. 'And God only knows where that son of mine is.'

Tommy thanked her, and as she left the room, he peered at the door with a mixture of hope and fear, ready to tell Sam everything: he'd been a dickhead, and he would put it right, look for a proper job, dress like a wanker if he had to. But he knew there was little he could do to put it right now. The drugs were gone, and he didn't blame Sam for getting rid of them.

Trevor Logan, his energy returned, had been at the rec at nine o'clock the night before as planned with some older fella with a mean mouth and greedy eyes. But Tommy had arrived empty handed, and Trevor had spat at Tommy's feet before telling him he was a useless fucker and storming off with his lacky in tow.

Eyes on the door, Tommy felt horribly alone. It was an odd feeling, like he'd been sucked into another dimension where he was invisible. Without Jed, he felt like he'd lost an arm; without Sam the other one was gone too, and the legs. He wouldn't survive this limbless life without either of them.

But instead of Sam's face, Frankie's appeared, his hamster cheeks full of Betty's breakfast. Tommy's heart sank a little, but he felt the relief of reprieve too.

'Jesus!' Frankie exclaimed. 'You look like Oliver Twist!'

Tommy rammed a half slice of toast into his mouth as Frankie strode in and raised a palm for a high-five.

'Soul brother,' Frankie said, grinning.

That word again, and Tommy's eyes searched Frankie's face, looking for any sign of his own mother in it. He was no astronaut, but Frankie would be as good a brother as any. But he was clutching at straws and he knew it, and seeing nothing at all, he raised his hand weakly to receive Frankie's palm.

'All limbs accounted for.' Frankie examined Tommy from a short distance. 'Mind, you should hear some of the stories. People getting blown up, arms and legs landing in people's gardens. Fucking Armageddon!'

Tommy's mouth was so dry, swallowing the toast made him grimace. 'Have you seen Jed?' he asked.

'I've been asking myself the same question all night, pet,' Betty said, coming back into the living room holding a cup of tea and a small pile of Jed's clothes. 'You,' she said to Tommy, 'upstairs and get in the bath. You can take that with you.' She indicated the toast and tea when Tommy's hungry eyes widened. 'But you'll have to take them off here,' she added, eying his filthy clothes. 'And you,' she pointed at Frankie, 'don't sit on anything, is that clear?'

'Yes, Mrs Foster,' said Frankie.

Fifteen minutes later, Frankie stood at the bottom of the stairs as Tommy trotted down, Jed's Beasty Boys T-shirt billowing around his waist, the football shorts hanging like a lamp shade around his skinny thighs.

Frankie howled. *'Thread legs!'* But his laughter was cut short as a key twisted in the lock and their attention turned to the front door.

'Oh, thank Jesus!' cried Betty, striding into the hallway.

Dropping his key onto the console table, Jed closed the door behind him with his foot. Betty strode past Tommy and Frankie, took Jed's chin in her hand, scouring his face. She spun him around and checked the back of him, then turned him back around to face her.

'Mam!' Jed hissed, pushing her hands away. 'I'm fine, get off.'

'Where've you been?' she demanded, 'I've been worried sick!'

'Nowhere,' huffed Jed.

'Not a thought for anybody. You could've been lying dead somewhere!'

'I stayed at a mate's. And what's he doing here?' He nodded at

Tommy and made for the stairs, but Betty stopped him.

'A mate's? A mate's?!' she said. 'Here's your mates; they didn't know where you were either!'

'I'm twenty-two years old!' Jed bellowed at her.

'Not yet, you're not.' Jed's father was at the kitchen door. 'Talk to your mother like that and you'll see the back of my hand.'

Jed rolled his eyes. Davie Foster was all talk and no trousers.

'You'll neither work nor want,' Davie said, finger pointing.

'Like you can talk,' muttered Jed.

'That's enough!' Betty snapped.

Frankie had started to shuffle and cough with embarrassment, and Tommy jerked his head towards the front door, Frankie more than happy to take his leave.

'The Crown, tonight,' Tommy murmured as he opened the door to let Frankie out. Even without the cash or the drugs, he'd have to try to get some sort of do off the ground, even if it was a shit one that would make enough money to pay back Paul Smart with interest. Perhaps then he'd get away with a duffing-up rather than bullets through his kneecaps.

When he closed the door, he heard Betty's stern voice, 'You two, in here.' She marched into the living room, now cleared of the mucky sheets, Tommy following, and Jed reluctantly bringing up the rear.

A minute later, the two friends sat eyeing each other across the living room in a simmering, resentful silence.

'I'll bang your bliddy heads together,' Betty scolded. 'Like a couple of bairns, the two of you.'

Jed scowled. 'Mam, just leave it, will you?'

'Don't you "mam" me. Now tell me what's so bad that two best friends can't even talk to each other?' She looked from one to the other. 'Money? Girls?'

Tommy watched Jed turn his head and stick his nose in the air, a gesture he usually reserved for toffs and wankers.

'That's all men fall out about, money and girls,' Betty said, 'unless it's their mothers, and yours is dead and you couldn't care less about yours.'

Jed was ignoring her.

'Money, then,' she said. 'How much do you need?'

Tommy hung his head, cowering under Betty's disappointed stare.

'More than you've got,' said Jed with a sniff. 'And anyhow, it's not just money.'

'I took out a loan,' Tommy mumbled.

The shake of Betty's head was regretful, her sigh laboured and sad. 'There's only one person you'd borrow money from round here.'

'Dickhead,' said Jed under his breath.

'That's enough from you,' warned Betty. 'You've got no idea how important your friends are. You'd know about it if one of you wasn't here anymore.' Her voice wavered, but she composed herself quickly as Tommy met her eyes. 'How much?' she asked again.

Jed glared at Tommy with a slight shake of the head. *Don't you dare.*

'Two grand would do it,' said Tommy with a glimmer of hope. Maybe Betty had a small fortune stashed away.

But Betty looked stunned, her mouth falling open then closing again, swallowing the hope in one big gulp. 'Oh my Lord, you stupid bugger.' She put a hand to her heart. 'Your mother would be turning in her grave, God love her.'

Tommy's head dropped once more.

'It'll be for one of these acid-house parties, is it?' said Betty.

Jed turned down the sides of his mouth and glanced at Tommy with surprised puzzlement, hiding a grin at the peculiarity of the words coming from Betty's mouth.

'I wasn't born yesterday. We were young once too, you know.' She pointed a finger at her son. 'And if there's a solution, two heads are better than one, and that's a fact.'

Tommy heard what he hoped was a sigh of agreement from Jed.

'I've got a hundred pounds put by for an emergency if you need it,' Betty said. 'And you.' She was still pointing at Jed. 'You don't abandon your friends when they need you the most. That's not how we brought you up.'

With that, Betty got to her feet and left the room, leaving only her lily of the valley scent behind.

It was Tommy who broke the silence. 'Where were you?'

Jed drummed his fingers on the arm of the chair and sniffed again. 'Shona's.'

'Shit. You're in love.'

'No, I'm not.'

'Yes, you fucking are.'

There was a pause as the accord settled, then Jed scrunched up his face. 'Nah,' he said. 'She's got bairns.' He folded his arms, satisfied with his decision.

'So?' said Tommy. 'What's that got to do with the price of fish?'

Jed didn't have an answer and his face settled in displeasure at not winning the point while Tommy sighed, all this talk of love leaving him feeling empty and alone.

'I think Sam's left me,' he said.

'Good.'

'You don't mean that.'

'I fucking do, you're a prick. I hope she gave you that.' Jed nodded at the bruise on Tommy's face.

'Aye,' said Tommy. 'Sorry, pal.'

'Hm.' Jed pursed his lips in a pout, and Tommy knew from experience he'd have to apologise at least three times before forgiveness came. And so, he did, four times to be exact, each one batted back with an insult before Jed held out a hand for Tommy to shake, his thumb quickly springing to his nose and fingers wiggling; their usual expression of bygones.

The gesture brought blessed relief. 'There's something I need to do,' said Tommy. 'Will you come with me?'

Jed looked at him and frowned with something akin to horror. 'I'm not going anywhere with you dressed like that, sunshine.' he said.

PEACH

The evidence bags from the search of Tommy's house lay scattered around him awaiting bagging and indexing, but with half the station's personnel in a riot briefing and the other half policing some demonstration in town, the station was agreeably quiet.

The search had turned up nothing. It was a disaster. There hadn't been time, and a new warrant would be out of the question; the potential disturbance a further arrest might trigger would be first and foremost in the brass's minds. The publicity would be too damaging; the politicians would be up in arms.

He pulled one of the evidence bags towards him and turned it over in his hands. Inside was a videocassette, its sleeve void of any information other than its Japanese manufacturer. He manoeuvred the video inside the transparent bag, so he could see the spine. He peered down at the writing: *"Tommy's Rave."*

He put the bag to one side and noticed a large, black portfolio resting against his desk. He looked at it with uncertainty before lifting it onto his lap. Opening it, he reached inside and drew out a sketch pad. He flipped it open: a striking scene from an alien invasion was drawn with fine detail in grey pencil, splinters of light bouncing off the roofs and gardens of every-day terraced houses, huddles of miniature people in the street, some staring up in awe, some running for their lives. In the foreground, a teenage boy's profile stared up at the ship, his hand outstretched. Seeing Tommy's face sickened him, and he threw the sketch pad to the floor.

He reached out for the evidence bag he'd put aside and tore it open, pulling out the videocassette and striding towards the VCR that still sat on the table, the building society tapes lying idly by its side. He switched on the TV and slid the cassette into the mouth of the machine.

A black and white fuzz filled the screen, but the image soon cleared and booming, rhythmic music hit his ears. The screen was awash with colour that cut through the smoky haze with laser fingers. The camera scanned over the tops of jerking heads and raised hands, moving forward and zooming in on the stage. Swirls, splashes, and shapes of all colours and sizes flashed across a screen at the back of the stage, dwarfing the silhouetted bodies that bounced and coiled, dancing as if it were beyond their control.

Captivated, he stood for several minutes, watching with a mixture of repulsion and curiosity as hundreds of bodies moved in a way that made no sense at all, until the lens rotated away from the stage and into the crowd, the white lights flickering so fast the dancers appeared to move in fitful bursts. Then the camera zoomed out and refocused, and Peach stood paralysed, blood draining from his face.

She was unaware of the camera, dancing slowly and sublimely, eyes closed, the long white dress hanging from her bare shoulder. White ribbons and feathers swayed in her blond hair, crimped and frizzed into a halo of light. Her face was blanched, her lips red, smiling faintly: an exquisite, heavenly smile. People danced around her, their jolting movements in contrast to her slow, unworried gestures. He scoured the scene, looking for any man of the right age who could profess to be her father. But Sally was alone, in her own secret world.

The camera stayed on her as if the person holding it was as mesmerised as him. Could it be him, the father, holding the camera? Or Tommy? But then Tommy was in the frame, the palm of his hand covering the lens and the black and white fuzz filled the screen once more.

Peach lurched towards the television, grasping its sides, shaking it as if the answer to his question would fall from the screen and onto the floor.

But he knew it was futile. He knew there was only one person who could help him with the identity of this man, and he was pretty sure she would be able to talk by now.

***

Only a couple of reporters remained outside the hospital, looking bored, probably the newbies desperate for their big break. The rest would be writing up other stories, Sally's recovery no longer saleable news.

'*Detective Inspector!*' They were in his face as soon as they spotted him.

'*Chief* Inspector,' he corrected them, and they fell away in disappointment as the hospital doors slid closed behind him.

Inside, he was greeted by the porter, an old military type with a turban, tattoos, and white chest hair curling from the neck of his green shirt. Other staff smiled or nodded a greeting at him, and he realised he would miss coming here every day where he was greeted with an acceptable level of solemnity.

Pamela had had her hair done, he noticed. It shone, soft curls resting on the collar of her nurse's dress, the roots gone, the frizz under control. Kathleen had always wanted him to notice when she'd had her hair done, and he did notice, he just hadn't cared to tell her every Friday for seventeen years. It hadn't mattered to him what her hair looked like. She had hair, and it was nice, what else was there to say about it?

She'd stopped getting her hair done on a Friday, and eventually it thinned so much she looked like a cancer victim. He'd wished, then, that she would go back to Maureen's salon every week and he would have happily told her it was wonderful. But she didn't, and he hadn't. He didn't say anything to Pamela now either, but he knew, even from the back, that it looked far nicer than before. Sally's hair, on the other hand, rested limply on her shoulders, a little mound of it sticking up at the back of her head in a tuft.

As he stood at the edge of the cubicle, he watched Pamela wipe Sally's face with a tissue, issuing *"there, theres"* in a soft voice. Turning when she heard Peach clear his throat, the nurse smiled, and he found his lips turning up at the edges without thinking.

Pamela patted Sally's hand, rose from the bed, and indicated the curtain with her head. Peach followed her into the corridor, and Pamela closed the curtain, speaking in a hushed voice. 'She's grieving, Mr Peach,' she said.

He was about to tell her she should call him Mike, but realised he'd be expected to call her Pamela rather than "nurse," and he wasn't too sure about that.

'You both need to grieve,' she was saying, her forehead sunk in sympathy.

Sally had clearly unburdened herself, told Pamela the whole story. But Peach had already done his grieving, in private, keeping strong for Sally, not wanting her to suffer any more than she had already. And it had worked – Sally had got on with her life once the grief of Finnegan's encounter with the bin-man's wheels was over; she'd grown up, blossomed, or so he thought.

'She needs a father,' he said, 'not some blubbing idiot.'

Pamela laughed a little, slapped him gently on the arm. 'She needs a role model, stupid, not a hero.' It wasn't a chastisement, just a statement of fact. 'Go easy on her,' she said, sliding the curtain open. 'Tea?'

'Strong, two—'

'Yes, yes, I know,' said Pamela, and she strode off down the ward towards the nurses' station.

***

Sally's eyes and nose were red with crying.

'How you feeling?' Peach asked, sitting on the bed.

Sally nodded. 'Bit better.'

'Can we talk? It's important.'

She nodded again, sitting up a little straighter. She was so pale, her eyes looked greener than ever; Kathleen's sunken eyes looking right back at him.

'I've been trying all week to find out who did this to you,' he said.

'Nobody did anything to me.'

The confident response was unexpected. 'Listen—'

'I knew what I was doing, Dad, I'm not twelve.'

Sighing, he paused, rubbing his chin in thought and looking at her carefully as he took Tommy's photograph from his jacket pocket and held it up.

'Do you know who this is?'

'Tommy. He's a legend.'

'He's a drug dealer.'

'No, he's not,' Sally said with a laugh which soon faded when she saw the gravity of her father's expression.

Putting the photograph onto the bed, he put his hand on hers. She was young, naïve, didn't know that wolves could dress in sheep's clothing.

He tightened his grasp. 'I know he gave them to you.'

'What?' She was hesitating, unsure what he knew and what he didn't, hedging her bets.

His hand was in his pocket again and he held up the seal bag with the small blue pills inside. 'Where did you get them?' he asked, and when she looked away, he took her chin in his hand, forcing her to look at him. 'Where?'

'A friend,' she blurted.

His eyes cut into her. 'Now is not the time to lie to me.'

'I'm not lying!'

He half stood and dug into his trouser pocket, pulling out the "*Little Raver!*" card. He opened it, showing her the message inside. 'Who is he?'

Sally stared at it, shook her head, a burst of fear making her face redden.

'Sally,' he kept his voice calm and even. 'Who did you take to the school with you?'

She gulped, a small whine emitting from her throat as Peach held up Tommy's photograph again.

'It wasn't him,' she said. 'I don't even know him.' She looked at her father with pleading eyes, but he carried on; he had to know, grief or no grief.

'But Tommy knows who he is, this "*Dad*" person,' he said. 'The two of them are using girls like you to do their dirty business.'

Her face fell with distress, and the words came flooding out. 'I don't know his name, I swear. He just said …' She began to cry. 'It was Selina, Dad, she started it.'

She wasn't wriggling out of this one. 'Started what?'

'He said we could have a free drink, jobs and stuff. That we didn't need to waste our time at school, and we could earn loads of money working for him.'

'Working?'

'Selling stuff.' Her breath came in short bursts. 'He said Tommy's bouncers wouldn't look at us twice. They could search your bag and your pockets, but they couldn't search your body, not if you were a young lass.'

Peach's chin fell to his chest as he listened to her confession.

'If we sold everything in two hours, we could have some for free and we'd get fifty quid. He said next time it would be a hundred, then three hundred if we were good at it.'

'And you agreed?' The tone was angry, and he regretted it the minute it came out of his mouth. It was as if he could never just shut up and listen; always on the opposing side, always trying to trip people up. It was his job. It was how he operated. But now Sally was scared and vulnerable. How could he have thought she was simply becoming independent, leading her own life? She was *sixteen*.

'I'm sorry, Dad, I didn't mean it, but I hate that school, and I didn't want to tell you.' Fresh tears came, and she started to sob. 'I hate it, I hate it!' she cried.

Letting her head fall against his chest, he stroked her hair until she'd calmed down and was able to sit back against her pillow again. He handed her a tissue from the box on the cabinet and she blew her nose, long and loud.

'Okay,' he said. 'Think. Did you ever hear his name?'

'Just called himself *"Dad,"*' Sally said.

Peach nodded; he knew this already. 'What does he look like?'

Sally shrugged. 'Old,' she said, sniffling and wiping at her nose. 'Not as old as you.'

Peach stifled a smile, despite himself. *From the mouths of babes.*

'His hair was brownish, kind of bushy.' Sally lifted her hands to the sides of her head to illustrate. 'Little glasses, old-fashioned ones.'

There was some relief in the fact that it wasn't Paul Smart, a man that had sat under his nose less than twenty-four hours ago. But he'd known that, in his heart. Smart had some standing in the community, a reputation of sorts. Exploiting young girls wasn't his style.

'Was he ever with anyone else?' Peach could see that Sally was tiring, but he kept on; he was running out of time.

'No,' Sally gulped back tears. 'It was just him.'

Peach held up Tommy's photograph. 'Think again,' he said. 'Have you ever seen the two of them together?'

Sally closed her eyes, forcing tears down her cheeks. She nodded her head grudgingly. 'But, he's all right, Tommy.'

'He's not all right,' said Peach. 'He's anything but all right.'

'Oh my God,' Sally sobbed.

'Come here.' Peach drew her into his arms again, kissing the top of her head. 'None of this is your fault,' he said. 'No one's blaming you.'

'You are,' she hiccupped. 'I bet mam wouldn't.'

'I'm not, and your mam blamed everyone for everything.' It came out like a fond memory, rather than an attack on her character, but still, he awaited Sally's rebuke. Instead, he felt her chuckle in his arms.

'She did, didn't she?' she said, pulling away from him, wiping her eyes. 'I didn't like him, Dad,' she said. 'Not Tommy, the other one. He got sort of … mean.'

Peach swallowed, the question that needed to be asked climbing reluctantly up his throat. He dreaded it, holding her at arm's length before he allowed the words to come out. 'Did he …?' He couldn't finish the sentence.

Sally's face turned from sad to horrified. 'No!' she said. 'God, Dad!'

'All right, all right.' He held up his hands in submission, feeling the question sliding back down his throat with relief. He had a description at least, something he could go on.

'Everything okay?' Pamela had made a re-appearance with the tea, and Peach fought to suppress the rising fury that made him want to pull the bushy, brownish hair from the man's head with his bare hands when he found him.

'I need to go,' he said, getting to his feet.

'But ...' The disappointment in Pamela's voice surprised him, so he took the tea from her, finishing it in a few gulps despite its stinging heat.

He handed the empty cup back to her. 'Nice hair,' he said, and left the cubicle.

TOMMY

Durham was a city known for its spectacular beauty unless you were spending time there at Her Majesty's pleasure. The waiting area was a surprisingly bright room considering, but Tommy's nerves were jangling like pennies in a jar. They'd been through security, frisked to within an inch of their lives, Jed glaring down at the guard when his hands wandered too close to his balls.

Tommy wiped his palms down denimed thighs; they hadn't been called, and only half an hour remained of visiting time. Staring down at the grey linoleum, he listened to the echoing sounds of clanging doors and voices from the corridor. His heart thrummed in his chest. He hadn't seen his father since the day DCI Peach had hauled him down the path five years ago. Tommy was in no doubt that Reggie was guilty, not only of his crime, but for his mother's despair and ultimate demise, for Trevor Logan's descent into drugs and crime. But something niggled, and he needed to know what contribution Paul Smart had made to the collapse of his family. It hadn't been perfect, but it was his, and it had been swept from under his feet in a matter of months.

When the call eventually came, Tommy jumped to his feet and followed the guard, Jed tight by his side. They were led into a yawning hall, prison guards lining the walls and pacing between the tables as if invigilating an exam.

'Table twenty-three,' said a chunky female guard pointing to one of tables set out like dominoes. Tommy followed the direction of her finger, not recognising anyone in that general direction, but Jed was already striding over to the table and Tommy had to run to catch up. Only when he was stood by the table did Tommy recognise the once handsome face of his father.

'Son,' Reggie said.

Two spots of heat ignited Tommy's cheeks while Jed's eyes, like Tommy's, stared unblinking at the ravaged face before them.

'What happened to you?' Reggie nodded up at Tommy's bruised face.

'Should see the other fella,' said Jed when Tommy's reply didn't materialise. It was one of Reggie's favourite punch lines, but it didn't crack a smile this time.

Jed sat down, and Tommy blinked with disbelief at the shadow of a man before him. Thick red lines ran from the bridge of his nose beneath cheekbones which sunk into a mouth now void of teeth. Aged and skeletal, his hands and face were raw, broken veins littering the skin like thorny scratches, his hair, once quaffed into a perfect Teddy Boy curl, hanging thin and grey to his shoulders.

Tommy felt Jed's hand on his arm and he sunk slowly onto the chair next to him.

The lack of teeth made Reggie's voice whistle and lisp. 'I was sorry about ya mam, son. I miss her every day.'

Shame he hadn't thought of that while he pointed a gun at Billy Logan. Shame he hadn't bothered coming to the funeral. Tommy knew he had the authorisation, but still he'd stayed away.

'Didn't think anyone would want me at the burial,' Reggie said. 'I had me own private do in me cell.'

'She was cremated,' said Tommy, finding his voice.

Reggie just looked at him, his irises starting to fade at the edges like an old tortoise. He wiped his mouth with the back of a tremulous hand and sat back into his chair, his head almost colliding with that of the baseball-capped visitor behind him.

'Well, this is very nice, son.' Reggie attempted a smile. 'What are you here for?'

The words in Tommy's throat were wedged in, and Jed filled the void once more, his voice bordering on fondness. 'How are you, Uncle Reg?' he asked.

'Oh, never better,' Reggie replied. 'Living the life.' There was nothing funny about the irony.

'Paul Smart,' Tommy blurted out. Only ten minutes left of visiting time; might as well get to the point.

Reggie's face turned to steel as he leant forward and growled, 'Keep your bloody voice down.'

Tommy moved towards him, teeth gritted. 'What did he do?'

Glancing to his side, Reggie crept further forward on his chair, his nose almost touching Tommy's, breath rancid. 'Nothing I can't handle. Now let's say no more about it.'

Tommy fizzed inside. 'You owe me—'

'I said, no more.' The finger Reggie held up shook – with rage or fear Tommy couldn't tell.

Reggie blinked his eyes away from his son towards Jed. 'How's the family?' His voice was suddenly loud and jaunty, but Tommy could see the tension in his face and body. 'Betty and Davie, and the young 'un?'

'Champion, aye,' replied Jed.

Tommy looked away, laughing to himself to halt the tears that threatened. He wasn't going to get answers, not from this man, but he'd find out somehow, even if it meant asking Smartie himself once Trevor Logan was safely back inside a cell and wouldn't become Tucker's new target. The smell of sweat and plastic food made his stomach churn. This place was the pits and Reggie deserved every inch of it. Why Trevor would want to come back was beyond him. But when looked back at his father, he thought he saw genuine concern.

'Are you in trouble, son?' Reggie asked, almost inaudibly. He extended a hand and Tommy drew away from it as if it were a lit flame. If Reggie wouldn't tell him about Paul Smart, at least he could enlighten him on another matter.

'I want to find my brother,' said Tommy, and he watched his father's shoulders fall, felt Jed's eyes on the side of his face. 'Do you where he is?'

Reggie pursed his lips, eyes flitting to Jed who sat stiffly.

'I need him,' said Tommy, hearing the desperation in his voice and feeling Jed's elbow nudge him.

'You've got me,' Jed muttered, 'and Frankie, and—'

'It's not the same,' said Tommy, knowing it would hurt Jed, but unable to keep quiet any longer. And it wasn't; it wasn't the same. 'Well?' he asked Reggie.

Reggie thought for a long while before saying, 'Maybe if you come back another time …'

The provocation was like a punch to the gut, and Tommy sprung from his chair, Reggie's hands reaching out towards his son, grabbing at the air as Tommy leant away from his father's outstretched arms.

'Stay a bit, howay.' Reggie's eyes were desperate. 'Gerald, tell him to stay.'

Jed's hand reached up to pull Tommy back down into the chair, but Tommy resisted, a finger pointing down at his father.

'Do you know what you did?' He raised his voice, not caring who heard. 'Are you even a bit fucking sorry?'

Reggie's fingers clawed at his lips, as if he wanted to speak out but couldn't. 'Sit down, son,' he said.

But it was too late; two guards were at Tommy's side and Jed was attempting to appease them.

'Your brother's looking out for you, son,' said Reggie, 'and all this is getting sorted, I promise you that.'

The chair behind him came slamming backwards, throwing Reggie forward.

'Time to go,' said one of the guards.

'He's here?!' Tommy was being pulled away, and Reggie was getting to his feet, flanked by two more guards who had their hands under his armpits.

As Tommy was dragged reluctantly backwards, a familiar cough drew his eyes towards the visitor sitting behind his father. The baseball cap was pulled down low over his face, but the gaunt profile was unmistakable.

Trevor Logan.

Reggie's eyes warned Tommy to say nothing. 'Nice to see you, lads,' he said as he was led away.

PEACH

'Durham, boss.'

Murphy had said it twice already, but he'd been unable to breach the DCI's thoughts.

Peach heard the click of Murphy's fingers in front of his eyes, heard him say that Tommy Collins and Jed Foster had boarded a bus at ten-thirty that morning. He tried to clear his clouded mind and concentrate on his sergeant who ate chips from newspaper, popping them into his mouth in quick succession. 'And you didn't follow them?' he asked.

'Undercover tonight, boss, don't want them recognising me.'

He sensed no hint of judgement or criticism in Murphy's voice, even though he'd royally messed up the night before. Normally there would be a raft of bitching and talking behind hands, an assignment of blame. 'Think it might be a bit late for that,' he said. 'I told you to stay in the car.'

'I saved your life, chief, you should be grateful.'

The titters of the other detectives were badly stifled, and Peach glowered at them, unsure whether they were sniggering at Murphy's exaggerations or the fact their DCI might show gratitude.

'Been onto the prison, though,' said Murphy. 'And guess what?' He handed over a smooth white roll of fax paper, a copy of entries into the visitor's book at Durham prison that morning – and there they were: Tommy Collins and Gerald Foster, the ink slightly smudged by Murphy's greasy fingers.

'The lad can visit his father,' said Peach.

'That's just it, boss, he never has before.' Shoving the last two chips into his mouth, Murphy scrunched the newspaper into a ball and lobbed it across the room into the bin, grabbing at the air with a '*Yesss!*' as it fell neatly inside.

Peach's eyes scoured the list where another name caught his eye, but the fax machine had cut off the name of the visitee. It piqued his interest. 'Find out who Trevor Logan was visiting,' he said, handing the fax paper back to Murphy and heading for the door. 'And see who else has visited Collins Senior recently.'

Murphy saluted with two fingers to the temple before picking up the receiver of his desk phone. 'Oh, and chief,' he said, before dialling.

Peach stopped at the door but didn't turn back.

'I had another look at the building society. It's on your desk.'

***

In his office, Peach tried to focus on his plan of action for the rave on Saturday night. With Collins still free, the party would go ahead. But the lad's time was limited. Just another twenty-four hours and Peach could have him just where he wanted him. And he wasn't going to mess up this time.

He ran down his list: road blocks, police dogs, riot vans, and protective gear, it all needed to be confirmed, but there was nothing else he could do until he knew the venue, and there weren't many options open to him on that score. He could wait until they knew the telephone number; it would be on the flyers, be broadcast on the illegal radio stations – easy enough to get hold of. But getting the number at the eleventh hour would mean joining the thousands of others and following the convoys of cars heading to the party. If he got there too late, the drugs would be divvied up between the dealers and too easily disposed of once their presence was known. If he knew in advance, he could time it to perfection with the right surveillance. Then the blockades could be put in place, the party shut down, the drugs seized, and the money and equipment confiscated.

Tommy Collins arrested.

But there were only two ways he could get intel on the rave's whereabouts in time: he could hope that Murphy would hear it from the horse's mouth that night when he trailed Tommy and his friends – a long shot, knowing how imperative it was to keep the venue a secret until the last minute.

Or he could do a deal with Paul Smart.

He'd never crossed that dangerous line before and he knew what it would mean for his career and his reputation should it ever come out. But maybe it was time he put his daughter first.

He opened the desk draw and picked up the business card Paul had slid into his hand. The call lasted less than ten seconds, and the meeting was set for two hours hence.

Dropping the receiver into its cradle, he breathed out his decision. Good or bad, in two hours he'd have his venue. He rubbed at his eyes, his mind wandering in circles once more, his attention back on the imposter. He wracked his brains, back through years of raids, arrests, punch-ups, and stabbings, but he could remember no one matching the description of this liar masquerading as him and recruiting young girls to do his dealing. He tried to picture him – a dealer, working for Collins to supply drugs to his wretched parties, but he could only see Paul Smart's face in his mind's eye.

He turned and faced the photographs on his wall, his fingers like pincers through his moustache. In his dogged mind, Tommy's eyes goaded him: *Catch me if you can.*

Striding over to the wall, he tore Tommy's image down and crushed it in his hand, then he reached up to the others. As he did so, his hand froze, suspended mid-air as he stared at the copied newspaper clipping of Jed Foster. Jed stood next to his brother, an arm around his shoulder. Next to Barry stood the mayor, fat and red faced, and next to him stood a pint-sized man in wire-rimmed round glasses, hair mushrooming from his head in a ball of frizz. He snatched at the picture and read the italic print beneath:

From left to right: Volunteers, Jed Foster, 21, Barry Foster, 15, Mayor Springfield, Newcastle
City Council, and youth worker, Darren Adams-Deighton.

***

It had taken forty-five minutes to drive the four miles to the youth worker's home. The traffic through the city centre was dense, a procession of fluorescent yellow jackets cordoning off the entrance to Pilgrim Street. Two mounted police officers had cast a dark shadow over Peach's car as he waited, lungs deflated with impatience. At the traffic lights up ahead, streams of people were marching by, banners and arms aloft, chanting. It seemed that every other day there was something to protest about: poll tax, nuclear disarmament. *Gay rights.*

Desperate to get moving, he'd switched on the car's police lights, and in less than five seconds the fist of a middle-aged woman with purple dreadlocks and bad teeth was bouncing off the windscreen.

'*Fucking filth!*' she'd screeched. '*Fucking bastard Tory cunts!*'

Peach had to stop himself leaping from the car and pulling her head back by her stinking hair. Instead, as spit hit the windscreen, he'd turned his face away, the horses snorting and staggering beside the car, but maintaining more dignity than this mob ever could. His eyes were focused on the footwell, and he'd noticed the edge of a plastic carrier bag protruding from beneath the seat – the takings from Tommy's rave. He was bending down to retrieve it when he heard the car horns blasting behind him. The traffic was on the move and he'd soon caught up with the car ahead of him, his mind back on the man who had relieved his child of her education.

Darren Adams-Deighton had been arrested only once before, back in the late seventies on a charge of possessing marijuana and LSD. Murphy had pressed a few keys on the computer which had produced as much information as Peach had needed in a matter of minutes. Maybe these machines had their uses after all. In his mug-shot, Darren was bearded and rake thin but had the same full head of spongy hair.

By two o'clock, Peach was standing outside Darren's home. It was a typical ground-floor Tyneside flat in Jesmond, a leafy part of the city prone to invasion by university students with affluent parents. The flat wasn't plush, but it wasn't a hovel either. It would take more than a part-time youth worker's salary to afford the rent in this part of town.

Peach bent down and opened the letter box, the stench of cannabis hitting his nose. Straightening up, he rapped the knocker, then grasped the door frames with his hands, ready to kick out as soon as the Yale lock sprung. It took a few hammerings, but spring it did, and Darren sprawled backwards as the door hit his face.

Without taking time to look at his assailant, the youth worker was quickly on his hands and knees, crawling down the hallway. *'Help! Police!'* he wailed.

Stepping inside, Peach kicked out again and Darren fell forward, prostrate on the floor, his hands covering the back of his head as if he were expecting blows. Peach placed his feet either side of him, crouching down onto all fours, bending over Darren's back as the little worm writhed, continuing to screech, *'Police! Police!'*.

He put his lips to Darren's ear, forcing his face into the floor. 'I am the police.' It was a line he'd always wanted to use, but he took no pleasure in it now.

'Wha …?' Darren couldn't get anything else out, his lips contorted as Peach pushed his face harder into the carpet.

'Do you know who I am?' Peach hissed. Gurgles was all he heard in response, and he turned Darren over, pinning his arms to the floor with his knees. Without his glasses, Darren's eyes were beady and a little crossed, flickering feverishly like the wings of a moth as recognition flashed in his dilated pupils. Peach's fingers grasped his throat. 'Who am I?!'

'That copper,' Darren rasped.

His fingers tightened around Darren's thin neck. 'And Sally Peach's father.'

Liquid was starting to force its way from Darren's eyes and down his temples, and Peach thought he heard an apology, a strangled, '*I'm sorry!*'

Darren's hands had been raking at his legs, but they started to fall away as he weakened, face crimson, teeth clenched. Lost in his need to cause maximum pain to the mongrel beneath him, Peach kept on squeezing until he felt something soft brush his hand, heard the soft purring of the ginger cat that rubbed its cheek against Darren's face. The animal trilled gently, its face now rubbing at Peach's fingers. He snapped his hand away from it, Darren gulping at the air before trying to speak.

'I didn't know,' he coughed, terrified, wretched. 'I didn't know who she was!'

Leaning down, Peach put his face next to Darren's burning cheek. 'Doesn't matter who she is,' he said. 'She's sixteen years old.'

Out of nowhere, Darren began to sob like a child, the snot and tears merging into a stream of salty slime. 'I don't want to die!' he cried.

If it was meant to evoke sympathy, the man had got Peach all wrong, because sympathy for criminals wasn't something he'd ever had the misfortune of feeling.

He put his fingers around Darren's throat once more. 'You'll die right now if you don't tell me everything.'

***

None of it was his idea, Darren insisted, targeting the vulnerable ones, the ones in care, the ones from troubled families. The horrible fact that Sally fitted into any of these categories stuck like a leech to Peach's gullet.

They sat in Darren's living room, their backsides perched on the edge of a sofa laden with cat hair, another black and white moggy curled up on an armchair, probably stoned off its furry head. Darren wrung his hands, the embodiment of a blubbering coward.

'The drugs,' said Peach. 'Where are they going tomorrow night?'

Darren looked back at him as if he was unsure what he should and shouldn't say. 'I don't know, Mr Peach,' he said. 'Honest. I just do what I'm told.'

'Liar,' Peach snarled.

The youth worker was shaking. 'I don't!' he insisted. 'He doesn't tell me anything, I promise.' His face took on an expression of extreme alarm. 'You're not going to torture me, are you?' He gulped at the end of the sentence, his hand shooting to his bruised throat.

'Don't be so bloody stupid,' said Peach.

Darren breathed a sigh of relief, his eyes closing.

'But you *are* going to tell me everything you know,' said Peach. 'Where he stores the drugs, where the money's come from, where the rave is.'

Darren's face puckered as he swallowed. He didn't know, he

stammered. He didn't know anything about the rave's whereabouts.

Peach had expected someone bullish, a shrewd operator with attitude and cheek, but instead, the man sitting next to him was a great yellow chicken who was ripe for a roasting.

He pushed out his lips in a thoughtful pout. 'Do you know what happens to rapists and perverts in prison?'

Darren shook his head. 'I didn't ... I wouldn't ...'

'That's not what my daughter tells me,' Peach lied. 'And there are others. Other girls who'll corroborate her story.'

'They're lying!' shrieked Darren. 'I didn't do anything like that!'

'Your word against theirs. Nice middle-class girls from good families. *Police* families.'

Darren's lips quivered. He wiped at his mouth, then sat up straight, eyes wide with fright. 'I want witness protection,' he demanded.

'Witness to what, exactly?' Peach waited; he had one hour to wait for Darren to grass on Tommy and give him the venue of the rave. Then there would be no need to compromise himself with Paul Smart.

Jesus Christ!' It came out of Darren's mouth like a mosquito's whine.

'Tell me what you know, then we'll talk about protection.'

Darren looked down at his hands, gritted his teeth. 'Fucking Tommy ...' he said.

Peach felt his muscles ease as Darren took a deep breath, then began to talk.

Paul Smart was trying to build up a new enterprise, Darren said. Paul had wanted to start small, test the market, so he'd put some of his men into Tommy's raves to sell ecstasy and coke. But the men couldn't get past Tommy's bouncers, so he'd had to think of a new approach, and the only way they could get the drugs in the door was to recruit the ravers themselves. Most of them refused, but there were some that were up for making a few extra quid.

Peach listened, feeling his insides start to roll. *Smart?*

Then an offer came along Paul couldn't refuse, Darren said, and he'd sunk everything he had into a consignment of ecstasy.

Peach held up his hands. 'Wait. You work for Smart?'

Darren's eyes darted around him. 'Yes,' he said, as if stating the obvious.

Peach found his eyes closing, and the story went from bad to worse. Smart had given Tommy a loan, Darren said, but when Tommy needed more, he gave him drugs instead of cash. Darren's voice had begun to turn bitter. It was profit that would normally have been his, by rights. He'd worked for Paul for years on the hush-hush; Paul trusted him, and he deserved some loyalty, right?

'Tommy can't sell drugs,' he heard Darren sneer. 'He hasn't even got rid of them yet. Even came to me, asking if I could find him a buyer, the daft twat. And when I say Smartie sunk everything, I mean *everything*. If Tommy doesn't raise that cash, there won't be any rave.'

And without the rave, thought Peach, Paul Smart wouldn't be able to sell his drugs.

Disgust churned like rancid milk in his stomach as he opened his eyes and focused on Darren. 'And what will Smart do if there is no rave?'

Darren wrung his hands, but there was little sympathy in his voice. 'Knowing Smartie, he'll go for Tommy's wife first. He's a cruel bastard.' He shook his head. 'She's his niece an'all. Nice lass.'

Peach held Darren's gaze, his eyes revealing his uncertainty.

'Smartie's big sister is Sam's mother,' Darren explained. 'Now there's a bitch if ever there was one.'

A sharp sigh escaped Peach's nostrils, and he thought back to Denise Morris' face, seeing the resemblance for the first time – the eyes, cold and blue, the wide set of the mouth. 'And Collins has nothing to do with him?'

'Not 'till recently,' said Darren. 'Not 'till he got some mad idea that he could actually get out of Valley Park unscathed.' Darren laughed to himself. 'Always been a dreamer that one. Hates dealers though. If you knew what I had to do to get that gear past him into those raves …' His voice trailed off, his smirk fading. Realising his mistake, he looked away, had a think, then put on his begging face and held out his wrists. 'If I'm going into witness protection, I'd rather it looked like I was getting arrested.'

Peach stared down at the youth worker's upturned wrists, the blue veins standing out like a river delta. But Peach remained stock still, the chill of clarity fully descended.

He'd got it wrong. He'd got it horribly wrong.

His gaze sliced through Darren's gutless stare, and he saw panic flash in the youth worker's eyes when the cuffs didn't materialise.

'There's more,' said Darren, inching forward. 'Billy Logan.' He stopped, glancing at Peach's coat pocket, waiting for the metal to snap around his outstretched wrists. 'He worked for Smartie. Collected money when he was out in the fish van. Thought he'd ask for a bit extra from the customers and pocket it, but Smartie got wind of it, made an example of him.'

Peach didn't move, and Darren's panic was making his voice gallop.

'Made Tommy's dad kill him.' Darren thrust his wrists further forward, so they touched Peach's chest. 'I'm the only one who knows, he trusts me, see?'

'Why did Reggie do it?' Peach urged him on and Darren

swallowed a whimper – he'd gone too far now to stop.

'Reggie owed Smartie ten grand, maybe more, and Smartie said he'd do the wife, and Tommy an'all, if Reggie didn't do it. So he did. Shot Billy dead and Smartie forgot the debt.'

Peach had known it, had known there was more to it, but no one would talk, their loyalties all to pot, his own distress at Kathleen's death six months earlier still overpowering his instinct to dig deeper.

'It's true. Every word,' Darren said.

'Where's the rave?' Peach asked.

'I don't know, I swear!'

'Doesn't trust you that much, then,' said Peach.

Darren shrugged, attempting a friendly smile as he swallowed down his cowardly fear and pushed his wrists into Peach's chest. 'I'm ready to go when you are.'

Peach looked from one of the youth worker's hopeful eyes to the other as he faced another decision. Protect Darren, or let him squirm? The picture of Sally that made the county listen burnt into his memory, and it didn't take him long to choose.

'Over my dead body.'

Peach stood, walked out of the flat, and left Darren just where he was. A sitting duck.

DENISE

The hangover was proving stalwart, and she popped another Polo mint into her mouth – anything to rid her tongue of the horse shit that seemed to have taken up residence there.

Sam was at the window, biting her nails and pacing back and forth, forcing Denise's head into a spinning mire. A night of drinking alone in the dark hadn't been the plan, and she worried the mixture of Tia Maria and vodka might regurgitate itself onto the new sheepskin rug at any moment. She knew her daughter well enough to know that she hadn't really left her husband; that this was just a warning shot, one Denise herself had used far too often with her own husband for it to have made any difference in the end.

As she watched Sam move from one end of the window to the other, she cursed Tommy Collins. She cursed the gobshite who'd given birth to him and the murderer who'd put his seed in her. She cursed Valley Park and the idiots who had burnt down that house last night, alighting renewed fear in her child for a man who was no good for her.

The night before, Sam had curled herself into a ball, listening vacantly to Denise's assertions that it was all bullshit, that Tommy would never amount to anything, that Sam had been duped just like she herself had been duped many times before. It was a rare thing indeed, she'd said, that a man came along who was of any value.

Sam had looked up at her with eyes on the verge of fret, then taken herself off to bed without a word, only to come running back down the stairs again when she heard the sirens and the helicopter and saw the flames in the distance. Sam had run out of the house in her slippers, sprinted across the estate to Holly Drive, only to be forced back by the police. She'd come back in tears and fallen asleep on the sofa, anxious fingers still in her mouth. The next thing Denise knew she was sitting at the kitchen table in the dark, the vodka finished and another empty bottle in the bin. The rest was oblivion. She'd managed to get herself to bed somehow, and the phone had woken her at nine-thirty that morning. She'd staggered downstairs to find Ashleigh playing on the floor with a coaster, and Sam clutching the telephone receiver with a smile of relief on her face. Tommy was safe. More was the pity.

But now Sam was agitated. Tommy had told her to stay put, not to come to the house under any circumstances, that he would be around later to explain everything.

'What's he going to explain?' Sam was asking as she paced. 'What's he up to?'

Denise knew exactly what he was up to, and she had a mind to tell her. She glanced at the sewing basket, the drugs still keeping the late payment demands company, and decided she would save it for later. She'd save it for when he was there, and she could produce the evidence. The element of surprise would not only humiliate Tommy but ensure Sam wouldn't be taken in by his excuses.

Denise rubbed at her temples. The afternoon was striding on and she needed to get a message to Paul to tell him to stay away, the time not yet right to tell Sam of their renewed relationship. Sam had witnessed one of Paul's outbursts several years earlier. He'd punched Denise, not once, but three times, loosening a tooth and bringing a slither of blood from her nose. It hadn't been the first time, and he'd called her things that she could hardly bear to repeat. It was as if he hadn't seen the child, even though she was right there, sitting on the floor doing a jigsaw puzzle. It was one of those times he forgot anyone else in the world existed other than his target. It was one of those times she'd seen her father's merciless face in his.

After that, he'd stayed away, refused to take her calls or answer her letters. At first, she'd imagined he was too ashamed to face her, but as time went on, and she heard how he was going up in the world, she realised that he'd simply forgotten her. It was only on her return to this shit-hole that she'd begun to hope for a reunion. Sam's insistence on moving into Tommy's house on Valley Park had been absurd, but that was what Tommy had wanted, and Sam was too blind to see the consequences. But she wouldn't leave her daughter alone in a place like this, so back she came, and that's when it started, the gnawing desire to put things right, the need to rid herself of the guilt and the sleepless nights it induced. It had occupied her mind day and night for over a year, but she'd never had the guts to instigate the first contact. It was Paul who made the first step, and that took balls.

Lost in her thoughts, Denise didn't hear the knock on the door or Sam's 'Oh my God!' until the Detective Chief Inspector was standing in her living room, staring at her, condemnation written all over his face.

'Mrs Morris,' he said.

Her blood ran cold. He was here to question her about the building society again and she scrambled her way through explanations in her fogged mind, wishing to God she'd stayed sober last night. Sam was looking from the inspector to her mother, wondering how he knew her name, no doubt, and Denise tried to hide the fear that peppered her face.

The DCI was offered a seat on the sofa which he took without question, Ashleigh crawling over to him and pulling herself up by his trouser legs, smiling, her chubby legs wobbling.

'She's lovely,' he said.

Sam's eyes were filling up. 'What's happened?' Her hands covered her ears in preparation for the answer she dreaded. Tommy was arrested, hurt, dead.

Denise, her legs as unstable as the baby's, lowered herself into the armchair, willing the return of composure and clarity of thought.

'I believe you might be in danger,' Peach said.

'How?' asked Sam.

Denise was going to throw up for sure, and she didn't hear what he said next, such was the sudden pounding in her ears, but she heard Sam's response.

'Drugs? I don't understand.'

'I think he was coerced into it, but yes,' said Peach.

Coerced? Someone was taking this inspector for a fool. Tommy had got himself mixed up with some nasty people and now her daughter was about to be collateral damage.

'My top priority is your safety if Tommy fails to do what's being asked of him,' Peach said.

Sam's voice trembled as she sat down on the sofa next to the copper. 'What will they do to him? Mam?' She turned to Denise who struggled to hide her *what-did-I-tell-you*? expression.

'Let us worry about Tommy,' Peach said. 'Do you know where this rave is happening?'

Sam shook her head, no.

'Do you know anything about a robbery?'

'What? No!'

Denise felt the pull of the knot in her stomach as the DCI's eyes turned on her.

'There may have been a misidentification,' he said.

'I don't believe it,' said Sam. 'It's just not him, he wouldn't, I swear he wouldn't.'

'Like I said, we want to make sure you're safe.'

'Who is it?' Sam asked. 'If we're going to stay safe, I need to know.'

Denise didn't realised how long she'd been holding her breath. She let the air out, relieved the conversation was being diverted away from the robbery. She waited for his answer as eagerly as Sam. As soon as she knew who it was, she would inform her brother. He'd take care of it. He'd protect them. Finally, they had a problem they could solve together.

But the inspector had a different story. 'Paul Smart,' he said, and she felt the icy cold return.

'Then I am safe,' said Sam, picking up Ashleigh and holding her to her chest. 'He wouldn't dare come around here. And Tommy wouldn't go anywhere near him.'

Denise's eyes were closed, and it was all she could do to keep the vomit down. The copper had it wrong – it was the Logans he should be worried about. The older lad had had it in for Tommy for years – a shocking family if ever there was one. But something in her – something she didn't want to acknowledge – knew her brother was more than capable.

Open, put inside, click.

'I think you'll find he's been very much near him,' said Peach.

'Jesus, Tommy,' said Sam, her face pinched with distress.

And then, as if the blinds in Denise's head were snapped opened, clarity returned. Tommy. Sam's weak point. She loved him.

Denise's legs were like springs and she was on her feet. 'We can't trust this lot, love,' she said. 'They're after our Tommy, and they'll put him away.'

Sam's brow furrowed through her pain. *Our?*

'His bairn's in hospital, remember? He thinks Tommy did it. He just wants to find him and make him pay. He wants you to turn him in. Don't trust him, Samantha.'

'Listen,' said Peach, 'as far as I know Tommy hasn't sold the drugs, but if he doesn't, and the rave tomorrow night doesn't go ahead, he's in trouble. And so are you.'

'Lies, Samantha, all lies!'

The inspector was wrong. Paul wouldn't hurt his own niece. She had to believe it, otherwise what would become of them all?

'You know Tommy wouldn't get involved in anything like that,' she said to Sam. Then she turned on Peach, eyes on fire. 'He's a nice lad, you stay away from him.'

She watched his face darken. 'Oh, really?' he said.

She knew what was coming, she'd led him right to it. But if she got in first, he wouldn't have a leg to stand on.

Out it came in a shower of lies as if she were born for it. Peach had tried to make her identify Tommy in the robbery at the building society, she said. But she hadn't; she wouldn't do that to Sam. He'd tried to force her, offered her money, but she hadn't turned up at the ID parade. She wouldn't betray Tommy like that, not when she knew how much he meant to Sam.

She watched aching perplexity spread across her daughter's face. 'I didn't want to tell you, love, you've got so much on your plate, and I thought you might not believe me.' She turned on the tears, surprising herself at her ability to do so.

'Now, hold on a minute—'

But Denise wouldn't let him speak. 'Get out of my house!' she yelled, pointing at the door. 'Go on! Out!'

'Tommy wouldn't have anything to do with him,' said Sam, putting Ashleigh back onto the floor. 'He promised me he wouldn't.' She looked to her mother for reassurance then turned back to Peach. 'You're lying,' she said.

'Mrs Collins ...' Peach was trying to appease her, but Denise was striding to the living room door.

'Go!' It came out like a dog's yelp.

'Do what she says,' said Sam, angrily. 'You're not welcome here.'

His face turning to stone, the inspector stood slowly like an old man who needed a stick. He walked towards Denise, telling her she should get her priorities right. Would she put her own child in jeopardy?

'I don't think you're in any position to give me parenting advice.'

Bam! She almost heard the words collide with his face, and she revelled in her sudden advantage. It felt good to be back in control.

'You people,' the copper said, his voice riddled with scorn. 'You'd rather die than turn in one of your own.'

With one last defeated look at Sam, the inspector left without uttering another word.

Denise drew back the net curtain and looked through the window, her heart leaping as she watched her brother locking his car door, his face surprised but relaxed as he stood at the gate and waited. But Peach opened the gate and walked past him, saying something that made Paul's face fall into an empty glare that turned to the window, his eyes resting there for a moment before he got back into his car and drove away.

Come back! Her heart pleaded. Perhaps now was the right time after all, now that she felt her daughter's loyalty once more.

'Thanks, Mam,' she heard, and she turned to see Sam's arms outstretched.

She melted into the embrace. 'Don't listen to him, love. It's got nothing to do with our Paul, he's different now.' She clung onto her daughter tighter, but she felt Sam stiffen then pull away.

'Have you seen him?'

Denise reached for her, but Sam stepped back. 'Just a couple of times,' she said, the nausea returning with a vengeance. 'He's changed, Sam.'

'Since when?'

'He's not the same, love, not now.'

'Are you mad?!'

Denise reached out again; why wouldn't she *listen?*

'Do you know what he does to people? What he did to you?' Sam was recoiling away from her, as if her mother had some sort of plague.

But she could explain. They'd put the kettle on, she said. They'd have a cuppa, and she'd tell Sam everything. She watched tears brim in her daughter's eyes.

'I don't even know who you are,' Sam said.

'He just wants his family back, love.' Denise could almost see inside her daughter's head, the battle going on within. 'He needs our help,' she insisted.

'People don't change, Mam,' said Sam, shaking her head.

Denise hovered, feeling herself on the precipice. It could go one way or the other. 'They do, love, they do.'

'That's what Tommy was looking for.' Sam looked into the distance, remembering something. 'The drugs. They've gone, and he thought I got rid of them. If he can't sell them—'

'They'll turn up, love, things always do,' Denise reassured her.

'Smarties.' Sam sank onto the sofa, then looked up at her mother. 'He called the drugs "Smarties."'

Denise hadn't made the connection, and yet there it was, staring her right in the face.

Coincidence. It had to be.

The sound of rattling had them turning their heads. Ashleigh was standing at the sewing basket, holding it open with one hand, and shaking a tube of Smarties with the other. She held the sweeties out for Sam to take, a gift that she would want back a few seconds later. Sam sprang from the sofa and grabbed the tube from Ashleigh's hand.

The precipice began to fracture, and Denise felt herself fall as Sam opened the tube's top to look inside, the sob of realisation escaping before her accusing eyes met Denise's.

'You cow,' she spat.

TOMMY

'Sorry, marra. I need the cash.'

Tommy still hadn't paid for the last lot of flyers from the printers and Macca, like the Iron Lady, was not for turning. Macca's eyes lingered sympathetically on the yellowing bruise on Tommy's face before directing his attention to his next customer.

'Howay, Macca.' Tommy blocked his line of vision. 'I'll pay you double tomorrow, I swear.'

Macca looked torn but said nothing.

'I thought we were mates,' Tommy hissed at him.

'It's not me, it's the boss,' said Macca in a hushed voice. 'I'll lose my job, man. I've got three bairns, and she's up the duff again!'

Tommy's agitation grew. 'Mate, if I've got no flyers … can I just take one box?' A small queue was forming behind him and he heard sighing and shuffling feet.

Macca's expression hardened. 'I can't, Tommy,' he said. 'Took me six months to find this job. I need the fucking cash, right?' He handed over the original flyer, looked over Tommy's shoulder and asked who was next.

Tommy left the shop and trudged through the city centre's Greenmarket. It smelt of raw meat and sawdust, echoing with the sounds of traders barking their *three punnets for fifty pence!* as the afternoon wore on and trade slowed down. He stopped at another printing shop, rickety and run down, standing at the door just as the woman inside turned the CLOSED sign over and pulled down the blind. He stepped back, almost falling over a man in a blue apron pushing a dead pig in a wheelbarrow. The stench of dead animal was making him nauseous and faint, and he headed towards the main street and blessed fresh air, obstructed every few seconds by excitable youths hanging around the piercing and tattoo stands.

Where's the rave, Tommy?

Rumours were rife that the next party was going to be as big as *Sunrise* or *Genesis*, and that Judge Jules himself would be making an appearance. The town's underground ravers were buzzing.

Jed and Frankie waited for him outside the travel agency in mutually acceptable silence. Even Frankie seemed anxious as he explained that almost every all-nighter in the region had been cancelled. Stout men with wide faces had paid visits to all known promoters and made it clear that any rival party would end in trouble. Guns had been pointed into the promoters' faces until they'd confirmed they understood. Every party-goer north of York would be heading their way on Saturday night.

That wasn't all that was heading their way. Tucker, his face a swollen mess of ugly stitching, was crossing the road and walking down the hill towards them, Terry and June straining in their studded collars, Tucker's stride about as demonic as the dogs'.

'*Fuuuuck!*' Jed still hadn't paid for the knock-off trainers.

Tucker stopped and hammered on the door of a nightclub that resembled a seedy hovel during daylight hours. Two men emerged, all chest and no neck, men Tommy recognised from the greyhound track. Perhaps they were all joining forces – a conglomerate of hard bastards trading in Tommy's misery.

After what looked like a friendly exchange of words, the door closed, and Tucker headed back down the hill in their direction.

The lads scarpered into the travel agent's and perused the shelves, one eye on the street, the other feigning interest in package holidays to the Costa del Sol. They turned their backs to the window as Tucker staggered by, and Tommy pulled a brochure down from the shelf, burying his head in it: *Majorca, and the Balearics*. He looked with wretched envy at the images of cloudless blue sky and sapphire sea, glancing sideways at the hoity-toity-looking woman in a blue neck-scarf who eyed them warily.

'It's free, you don't have to nick it,' she said, coldly.

Outside again, Tommy tucked the brochure into the back of his jeans and lit a cigarette while they all glanced around them to make sure Tucker was well out of sight. His nerves were ragged. He needed those flyers even if he had to break into the printers to get them. The rush of nicotine did nothing to ease the tension.

'On the positive side,' Jed was saying with a smile, 'with everything else cancelled, at least there's plenty personnel knocking about.'

Tommy and Frankie exchanged a glance of amusement, and Tommy nodded his agreement, not wanting to discourage this new-found optimism. Jed had already put in the calls, he said, just a matter of time.

'And hey,' Jed dug into his bag and brought out a chunky black handset about the size of Tommy's foot. 'Mobile phones,' he said, 'they're mint, look.' He passed it to Tommy who turned it over in his hands. He'd seen them on TV, on news items about yuppies and the rise of wealth he wouldn't ever get a sniff at.

'Where you supposed to put it?' Frankie had snatched the phone and was trying to shove it into one of his pockets. Not so mobile after all.

Jed retrieved the handset from Frankie and tucked it into the back of his jeans. *Ta-dah!* his free arms said.

Tommy's smile was as false as Freddie Laker's. Jed could phone all the personnel he liked, but Tommy didn't have the money to pay them, and now he had to tell Jed he didn't have the flyers either.

'Here's wor lass.' Jed was putting the phone back into his man-bag, staring up the hill towards the towering Monument of Earl Grey, where a long line of young women, headed up by Shona, were marching towards them. They were a motley crew, some dressed androgynously in baggy joggers and long T-shirts, others in skimpy skirts and tops, one or two Goths thrown in for good measure. Two things they all had in common was a rucksack thrown over their backs and white trainers with lightening streaks up the side on their feet. 'Our flyer distribution team.' Jed folded his arms and grinned like a man who loved being Jed.

Tommy gave him a thwarted look and shook his head, Jed's satisfied expression turning into a frown of disbelief. But Shona was already beckoning three of the girls forward. Marie, she said, would be responsible for Newcastle; Emma, County Durham; Lisa, Carlisle and Whitehaven. The girls chose their teams as they would a school netball squad and assembled into three eager groups while Shona stood like Cleopatra, hands clutching bangled biceps.

Tommy took Shona to one side. The team would have to wait while he tried to find another printer in the next half an hour who would do the job quickly on the promise of three of four times the payment. He found himself looking into Shona's sunflower eyes – they glittered and twirled in spellbinding flashes, a deep amber, round, and unblinking. He couldn't speak, and he felt himself float from the ground.

The click of Jed's fingers brought him back down again with an almost audible thud.

'Told you she could hypnotise anyone,' smirked Jed.

Tommy held onto Jed's arm to steady himself and smiled at Shona. 'Follow me,' he said.

***

A few minutes later, Macca sat on his stool at the counter of the printers reciting the alphabet forwards and backwards on Shona's command while a chattering bunch of girls loaded their rucksacks with flyers.

'Belter,' said Tommy, slapping Jed on the back. 'She's a keeper.'

Jed looked on, proudly, while Frankie stared at the arses of the girls as they bent over the boxes to fill their bags.

The niggling fear was beginning to abate, and Tommy thought that maybe, just maybe, the universe and the aliens that inhabited it were sending cosmic stardust his way. He looked up at the ceiling and prayed silently to them.

'What do you think my chances are with that Emma?' he heard.

Tommy brought his attention back to the shop where Emma, catching Frankie leering at her, was drawing her eyes over him with open disgust.

'Bit of a long shot,' Tommy replied.

'Aye,' agreed Frankie, shooting a glance at Shona who still held Macca's wide eyes with hers.

'Don't even think about it.' Tommy slapped him on the arm and pulled him out of the shop before Shona brought Macca out of his stupor.

***

The Haymarket bus station was packed with hobos, shoppers, and commuters.

'That's me out of cash.' Jed turned out his empty pockets, Betty's hundred pounds now in the hands of the flyer distribution team for their fares and their drinks.

'Aye, me an'all,' said Frankie. 'Had to pay the coach deposits out the petty cash. I'm sacked if Jim finds out.'

'You can't get sacked from a fiddle job,' said Tommy.

'Oh,' said Frankie, thinking.

Jed regarded Frankie with a mind-boggled face that made Tommy smile. Hearing the low drone of Jed's mobile phone, he drew in a long breath. Jed winked at him – *the personnel* – and Tommy felt the zing of positivity once more. They might pull something off, even without the drugs. He looked around him at the hustle and bustle of the bus station as Jed walked away to take the call. He closed his eyes, his mind transforming the queues of passengers into long lines of people waiting in anticipation at the entrance of the club that would one day be his.

'One in, one out.' Hadgy Dodds was on the door, dressed like a penguin and lording it over the other bouncers. Inside, the place was heaving, the hisses and low rumblings of the buses mutating into the steady beat of house music, the atmosphere electric, not an inch of the dance floor bare of feet.

'Spare us some change?' The voice brought Tommy back to the Haymarket, the tramp in front of him holding up his dirty palm like a modern-day Fagin.

'I wish,' he said, turning to Jed who was facing him now, holding the mobile phone by his side, his face one big, fat sourpuss.

'No lighting, no sound,' he said.

***

The house opposite Tommy's was still smouldering as he turned the corner onto Holly Drive, the yellow tape around it fluttering where it had come loose from the lampposts. Small clusters of youths were congregating in their usual places, sharing spliffs, their collars turned up against challenge.

Trevor Logan stood alone, leaning against a wall, one hand down his grey jogging pants as he awaited his customers. There had been a time when you didn't shit in your own back yard, but times were changing.

The three friends had parted in gloomy silence. Twenty-four hours to go and all Tommy had was DJs and artists and a promise from the riggers and chippies that they'd turn up the next morning for the few hundred quid deposit Tommy didn't have to give them. Without it, he was sure they'd turn right back around and spend their Saturday doing something else. The sound and lighting were another story all together, not a single professional willing to drive their gear all the way to Hexham on the promise of nowt.

Tommy pushed his hands deep into his jeans pockets, fingering the loose change that lay there. He passed Trevor without a word but felt his presence behind him as he opened the gate.

'Found them yet?'

Tommy turned, tasting venom. 'The prison?' he spat.

'Visiting my cousin,' Trevor said, all innocent. 'The venue?'

Clearly there was no point, and Tommy thrust the gate into Trevor's stomach, winding him, bending him double.

'Ye knaa what'll happen!' Trevor squeaked through empty lungs as he backed off. 'Bye bye, Tommy!'

Tommy's broken windows had been secured with plywood by the council, already obscured with black graffiti, the door patched up with the same lock. He tried the key; it still worked, and he gave the door a hefty shove to open it. He stepped inside and pushed the door closed, standing in the hallway and breathing in the familiar scent of damp and lavender furniture polish.

Despondency settled in his chest. He could hear Sam's cheerful banter in his mind, could hear Ashleigh's gurgling gibberish.

Opening the living room door, he stopped dead in his tracks. Ashleigh's gurgling hadn't been in his mind at all because there she was, sitting among the sofa cushions on the floor, her wide smile almost bringing tears to his eyes.

He swooped her up into his arms, calling Sam's name. A second later, she was at the kitchen door, her hands in the pockets of her short summer jacket, the pink one she loved so much. Her eyes brimmed, her chin quivered.

'I went to the police,' she said.

'Wha? Why?' She couldn't let him down, not now.

'He told me something,' she said, 'that Chief Inspector. Something about your dad and Billy Logan. And my Uncle Paul.'

She told him quickly, not mincing her words, and Tommy felt the walls of the house collapse around him. He hung his head and tried not to scream.

'I know about the drugs, Tommy,' Sam said when she'd finished.

Unable to look her in the eye, Tommy focused on a spot just behind her knee, his heart climbing up his throat when he noticed the holdall behind her heels, open and displaying clothes he'd seen her wear a hundred times.

'No, no, no,' he said desperately. 'Come on, Sam.'

Tears coursed down her cheeks, the sight of them making his own eyes wet. She took her hands from her pockets and held up four tubes of Smarties.

'Let's get the hell out of here,' she said.

PEACH

'Amphetamines, ecstasy, LSD, cocaine, crack ...'

Murphy was handing out seal bags containing pills, powder, and crystals. Around twenty officers, a mixture of uniform and detectives, sat theatre style in the room, passing the labelled bags to each other like a game of pass-the-parcel. They held them up to the light, felt the consistency of the drugs before handing them on to their neighbour.

The atmosphere chimed with anticipation and the expectation of a few extra quid overtime. Twenty more officers and dog handlers would join them the next day, along with air back up and armed response. Their aim was a simple one, Peach had explained at the start of the briefing: to prevent a large-scale, drug-fuelled acid-house party taking place in their region: the first of its kind in these parts, and the last. *Operation Red Kite* would pave the way for a mass crack down on illegal all-night gatherings.

'The biggest threat our young people have faced in a generation,' he'd said. They'd lapped it up, hung on his every word.

DCI Peach stood back now, his shoulders against the wall, his thoughts entirely elsewhere. As Murphy crouched at the end of the front row, explaining the contents of a bag of drugs to a confused-looking officer, Peach caught his eye. Murphy was his only hope now of identifying the venue, all notions of a deal with Paul Smart banished. Instead, a plan was forming in his head.

Murphy gave him a reassuring nod, the sort of gesture that would have made the hairs on the back of his neck stand up in defence not so long ago. Over the last six years he'd preferred to work alone, delegating only when necessary or when ordered to by Superintendent McNally on pain of suspension. It kept him busy – more than busy; *besieged.* Burden had become his haven, permission to disregard his own self-loathing, his failure as a husband, as a father, as a human being capable of even the most basic of friendships. There was something about Murphy that withstood his coldness, didn't rile against it or complain. There was something unfathomably loyal about him. He realised suddenly that Murphy might actually *like* him.

'Listen up.' Murphy had left the officer none the wiser and was clapping his hands, standing in front of the horseshoe of chattering officers, taking charge. 'We'll have three teams. You should know which team you're in, and if you don't, then you 'aven't been fucking listening, 'ave you?'

He could still lose the language, however.

'Team A, you'll target the high-rises,' said Murphy. 'We need to limit numbers, so there's to be no pirate radio over the next twenty-four hours.'

'Ooh arr, shiver me timbers,' said a uniformed officer, eliciting a few sniggers. Peach noted his idiot face, red and shiny like the class fool. He recognised him, *Cinderella*, the young officer who'd handed him Tommy's trainer almost a week ago. How much had changed since then. It was as if he was seeing clearly for the first time in years. He knew exactly what needed to be done.

'Team B. You'll go round the clubs tonight and confiscate as many flyers as you can, preferably from the distributors themselves. Collect information, get them while they're pissed, and try not to look like coppers. Team C,' Murphy extended his chest, 'the *sexy* team, will be with me.'

Cheers from half a dozen officers brought a thin smile to Peach's lips, and after Murphy had identified team leaders, a hand shot up. Peach nodded to the owner of it, pushing himself away from the wall, back in the game.

'If *we* don't know where it is, sir, how do the punters?'

'There'll be a telephone number on the flyers,' Peach replied. 'People will ring it and get information on meeting points, then they'll ring the number again and a new message will tell them where to go.'

'Can't we just get the phone line stopped, sir?' said another voice from the front row.

'Multiple lines into one BT answering service,' Peach said.

The officers furrowed their brows.

'The sort used by sex lines,' added Murphy, and enlightenment ensued in the form of nodding heads, blushes, and slaps on arms.

'Jeez, they've got it all sussed, eh?' said a middle-aged detective amidst the low hum of voices.

'Oh, they're not daft,' said Peach. 'But neither are we. We'll have some of you ringing the numbers on the night to determine the venue.' He glanced at Murphy and added, 'If we don't have it by then.'

'How many are we talking about?' he heard.

'Could be five or six thousand,' said Murphy.

Another murmur rumbled through the room as Peach headed towards a notice board on wheels displaying headshots of Tommy, Jed, and Frankie.

'Here's who we're looking for,' he said, pointing to Tommy's photograph. 'This man is the promoter, along with his friends, here. These events are illegal, remember, so all proceeds are confiscated.'

While Tommy had been exonerated as a supplier of drugs, Peach was still determined to put a stop to any future parties. He'd kept Paul Smart's image to himself. He had his own strategy to deal with him, one he had yet to test out with Murphy. He'd soon gauge how far his DS's loyalty ran.

He looked around the room. 'They talk about freedom of expression, the right to *party*.' He said the word with a flourish that brought more sniggers. 'But what about the rights of decent, law-abiding people who just want to sleep at night and not have to clean up needles and human faeces from their gardens?'

'Just go to Valley Park, sir,' said Cinderella. 'Standard practice.' Peach watched Cinderella and his neighbour high-five each other. Just yesterday, he would have agreed, but something about the gesture didn't sit well with him. Collins's young wife had surprised him with her dignity and her obvious dedication to her child who was well cared for, happy. She was only nineteen he'd realised, just a few years older than Sally. He'd found her mature, sweet-natured, brave even - a world away from her mother who was clearly selfish to the point of delusion. Perhaps that was what Valley Park did to you, perhaps one day, there would be rescue for the place, an estate that was responsible for twenty per cent of the city's crime.

'Any more questions?' He surveyed the room, and silence fell, some of the officers already on their feet, five minutes past the end of their shift.

Peach dismissed them, and they filed out, dropping the seal bags into a plastic tub while Murphy unpinned the photographs from the board.

'Good bunch,' said Murphy, holding the photographs to his chest.

'I've seen worse.' Peach wondered whether he should divulge the plan now or wait until tomorrow when Murphy wouldn't have time to think about the consequences – the potential for disciplinary action and the ensuing black mark on his record. He'd wait, he decided, the desire to see Paul Smart rot behind bars outweighing his concern for Murphy's career progression.

Murphy stood motionless, as if awaiting instructions.

'Get yourself away for a couple of hours before tonight,' Peach said. 'And remember, all I want is the venue. If Collins has drugs on him, let him sell them. We need this rave to go ahead.'

Murphy didn't move, raised his eyebrows expectantly, and it took a few seconds for Peach to realise what he wanted. He thought about it, then nodded at the empty room. 'And that was … well …'

Murphy smiled, a warm smile, just a hint of cheek.

'Now, don't be getting all mushy on me, boss,' he said.

***

In his office, Peach stared at the computer screen as he reached out a finger and pressed the button he assumed switched it on. It whirred into life, the screen turning black, lines of incomprehensible numbers and letters rolling upwards until they came to a stop and a small green rectangle flashed, asking him to do something. He pressed a few keys but heard only warning honks.

He took the form for the computer course from his in-tray and a pen from his shirt pocket, pulling a folder towards him to lean on. It was the building society file Murphy had reviewed, and he pushed the form to one side and opened the folder. Curious to see what Murphy had come up with, he flicked through the CCTV stills – pictures he'd seen before, nothing new. On one of the stills from outside the building, however, Murphy had drawn a ring around the head of the tall robber in the coat and hat. Peach picked the print up and looked closer, focusing on the robber's neck. He'd been so intent on the skinny one, on his need to put Collins at the scene, he'd missed it: the tip of a bird's wing, Paul Smart's tattoo of the dove in flight.

Flipping over to the next image, he faced the mug-shot of a girl of about eighteen, thin and pale, the bags of an older woman under large blue eyes. Murphy had attached a Post-it note to it: *"Lassie's eyes."*

Next was a picture of the round face of a young man, eyebrows, nose, ears, and bottom lip pierced. The face was riddled with acne, bum fluff trying to find life through the scars and yellow pimples. Another Post-it: *"Our Janice's lad."*

Peach skipped to the transcript of the interview with Mrs Bailey and Denise Morris where Murphy had highlighted Mrs Bailey's words in yellow. Closing the folder, Peach wondered how much Mrs Bailey knew or didn't know, and as he pushed it to one side, he suspected the old woman had been had – another vulnerable person taken advantage of. He had a feeling that Janice and her lad wouldn't be dropping Paul Smart in it, but the tattoo might be all the evidence he needed. On top of a conviction for drug dealing, Paul Smart wouldn't be bleeding any poor people dry until the Millennium.

Lifting his head at a knock on the door, he shouted his "come in" and Murphy stood in the doorway.

'Just got off the phone with the prison, boss,' he said. 'Trevor Logan has visited Reggie Collins twice these last three months.'

Peach frowned. 'Why?'

'Dunno. Took us ages to get through, coz the prison's been on lock-down.' Three guns had been smuggled into the prison, Murphy said, but they'd only found two of them, so the place was a no-go zone. 'But there's not been any argy-bargy between them, boss. Seems they've kissed and made up.'

'I doubt it,' Peach murmured. Guns, drugs, violence, exploitation. It didn't stop when they got banged up.

Something sat heavy in Peach's gut; an instinctive sense of

providence. 'Everything ready for tonight?' he asked.

'Yup. I even ironed me jeans, boss.'

'You've got an iron?'

Murphy looked hurt. 'I've got all mod cons, thank you very much.'

Peach hmphed. 'Good, well make sure you use it more often in future.'

***

As the evening drew in, Peach left the station and approached his car but stopped at the sound of crunching glass underfoot. He cursed under his breath as he noticed the smashed windows and the deflated tyres. Eyes darting around the car park, he spotted a young boy sitting on a low wall, digging at the soil behind him with a garden trowel. His bare legs were grubby and bruised, the sole hanging off one of his sandals. When the child looked up, Peach recognised him: the youngest of the Logans, Carl, who was regarding him with a vacant stare. He had the deep reddish-brown hair and black eyes of his father, Billy, the man Tommy Collins' father had murdered, though not in the cold blood Peach had originally thought.

Carl jumped soundlessly from the wall and meandered past him, the trowel and a plastic carrier bag hanging loosely in his hands. Peach felt his eyes drawn to the child. He was small and frail, the slow walk reminding him of Sally when she was his age, tired from walking and wanting a carry.

When Carl was beyond Peach's reach, he swivelled around and lifted the carrier bag over his head. 'Best little thief in Valley Park!' he shouted.

When Peach wrenched his car door open and looked under the passenger seat, the takings from the rave were gone, and Carl

Logan was dragging the trowel firmly along the sides of parked vehicles before sprinting out of sight.

DENISE

Hovering next to the ceramic pit bulls, Denise looked towards her brother's house with wary eyes. She walked up the gravelled drive, past the Range Rover and the silver MG to the door. She spotted his face at the living room window, and a few seconds later she was dragged roughly inside by her arm. Paul slammed the door and walked past her into the living room, throwing himself onto one of the swivel chairs where he sat rigid, palms clinging to the edge of the arms.

Denise stopped in the doorway, her hand springing to her mouth. The room had been trashed, the bar shattered, the floor littered with broken glass, most of the floorboards upended.

Her voice wavered. 'Is it true?' He didn't look at her, so she asked again. 'Did you give Tommy drugs?'

It was then she noticed the suitcases, three of them piled on top of one another, their edges just visible behind the slashed leather of the bar.

She took a few steps towards him. He was deep in thought, his face desolate, and she felt a flutter of pity, followed by an overwhelming need to give him comfort.

'Take me with you,' she said, her voice hopeful.

Paul just stared at the bar. 'He's taken everything.'

It wasn't the response she wanted, but she kept her voice kind, sympathetic, just like Oprah. 'What do you mean, love?'

'That bastard darkie,' he said, indicating the devastation around him. 'Kept me safe, kept my money safe, what was left of it. And now he's gone to work for another bunch of apes.' He looked up at her. 'No fucking loyalty.'

Denise took another step towards him. She could be loyal, she could protect him.

'Even took the fucking dogs.' Paul leant forward, his head falling into his hands, his shoulders starting to shake. 'I loved those dogs,' he whimpered.

Denise clutched at the knot that grasped her stomach; forgiveness, compassion, empathy – she could feel those things again if he would let her.

She ran to him, kneeling in front of the chair, her hands on his knees, imploring him to look at her. They'd be fine, she said, they'd start afresh, together, they'd build a life if he would take her with him. But Paul was shaking his head, his fingers still spread across his face.

'I've got nothing,' he cried. 'And I couldn't take your money.' He closed his fingers tighter across his eyes and hiccupped a great sob.

The sound made her heart leap, the vulnerability of it. She held his arms, shaking them firmly. She had a few hundred pounds credit on one of her cards, she said. She could get more in a few days. They could go abroad. They were both resourceful people, they'd soon be back on their feet.

'Card?' The voice was suddenly clear and steady, the shoulders taut and unmoving.

'I haven't got much,' she said. 'But what I have got – it's yours. Ours.' She brought her hands to his, pulling his fingers from his face, but when he lifted his head, she saw no tears, and the fingers had grabbed her mouth before she could say, 'What are sisters for?'

His face loomed, and he squeezed, forcing her lips into a painful pout, then he stood, pulling her to her feet and marching her backwards until she fell to the floor. He straddled her, grabbing her hair, and pulling her head back, no amount of clawing at his hands relieving the stinging pain in her scalp.

'You think I give a fuck about Tommy?' He pulled harder, his face a mask of rage. 'It's your kid you should be thinking about. She's my currency.'

She began to speak but his hand covered her mouth, finger and thumb nipping her nostrils, halting the words that now vibrated against his palm, muffled and futile.

'I need this rave to happen tomorrow night,' he said, 'and you're going to make sure my drugs get there, do you understand?'

Her eyes were wide, frantic.

'What was that copper doing at your house?'

She wanted to tell him she'd got rid of the copper, shielded him, but she couldn't breathe let alone speak. She squeezed her eyes closed against the pain in her head and lungs, tasted the iron tang of blood.

'If the police are anywhere near the place tomorrow night, you'll be sorry.' His nails dug into her cheeks as his eyes scoured her face.

She nodded, sobs of humiliation obstructing her throat.

'What did you tell him?'

She shook her head, it was all she could do.

'Does he know anything?'

She shook her head again, and finally her mouth was free.

She gasped, filling her lungs two or three times before she was able to speak. Her daughter, her Samantha. Would he really hurt her? The answer was written all over his soulless face.

'If I do what you want, you'll leave her alone?' she managed.

'I'll be gone, sweetheart.' He bent down to her ear. 'Tucker didn't know where I stashed the drugs.' And then he sang in a cruel chime, '*Oh, my love is like a red, red rose.*'

The realisation hit her hard. She wanted to scream, scratch her nails down his face, but looking into his eyes, she realised they weren't her father's at all, but her mother's blue eyes, sad and empty. Grief seized her heart, grief for this lost boy she'd once held in her arms, the tiny baby she'd fed with a bottle when her mother's fingers were broken and useless. With a tear rolling down her temple, she held her hand to his cheek, and for a moment, he closed his eyes and leant into the touch. 'Forgive me,' she whispered.

He lifted his hand, rested it over hers and she felt a surge of love. There was still hope for him.

Grasping her fingers, her brother squeezed the love right out of them. She froze as she felt one of his knees force her legs apart, the '*No!*' snared in her throat with fear, and his breath warm on her ear.

'Guilt will be the undoing of you, sister,' he said. 'And I'll tell you this. You can rot in hell.' His knee pushed further into her thighs and she managed to get the '*No!*' out.

Not this, please not this. Some people had called him "evil," and now she knew why.

His knee slid back, and it collided with her groin with such force she felt her pelvis stab into the bones of her hips.

Her face scarlet, her breath trapped, she rolled over as Paul stood in one graceful movement.

'As if,' he said.

Saliva was pouring from the side of her mouth onto his shiny white shoes. She couldn't stop the drooling, she couldn't breathe, but she could hear her brother's words.

'Currency. Remember that.'

TOMMY

Newcastle was dressing itself up to the nines for its Friday night out. The mood was intoxicating, laughter spilling out onto the streets from the hot, boozy air of the pubs. It was eight o'clock and the city centre streets were teaming with townies, students, couples, and arty-types, drunken knots of leather-look trousers and spangly tops whose wearers had had their fill of Happy Hour's three shots for a pound. They poured from the Metro stations and the buses with one thing and one thing only on their minds: to get as hammered as possible by home time, if not before.

The streets were classless, a fusion of those with, those without, and those who couldn't care less. The pubs and clubs had their loyal clientele, each faction filtering off at the city's junctions to spend the night with their own kind. The students crammed into the darker, dingier establishments with gig posters for wall paper. Graduates and young professionals would head for Central Station or the old Quayside bars that stocked German beer they could drink straight from the bottle. The good-timers headed to the Bigg Market where they could drink and cop-off, cry in the toilets with their friends and not have far to stagger for a kebab and a taxi at the end of the night, and all for under a tenner.

The Crown was a traditional alehouse, caught between the crowded, rickety bars of the old Quayside and the contemporary new construction of the Law Courts and its imposing regeneration that threatened to bring a different kind of drinker to the riverside. Valley Park had little to offer young people like Tommy and his friends, only the Nag's Head and its meat raffles and pissy old men. The Crown offered the best of both worlds: working-class people with ideas, and the opportunity to talk to those who were doing better than yourself, but who weren't twats.

'Me mam's been to Benidorm, like,' said Frankie, the holiday brochure open on the table. 'Came back like a fucking radish.'

Despite the heat, Tommy kept his flying jacket zipped up to the neck. He touched his chest now and then, convinced the tubes of ecstasy in his inside pockets were rattling audibly against the pounding of his heart. Feeling tiny spiders of sweat running down his back, he glanced at the door of the pub where Hadgy Dodds stood back to allow a couple into the bar.

Tommy tightened his lips and looked at his watch. Jed was outside on the mobile phone, talking to the sound and lighting guys, trying to convince them the money would be in their pockets by the morning, money Tommy wouldn't have until he'd relieved himself of drugs under the noses of men who would take great joy in punishing him for it. Jed had offered to help, relief evident in his face when Tommy had refused point blank to involve anyone else.

Frankie coughed, unused to the tense silence. He closed the brochure and began flipping a beer mat from the edge of the table with his fingers, catching it then repeating the process until Tommy snatched it away in irritation. The pub was filling up, the couple taking the last empty table next to them with their pints of Guinness, their hands all over each other, blocking Tommy's view of the door where he could see the heads of more drinkers streaming in. He watched half a dozen men gathering at the bar. He could spot them a mile off; they were too clean shaven, perfect short back-and-sides hair-cuts. They looked way too *employed*.

He nudged Frankie and nodded towards the bar.

'Filth,' muttered Frankie.

Tommy lifted himself halfway from his stool and strained his neck, his face falling into a frown when, instead of Jed emerging from the growing crowd of drinkers, Tucker appeared and stood still for a moment as if bracing himself before walking towards him.

'Aye, aye, here's trouble,' said Frankie.

Tucker stood over them, his face grisly and misshapen.

'He hasn't got your trainer money yet, you'll have it tomorrow,' said Tommy on Jed's behalf.

Tucker bent forward into his face, and Tommy strained his head back. 'Give over, Tucker, you'll be giving people nightmares.'

'I've got cash.' Tucker straightened up and flicked his head towards the vestibule that housed the pub's toilets.

Tommy thought for a moment. Perhaps Smartie had relented, or maybe Tucker was there to bundle him into a car again. He touched the bruise on his face, the tip of the iceberg of pain. But cash trumped selling drugs any day. With a glance at Frankie, he stood up, Frankie's hand springing to his arm, a look on his face that asked what the hell he was doing.

'I'll be fine,' said Tommy, although he didn't quite believe he would be.

A minute later, Tucker stood with his back to the payphone outside the gents, Tommy keeping a safe distance, his instincts on full alert.

Tucker produced a roll of notes, no more than sixty quid. 'You need to go,' he said.

Rubbing his hand over his mouth, Tommy stifled a sceptical laugh. He'd heard it all now. 'Why would Smartie want me gone?'

'He doesn't. I do.'

Aye, right. It was some sort of test of his metal. Run away, and he'd be forever listening for footsteps behind him, forever expecting the blow to the head, the bullet in the chest, the hammer to his knees. If he was going to do a moonlight flit, it would be further away than Sheffield.

'Do you want it, or not?' said Tucker.

'Sixty quid?' Tommy laughed. 'What we gonna do, live on the streets? Fuck off, Tucker.'

Tucker held the money up. 'There's eighty, and it's all I've got.'

Tommy creased his face in irritation. 'Hey, I might look it, but I'm not daft—'

'I want to fucking help!' Tucker looked around him as if surprised at his own raised voice. 'Just fucking take it.' He shoved the money into Tommy's chest, but Tommy kept his arms by his sides.

'Paul Smart's bitch wants to help?'

Tucker drew air in through his nose, let it out slowly through his mouth and said, 'Why do you think I'm here?'

'Haven't got a clue,' Tommy replied. 'So, if there's nowt else, I've got your boss's drugs to sell.' He made to move but stopped at Tucker's '*Wait!*'

There was more heavy breathing, as if Tucker were preparing himself for a big fight, his fists opening and closing by his sides.

'He's not my boss anymore.' Tucker looked at his feet, then back up at Tommy, who saw something in his eyes he'd never seen before: sadness. 'I was too late,' he said.

'Eh?' Tommy was beginning to wonder if Tucker had taken a few too many blows to the head.

'She was already dead.' He continued to look at Tommy, his eyes strange, his glare so piercing Tommy could only stare back.

'Can you not see it?' Tucker said, grabbing Tommy's arm.

'See what, man?' And as he looked into Tucker's green eyes, the noise of the pub became muffled, and it was as if he knew what was coming next.

'You're my fucking brother, Tommy.'

There was a beat before Tommy laughed behind the back of his hand, a sound with a bitter edge. He looked Tucker up and down, unconcealed disappointment and disgust shrouding his face. His brother was someone important, someone who would change the world one day. Tucker Brown maimed and killed for Paul Smart, was as savage as the great Jaws himself. His mother could never have given birth to such a creature.

Slowly, he pulled his arm from Tucker's grasp and stepped away from him, disbelief turning to anger. But Tucker's eyes stayed steady.

'It's true—'

'Liar.' Tommy snarled. He'd never been an angry man, never felt this kind of strain and burden. But now, it overwhelmed him, and he thought he might explode with it. 'Look at the state of you, man!' he yelled, pushing Tucker back against the payphone. 'You're nothing, you're a nowt.'

'I've got my birth cert—'

'You're a fucking animal!' Tommy spat, finger pointing, 'and even if you were my brother, which you're *not*, I'd fucking *disown you!*'

He watched Tucker's face lose its earnestness, the armour returned, protecting the defences he'd let slip for just a few minutes. Then, resisting the desire to spit at the animal's feet, Tommy stood back, straightened his jacket, and pulled open the door that led back into the pub.

***

Jed was sitting on a stool, looking up at Tommy with a relieved smile and a nod of the head. The sound and lighting guys wanted paying by 9.00 a.m., the full amount, he said as Tommy flopped down next to him.

Tommy sighed and rested his forehead on the balls of his

hands, his fingers grasping at his head as he watched Tucker railroad through the pub, pushing people out of his way to get to the door.

'The antennae's gone from the flats,' said Frankie, 'but that lassie was all right, before she got cut off.'

Tommy didn't answer, so Jed stepped in.

'Did she get the message out?'

'Aye, loud and clear.'

'Generator company's pulled out, though,' said Jed, nudging Tommy for a reaction. 'And this place is full of pigs.' He nudged Tommy harder, frowning. 'Look, man!'

Tommy followed his eyes to the bar, his mind still on Tucker. 'Jimmy's got an old generator,' he said, mechanically, 'but it won't last all night. We'll have to use the one at the farm.'

Frankie shifted in his seat away from the couple next to him, embarrassed by their smooching. 'Where's your lass, like?' he asked Jed, who answered him with a blank stare. 'Just asking. Nice lass, that's all.'

Jed leant forward. 'She's gorgeous,' he said, voice teasingly wanton. 'Really nice tits, lovely wet bits.' He licked his lips as he said the word *"lovely."*

Frankie swallowed, and Tommy gazed heavenwards. 'Pack it in,' he said. 'And you, put your hands back on that table.'

Frankie obeyed, sheepishly. 'Why does he get to manage the lasses, like?' he asked.

'Because he's married,' said Jed, 'and you smell.'

Tommy should have laughed but he didn't have it in him. The coppers at the bar were laughing, he noticed, pretending to have fun. Tommy even recognised one of them – the boulder of an officer who'd taken him in for the line-up.

Divs.

'Giz a tab, Frankie,' he sighed. He needed to concentrate on other things, and he shook his head free of Tucker's eyes, the same colour as his mother's.

Frankie doled out the cigarettes and Tommy held up his hand for the lighter which Jed lobbed to him across the table. It dropped from Tommy's hand onto the floor.

'Let's hope Farmer Dawson's stocked up on generator fuel,' Tommy said, bending down to pick up the lighter. As he reached for it, another hand got there first and picked it up. He looked into the droopy brown eyes of the Guinness drinking lover boy, a dead roll-up hanging from his lips.

'Cadge a light, chief?' the man asked in an accent that reminded Tommy of *Coronation Street*. The fella looked directly at him as he took the lighter and sat up, lit his roll-up, and turned back to his girlfriend. Only the smile he was giving her now wasn't dreamy and amorous, but shrewd and victorious.

***

It was gone three in the morning and Tommy approached Holly Drive with the weight of the night's failures hanging over him like a monsoon about to break. He'd been denied entry into every club. Huge men in black suits held their hands against his chest, no eye contact required. They bent down to his ear.

Fuck off home.

Even Hadgy Dodds was absent from the door at Phutures. Tucker had put the message out, and every bouncer had been given Tommy's name and description.

It had taken him over an hour to trudge home, his legs leaden, his body heavy as a millstone. He stood regretfully at his front door, the house across the street exhaling a death rattle, the smell and taste of scorched timbers feeling woefully ordinary.

He put the key in the door and pushed it open.

Inside, the house was painfully quiet, void of any comfort, Sam and Ashleigh tucked up in Jed's bedroom out of Paul Smart's reach. Tommy fell onto the sofa, pulling the bent and battered Smarties tubes from his inside pocket. He looked at them blearily and wiped at his nose. He lay down, closed his eyes, and prayed for a miracle, for there was nothing else that would save him now.

SATURDAY

TOMMY

The morning announced itself in a bulldozer of light, springing his eyes open. He sat up sharply, one of his feet still flat on the floor where he'd left it a few hours earlier, sleep finally taking him as the sky began to brighten. On the carpet, the tubes of ecstasy lay in a small heap, and the night came flooding back with painful clarity: the bouncers' whispered threats, sound, lighting, deposits for the chippies, all out of reach without the cash. Tucker's below-the-belt lies, and Loverboy's eyes looking into his with the gratified smugness of someone who'd got exactly what they came for.

Tommy had mentioned Farmer Dawson's name.

The cops.

They knew.

He dug into his back pocket and brought out a fiver and a few coins. It was all he had to his name. Might cover the bus fare to Berwick; sixty miles north, not far enough away from Paul Smart.

The living room was still a mess from the police raid. The videos were scattered in front of the television, Grandad's photograph face down next to the gas fire. Tommy rose stiffly from the sofa and bent down to prop the photograph up against the fire. The glass was broken, pieces of it falling onto the fireplace. He picked the picture up, loosened the frame and pulled the photograph from it, remembering the stroke that had the grumpy old bugger confined to a bed in the living room for weeks while the powers that be decided what to do with him. Tommy had just turned eighteen, and Jed's mother had once again risen to the challenge, bringing gallons of soup and plated corned-beef pies daily, happy to order the district nurses around to her heart's delight. Just a week after Tommy met Sam, the second stroke took Grandad before the council had to spend any money on him.

Tommy slid the print from the broken glass and looked down into Grandad's proud, young face, his shadowy eyes looking directly at him. In the clarity of the picture, now free of its yellowing glass, Tommy saw something new in those eyes: challenge, bravery, and not a small amount of cunning.

One: work hard, play hard.

The rapping on the front door made him start and the photograph fell to his feet. With a rush of dread, he stumbled into the hallway and opened the door, expecting Paul Smart's fist to hit him square in the face. Instead, he looked down at Trevor Logan who squinted up at him as if he too had just woken up.

Trevor pulled a plastic carrier bag from the back of a pair of jeans that hung from his thin hips. He held it up. 'Where's the venue?'

Bank notes revealed themselves through the thin white plastic, and his heart began to thud.

'It's your fucking money, man, howay,' said Trevor.

Tommy's mind did cartwheels. Peach would know the venue by now; not many Farmer Dawsons to choose from. So, what was the point if he couldn't even get the rave started? Paul Smart would be there with his henchmen, and now Trevor Logan could rack up with whatever he had up his sleeve. He could be brave, cunning, like Grandad, or he could run for his life.

'The venue,' said Trevor.

Tommy stared at the bag in Trevor's hand. The money … *his* money. *His* profit. It would get them further than Berwick.

'Groat Hall Farm,' Tommy said. And the money was in his hands.

'And don't you be worrying about the pigs, neither.' Trevor

grinned and touched his nose. 'We've got that sorted.'

That "we" again.

With that, Trevor turned and sauntered down the path, and Tommy walked into the living room on hollow legs, sinking onto the sofa, Grandad staring up at him as if egging him on.

And then, it was if someone had flipped a switch. He saw it. It dominated the photograph, vast and magnificent, Grandad dwarfed to insignificance by its presence.

The aircraft hangar.

'What you doing?' The doorway framed Jed's silhouette. 'You're door's wide open, man. You should've come to ours, you wazzock.'

Getting to his feet, Tommy held out the carrier bag to Jed who took it and peered inside.

'You sold them?' His eyes were wider than his mother's hips.

Tommy shook his head, trying to suppress his giddiness. 'Trevor Logan,' he said.

Jed's face collapsed. 'Jesus, man, Tommy. More wankers to deal with.'

'It's ours,' said Tommy, 'the takings from last week.'

'Ha!' Jed laughed, but then his face turned serious, his eyes sombre as if trying to read Tommy's thoughts. 'What you gonna do?'

Tommy looked back at his friend, a man who'd been more than a brother to him his whole life. He could run away, live somewhere else a pauper.

Or they could pull off the biggest party to hit the north-east.

Tommy picked up the photograph from the floor and held it up to Jed, his finger tapping at the inscription under Grandad's picture:

Evershott Airfield, Northumberland.

Jed's eyes scanned it, his initial confusion turning to realisation. 'Are you taking the actual piss?'

The reply rested in Tommy's face.

'You know what this means?' Jed's face was grave, but Tommy sensed the exhilaration that zinged between them. He knew exactly what it meant. If he cheated Paul Smart, he'd never be able to show his face in Newcastle again; the city where he was born, the city he'd been proud of all his life. Though now, he wasn't so sure. There were too many risks, too many memories. Too many people that made it lousy.

'You better fucking come with us,' said Tommy.

But Jed swallowed his reply, breathing deeply before putting a hand on Tommy's shoulder and looking him straight in the eye.

'We're gonna have that bastard, comrade,' he said.

PEACH

Murphy had found the nearest telephone box to the pub, had been through the *Phone Book* and located the only Farmer Dawson in the region, delivering the message to Peach in three short words: *Groat Hall Farm.* Murphy had driven down there in the dead of night, found a note pinned to the front door of the farmhouse in a misspelt scrawl: "*Back Sunday nite. Anyone touches my cows, your dead.*"

The DCI leant over his desk, circled the farm's location on the road map he'd spread out next to a pile of two hundred or so flyers: "*Space Generation*" they read, and Peach recognised the alien faces from Tommy's sketch pad which still lounged by his feet.

Placing the pen next to the map, he checked the clock, the minutes ticking towards nine o'clock as slowly as January. Sally grinned up at him from the framed photograph, and his eyes absorbed her placid face. Her cheeks had had colour earlier that morning, her eyes brighter, her mood cautious but cheerful, Pamela just arriving for her shift and handing him the tea without him having to ask – and in a proper mug, too, not the half-measure nonsense of a polystyrene cup. The woman made good tea, he'd give her that, and he'd found himself wondering what her mince and dumplings tasted like as he watched her chatting to Sally.

Peach sat back in his office chair, his foot catching on the portfolio of Tommy's drawings. He blinked at it for a moment before bending down to pick it up, needing something to occupy his mind while the clock *tick-ticked* in time with his impatience.

He opened it and drew out the sketch pad, flipping the paper over to the image of the alien invasion. His fingers hovered over the face of the boy, desperately ogling the retreating spaceship. Looking at it properly this time, he focused on Tommy's teenage face: *Please!* it cried. The epitome of painful longing.

He turned slowly to the next page, his head lurching away from the image. Paul Smart stared brutally back at him. It was an uncanny likeness and he drew the pad closer to his face to admire the detailed lines of Paul's features, the shadows under his squat chin and the perfect curling of his earlobes. But it was the eyes that drew him in, eyes so alive that Peach half expected them to blink. They were eyes that lied with frightening conviction.

He lifted the page carefully and flicked it over the top of the pad: a young woman holding a tiny baby, their noses and foreheads touching. Sam Collins's eyes were closed, lashes gently brushing the top of her cheek. She was so young, just a hop and a skip away from Sally's age. The newborn, lips slightly parted, slept unperturbed, arms falling by her side in a peaceful lull. It was almost religious in its purity, love oozing from the paper: baby, mother, and observer.

Peach felt his throat constrict, wanting to tear his eyes away from it, but unable to control the focus of his gaze. He dropped the pad as if it had stung him, and he grasped his mouth with his hand. Hadn't he wanted the best possible life for his daughter? Hadn't he dreamed of her success and happiness? A life free of want, hardship, violence? Hadn't he vowed, when she was a tiny innocent like the child before him, that he would protect her from those things? He'd failed; his own selfish grief consuming him to the point of neglect.

His office door swung open and Murphy entered wearing a gaping yawn and a pair of khaki trousers sporting more pockets than the *Little Match Girl's* frock. Murphy drew a white paper bag from one of the pockets and threw it onto Peach's desk. It smelt better than good, the vapours of sausage, egg, and brown sauce reaching Peach's nose in seconds. All he needed was a bucket of tea to wash it down with, and, as if by magic, Sharon was at his door with a tray of two steaming mugs.

'The answer's "no", chief,' said Murphy, 'I can't marry you, it's too soon.'

'Very funny,' said Peach, drily, putting the sketch pad down and reaching for the bag.

Sharon had put the mugs down and was picking up the drawing of Sam and Ashleigh, her expression turning to one of reverence. 'Oh, sir, it's beautiful,' she gasped. 'Did you …?' She looked at him with astonishment, hope even.

'Don't be ridiculous,' said Peach, snatching the sketch pad back. 'Haven't you got anything better to do?'

Indignation settled in her face, and she turned and walked from the office giving Murphy a *sod-you-and-your-favours* look.

'Sit down,' said Peach.

Murphy obeyed, not before bending to one side and extracting another greasy bag of fat from a pocket. He tore it open and tucked in. 'What's the plan, chief?'

The plan was this, Peach began: they'd make their way to the farm in the next hour, be there before anyone else, hide out in one of the farm house's upstairs rooms and wait for Paul Smart and his drugs to arrive.

'What about the boss, boss …?' Murphy looked over his shoulder towards Superintendent McNally's office.

McNally was on a trip to the Welsh coast to visit his new grandchild. The timing couldn't have been better, and the message in Peach's eyes was clear when Murphy turned back to him.

Murphy whistled, whether in agreement or unease Peach wasn't sure.

'We'll arrest Smart,' said Peach, 'and Tommy will pay his dues when he arrives.' Every penny and every piece of equipment would be confiscated. No one would ever work with him again. 'There'll be no more all-night raves in Tyneside.'

Murphy was quiet, looking at his butty before taking a bite. 'Thing is,' he said between swallows, 'looks to me like he's just trying to make something of himself, you know, for his wife and kid. It's nature, ain't it? That your kids have a better life than you.'

Peach wasn't up for a lecture. 'There's people in danger because of him.'

Murphy continued to chew, unmoved by Peach's claim. 'Has anyone ever told you, you don't listen, boss?'

Peach drew back his chin. McNally had done so, repeatedly, but never his inferiors. They wouldn't dare.

'Look, why don't you rethink things,' said Murphy. 'You could set up a meeting with the council or summat. Maybe get the raves run legit, licenses and all that. Then you could police them properly.'

Peach recoiled at the suggestion. Drug dens run as legitimate businesses?

'Listen.' Murphy's expression was thoughtful, even a little patronising. 'Times are different now, know what I mean? There's been drugs long before there's been raves. Youngsters …' He waved his arm around the room as if it were occupied by grisly teenagers. 'They just want to be free, y'know? They want to do what they want to do, party if they want to party. Shouldn't we be making sure they do it without killing themselves?'

Peach understood the implication. If the rave last Saturday night had been policed, if it had been legal and organised, Sally wouldn't be where she was. Or would the likes of Darren Adams-Deighton and Paul Smart simply find another way to make their profits? The city's night clubs were hardly drug free. He drew the sandwich from its bag, lifted it to his mouth. Negotiation was not on the table. He was going to put Paul Smart behind bars, put a stop to the parties, confiscate the takings, and anything else he could get his hands on.

He kept his eyes on his food as he spoke. 'You're either with me, or you're not.' He bit into his sandwich, heard Murphy's heavy sigh and imagined his rolling eyes.

'I'm a copper,' said Murphy. 'And what copper would say no to a fucking full-on stakeout?'

Peach chewed silently. Job done.

'She's right, though, Shazza.' Murphy nodded at the drawing of Sam and Ashleigh, still lying face up on Peach's desk. 'It's stunning, that.'

Murphy stood, picked up his bacon butty and his tea and left the office, leaving Peach to stare down at Tommy's drawing.

The man was talented, no doubt about it. But talented people had to abide by the law, just like everyone else.

TOMMY

He sat silently with Sam, Barry, and Davie Foster, Ashleigh in her highchair and Betty in her element, replenishing the plate of hot breakfast in the middle of the kitchen table, telling Tommy he'd need his sustenance.

Jed had given his family a half-story earlier that morning before heading out with the cash to pay the personnel. They'd recovered the takings from the last rave, he'd said, and the party was going ahead. Just a small affair, probably their last.

'About bloody time,' Davie had said, flicking his newspaper. 'Time and tide wait for no man, Gerald.'

'Will there be gangsters?' Barry had asked. He'd seen the news items too over the past few days, and Betty had given Tommy a look of concern.

Sam's smile was anxious but resolute now as Tommy sat opposite her, Grandad's photograph rolled up in his back pocket. He picked up a fork and jabbed at a fat sausage. They couldn't discuss the plan, not until they had the money in their hands. London, they'd decided. Tommy could pick up work on the building sites and go from there. The money would pay the extortionate rent until he got qualified and could earn more. It would buy Sam a car and she could start her hairdressing business. Anyone could walk into a construction job in London, everybody said so. Anyone could disappear. Still, something about the nation's Capital seemed foreign to him, more alien than the Martians he imagined making friends with one day. He tried to place himself there, with Sam and the baby, amidst the torrent of people, the towering buildings, the tourists, and the traffic jams, but the whole place was a big blur to him. He would be a nobody there, a cog in the wheel. But they'd be safe.

With Davie's head in his paper, Barry lost in his Walkman, and Betty at the sink, Tommy took Grandad's photograph from his pocket and placed it on the table, nodding down at it subtly. Sam looked at it, comprehension making her eyes flash: first fear, then composure, her faint smile and long intake of breath denoting her understanding and agreement.

Hearing the front door open and close, he put the photograph under his arm. Jed appeared in the kitchen doorway, the buoyant smile on his face assuring Tommy that the sound and lighting was sorted, the chippies paid their deposits, and Hadgy Dodds given the cash he needed to round up his gang of uglies.

'Generators are sorted,' Jed said, giving Tommy a wink and a horsey click of his cheek. 'Jimmy will meet us there, and Frankie's on his way.' Jed picked up a piece of black pudding and fed his face, ravenously. 'Shift 'owa.'

Tommy slid his backside across the dining chair so Jed could perch on the edge. It was how they'd all fitted around Betty's kitchen table as children, crammed in, Barry demanding his own seat on pain of tantrums from hell that weren't worth it.

Tommy bit into his sausage and leant over the table to stroke Ashleigh's cheek with his thumb, catching Sam's eye as he heard the tooting of a horn outside.

'Be careful,' Sam said.

There were no tears, just a nod of consensus, and her eyes didn't leave his as he got to his feet. He was quickly joined by Jed who saluted Sam before pulling Tommy down the hallway to the open door where Betty stood ringing a tea towel in her hands. She grabbed Tommy and Jed in a vice-like embrace, pressing them tightly to her chest.

'Mam …' Jed growled.

'Don't do anything stupid,' she said, letting them go.

As Jed disappeared outside, Tommy felt Betty's hand on his arm.

'Watch over my lad,' she said. 'I don't know what I'd do without him.'

Tommy's eyes followed Jed, who was flinging his arms in the air at the sight of a huge, pink open-topped car.

'I will, Mrs Foster.' And he closed the door behind him.

***

Frankie lounged in the driver's seat of the pink Cadillac, dressed in a two-tone suit, complete with white socks and Ska hat. He fixed his piano-patterned tie into place and removed his sunglasses. 'Your Lady Penelope awaits,' he said.

'I said inconspicuous!' Jed surveyed the car, exasperated.

'Shut up and get in.' Tommy took the photograph from under his arm and vaulted over the door of the Cadillac, falling expertly onto his backside next to Frankie, his heart thudding with the thrill of euphoric terror. What if the aircraft hangar wasn't there anymore? What if it was inhabited by livestock or combined harvesters?

'Is that it?' asked Frankie, nodding at the photograph.

Tommy handed it over, and Frankie grinned down at it.

'Mint,' he said, turning the print over in his hands. 'What's this?' Frankie's fingers were picking at a small square of white card stuck to the back of Grandad's picture with old, yellow tape that Tommy hadn't noticed. Removing it, Frankie turned the card over and Tommy looked down at a black and white photograph of a newborn baby, the stark white of the frock and booties contrasting with the darkness of the baby's skin and the shock of black, fuzzy hair. Underneath it, in Jean Collins's handwriting, was written:

"*Tony, 1963.*"

'Who's that?' Jed's head was at Tommy's shoulder.

Taking the photograph from Frankie, Tommy stared down at it.

Four: expect the Unexpected.

'Fucking Tucker,' he said.

Tommy sensed two pairs of quizzical eyes darting between each other before Frankie turned the key in the ignition. He wanted to laugh, he wanted to cry, wondering if a brother like Tucker Brown was better than no brother at all. He slid the photograph into the pocket of his jeans; he'd think about it later. He had a rave to pull off.

'Drive on, Parker,' he said.

'Yes, m'lady,' said Frankie, donning his hat and sunglasses.

Today, they were doing it in style.

***

Frankie drove through the country roads like Lord Muck. The roadworks on the A1 north of Alnwick had put them an hour behind, men standing with "*stop*" and "*go*" signs without supervision, having a laugh as furious motorists stuck their fingers up at them from their open windows.

'Are we nearly there yet?' Jed was turning pale, his cheeks puffed out, one hand clasped at his mouth.

'Left, man, left!' shouted Tommy.

'We've been down here before!' wailed Frankie.

He was right, and Tommy sucked in his lips in apology as Frankie looked with dismay at the unending road ahead, flanked by open, unfenced fields, sheep straying from their grassland onto the tarmac.

Tommy flattened the map against the dashboard, studying it, wishing he'd paid more attention in his geography lessons.

'Definitely back that way.' He pointed his thumb over his shoulder.

Frankie drove off the road into a field, taking the car full circle over the grass, blasting the horn at stray sheep who stared stubbornly while Jed groaned that he was about to puke his ring.

'Do *not* be sick in this car,' Frankie warned, driving back in the direction they'd just come.

Ten minutes later, they were climbing a steep, winding road, the engine roaring, Frankie's nose almost touching the steering wheel as he willed the car on.

'*Come on, come on!*' Tommy hissed under his breath, wondering if it was possible to die of anticipation.

The road bent sharply to the right at the top of the hill, and as they turned and faced the steep incline on the other side, Frankie stamped on the breaks.

And there it was in all its splendour: Evershott Airfield, a criss-cross of weedy runways and rusty shacks, in the centre, the hangar, spectacularly gloomy and grey, its corrugated doors already wide open in welcome. It dwarfed the redundant outbuildings that scattered the airfield's edges, its domed roof intact bar one or two missing sections. It was a thing of beauty.

Frankie grinned at Tommy for a second before they heard agonising retching from the back seat, and Jed promptly threw up over the side of the car.

Tommy jumped out and walked to the edge of the hill, staring down at the airfield, emotion swelling in his chest, the sort of emotion he hadn't felt since he held Ashleigh in his arms for the first time.

Like her, it was perfect.

DENISE

She'd heeded Paul's instructions with tacit hatred. She was to take the drugs in the Range Rover to Groat Hall Farm, make sure there were no police around then call him at the Joiner's Arms in Hexham when she knew the coast was clear. He wasn't taking any risks, he'd said. He didn't trust Tommy, or her or anyone else.

Her garden had been dug up, the parade of colours now trampled and soiled. The black bin bags had been emptied out onto her kitchen table, the individual seal bags of a hundred or so pills in each crammed into a Head sports bag that was too heavy for her to lift. But lift it she would, for if she didn't …

Paul had held a knife to her cheek as he explained how he could cut someone's face to shreds with a few quick flicks of the wrist, the tone of his voice firm enough to remind her she had no choice.

He was gone now, and she stared down at her filthy kitchen floor, feeling like she could mop the linoleum with her dignity. Inside the holdall was a separate Super Savers carrier bag containing twenty seal bags of drugs. The carrier bag had Tommy's name on it.

'Just in case Peach sees the light,' Paul had said. He looked like he was off to a funeral; her brother was quite literally dressed to kill. 'Either way, the lad's finished. Too fucking stupid.' He'd patted the breast pocket of his black suit jacket, his face grotesquely pleased as his ring hit the jutting metal of the knife that lay there. She'd heard over the years that Paul had no time for guns. He liked to get close, smell the blood for himself. She believed every word of it now.

A rolling sickness gripped her stomach, bending her double.

She wanted Tommy out of Sam's life, but she didn't want him dead. She had enough guilt in her life.

She had to warn Tommy. She had to warn Sam. She had to do the right thing, otherwise she was finished too.

***

But Tommy wasn't home, and neither was Sam. When she turned away from her daughter's front door, little Carl Logan was standing at the gate, gawping at her, his face streaked and dirty.

'Where is she?' She marched towards Carl who stood motionless, not a glimmer of fear.

Carl gave an exaggerated shrug, his face set in a mocking *fucked if I know.*

The palm of her hand had walloped his small cheek before she could even think. It frightened her more than him, and though he staggered with the force of it, he regained his balance like a pro and stared up at her, staunchly. It unnerved her, making her feel small and useless, and him only seven or eight years old.

'Does your mother never wash you?' she spat. 'You *stink!*'

It hurt more than any slap, she could tell by the way he flinched at her words. But the pain was short lived and Carl brought back one of his skinny legs and kicked at her shin with the force of a striker aiming a penalty. The agony was immediate and intense, bringing tears to her eyes and a barking yelp from her mouth.

'The fucking Fosters, you fat bitch!' he squealed in his little-boy voice. Laughing, he ran away from her across the road and into the blackened garden of the burnt-out house.

She limped towards the Fosters', cursing with every step. She was greeted at the door by Jed's father, a man with Lego-man hair and a jumper thrown over his shoulders. He brought to mind her ex-husband and she felt herself bristle as the man looked down at her like she whiffed.

'I need to see Samantha,' she said, trying to sound authoritative.

'Betty!' Davie called over his shoulder.

'It's all right.' Sam was behind him and Davie stepped aside, still eying Denise warily.

'Can I come in, love?' The sight of her daughter brought a lump the size of a golf ball to her throat. She looked a spectacle, she knew it, her hair unwashed, mascara streaked, a warm trickle of blood making its way down her shin to her ankle. The look of shock on Sam's face brought fresh tears to her eyes. Perhaps she could stay here with the Fosters. Perhaps she could be safe, too.

Sam stood back, and Denise stumbled into the house, the cosy warmth of the chintz swathing her in both relief and disgust. She followed Sam into the front room, listening to Ashleigh's infectious laughter from the kitchen.

'What do you want?' Sam stood at the fireplace, her arms folded.

Her legs unstable, Denise looked towards one of the high-backed chairs, the sort you find in old people's homes and hospitals. Imagining a faint odour of piss, she decided against sitting, so she steadied herself instead against a glass-fronted sideboard full of china thimbles.

It was Tommy, she said, he was in danger.

'Danger you put him in. Why can't you just keep your nose out of our business?'

'It's your Uncle Paul, love, I got him all wrong.' Denise heard the bitterness in her own voice.

'For God's sake, Mam, you always get them wrong. There's always something, it's never you, is it?'

It wasn't. She'd just had bad luck. But Sam was on a roll.

'My dad couldn't stand you. Drove him away to the other side of the world. Couldn't get far enough away from you. And Marvin.

I loved him, he was my dad in every sense of the word and you didn't bat an eyelid when he fucked off with all your going on and on and on.' Sam gave her the 'Birdy Song' gestures, 'Nag, nag, bleedin' nag. And then who did I get? Adrian? Oh, he was just dandy, the pervert, but oh no, you didn't believe me, did you? Had to wait for him to expose himself to some poor cow before you got shot of him.'

Denise had never heard Sam so angry, so *articulate*. She got that from her mother.

'And then Kevin did a runner with all our money, and now your precious brother is back in your life. You haven't got a clue, have you?'

Denise felt the sting of undeserved blame. 'He lied to me,' she said, her defences unleashed. She couldn't help it. It was in her bones. She was the victim here.

'They all lie to you, mother, everything you don't agree with is a lie. All you think about is yourself.'

The insult cut Denise's gasp in half. She'd come here to tell Sam that Tommy should stay away from Paul and the drugs. She was there to warn them both after which Sam would fall into her arms in gratitude. 'I don't think you can lecture me on men,' she said, still aghast. 'Look what you landed yourself,' and she felt the electricity of Sam's fury.

'I love him!' Sam was pointing out the window at the street and Tommy beyond it. 'I don't want him for what he's got, Mam, I want him for him! Do you know what that even means? Do you know what that feels like?!' It was like a barb jabbing at her heart. 'Well? Do you?'

Sam's eyes flashed as she contained the tears, not allowing them to flow. She got that from her mother, too.

'I love him, Mam, and he loves *me*, all right?' she crossed her hands over her chest. 'Just accept it.'

Denise squeezed her eyes closed as if to stop the words in their tracks. Sam wasn't getting it; the sacrifices she'd made, the dreams she'd had. All the things she had planned for their future. She opened her eyes – one last try. 'We could go away, you, me, and Ashleigh, get out of this hole—'

'I don't want to go with you!' Sam butted in. 'I want to be with my family!'

Her family? It choked her, stung her eyes, but when she spoke again, her voice was calm and measured. 'There's something I've got to do, love,' she said, 'please don't hate me for it.' She thought Sam would look at her as if she hated her already, but she didn't. She simply looked exhausted. 'I've got to go to the farm, make a delivery.' She knew Sam understood, but she saw indecision, hesitation. 'I can't say any more than that, but I'm doing it for you, sweetheart. And Tommy.'

Denise reached out, but Sam's face darkened like night falling in the desert, swift and unforeseen. She knew then that her daughter had been told; that she knew about the robbery, the identification of Tommy's eyes. She knew then that forgiveness was impossible.

'We're leaving.' said Sam. 'And we won't be coming back, thanks to you and your shithead brother.'

'Don't, Samantha, please ...'

Sam was looking towards the door, listening to her baby's faint cries.

'Wait.' Denise grabbed her daughter's hand, and Sam didn't pull away. It gave her some hope, some semblance of redemption. There was one thing left she could do, and it might save her daughter's life.

She rummaged in her bag, took out her purse and opened it,

running her fingers over the line of cards inside. 'Here.' She handed a credit card to Sam. 'There's five or six hundred on there, you can fake my signature, I know that.' All the notes asking to be excused from PE and showers that she'd never written. 'Just in case,' she said. 'Please, be careful, love. Use it if you have to.'

Sam's eyes questioned hers, so she had to explain. 'If you have to get away, even without Tommy.' Denise closed her hands around Sam's.

'I'm not going anywhere without my husband.' Sam withdrew her hands from her mother's but held on to the credit card. 'Bye, Mam,' she said.

And she was gone, running from the room with a gulping sob. Sam wanted her *family* more than she wanted her mother. She'd made her choice, and Denise felt a sharp slice of fear cut through her.

TOMMY

'Your brother?' Frankie squinted up at the hanger, hands folded into his armpits.

'Half-brother, obviously,' said Tommy.

'I've heard everything now, like.'

Tommy had spent the last few hours considering ways to approach Tucker, now the reality of it had sunk it. Maybe they could call a truce, even have a drink together. Maybe Tucker could turn over a new leaf. But it didn't feel right. Tucker was too unknown, too far removed from Tommy's life to be part of it. Too much of a thug. *Perhaps not such a nice family that took him after all,* he thought, remembering his mother's words. But how was she to know what Tucker's life had been like in Liverpool? If he had stayed a Collins, would he have turned out any different? Or would he have been an outcast, an embarrassment? It was hard enough not being white on Valley Park now, so Christ knows what it would have been like back in the sixties.

Still, Tommy had tried to summon brotherly affection, something akin to what he felt for the astronaut, some sort of implicit bond that could unit them. But, when he truly thought about it, he'd only ever felt that kind of attachment to Jed. And, besides, Tommy and Sam would be gone by the morning, and it had begun to sink in that his life was about to change forever. He'd never visit the garden of remembrance where his mother's ashes were scattered again; his home would be occupied by some other family with nowt. He might never again spread Stork SB over one of Betty's warm cheese scones. His father would be released to no one. It had occupied his mind to the point of distraction all afternoon, sending Jed into a panicking squall. Nevertheless, the afternoon was going like clockwork, everything falling into place, or so he thought.

'We're running out of power!' Jed was breathless, approaching Tommy and Frankie with a look of holy hell.

'How?' Tommy asked.

Jed hadn't said a word about Tucker. Once he'd regurgitated his breakfast, he'd avoided eye contact with Tommy, walking away and busying himself when Tommy asked his opinion on the matter.

'Three generators didn't show,' said Jed, looking over his shoulder. 'The farm one's a hundred years old and there's no frigging fuel.'

'Speak to Jimmy,' said Tommy. 'He knows how they work.'

'Can't find him, can I?!'

Tommy nodded in the direction of a line of three portaloos that would have to serve thousands, and where Jimmy was quite literally shitting himself, his impending night of MC fame taking its toll on his bowels.

'And these,' said Jed, holding up his precious, brick-like phone, 'don't work in the middle of frigging nowhere.' He threw it over his shoulder, his face searching Tommy's for answers that didn't come, not for a few amusing seconds, anyway.

'Good job I brought walkie-talkies, then isn't it?' said Frankie. 'They're in Lady Penelope's boot. Back to basics, Gerald.'

Jed put his hands on his hips, as if he didn't want to hear solutions, as if he was due a good moan.

'Listen mate,' said Tommy. 'About Tucker—'

'And where's the lighting and the sound gear?' Jed wasn't interested in a conversation about the usurper. 'I've got riggers sitting on the stage doing sweet Fanny Adams.'

Tommy sighed and looked around him. The sun was sinking. It would be pitch-dark in a few hours. 'They should've been here by now,' he said, too calmly for Jed's liking.

'Tommy!' Jed raised his arms. 'I'm stressing my tits off here!'

'It'll be fine,' said Tommy, holding Jed's arms and bringing them back to his side. 'Enjoy it, this is going to be the best night of our lives.'

'Jesus.' Jed put his head in his hands. 'Please, God, send power.'

The portaloo door swung open and Jimmy strode out, zipping up his flies.

'Thank Christ!' Jed strode off in Jimmy's direction, arms gesticulating at all the things that were going wrong while Tommy walked away from Frankie towards the hangar. It was epic, remarkable, people bustling around its vast mouth like a scene from *Close Encounters of the Third Kind*. The stress was gone, the fear evaporated. The plan would work, it had to.

Inside the hangar, he stared up at the floodlit walls. Great sheets of white were being staple-gunned to the wooden beams, giving the interior the appearance of the inside of a billowing tent. Mobz's army were working their way efficiently around each sheet, some of the artists hanging from the rigging, some on great, wheeled ladders, others reaching up precariously from piles of empty crates. Each white sheet was imbued with an evocative alien, interspersed with iconic, smiley faces at various angles. Any spare piece of wall not covered by a sheet was being slathered in luminous, neon paint.

Tommy stood next to Mobz who tugged slowly on a joint, his oily curls fingering the edges of his back-to-front baseball cap.

'Few hotels didn't get their clean sheets,' said Mobz, grinning in a way that hid his stained, rickety teeth.

Tommy had no words, and Mobz had little need of them. They

stood, side by side, cocooned in the echo of hammering, drilling, shouting, and laughter. He was about to burst with pride when the generator's hum faded, and the floodlights died.

'*Fuuuuck!*' Jed's wail filled the hangar, but somehow, Tommy didn't flap. He decided to add another rule to the billionaire's list.

Six: trust your instincts.

He patted Mobz on the back and walked outside to find two minibuses parking up, great hulks of men pouring from their sides. Hadgy Dodds was at the helm, taking considerable pride at overseeing such a healthy bunch of specimens.

'Hey, these better not be hooligans.' Jed had sprinted to Tommy's side, his voice fraught. 'Christ, that one's in a 'Boro shirt!'

'Behave,' said Tommy, striding up to Hadgy.

'Where do you want us?' Hadgy asked, back straight, hands clasped at his groin.

'Back on the A1,' said Tommy. 'We need power and diesel. Some Valium for Jed would be champion.'

Hadgy nodded, as if he was asked regularly to find such things. He whistled, and his men gathered around. He picked half a dozen, dishing out the orders before they climbed back into the minibuses which headed back off in the direction of the roadworks, the bane of every northern driver's life, and Tommy's electricity salvation.

Tommy put a hand on Jed's shoulder. 'Show these boys their stations, then.'

Jed was frowning at the bouncers, and he cleared his throat, drawing his shoulders back and flexing his muscles before leading them away.

Looking back at the hangar, Tommy saw Jimmy waving him over.

'Where's the lights and the sound? I'm getting worried,' Jimmy said when Tommy reached him.

'Aye,' said Tommy, looking at his watch. It was gone eight o'clock. The trucks were two hours late. 'Where's Frankie?'

Jimmy nodded his head towards the pink car where Frankie was bent over the bonnet with a handkerchief, rubbing at spots of dirt.

'Maybe they've gone to the farm,' said Tommy.

'Christ, Tommy, it's a hundred-mile round trip,' said Jimmy, his red face suddenly flushing redder. 'Oh, Jesus …' A loud gut-groan had Jimmy heading for the portaloos once more.

Tommy watched Frankie as he uncurled himself, stretched his back and waved, happy as Larry and completely out of place in his dated two-tone finery. A hundred-mile round trip. If he avoided the roadworks, he could be back just in time. Then there was Peach to consider. Peach thought they would be at Groat Hall Farm, and he'd probably be there by now, and Tommy didn't want Frankie leading the police back to the airfield. But no lights, no sound – no rave.

Jed was back at his side, considerably calmer, like a dog who'd been scolded by its pack leaders. Tommy explained the dilemma.

'Jesus,' Jed whined. 'I told them the new venue.'

Frankie was walking across the tarmac towards them. 'How's it gannin'?' he asked. 'Need 'owt doing?'

Tommy and Jed exchanged a brief glance.

'He can't take that car,' said Jed under his breath.

'What?' Frankie looked puzzled until Jed enlightened him. They needed someone to go to the farm in case the sound and lighting had gone there by mistake.

'Nee bother,' Frankie said. 'But I'm not leaving Her Ladyship here. More than my job's worth.' He looked back at the car with something akin to tenderness. 'Where I go, she goes,' he said.

Jed sighed and looked at Tommy who shrugged his agreement. Who was he to separate a man from the woman in his life?

'Right,' Frankie smiled. 'What do you want us to do?'

PEACH

'Great party, boss, fancy a dance?' Murphy sucked thirstily at a can of Irn-Bru, the liquid echoing down his throat in noisy glugs.

Peach could barely contain his frustration. Had they been duped?

Silence reigned, the shadows of tree branches dancing on the walls as the sun began to sink. They'd been sitting either side of a filthy window they'd had to wipe clean with toilet roll and spit for almost nine hours. Peach's top lip burned, his fingers clawing at the hair of his moustache harder than ever. The stench of the farmhouse – mould, damp, and wet dogs – turned his stomach. Even the sandwiches Murphy had brought seemed infused with a hint of manure flavouring.

Peach lifted his radio to his mouth.

'Any activity at the petrol stations?'

'No, sir,' came the bored response four times over.

The patrols had been at the service stations for four hours, others on standby at every conceivable entry point within ten miles of the farm. Riot and dog teams, armed response and air patrol were awaiting orders. Chief Superintendent Forbes was not going to be a happy man come Monday if Peach didn't get a result, and McNally would have every reason to put him on the backlog of unsolved crimes that were accumulating at a rate of knots – if he wasn't sacked outright for disobeying orders. This was his one chance, and something had gone very wrong.

Murphy crunched the empty can in his hand and flung it across the room while Peach eyed him doubtfully, wondering if Murphy had heard wrong, whether his confidence that the set-up would happen in stages was unfounded. Not everyone would arrive together, Murphy had said, they wouldn't want to draw attention to convoys of vans and lorries. It would all start at midday and go on until past ten when the phone numbers would go live. Then they could move in.

But there was nothing to move in on.

Peach looked back at the streaky window, the flicker of stars becoming visible as the sun made its slow descent. He heard a rustling, Murphy digging into one of his voluminous trouser pockets for his tobacco and papers. As he drew out the machine he used to roll his cigarettes, Murphy's wallet fell to the floor, falling open, displaying a photograph of his younger self. The picture was around ten years old judging by Murphy's flares and the wide necked shirt. In his arms he held a toddler, a little boy wearing a white sun hat.

Peach leant down and picked it up. 'He yours?' he asked, surprised that Murphy was mature enough to father a child.

'No, that's our kid,' said Murphy. 'Bit of an age gap, eighteen years.' Murphy pressed the tobacco into the roller, slotted the Rizzla behind it. 'Let's just say he was a surprise for my parents. Good kid, though, proper angel. Well, most of the time.' He laughed gently.

Was? Peach closed the wallet, held it in his hands. 'Was he killed?'

'You could say that. Cancer,' said Murphy, licking the edge of the Rizzla with the tip of his tongue. 'Fuckin' 'orrible, it was. Six-year-old when he went.'

Peach found himself concentrating on Murphy's hands.

'Broke me mam's heart,' said Murphy. 'She was never the same after that. Or me dad. Moved down south and threw themselves into their work.' He lit his cigarette, eyes squinting at Peach over the flame. He took a long drag, blowing out a plume of smoke as he put his lighter and paraphernalia back into his pocket. 'I've seen what losing a kid does to people,' he said.

Handing the wallet back to Murphy, Peach exhaled his relief, feeling unexpectedly lucky. Sally would be home soon – tomorrow if Doctor Flynn gave her the all clear. He felt something he hadn't felt in a long while – the need to share.

'It's like …' But he couldn't finish. He felt it in his heart but couldn't find the words.

'No need to explain, boss,' said Murphy. 'No need at all.'

Peach nodded, grateful of the reprieve, his eyes turning back to the window and the grey dusk beyond it. No red sky tonight, no shepherd's delight in the morning. Perhaps the long dry summer was finally over.

Leaning forward, he spotted a flash of light in the near distance.

'Ay up,' said Murphy, suddenly alert.

The lights flickered through the hedges that lined the road, drawing closer until the vehicle slowed and turned onto the track that led to the farm. A black Range Rover approached, the darkening sky glaring off the windscreen. Peach squinted, trying to see beyond the glassy sheen, unable to see inside the vehicle. But he knew the car, and he knew the owner.

The wheels bounced over pot holes and the car came to a stop a few feet from the gate of a fence that enclosed the overrun garden. If it would just inch forward into the shadow of the house, he'd be able to see inside. Instead, it remained stationery, engine turning.

'*Sir.*' Peach heard an urgent voice crackle from his radio. '*Reports of two firebombs in the Byker Wall, an armed robbery in Gosforth and three stabbings in the city centre. We need officers.*'

What? Peach rubbed at his eyes with a finger and thumb. 'How many do you need?'

'*Six units… Sorry, make that seven, we've got a jumper on the bridge.'*

'For Christ's sake.' Peach clenched his lips together in frustration. 'Take them from the service stations, I need the others.'

'*Roger.*'

'Boss.' Murphy was on his feet and Peach joined him, looking down at the car, the driver's door now open. A foot emerged, then another – red peep-toe sandals with a short heel. A few seconds later, she was standing by the car and pulling a sports bag from the back seat.

'What the hell …?' said Murphy.

Denise Morris was clutching the sports bag in her hand, bending to one side with the weight of it, surveying the farmhouse with anxious eyes. She staggered at first, then began walking towards the building with small, nervous steps.

Peach switched off his radio and indicated to Murphy to do the same as they heard the latch clunk and the front door creak open.

'Don't move,' Peach whispered, and he walked carefully to the bedroom door, avoiding the creaky floorboards he'd already tested. He eased the door open a crack and listened: shoes on lino, then a grunt and the sports bag hitting the kitchen table.

'*Sweet Jesus,*' he heard, then footsteps echoing again, in and out of rooms, the sound of panicked breathing, then the faint tinkle of a bell as Denise picked up the receiver of the telephone on the hallway wall. He heard the rasp of the telephone's rotary dial and the painfully slow click of its return as she dialled a number. The silence was so dense he could hear the ringing of the recipient's phone from the earpiece.

Denise's voice was hushed, verging on hysteria. '*Paul Smart, get Paul Smart.*' There was a long pause before she spoke again. '*There's no one here! …Yes, I'm at the right place … No, no other* cars ... I don't know! ... Nobody, it's completely empty.' A long silence followed where Denise tried to speak but was cut off at every attempt. Finally, her voice trembling, she said, *'The barn? ... okay, okay, I'll go and look.'* She hung up, and the front door opened and closed once more.

'Who is it?' Murphy asked, watching Denise reappear as Peach reached his side.

Murphy whistled when Peach enlightened him: Paul Smart's sister, Tommy Collins's mother-in-law, one of the witnesses from the building society robbery.

Outside, Denise was standing amidst the weeds, looking about her before disappearing around the side of the farmhouse. While Peach's car was being repaired, he'd picked up a temporary vehicle from the depot, ten times better than his own, and had parked it behind some trees off the public road half a mile away, so if it was vehicles she was looking for, she'd find nothing.

'Control?' he said when he switched on his radio.

'Sir, we've been trying to get hold of you. There's a shit storm going down here, we've had to take all your units.'

'What? Listen to me—'

'Reports of gun-fire in three locations, two hostage situations, another armed robbery.'

Peach dropped the radio from his mouth and Murphy slumped down into his chair. 'They've got to be hoaxes, boss,' he said.

'Sorry, sir, but we've got to respond.'

Peach struggled to hold back the convoy of expletives that herded in his throat. 'I need at least four units,' he said.

'Superintendent McNally's orders, sir.'

Peach's furious eyes met Murphy's. Could the man not have a weekend away without sticking his nose in?

'We had to contact him, sir—'

Peach switched the radio off and flung it onto the farmer's unmade bed as a long '*Shhhhit!*' slid from Murphy's mouth.

Peach peered around the window frame as a pale blue Jaguar pulled up alongside Paul Smart's car. The sun was low enough now for Peach to see inside: white baseball cap pulled low over the driver's face. A cigarette was flicked from the window before the door opened and Trevor Logan stepped out, the butt of a pistol sticking out the front of tracksuit bottoms that he hiked up before looking towards the bedroom window. Peach and Murphy snapped their heads away, and when they looked back, Trevor Logan was out of sight.

'Armed response, Groat Hall Farm,' said Murphy into his radio.

'*All units are out, man, I've just told you!*' The tone was stressed against a background of raised voices and ringing phones.

'Switch it off!' said Peach, straining his neck to see out the window.

Murphy obeyed, and the farmhouse door opened, Peach indicating to Murphy to keep watch at the window while he made his way to the bedroom door once more.

Footsteps shuffled down the hallway, then in and out of the downstairs rooms, the pace quickening as Trevor walked to the bottom of the stairs.

Peach edged the door open another inch, put one eye around its frame. Trevor had his foot on the bottom stair, looking down at the gun which was now in his hand.

'*Boss!*' Murphy hissed, and Peach turned to him angrily with a finger to his lips. '*We've got no back up,*' Murphy mouthed, pulling a finger across his throat.

Peach hesitated, thoughts of Sally, fatherless as well as motherless, forming a nub of indecision in his throat.

A stair creaked, and he heard the soft padding of footsteps. Trevor reached the landing, and Murphy pulled the long curtain around him while Peach put his back to the wall behind the door. It opened, and Trevor's short, raspy breaths could be heard as he stood in the doorway. Peach closed his eyes, held his breath, and the footsteps crept away, three other doors opening and closing before Trevor's low, seething voice could be heard.

'*Come out, you fffffucker, I'll blow your bastard brains out!*'

The sound of feet on the stairs again drew Peach's breath from his lungs. A few seconds later, he heard the grating of the sports bag's zipper, then a short laugh and the scraping of a chair on the kitchen floor. The gun rattled as it hit the kitchen table, then there was nothing but silence for a while.

The sniffles were quiet at first, growing louder until the sobs became long, angry howls. The chair scraped back, and Peach heard it fall to the floor.

Trevor Logan raged. Glass and crockery smashed to the floor, windows shattered, wood splintered on wood. Trevor's cries came from the depths – long, anguished roars.

Murphy pushed his hands into his pockets, his eyes closed, head bowed as if witnessing Billy Logan's drawn-out death in real time. On it went for several long minutes, until Trevor's cries started to abate, reduced to exhausted moans, rendered more sorrowful by their maleness.

'*Come on! I'll fucking kill you!*'

Trevor's feeble sob was cut short, the sound of rapid footsteps approaching the front door bringing him back out into the hallway.

Peach pulled the bedroom door open and, before Murphy could protest, he was on the landing, now in gloomy darkness, only the kitchen light illuminating the hallway below. Murphy was by his side a few seconds later, his face agitated at his boss's rashness.

The latch of the front door clicked open and Denise appeared in the doorway. Trevor stood stock still, the sports bag in one hand, the gun outstretched in the other. Denise stepped back in fright, her hands darting to her ears.

'Put the gun down,' said Peach from the top of the stairs.

Trevor spun around, pointing the gun up at Peach. It shook in his hands, and Peach lifted his arm instinctively to protect Murphy who pushed through it and took a few steps down the stairs.

'Do what the man says, mate,' he said.

Trevor's terrified eyes bounced to Murphy before he turned the gun back on Denise who still stood in the doorway, face rigid with terror. She gasped, her legs buckling beneath her, and she sank to her knees, one hand held up as if it might halt the course of the bullet.

'Come near me and I'll kill her,' said Trevor, striding to Denise and pointing the gun at her head.

Peach took a few tentative steps down the stairs, stopping when Trevor began to bellow. 'Where's Paul fucking Smart?! Eh? Where the fuck is he?!' Trevor swung the bag viciously at Denise who fell sideways and curled into a ball, not flinching at Trevor's kicking feet as if she knew exactly how to protect herself.

'We were wondering the same thing, weren't we, boss?' said Murphy.

'Fucking shut up!' Trevor turned, dropping the bag, and lifting the gun with both hands, pointing it at the two detectives who were halfway down the stairs, palms raised.

'Back up's on the way,' lied Murphy. 'They'll be here any minute. Just put it on the floor and kick it towards me.'

Peach watched Murphy walk down the stairs, stopping at the

bottom just a few feet from Trevor. His DS was braver than he thought.

But Trevor's face was set in fury. 'Get up,' he ordered Denise.

Denise stayed motionless, her muffled whimpers barely audible.

'Fucking get up, man!'

'Trevor,' said Peach, his hands still raised as he joined Murphy. 'I know what happened, I was there.' In any other circumstance, he would have said Billy Logan didn't suffer, that he died instantly, but Trevor had witnessed the whole sorry affair through his living room window.

The circle was closing in Peach's mind. Trevor Logan and Reggie Collins, the visits to the prison, the gun runner who'd supplied the weapon in Trevor's hand, meant to assassinate Paul Smart. Trevor had nothing to lose in taking his vengeance. His life was over, ruined already by the things he'd seen and done.

Trevor took hold of Denise's arm, dragging her to her feet with one hand, the gun wobbling precariously in the other. If he pulled the trigger, the bullet could hit any one of them.

'Get the bag,' he said.

Denise picked up the sports bag, held it loosely in her fingers.

'It's not worth it, mate,' said Murphy, stepping forward.

'It's nothing to do with me,' Denise protested, turning her pleading eyes on Trevor. 'I know where he is—'

Eyes red with hate, Trevor pulled Denise to him, put the gun to her temple, his arm hooked around her neck as he dragged her backwards towards the Jaguar, opened the passenger door and shoved Denise inside with the bag. With the gun aimed at Peach, he jumped into the driver's seat and started the engine, the three-point turn sending a shower of gravel their way as he sped off.

When the car reached the end of the dirt track, the passenger door flew open, and Denise came tumbling out.

Peach was the first to reach her. 'Where are the car keys?'

Denise's breath rasped, speech beyond her.

'Where are the keys?!' he repeated, raising his voice and pulling her into a sitting position.

She pointed at her pocket.

'And where's your brother?'

She whimpered, finding her voice at last. 'He's coming here. He should have been here by now. Please, he'll hurt my Samantha!'

Peach put his hand in her jacket pocket and drew out the Range Rover's keys, tossing them to Murphy.

'I hope you're pleased with yourself,' he said to Denise before she fell back to the ground and he jumped into the car with Murphy.

TOMMY

Tommy and Jed sat together on crates in the hushed blackness, the moon and the tip of their cigarettes their only light. The silhouette of the hangar loomed in front of them.

'Maybe we should move to Scotland.' Jed's nerves were still on edge.

'There's some hard bastards coming from Glasgow,' said Tommy.

'Howay, Hadgy. Where is he?'

They still had no power, but the sound and lighting had arrived just twenty minutes after Frankie set off on his recce to the farm.

'Don't go into the grounds,' Tommy had said to Frankie. He was to drive past the farm entrance, and if the trucks were there, he was to park up somewhere, find the crew and give them directions.

'You can count on me,' Frankie had said.

'Hundred per center.' Tommy had slapped him hard on the shoulder, his hand resting there a while before Frankie jumped into the Lady Penelope and drove off, the box of walkie-talkies still at Tommy's feet. It had been too late to chase him down; Frankie was out onto the road in a few seconds flat and incommunicado.

That was two hours ago, and Tommy felt Jed's tug on his arm. They stood slowly as the twinkling of a single set of headlights in the distance came into view. The lights grew larger, another set appearing behind them, and the people lounging around the hangar began to stir.

'These better not be punters,' said Tommy.

Jed swallowed. 'The numbers have been live for an hour.'

'Hadgy,' said Tommy, grabbing Jed's arm and pulling him

across the tarmac.

The minibuses pulled into the airfield, grinding to a halt at the doors of the hangar. Hadgy emerged and pulled the sides of the first minibus open. Two men hauled a generator from it, carrying it easily inside, followed by another man who carried a barrel of fuel.

'You *beauty!*' exclaimed Jed, approaching the second minibus where three more men were lugging another generator from its interior. Jed crossed himself and held his palms together in prayer. 'Please work, please work, please work.'

'Pray harder,' said Tommy.

Another set of headlights shone in the distance.

'Hail Mary, full of grace ...' Jed's panicked voice trailed off as they watched the headlights approaching, one after the other, from the roads to the north, south and the east. They heard the distant pounding of bass, people already pumped up, high on the anticipation. 'I think I'm gonna piss myself,' said Jed.

The sound of a helicopter approaching had them turning their faces skyward. Not the cops, *please not the cops.* They watched its flashing light pass over them, heading south, dissolving into the distance.

As they brought their heads back down, the aircraft hangar burst into light, beams of silverish white slicing through the roof's void panels in strobes that pierced the darkness. Cheers rose up from inside the hangar and they heard the buzz, felt the vibrations, of the sound system revving up. The first few bars of the 'Hallelujah Chorus' blasted out and a mass of coloured lights rebounded from the beat before the piano riff of 'Strings of Life' drew Tommy and Jed into each other's arms.

'I believe in God! I believe in God!' yelled Jed.

They jumped up and down, fingers grasping at each other's

backs, then they ran hell for leather towards the hangar.

***

The coaches and cars didn't stop. They crawled into the airfield like a troop of illuminated, giant caterpillars, the roads lit up as far as the eye could see.

Shona and her gaggle of girls, wearing fluorescent jackets robbed by Hadgy from the workmen's portacabins, waved cars and buses into spaces across the runways and beyond onto the fields.

Tommy and Jed, flanked by Hadgy and three other beefy men, stood at the entrance to a long, coiling tunnel fixed to the huge doorway of the hangar. It was lit in neon ultra-violet, forming an umbilical corridor which punters stared at in wonder as they parted with their twenty-quid. Mobz had come up trumps.

'You didn't see Frankie, did you?' Tommy asked Hadgy.

Hadgy shook his head. 'Wouldn't get back in anyway,' he said, nodding towards the queues of traffic.

''Suppose not.' He wouldn't leave the Lady Penelope out on the road either.

Tommy looked up at the ceiling of stars, piecing together the face of an alien. But its face wasn't friendly. If anything, it looked a little too much like Paul Smart for his liking.

PEACH

The Jaguar was speeding ahead of them, lights on full beam as the sky finally gave up its grasp on daylight. Peach fumbled in his pocket, cursing silently when he realised his radio was still lying on the farmer's bed.

'Here, use mine.' Murphy passed his radio to Peach.

'Control,' said Peach. He had to repeat it twice more before he got a response.

'*Go ahead,*' came a frazzled voice.

'In pursuit of a blue Jaguar, probably stolen, heading north from Groat Hall Farm, Hexham, on the B6306. Driver, Trevor Logan, that's Trevor Logan, we know him well.'

His hand fell away from his mouth as he noticed the tail lights of another car just a few yards ahead of the Jaguar. It looked small and sporty, and it sped up as the Jag got closer.

'Paul Smart had a silver MG on his drive, boss,' said Murphy, and he pushed down further on the accelerator.

'*Is anyone in immediate danger?*' the radio sputtered.

Peach held the radio to his mouth, kept it there, the speaker button un-pressed.

'*Is he armed, sir? Is anyone in immediate danger?*'

'Boss?' Murphy was keeping his eyes on the road while he drove, glancing intermittently at Peach.

The only person in danger now was Paul Smart.

Peach pressed the button. 'No.'

'*Downgraded, over and out.*'

Murphy's glances became more frantic. 'What you doing?'

Peach stared straight ahead. 'Turn back.'

'Wha?!'

Murphy didn't understand after all. Paul Smart was clean as a whistle now as far as his drugs were concerned, and when someone harms your child or puts them in danger, you would happily see them destroyed by whatever means necessary.

Peach didn't flinch when Murphy's hand slammed on the steering wheel, a vein in his neck throbbing as he lifted his foot from the accelerator and pulled into a layby to turn the car around.

They coasted back towards the farm in silence, until Murphy's face shot forward, his eyes on something in the field to Peach's left as they slowed to take a bend.

'What the …?' Murphy stopped the car and reversed, parking up on the grassy verge. In the field, what looked like the back end of a pink Cadillac jutted from a shallow ditch, surrounded by a herd of curious cows. The passenger door was hanging open, a man lying on his back just a few feet away, the bloodied face glistening in the beam of the Cadillac's headlights.

Shooing the cows away, they approached the car, Peach hunching down next to the man's body, the back of Murphy's hand springing to his mouth when he saw the driver's face, beaten and swollen to a pulp. The fingers of one hand had been crushed and forced into the rocky soil, and blood soaked his chest.

'Get an ambulance,' said Peach.

As Murphy strode towards the pink car with his radio to his mouth, Peach felt for a pulse; it was faint, but present. He tore open the man's shirt which revealed two stab wounds that oozed blood with every shallow breath.

'Can you hear me?' Peach urged.

One of the victim's eyelids fluttered open despite the swollen mess.

'Don't move, help's on the way,' said Peach.

'I didn't tell him.' The man's lips barely moved. 'Didn't tell him where it was.'

'Who?' asked Peach. 'Who did this to you?' But he had a good idea.

'On their way, boss, air ambulance,' Murphy said, getting down onto his haunches by Peach's side.

'Loverboy!' The man smiled a weak, bloody smile, and Peach heard the gurgle of fresh blood from the wounds. He put his hands over them to stem the flow. 'I'm not telling you either,' the man said.

'I think it's Frankie Donahue,' Murphy said. 'The hair, boss. He was in the pub last night.'

Frankie's laboured breathing faltered, the white of the one eye he could barely open like a tiny light bulb amidst the crimson of his face.

'Needs to get away,' he said, straining his neck.

'Don't move,' said Peach, pressing down harder on the wounds.

'Who, mate?' asked Murphy.

Frankie's head fell back with a thud. 'Tommy.'

He was trying to say something else, lips moving but no sound coming out, and Peach put his ear to Frankie's lips.

'He'll kill him,' Frankie whispered. 'Smartie …'

But Peach knew there was someone else he would target first. Paul Smart's drugs were in the hands of Trevor Logan and Tommy Collins had deceived him. If Trevor Logan hadn't already run him off the road, he knew where Paul Smart would be headed.

'Where's the girl and the baby?' asked Peach, his voice gentle but urgent.

Frankie's eyes were closed, bubbles of blood forming at his nostrils. 'Jed's.' It came out in a single breath, and the blood seeped through Peach's fingers.

Indicating for Murphy to take over stemming the blood, Peach grabbed Murphy's radio from his hand and called Control.

'Get a patrol car to 10 Elm Street on Valley Park,' he said, 'it's urgent.' He didn't give them the chance to refuse, told the controller he'd kick his arse halfway to Scarborough if he didn't do what he asked. Now.

A pause, then a *'Yes, sir.'*

'And stand down all officers on *Operation Red Kite*.'

They already had.

With the distant *put-put* of a chopper at the edge of his hearing, Peach's eyes were drawn to the distance, miles away to the north, where two beams of white light suddenly sliced through the night sky.

'He's trying to say something, boss,' said Murphy, and Peach crouched down, putting his ear to Frankie's mouth once more.

Frankie lifted his crushed hand, attempting to point in the direction of the distant beams. 'Looks like the lights turned up,' he whispered, and the bloody bubbles at his nose stopped inflating.

TOMMY

Three hours passed. Eight thousand people were inside, spilling out onto the surrounding tarmac; and still they came, in cars and double-deckers, camper vans, Transits and motor-cycles. When there was no more room for vehicles they came on foot, abandoning their rides on the road and running through the fields, their glow torches like a swarm of fireflies.

Inside, the hangar pulsed like a beating heart, white strobes moving across the heads of the dancers like celestial fingers. Alien faces drifted above them, breathing misty, dry ice from their paranormal lungs, their neon eyes flashing in hypnotic time to the pounding bass. Hadgy pushed his way through the smoke and the bodies with bin bags full of money to the safe that stood guarded by four burly Sunderland supporters behind the stage, the stage where Jed was preparing for his first set, a bundle of nerves and excitement to be joining DJs he'd been idolising for years.

Tommy moved to the back of the throng and watched Jed take his place at the decks. He spotted Shona in the wings, tiny in the distance, a thumb and finger at her lips as she whistled in support of her new man. Jimmy Lyric and another MC joined Jed on stage for the hand-over. It was seamless, professional, Jed's face elated, his ego pumped as he spun his first tune, Lil' Louis's 'French Kiss'. The crowd went wild and Tommy raised his arms along with the masses, his body alive with the drumming rhythm.

He felt arms around his waist and he turned. 'Sam!' He hugged her so tightly she had to thump his back hard.

He let her go, grabbed her hand, and led her outside, through the crowds of outdoor dancers, one with a leg in plaster, crutches flailing in the air, another dressed as an African prince, holding onto his white skull cap as he jerked his elbows and knees. They peeked around the back of a caravan where a couple sat in camping chairs smoking joints, a beatbox supplying their very own chill-out tunes.

He pulled her behind a tree where she put her arms around his neck.

'I had to come,' she said. 'The police turned up and Mrs Foster's barricaded the door. She's got half the street in there for protection.'

Her eyes were sad, he noticed. 'Sam ...'

'I know,' she said. 'We've got to go. I want to go.'

Tommy looked away from her, the apology on his lips, but Sam's hands were stroking the back of his head.

'Look, Tommy,' she said, turning her head towards the hangar, throbbing with life. 'Look what you've done.'

He followed her eyes, and he saw the rave in all its glory from a whole new perspective. 'Yeah.' He couldn't help but smile.

Sam was smiling back at him, and she slid her hand into her shoulder bag, handing him a small bundle. He stepped back, holding it up to the moonlight: their passports and tickets.

'Ibiza,' she said.

'Eh? You want a holiday?'

She shook her head. 'They're one-way, Tommy.'

It took a few moments to sink in. 'Ibiza?'

'Yes!' Her eyes were wide. 'Sod building sites,' she said. 'Do what you love.' She cupped her hand and drew it across the air. '*Tommy Collins, Pioneer of Music.*' And, for a heavenly moment, he saw his name in lights.

'How?' he asked.

'Me mam's credit card. Got to the travel agent's just in time.'

Sam looked down at her feet. 'Long story.'

He was too happy, too elated to think about Denise.

Ibiza. The birthplace of raves, the Mecca of everything House Music.

'She can always come and visit,' he said, his joy interfering with his judgement.

Sam looked up at him, eyes sad but determined. 'We'll see.'

His hands cradled her cheeks, and he kissed her upturned face. 'I fucking love you,' he said, 'and Ashleigh.'

Sam smiled at him. 'We are pretty awesome, aren't we?'

At that moment, it didn't matter where he was. He could be living in a shack on the moon and he wouldn't care, so long as he had his family with him.

'Hang on,' said Tommy, 'how did you get here?'

'The inspector brought me.'

As if he'd landed in Antarctica, Tommy's skin froze.

'We had to walk for miles,' Sam said.

He closed his eyes and Sam's voice became concerned. 'He said I would be safer here …'

'Oh, Sam …' It was all he could say, and he opened his eyes to find her face frightened. Peach had said the patrol car would stay there all night to protect Ashleigh, and the Fosters until they were ready to leave, she said.

'He knows about this?' Tommy held up the tickets and the passports.

Sam nodded, yes, eyes brimming, and face creased with the knowledge she'd done something terribly wrong. Her voice trembled, 'Oh my God—'

But Tommy held a finger to her lips. A shack in Ibiza would be just fine. 'It's okay,' he said. 'Come on.'

He took Sam's hand and led her away, past the couple by the

caravan whose heads where now resting together, mouths hanging open in cannabis-induced smiles. They walked through the neon-lit tunnel, hands slapping off Tommy's shoulders and back, making him feel like Paul Gascoigne about to emerge onto the pitch at St James's Park.

At the end of the tunnel, Peach stood in the beige Mac, legs apart, hands in his coat pockets.

'This is quite the spectacle,' Peach said when Tommy reached him.

'Didn't have you down as a raver,' replied Tommy, warily.

'No. It's way past my bedtime.'

Tommy looked around for the rest of them – hundreds of coppers who would literally pull the plug and take everything.

'It's just me,' said Peach. 'Thought I'd come and see for myself.'

'So, what do you think?' asked Sam.

'Bunch of raving lunatics.'

'People just want to escape,' said Tommy, 'feel good for a while.'

Peach nodded. 'Yes, but at whose expense?'

Sam was looking at Peach, and he back at her, and Tommy thought he felt some kind of weird connection between the two of them.

'Thank you,' said Sam. 'But I think I'm going to be all right now.'

Peach nodded again and didn't follow when Sam pulled Tommy away towards the riot of colour, and when Tommy reached the throng of dancers and weaved his way among their flailing arms, he turned back, and Peach was gone.

SUNDAY

TOMMY

'It's not safe here, pet.'

Betty's hands grasped Tommy's across the kitchen table. They talked quietly, Davie and Barry asleep upstairs, half a dozen neighbours in sleeping bags in the front room. Betty didn't trust the policemen in the car outside not to doze off. She'd spent the last half an hour wringing her hands around her tea towel as she recounted tales of Paul Smart driving past the house three or four times until the police came calling. The officers had made sure all was well inside before parking up on the pavement and taking their fill of Betty's rock cakes and flasks of tea. She might not trust them, but she wouldn't see them go hungry.

The party was still going, Jimmy and Hadgy left in charge, but the elation of the night was over. News of Frankie had reached Tommy via Hadgy, the DCI relaying the details to him rather than directly to Tommy. His night had ended then, Hadgy hot-wiring a car parked two miles away, and Jed driving like a madman back to Valley Park. They'd fallen through the door at 5.00 a.m., and Betty had phoned the hospital to be told Frankie was critical, but stable.

'She's right,' said Jed. 'Just go, man, look at the time.'

Sam was sitting next to him, one arm cradling Ashleigh, the other holding the handle of her holdall. But Frankie was fighting for his life. He couldn't leave him.

'But, I sent him,' he said.

'*We* sent him,' said Jed. 'Look, what would Frankie say if he was here now?'

'He might have come with us,' said Tommy.

'Narrr,' growled Jed. 'His mam wants the kitchen doing. He's got pink paint and everything.'

'I know, I gave it to him,' said Tommy, sadly.

'Go, son. We'll make sure he's all right.' Betty carried on in the same quiet voice. 'He'll be right as rain in no time.'

Tommy thought he saw a glance between Betty and Jed. 'But what about you?' he asked. Paul Smart would come for them.

'Us?' said Betty. 'We've got Starsky and Hutch outside, pet.'

'The inspector said they could have protection,' said Sam.

Tommy frowned. 'Peach?'

Sam nodded, and a horn tooted outside. 'That's the taxi,' she said, her eyes on the flight tickets on the table in front of her.

'If your mother was here, she would never forgive me if I let anything happen to you and her grandbairn,' said Betty. 'You need to do the right thing, son. We'll miss you, but now's your chance. You won't get another one.'

Tommy looked down at Ashleigh's pouting mouth, sucking at her bottom lip in sleep. Paul Smart, Trevor Logan, Peach, Denise. Tucker. Their faces seemed to merge into one grisly image.

He got to his feet.

'Good lad,' said Betty. 'Jed, tell the taxi driver to wait.'

Tommy took Sam's holdall with one hand and picked up the rucksack at his feet with the other. It was all they had. A bag full of cash, enough to get through customs and a hotel until they got themselves sorted. The rest, Jed would take care of; all one hundred and twenty grand of it. Jed would take his cut, give Frankie his and pay whoever needed to be paid. The rest would be invested in whatever new venture Tommy could find on the sunny shores of the Med.

'Take care, son.' Betty hugged him when they reached the front door, held on as if she didn't want to let go. Tommy felt the warmth of her, smelt the familiar lily of the valley scent, and felt the needles pricking his heart.

Outside, Jed was leaning into the passenger window of the taxi while Tommy and Sam walked down the path, and Betty closed the door to let them all say their goodbyes, not before rolling her eyes at the sleeping officers in the squad car.

Sam climbed into the back seat of the taxi with Ashleigh and closed the door. The sun was gone, great leaden clouds rolling towards them, the heatwave finally broken.

Tommy and Jed faced each other.

'Come with us,' said Tommy. 'Loads of lasses in bikinis, howay.' He'd been wanting to ask, but he wasn't sure he wanted to hear the answer, not out loud.

'Got an interview with Nissan next week.'

'Jesus, congratulations,' Tommy said, not meaning it one bit. He knew that Nissan wasn't the only thing keeping Jed here.

He put his hand on Jed's shoulder, his friend mirroring the gesture. 'Divven't bubble, man,' Tommy said.

'Just got something in my eye,' said Jed, blinking rapidly.

Tommy smiled as well as he could, dropped his arm and turned to the taxi, his fingers on the handle of the car door when the shot split the air and a bullet whizzed over his head.

They both fell to the ground, Sam's muffled screams coming from inside the taxi.

After a few moments, Tommy lifted his head in the direction of the shot, sitting up as he saw Tucker step out from behind a parked van, eyes fixed on Tommy's, shotgun pointed straight at his chest.

'The trainer money!' Tommy heard Jed whimper.

Tommy glanced at the squad car, the officers nowhere to be seen. They'd ducked out of sight, frightened for their lives. But they'd be calling for armed back up who would be there in minutes, minutes Tommy didn't have.

Arms still clutching the rucksack of cash, Tommy looked straight at Tucker. 'We've got your money, Tucker!' he shouted. 'Five hundred, plus a bit more for your worries!'

'Never mind his money, where's mine?'

The voice sailed over Tommy's head, a pair of white, patent leather shoes appearing inches from his feet before he felt himself being hauled from the ground.

Paul Smart's unshaven face was red and blotchy, one side of his hair slightly out of sync with the other. His shirt was smeared red, his fingernails rusty.

The rain started to fall as Paul held out his hand for the rucksack and Tommy pulled it closer to him.

'And the rest,' Paul said to Jed who still lay on the ground.

But Jed's face was a picture of dismay as he strained his neck to look beyond Tommy and Paul. Tommy leant to one side, looked around Paul and saw him too, emerging from a car and pulling his Mac closed at his chest.

'You all know the score. Illegal do, the proceeds get confiscated.'

Peach walked right up to them, didn't bother holding out his hand for the rucksack, just grabbed it, one eye on Tucker who took a step towards them and stood at the bonnet of the taxi, gun still aimed at Tommy.

Tommy felt his plan, his money, his future sliding through his fingers like sand. There was only one last hope.

He turned to face Tucker, and, blinking through the falling drops of rain, he said his name: *'Tony.'*

Tucker's one open eye held Tommy's gaze for a few long seconds.

'Do the right thing,' Tommy said.

Tucker's shoulders seemed to relax, just for a moment.

'Brother,' Tommy added.

The rain was falling heavily now, a quiet rumble on the roof of the taxi. Tommy watched Tucker's Adam's apple rise and fall as he swallowed a decision that could change the course of Tommy's life forever. Or end it.

In one swift move, Tucker turned the gun on Paul Smart, and Tommy sensed the years of hatred and spite gathering in the tips of Tucker's forefinger as it twitched on the trigger.

Then, in the blink of an eye, Tucker turned the gun on Peach, and Tommy heard Sam's piercing '*No!*' as the shot rang out and he fell to the ground once more.

PEACH

He could hear sirens in the distance, but it was too late. The bullet would take his life in just a few minutes, if not sooner, his daughter an orphan before he had the chance to put things right. His daughter who was coming home today.

In a flash, the future was laid bare. Murphy would return to Manchester with exaggerated tales of his spell in the Geordie capital, working for a man who never cracked a smile; a hero, the first victim of a craze that just about destroyed a generation. McNally would retire and someone else would take Peach's place, probably his sick female DI, just to meet the quota. The nurse, Pamela, would cry for a while then get on with her life. Perhaps she would befriend Sally, become a role model. And Sally – he hoped she would fight on, not be ground down by grief, that she would find guidance and the love she so craved.

Someone will die. Paul Smart's words drifted like feathers around him, and he opened his eyes for one last glimpse of the world while he waited for pain and death.

But neither came. The only pain he felt was the handles of the rucksack pressing into his ribs.

He focused his vision. Before him lay Paul Smart, the smooth grey stones of his eyes the same in death as they were in life. Hollow.

Sitting up stiffly and rubbing the grit from his palms, he saw Collins, his arms around his wife and child, both staring over Peach's shoulder. The lad, Foster, was leaning on the bonnet of the taxi, shouting at the driver, telling him to wait just another minute, his mother by his side, doing the same thing.

Tucker was gone, and the sirens came closer.

Peach got to his feet slowly and wiped down his Mac, following Tommy and Sam's stunned eyes and looking behind him to find Trevor Logan standing in shocked stillness, the pistol hanging loosely in his hand.

'That was for your da,' said Trevor, his bloodshot eyes on Tommy. 'And mine.'

Then everyone was looking at the rucksack at Peach's feet.

He was alive. He could feel his heart beating, the blood in his veins. Looking towards the taxi, his eyes fell on Sam, holding onto her baby for dear life, her eyes pleading with him. Like Kathleen's. Like Sally's.

Peach bent down, picked up the rucksack and walked to the taxi, opening the boot and dropping the bag inside. He slammed it closed and stepped back.

The sirens were close, just seconds away.

He jerked his head towards the taxi and watched Tommy open the back door and bundle the girl inside with the baby, jumping in behind her. The door closed, and the taxi screeched away, leaving them all standing in the puff of the exhaust fumes.

Peach turned away from the scene and walked back to the car while armed response officers poured from their vehicle, barking at Trevor Logan to throw the gun away and get to his knees. Trevor did so without question and put his hands behind his head while the two officers from the squad car emerged, their faces red, their chests puffed out as if to rebut their own cowardice.

Peach closed the car door, the silence and the salty smell of its new interior enveloping him. He held a thumb and finger to his eyes, eyes that could still see in a face that was still alive.

'Is there anybody there?'

He frowned down at his car radio. The voice was weak,

pathetic.

'*Can somebody help me?*'

A smile formed as he remembered throwing his radio onto the farmer's filthy bed. Denise Morris could stay at Groat Hall Farm for a few hours longer. He was going home, and when he got there, he would stay there. He would sleep for a while and then he would pick up Sally from the hospital, maybe get Pamela's phone number, take her out somewhere nice to say thank you.

Thank you.

It didn't sound so bad after all.

He took the car radio from its cradle, turning the dial to control. 'I'll be taking the rest of the week off,' he said. 'Stick a note on Superintendent McNally's desk, will you?'

'*Will do, sir. I've got DS Murphy here, wants a word.*'

'Put him on.'

'*One of the murders last night wasn't a hoax,*' Murphy said. '*A Darren Adams-Deighton was found stabbed to death. Looks like he was a serious dealer judging by the amount of drugs in his house, boss.*'

Peach heard the understanding in Murphy's voice.

'*And, chief, not good news on Frankie Donahue.*'

Peach sighed and hung his head.

'*Passed away an hour ago, the family's been informed.*'

Somebody would die all right. It was only a matter of time.

As he put his radio back into its cradle, Peach soaked up Valley Park, its narrow roads and uneven pavements, the shopping trolleys, the graffiti, the boarded-up windows and doors. He wound down his window despite the falling rain, and he could swear heard Valley Park creak under the weight of poverty, crime, and disregard. It seemed to breed badness while the world around it pursued progress. Paul Smart was gone, but Peach had a feeling that something much more dangerous was about to take his place.

To his right, Trevor Logan's baby brother, Carl, sat on a wall in a pair of Spider-Man pyjamas. As he turned the key in the ignition, Carl formed his fingers into the shape of a gun and pointed them at Peach.

Carl closed one eye. *'Bang, bang,'* he said.

EPILOGUE

Ibiza
May 1990

Tommy and Jed lay side by side on their loungers holding Tom Collins cocktails like a scene from *Club Tropicana*. Behind them, Shona and Sam held out their arms in the pool as the children jumped in, hoping to be caught, revelling in the potential of being dropped. Hadgy Dodds, his thick, naked chest barely free of hair, shook cocktails for a line of middle-aged women whose sarongs were just low enough to bare their wrinkly cleavages.

By day, Frankie's Bar was a family haunt, serving pina coladas, chips, and pizzas – the odd Spanish omelette for those with an appetite for foreign food. By night, its beach parties were legendary across the island, DJs flying in from far and wide to play to the crowds of clubbers who flocked to their all-night extravaganzas. Tommy and Mobz worked day and night to ensure they were the best, unrivalled among all other open-air clubs on the Mediterranean. The merchandise sales were booming, and Tommy had bought the plush sofa for his villa just the week before.

Jed supped his cocktail, straining his sunblock-smothered face forward to reach the straws. He didn't want to age prematurely, he said. He might be a married man, but he wasn't going to let himself go.

'How's the car industry?' Tommy asked.

'Cushty.'

Project management hadn't been the offer. Jed was on the

production line, earning a pretty penny as it happened.

'Must be nice, all them Japs in blue suits,' Tommy chirped.

'Fuck off.'

Vanilla Ice began to blare from the stereo behind the bar. Hadgy turned it up, dancing and rapping as he put paper umbrellas into glasses of white mush.

'Pile of shite,' griped Jed.

'Could play anything you wanted if you were here.'

Jed's family had been rehoused up in Wooler in Northumberland, Betty working her dream job in the school kitchen, feeding the hungry mouths of babes five days per week. Davie was the local postman, his pride returned, a working man again, Barry his trusty, if unofficial, apprentice.

'Jed! Jed!' One of Shona's girls was at Jed's side, a dripping-wet bundle of six-year-old energy. 'Watch this!' She did a handstand and Jed reached out to steady her feet as she balanced.

'*Anything* I want?' Jed took another gulp of his cocktail.

'Anything.'

Jed thought for a while. 'Them blue trousers don't half crush my balls.'

Tommy grinned, squinting at his friend, sucking at his straw, and emptying the glass with a gurgle.

Jed released the girl's feet; and she sprang up onto her toes, screeching as she ran towards the pool once more and threw herself in. 'I'll have to talk to wifey, like,' he said, 'she might take some persuading.'

Tommy sat up on his lounger and looked towards the pool where Sam and Shona whispered to each other as if in cahoots, looking his way and laughing behind their hands. Shona had already been primed by Sam, the school places as good as booked for September, the deposit on an apartment already paid, her spot as the resident hypnotist in the local hotels sorted.

'Aye,' said Tommy, sitting back. 'Best to check first.'

The voluminous cocktails on Hadgy's tray glinted blood-red when he placed them on the table between the loungers.

'Ah, man,' moaned Jed. 'Can I just have a pint?'

'Shut it, mardy arse.' Tommy took the glasses from the tray and handed one to Jed, nodding his thanks at Hadgy, who waddled back to the bar.

'To Frankie,' said Tommy, raising his drink.

'The biggest pain in the arse to ever walk the planet,' said Jed, clinking his glass against Tommy's.

Tommy felt pain sting his chest. But he smiled nonetheless.

'Hundred per center,' he said.

༄

I hope you have enjoyed The Rave! If you would like to stay informed about new releases, you can sign up to my mailing list at www.nickyblack.co.uk

If you've enjoyed this book, now is a great time to let other readers know your thoughts. Please consider leaving a review on Amazon.

ACKNOWLEDGEMENTS

It's hard to know where to start when it comes to thanking people. This book has been a rollercoaster, and a massive learning curve, only made possible by the support I've had from friends, family and professionals alike. So, I'll have a go…

Firstly, to Julie Blackie – the Black in Nicky Black – for allowing me to take a fantastic movie script she wrote many years ago and transforming it into this story. I've always loved it, and many of these characters are hers. I hope I've done them justice.

To Louise Ross, fellow North-East author who has been more than generous with her support and advice. (If you haven't read the DCI Ryan series yet, why not?!). The next coffee and muffin is on me, lass.

I'd like to say a big thank you to Pauline Murray, retired CID detective, whose recollection of the eighties is second to none. All the little nuances in here that relate to the way the police operated back then is mostly down to her. I look forward to more scampi and chips in the future.

Where would we be without book bloggers? They are the rock upon which writers like me and many others build their audience. I've met many of you, and you're great company, too. Thank you to you all – too many to mention here and I'm terrified I'll miss someone out. But you know who you are. Special mention to Noelle 'Crimebook Junkie' Holten, though, for her "Eeeeeks! and cover reveal.

A special thanks to all the people involved in running social media platforms that make it possible to share readers' thoughts and reviews: to Helen Dillon-Boyce, Tracy Fenton and all the team at The Book Club on Facebook, Shell Baker from Crime Book Club, Anne Cater from Book Connectors, David Gilchrist, UK Crime Book Club, Deryl Easton, a sweary NotRighter, and Betsy Freeman-Reavley and her team at Crime Fiction Addict. I'm truly grateful for your support (and the gin).

Having been through many, many rewrites, this book has had several professional editors involved. Thanks to Sheila McIlwraith at The Literary Consultancy, Emily Ruston, and Emma Mitchell for her meticulous copy edit. Your honesty has been much appreciated (and acted upon – mostly…).

Shout out to Daz Effect from Ultimatebuzz.net and Jason Busby, two guys who shared their experiences of their love of raves and house music with an old woman who has never been to a rave in her life. Your stories are instrumental in some of the scenes in this book. Thank you.

Sarah Bidder. What can I say? Not only is she the best friend a woman can have, but she is also an unsung hero when it comes to editing. She has read several incarnations of this book, and always given me honest, helpful feedback. This book wouldn't be what it is without our Thursday night chats. I owe you big time, you fabulous woman.

To my family: my sisters and brothers, my mam and my dad (now sadly no longer with us) just for being my family – we rarely express it, but we love each other dearly.

In 2016, I left London and moved back up north, so I'm saying a special thank you to my sister, Clare, and her husband Robb, who put a roof over my head, and gave me the time I needed to recover from the trauma of turning my life on its head. It also gave me a few months to write non-stop. I couldn't have made that change without you.

Finally, of course, to all the thousands of readers who enjoyed

The Prodigal, and hopefully will enjoy *The Rave* too, thank you for the #booklove.

Rave on x

AUTHOR'S NOTE

The Criminal Justice and Public Order Act of 1994 as good as ended the illegal rave scene in the UK. Many will remember the second Summer of Love and the years that followed fondly, others will have been affected by it differently. But whatever our experience was, it can't be denied that the Acid-House movement had a powerful and lasting impact on youth culture and Electronic Dance Music in all its forms. It gave rise to the Super Club and gave DJs a platform to climb to the status of celebrity.

There was a small but thriving rave scene in the north-east back in the day, nothing like the size of the rave Tommy and his friends pull off in this novel, and I hope I'll be forgiven for dreaming up locations and events that simply never existed or happened. This is, after all, fiction, and I reckon I can take some artistic license…

I was only in my early twenties back in 1989, and I was aware of the scene but didn't participate in it (aside from a few memorable nights at the Hacienda in Manchester). It is pure nostalgia that has inspired me to write this book, alongside Julie's funny and poignant script. Now, having listened to rave music for the best part of two years, I'm not sure if I regret it or not. But one is for sure – it doesn't half create the backdrop for some pure, unadulterated drama.

I hope you have enjoyed this story. If you would like to know more about Nicky Black, visit the website at www.nickyblack.co.uk

ABOUT THE AUTHOR

Nicky Black is a collaboration between two friends, Nicky and Julie. Julie originally wrote The Rave as a movie script called "Heads" back in the late nineties, and Julie kindly allowed Nicky to turn the story into their second novel.

Julie has written for TV in the past, notably Hollyoaks and Casualty, and this is Nicky's second novel. Both met when they worked in the urban regeneration industry twenty years ago.

Nicky was brought up in Northumberland and worked in Newcastle upon Tyne for twelve years before moving to London in 2002, then back home in 2016. Julie is a born and bred Geordie, and still lives in the Toon.

CONNECT WITH ME
Facebook: Facebook.com/AuthorBlackNE
Twitter: @AuthorBlackNE
Email: nickyblack2016@gmail.com
Website: www.nickyblack.co.uk

Printed in Great Britain
by Amazon